Quilling Me Softly

Nigel May

Decoupaged layers of love to every person who has created and crafted.

Nigel

X

Chapter 1

'Killing me softly with his song, with his sonnnnng...'

Sheena Pollett elongated the last note of the song as much as she could to milk every glorious nanosecond from her pitch-perfect singing. It was how they did it on those telly talent shows, so it was definitely how she was going to do it in front of a small but appreciative audience at Rooney-at-Burrow's number one pub, The Six Pennies. The fact that it was the sleepy village's only pub was neither here nor there.

Sheena took a bow as those gathered around the tables and fruit machines in front of her clapped loudly and whooped in her direction. A few of the local lads wolf-whistled and did that thing where they whipped the fingers of one hand together in waggly appreciation. At twenty years of age, Sheena thought that it was really something that perhaps she should be able to do herself by now. She'd tried with no luck. But then her talents lay in her vocals, not her finger whipping. Hopefully one day her golden-noted singing might be her ticket out of Rooney-at-Burrow, the village that had been her home since birth.

Not that she disliked the village. Far from it. She loved the people she had grown up with, but surely there had to be more to life than just her weekly singing spot at The Six Pennies. Although the £25 she pocketed came in very handy when it came to buying make-up and the gossip magazines she loved to read about the celebrities she loved to watch on the telly. It was a world that she wanted to be part of, but on her own terms. Sheena knew she could probably go on one of those TV dating shows and become famous overnight. Everybody said so. She had the looks. You weren't named Ravishing Rooney Queen at the annual village pageant five times on the trot if you weren't blessed with a natural beauty. But that wasn't her style. She wanted to be winning Grammys and music awards, not preparing a speech for her award as Best Cleavage Of

The Year In A Reality Show. Sheena knew she had the looks and the talent and one day she would use it. She just hadn't as yet.

Sheena looked at the array of smiley faces in front of her and felt a surge of warmth and love run through her as the crowd heckled for an encore. They were a huge part of the reason she was still loving village life. These people were her friends. An odd but deeply likable bunch of villagers who all held a special place in her heart.

Sitting cosily around a small circular table to her left were Violet Brewer, Margaret Millsop and Pearl Wheeler. She could tell that Violet, the sixty-something owner of the village wool shop where Sheena liked to help out, had maybe had one too many sherries as her cheeks were flushed the colour of beetroot and her smile, adorable though it was, now seemed a little wonky across her features. Margaret, also in her sixties, was Violet's best friend and had a heart of gold. She was stinking rich, so people said, as she had fleeced her ex-husband for every penny in the divorce courts after he had run off with Cheryl, the twenty-something barmaid who used to work here at The Six Pennies. Apparently, their affair had started during one of the pub's infamous lock-ins. A simple spot of after-hours poker had become so much more, when Margaret's hubby found he had more than just a royal flush in his hands. Margaret now owned a few cottages in the village and rented them out to people that she liked. Pearl, just slightly younger than the two other women, was one of her tenants. She shared a cottage with her husband Noah. They were originally from Barbados and Sheena loved to listen to their tales of life growing up in the Caribbean. She'd love to go one day. The closest she had experienced to tropical was taking aim at the coconut shy at the village fayre.

Over by the bar, Sir Buster Burniston was holding court with Phill Brooks, one of the co-owners of The Six Pennies. An ever-present tankard of lager sat in Sir Buster's giant hand. Sir Buster was a barrel of a man. Not as in he was carrying an excess amount of timber. Oh no, he was as solid as any man could be. He'd played rugby for the country back in the day. He was built like an ox. Which for a man who was now seventy-plus was pretty remarkable. Sheena loved Sir Buster. His massive beard and luxurious wavy rolls of ice-white hair gave him a real look of aristocratic gravitas, which was totally unsurprising given that he owned Burrow Hall, the manor house that sat atop Rooney Mound, the hill that stared down at the village. Sheena worked there part-time too, helping out with cleaning duties and catering when he had events. She'd often found herself talking to him after an event right through to the wee small hours of the morning. He was captivating to listen to and had many a tale to tell. His wife had died in a shooting accident at Burrow Hall a decade earlier. He'd never remarried, but if rumour was to be believed, he certainly had an eye for the ladies. Sheena had often felt a stray hand patting her backside as she wished him goodnight after one of their chats. If any of the lads in the village had done that she would have put them squarely in their place, but somehow with Sir Buster, it seemed anything but predatory.

She watched as Sir Buster erupted with a huge belly laugh at the bar as he chatted to Phill, who had now been joined by Stephanie, his wife and the other co-owner of

The Six Pennies. The two of them had been running the local boozer for as long as Sheena could remember.

Sheena had first been brought to The Six Pennies as a babe in arms by her dad Samuel and her mum Rita. Samuel, now Sergeant Pollett and the go-to-police officer in the village, was furiously and proudly clapping his daughter's beautiful tones standing by the bar's pool table with Rita, who managed the village's supermarket. Well, corner store. It had fruit, veg, milk, bread and a selection of tinned goods, but if you were wanting pitted olives or pain au chocolat, then the shelves were bare. Alongside her parents was WPC Paula Horton, the only other police officer in the village and Samuel's right-hand help, and Jimmy Coates, the affable owner of Coates Farm who supplied the village with not just the most incredible meat but also provided some of the wool that ended up in Violet's wool shop. The shop had originally been opened back in the 1990s by Violet and her sister, Betsy, who just happened to be Samuel's mum and, of course, Sheena's grandma. Betsy now lived on the other side of the world in Australia with her second husband, a famous telly soap actor. Again, Sheena dreamt of visiting her grandma one day very soon.

Yes, there was certainly life beyond the sleepy confines of Rooney-at-Burrow that Sheena ached to see, but she had to admit that life in one of the English countryside's quaintest and seemingly forgotten villages was as good as it got right now. And that was pretty good from her vantage point on the pub stage.

As the clapping subsided, Farmer Jimmy Coates placed his hands to his mouth and bellowed across the bar. 'Sheena, love, can you sing "Evergreen". It's my utter fave.'

Sheena smiled broadly from ear to ear. 'Thank you, everybody. And for my final number, especially for my good friend the Streisand fan in the corner over there, here's "Evergreen".'

She knew Jimmy would ask for Streisand. He was her number one fan. It was one of the many things discussed at the weekly craft group in the room at the back of the wool shop. Once a week, she, Margaret, Pearl, Violet and Jimmy would all get together for a knit and natter, a glue and coo, a quill and spill, a stitch and witch. Call it what you will. It was their craft group – the Crafters of Rooney-at-Burrow – Team C.R.A.B. for short. And it was another reason why Sheena found herself unable to quite tear herself away from village life just yet.

As Sheena eased her smooth vocals into the first line of the final song of the night, she stared around the room. Her eyes landed on Jimmy. His eyes were stained with tears, overcome with emotion, hand clutched to his chest in euphoria. It was always the same when he heard Barbra. Sheena let her gaze run across to Violet. She was also teary. But that was probably her last sherry. It always made her a little overemotional if she had one too many.

Halfway through the song, Sheena decided that it wouldn't be her final song of the night. She'd give the adoring crowd another one, something rousing, to send them on their way. Maybe a stirring chorus of 'Happy Days Are Here Again'. She knew Violet loved that.

Happy days are here again, your cares and troubles are gone... Yes, that would be a perfect finale. Sheena may not have been winning Grammys or sunning herself on a Caribbean beach, but right now there was nowhere the twenty-year-old would rather be than singing in front of her friends in a local boozer in the carefree village she called home.

Chapter 2

'Well, I thought your songs last night were bloody marvellous, as ever. That last number got the whole pub going,' boomed Sir Buster Burniston, swinging his gold club in a furiously impressive arc and sending the little white ball in front of him into the rich blue summer sky. He watched it, an inquisitive glance regarding its destination painted across his distinguished features as it sailed out of view into a wooded area on the grounds of Burrow Hall. 'Oh buggeration, that's probably gone into the bloody lake in the woods. Oh well, plenty more where that came from.'

He reached into his pocket and pulled out another ball. He placed it on the ground and turned to Sheena, who was standing behind him, close enough to talk but far enough away to avoid any chance of contact with his hefty golf club. She had just finished a Friday morning shift cleaning some of the many rooms the manor house contained and had come outside to see Sir Buster to say goodbye before leaving.

'No, I mean it, Sheena. You were really rather good again last night. You should sing for a living. You're better than some of the flaming noise I hear on the radio. Right old racket. You're wasted polishing my knick-knacks.'

'Thanks. I love it. The singing, I mean, not polishing your knick-knacks.' She felt her skin heat up as she realised what she had said. 'Not that I don't like cleaning and working here. I really do. It's great and every penny counts.' It was true. Nearly every penny she could earn from her many jobs went into her future fund. One day she'd use it, she was sure. 'I've finished for the morning. Is there anything else you'd like me to do before I go? I've cleaned some of the bedrooms, including yours, and the main hall itself. I can do some of the others if you like, or can they wait until next week?'

Sir Buster swung his golf club again and watched

happily as the ball rainbowed across the lawn in front of him and landed in sight, short of the woods. 'That's more like it. I don't want to even contemplate that my swing could be getting a little rusty.' Happy with his shot, his thoughts returned to Sheena's question. 'Oh, it can wait until next week. You always do such a marvellous job. Leave the other bedrooms. I've actually no damned idea how many there are. I don't think I've ever counted. The wife used to look after all of that back in the day. May she rest in peace. It's ten years this year, you know. Since the accident. I've no idea where that time's gone, or indeed what I've done with it.' For a moment, Sir Buster sounded a little overcome with emotion.

'You've made this place look incredible,' replied Sheena 'I've been coming here all my life and I've never seen it look better.'

'That must be your cleaning, my dear!' guffawed Sir Buster.

'Hardly, I run a duster around and clean a few surfaces with an anti-bacterial wipe every few days. That's not what's kept this place afloat. It's you. You've managed to keep the spirit of Burrow Hall alive even though it could have easily died when your wife passed away.'

'I do miss her, you know. Fiona was bloody remarkable, really. Running this place. She'd raised two kids, Alexi and Belinda, not that either of those two were ever grateful about the things life gave them. I've not seen either of them for years now. Other than the odd Christmas card and a letter once in a blue moon telling me to sell this place, I might as well not exist. Hardly team spirit, is it. I'd have chucked them off the team in my rugby days for not playing ball. No, Fiona was incredible, she did it all. I still love her. Even though I'm fully aware about the rumours that go around about me.'

Sheena couldn't help but smirk at his words. 'I don't know what you mean.' Her sentence was enveloped in sarcasm.

'To be honest with you, I love the fact that people still talk about me as some athletic Casanova at my age. Seventy-two next birthday. Can I help it if there's so many attractive women around? Look at you. If I was half my age...' He let his lips curl into a playful smile.

'You'd still be way too old for me,' smiled Sheena. One of the things that she adored about Sir Buster was that she could give him as good as he got. She could be cheeky with him and he loved it.

'Oh, you know how to break a poor man's heart, don't you?' he laughed. 'C'mon, walk with me to the ball. You can act as my caddy. Not that I'll make you carry anything, of course.' He picked up his golf bag and swung it over his shoulder as if to prove the point. 'Unless you need to run off. An important lunch date or something. With some tattooed youth more suitable to your age.' It was now Sir Buster's turn to be jokily sarcastic. 'I'll double your pay for today. You deserve it.'

Sheena was never one to turn an extra payday down and seeing as she enjoyed Sir Buster's company immensely and had no such youth waiting – truth be known, she didn't really consider any of the single lads in the village even remotely her type – she was happy to keep him company for a while longer. She ran a little to catch him up as he strode off. She'd never met such a speedy pensioner. Even with a bag full of heavy golf clubs over his shoulder, he was out of first gear in a heartbeat.

'People do talk about you having an eye for the ladies,' Sheena admitted as she caught up with him. 'It's only natural. You're up here in this house all by yourself. And, let's be honest, the village grapevine does like to have some juicy titbits to mull over. It's either you or discussing the new piggy arrivals on Coates Farm.'

'Well, I'm glad I'm deemed more stimulating than the pigs,' he grinned before letting the conversation turn more serious. 'I'm not going to say I've been a saint since Fiona died, but the truth is that I've never met anyone who could fill the hole that she left in my life. She was a one-off. She put her heart and soul into everything. Look at how she organised the village fayre every year and kept the village church in order. I'm buggered if I would even know where to begin with hiring marquees and organising judges and finding someone to tile the roof of St Charlotte's when it gets all leaky. Fiona used to do all of that. I adored every bone of her.'

Even though Sheena had not even been old enough for senior school when she'd attended the fayres organised by

Sir Buster's wife, she could still remember what a force of nature she was.

St Charlotte's Church was a disused place of worship on the grounds of Burrow House. It had also always been used as one of the focal points of the annual Rooney-at-Burrow village fayre. Instead of letting the church fall into a state of dilapidation, every year it would be decorated with flowers for the fayre by the villagers and the annual prize marrow competition would be judged in front of the church. Or in a marquee, should the British weather decide that August was to be wet, windy and woeful. The church would also provide the backdrop for the annual Ravishing Rooney Queen pageant, where the females of the village would compete for the crown.

In reality, the church should have fallen to the ground decades ago, but thanks to Fiona's dedication, and indeed to the couple's bank balance, the church was still standing. St Charlotte's may have been a rather ramshackle pile of bricks, stones and memories from days gone by, but for ninety-five per cent of the inhabitants of Rooney-at-Burrow, it was a symbol of hope, joyousness and tradition and was part of the very glue that stuck the strength and spirit of the village together.

'Were you worried that the fayre would fall by the wayside when Fiona died?' asked Sheena. Again, she was struggling to keep up with Sir Buster's vigorous stride. How come one of his strides seemed to equal at least two and a bit of hers? She could feel herself getting a little breathy as she followed him across the lawns towards the golf ball.

'Of course I was. But Fiona was very much loved by the villagers and there wasn't any question of the fayre not happening anymore. We'd have never had the chance to see your pretty face being crowned Ravishing Rooney Queen for eight times or whatever it was if we'd have stopped the fayre.'

'Er... five actually,' mumbled Sheena, a little embarrassed. She was fully aware that she had actually won the title for the last three years as well but had asked for her votes to be secretly discarded in order to give others a chance. Plus, the novelty of wearing a crown of colourful gerberas and helping to judge whose marrow was the girthiest had worn off long ago. Also, there were only so many metaphorical daggers from the other females in the village that a girl just out of her teens should have to put up with. It seemed that being the queen was a pretty big accolade.

'Which is why Margaret Millsop taking it on was an absolute godsend. That woman is incredible. How that stupid dimwit of a husband could have left her for a slip of a lass from the boozer half his age is beyond me,' Sir Buster reproached.

Sheena smiled. 'Says the man who flirts with me on a regular basis even though I could be your granddaughter. Maybe even great—'

'Says the man who won't be paying you this week, you cheeky thing,' volleyed Sir Buster straight back at her. 'No, Margaret reminds me greatly of Fiona. She will never take no for an answer. She has been the driving force in keeping the fayre as wonderful as it's always been. She and Violet have always made sure it happens. Even in the summer floods and rain of a few years ago, they still managed to bring marrows and merriment to the people of

Rooney-at-Burrow. Having that fayre on my grounds is one of my greatest pleasures in life. It's one of the reasons I'd never sell this place. Too many joyful memories. Mine and other people's.'

'Plus, Margaret loves any excuse to get her hands on a marrow. It's common knowledge they're her favourite food. We often discuss it at C.R.A.B. – that's the crafting group we hold at Violet's wool shop. Jimmy even brought in marrow chutney one week. He'd spent hours making it, maybe even days. Margaret loved it. She was spreading it over HobNobs and a packet of fig rolls. That is not normal behaviour. She's obsessed. I thought it was rank. She eats it as often as she can now.' Sheena felt a shiver run over her body at the mere thought.

'She is a tad obsessed with said vegetable, it must be noted. Mind you, I shall once more be entering my very own prize marrow this year. There must be something lucky in the soil for me right now because my crop seems to be bigger and more bountiful than ever. I have a sneaking suspicion I may be adding another first-place rosette to my collection. It's been three years since I last won, but I have a feeling the luck of the marrow gods is definitely on my side. How long is it until the next fayre now, two and a bit weeks? I know I've seen Margaret buzzing about on the grounds recently with a mobile phone glued to her ear, so she must be organising something. She's like a tornado, she never stops.'

'It's two weeks tomorrow. And hopefully this sunny weather is set to stay. I think you'll have some stiff competition in the marrow department, though. Jimmy was telling us that he has a particularly good batch on the go this year and Phill at the pub said the same. And Margaret will be pulling out all of the stops to make hers as impressive as ever.'

'Well, I'm sure mine is much bigger than both Jimmy and Phill's and you can share that information with as many ladies as possible.' Sir Buster burst forth with another deep and cavernous laugh and winked at Sheena.

Sheena rolled her eyes but couldn't help but giggle at his cheek.

They arrived at the golf ball, a fact that Sheena was more than happy about. How come Sir Buster wasn't puffed out like she was. A man in his seventies who was clearly fitter than her. Kind of awkward. Sheena made a mental note to try harder when it came to her visits to the village Jazzercise class. She'd not been in weeks and Hannah, the class instructor, had made it quite clear to her at the pub the night before that it had been noted that her enthusiasm was waning. Nothing of Hannah's ever waned. She spent her days working as a farmhand at Coates Farm shearing sheep and cleaning out pig pens and then still had enough energy to whip on a leotard and wave her body parts around furiously to the beats of Glenn Miller. Especially to her favourite tune, 'The Booglie Wooglie Piggy'. The obvious connection to Hannah's own life on the farm always brought an extra smile from those gathered and surplus gleeful exertion from Hannah. And she never seemed puffed out at the end. Sheena needed to take note. And also ask Hannah if she could swap Jazzercise to a night that didn't clash with her favourite reality show on TV. She doubted she would.

'Thank God, we've reached your ball. You tore across that lawn like an Olympian.' Was that a slight stitch

Sheena could feel in her side? She suspected so.

'If there were Olympics for the over seventies, I'd be gold medal all the way. Now, stand back and let me take a swing at this. Let's see if I can clear the lake.'

Sheena stepped back a pace and watched as Sir Buster took one of his clubs and lined it up against the ball. She could see every line of concentration on his face as he swung to hit the ball, sending it sky-high again. It sailed over the trees gathered at the bottom of the Hall lawns but fell short of clearing them, a fact that displeased Sir Buster immensely.

'Bloody hell, not strong enough on that one. That'll have ended up in the lake too, I guess. Hopefully, it stunned one of the trout on the way in. It'll make the blighters easier to catch when I'm next fishing. Right, onwards.' He placed the club back into his golf bag and curved it onto his shoulder again. He began to march towards the woods. He took a few steps before turning to look at Sheena, who had not moved to follow him. 'Are you coming, dear girl?'

The definite stitch in her side told her that would be a

no. 'Mind if I don't. I've just remembered I need to do something in the village.' It seemed easier than saying she was totally pooped already.

'Of course, thank you for your company as ever.'

He waved his hand cheerily as he marched off without her.

'Such a marvellous girl. I knew it. She does have a tattooed youth waiting for her somewhere, of course she does, pretty young thing like her,' muttered Sir Buster to himself as he wandered off.

Sheena took a deep breath and turned back towards Burrow Hall. As she walked, she couldn't help but ask herself where on earth Sir Buster found his boundless effervescent energy. And if he could possibly share some with her.

Chapter 3

Violet Brewer turned the key and opened the door to Brewer's Loop, the highly successful wool shop she had owned for over thirty years, and smiled. The feeling of cosy satisfaction she felt from seeing the shelves of multicoloured yarns all lined up and ready for knitting never left her. From the moment she and her sister Betsy had first decided to open a wool shop when they were both in their early twenties, she knew that she had found her woolly calling for life.

When they had first started, the shelves had been pretty sparse and much easier to organise than they were these days. One shelf would be stocking yellow wool, one white, one red... it was easy and remarkably formulaic. But now it was a completely different matter. There were so many different wools to choose from. Merino, cashmere, lambswool. The list went on. Plus such a vast array of colours. There were about twenty types of green alone, including one called spinach pie. There was everything from apricot to walnut, Parma violet to mushroom – why were they all named after foodstuffs? And only the other day someone had come in asking for a glow-in-the-dark yarn, which Violet had discovered was actually a real thing and not a prank.

Wool yarn was still the classic, of course, and fabulous for winter clothing. Most of Violet's winter wardrobe, and indeed that of her best friend Margaret, had been knitted using wool yarn from the store. It was incredibly forgiving when it came to staining – not even a disobedient spoonful of one of Pearl Wheeler's marvellous curries that had landed squarely on Violet's cardigan one supper evening had left a tell-tale mark after the wool had been put through the wash. Sure, it could be a bit scratchy now and again, but that was surely first-world problems. It had much more durability than most of the stuff you could buy on the high street. Who wanted a garment that looked like it had been pulled through one of Farmer Jimmy's digger's blades after just a couple of wears? Which was why, nine times out of ten, Violet chose not to visit the high street. Unless it was for decent tights and underwear. That was a different matter.

Violet shut the door behind her and turned the key to lock it again. Today was not for opening. Today was not a regular Friday. Today was stocktaking day. She'd told as many of her regulars as possible that if they needed anything from the shop, then they would have to wait until tomorrow morning when the doors of Brewer's Loop would be open again. She was sure they could cope for one day without their eggplant alpaca.

Violet walked through the shop, lifted up the wooden flap that allowed her behind the serving counter and then opened another door that led out to a large rectangular room at the back. This room served three purposes. Firstly, it was a stockroom and three sides of it were floor-to-ceiling shelves crammed with wool and yarn, plus numerous craft supplies that she had introduced to the shop over recent years. Ribbons, threads, buttons, zips and patterns were standard in any decent wool shop, but what made Brewer's Loop the most successful wool shop in the area, and indeed made some crafting enthusiasts come to it from way beyond the borders of Rooney-at-Burrow, was the fact that Violet had taken the very wise decision a few years back to branch out slightly and stock other craft items that seemed to be growing in popularity. She had a section for fabrics – everything from fat quarters and charm packs through to jelly roll packs of patchwork strips for quilting. There was the crafting library of books covering all subjects from felting and quilling through to sugar craft and pyrography. Violet had been very confused about that last one initially, having mistaken it for pyromania, and was worried whether the book should have come with a danger warning sticker. Then there were the copious amounts of paper packs, cardstock, glues, glitters, powders, pastes, paints and tools needed for quality creativity. And these days it seemed that most crafters of note had to have a machine to do their die-cutting and embossing, so virtually one wall was full of boxed machines, a host of packets of metal dies in various shapes, sizes and concepts and packets of plastic embossing folders too. And on top of that there was row upon row of stamps. Not the kind you placed on envelopes, of course. Oh no, these were the rubbery silicone type that allowed you to do all sorts of fantastic things with your card making or home décor.

Violet had first seen all of this fabulous stuff whilst browsing a crafting magazine that someone had left at Dr Roberts' waiting room at the village surgery. She'd shown it to Betsy and within weeks the pair of them had been heading off to a crafting trade event to expand the possibilities of Brewer's Loop. Once stocked, word started to spread and before the sisters knew it, revenue and productivity had gone through the roof. Not that Violet would ever let the shop lose its village feel and become another soulless store. That's not why they'd opened it and that was never going to happen. It was still very much a wool shop, that just happened to also cater for so much more.

The second reason for the large room was that it was the venue for the village's weekly craft group meeting –

Team C.R.A.B. The name had been Violet's doing. She and Betsy had advertised that they were starting a crafting group in the back room with a poster in the window of the shop quite a few years ago now. Betsy had written it out in bright colourful letters. 'Come and be one of the Crafters of Rooney-at-Burrow. Weekly craft group, £3 a session. Bring your own craft stuff, we'll supply the coffee... or wine depending on the time of day!' Betsy had underlined the words Crafters of Rooney-at-Burrow and coloured the C, R, A and B in bright hues. As soon as Violet saw it all, she could focus on was the word CRAB.

The first meeting of C.R.A.B. took place a week later. Those present included Margaret Millsop, Violet's best friend and organiser of pretty much anything that happened in the village. Violet knew she would come, given both her love of needlework and knitting and also, and perhaps more pertinently, her love of a good glass of wine. Pearl Wheeler had signed up straight away too. She wasn't really a crafter but wanted to learn more and it also gave her a chance to spend more time getting to know the locals.

Pearl and her husband Noah, a landscape gardener, had moved to the village from London only a few months earlier, which, despite being their choice, had been a massive culture shock. In London, they had seemed to be always surrounded by people, whereas in the rural peace of Rooney-at-Burrow there weren't so many to choose from. And Pearl was a highly sociable person. She loved entertaining – it was her Bajan roots. Having grown up in Barbados, she was used to cooking for people, partying and having a euphoric time. And with Noah away a lot of the time with his work, getting to spend time with other villagers was just what she needed.

The other member of the crafting group who signed up straight away was Farmer Jimmy. Apparently, he had a hidden love of cross-stitch that he'd been secretly indulging in for years. It was his little bubble of 'me time' after a busy day on the farm. Just like Pearl, his other half, a flamboyant interior designer to the stars called Bailey Frazer-Ferguson, was away from home with his work a lot of the time, and C.R.A.B. gave Jimmy the chance to have a good natter. The villagers loved Jimmy and Bailey, finding them both unique and fascinating. On paper, the two of them shouldn't have worked as a partnership as they couldn't have been more chalk and cheese. The chalk being covered in pig poo and the cheese dipped in opulent texture and design. But the odd male pairing worked and had done for many years. But with Bailey away creating grandeur and majesty for some D-lister, Jimmy was keen to share his love of cross-stitch with others.

Sheena had joined the group too. But only over the last twelve months. Ever since she'd had started working part-time at the shop in fact. With business booming and no Betsy anymore these days, Violet had definitely needed a helping hand. She hoped that Sheena would swing by later to help with the stocktake. Had she mentioned it to her? She couldn't actually remember. The sherry from last night had obviously clouded her brain slightly.

The third reason for the large room at the back of Brewer's Loop was to accommodate a kitchen. Violet lived in the flat above the shop and had done for many years. But the flat had a separate entrance and nipping upstairs to fix a brew during working hours, especially on a busy day, was not always convenient. So having a kitchen area out the back with a kettle, microwave, toaster, sink and suchlike was highly beneficial. Plus, there may have been a shelf or two housing a bottle or three of wine or Violet's favourite rhubarb gin. The crafting nights had proven that gin, gossip and glitter were a winning combination, and who was Violet to argue with that.

Moving into the kitchen, Violet picked up the kettle, filled it with water and flicked it on, waiting for it to boil. If she was to stocktake, then many a brew would be needed. And if it did go into the evening hours, then perhaps a sneaky glass of the rhubarb gin would be more than agreeable. She'd need to keep refreshed, after all, with so much work to do.

Brew made, she sat down at the big wooden table. She felt pleased with herself. Proud that the shop was still going strong. She did miss Betsy, though. She'd moved to Australia about two months after the first meeting of C.R.A.B. Terrible timing, but it would take more than a stack of yarn and a collection of knitting needles to stop the force of a whirlwind romance. She and Violet had been at another crafting event at an arena in Birmingham and one of those sci-fi fan-fests was taking place in the next hall. Betsy loved a bit of sci-fi. It was one of the areas where the two sisters really differed. Violet hardly ever watched TV, although she did like anything to do with upcycling, but she wouldn't know a Klingon or a Vulcan if one intergalactically fell on her, whereas Betsy loved it. Violet guessed it was something that family life must have strangely pushed upon her. Doubtless, Samuel must have loved them when he was young and Betsy must have become embroiled too. Violet herself had never married. It just hadn't happened sadly. But she loved being an aunt and great-aunt. Family meant everything to her.

When Betsy had seen that some of her favourite actors were doing meet 'n' greets, she couldn't resist buying a ticket. Long story short, Betsy had fallen madly in love with an Australian actor who had once played a crew member on some moon-based TV show and was now starring in a highly popular soap opera down under. Violet could never remember which one, but she knew it wasn't *Neighbours* or *Home and Away*. With Betsy's first husband long gone, he wasn't dead, he and Betsy had just fallen out of love and he now lived with his second wife in Mevagissy, the coast was clear for Betsy to fall head over heels. Nearly three years on and Betsy was the happiest she'd ever been. And this pleased Violet greatly even if she did miss her like crazy.

Violet and she spoke on FaceTime, or on the phone if Betsy hadn't done her hair to her satisfaction, virtually every other day. The time difference between Rooney-at-Burrow and Willow's Spit, the remote Aussie suburb where Betsy and her husband Rod now lived didn't always allow for the most convenient of chats, but they did what they could. Betsy was always keen to hear about the shop and what was happening back in Rooney-at-Burrow. Especially if there was any juicy tittle-tattle. Which normally there wasn't. Betsy also liked to share Rod's latest news from the set and his storylines. In his time, he'd been attacked by a Tasmanian devil, married his neighbour's wife and been arrested for fraud – on the soap, not in real life. And he'd been making a film as well, if Violet remembered correctly. Some grisly murder horror thing.

Another of Betsy's favourite things to watch. Odd woman. How did that even compare with the joy of seeing a broken old tea chest turned into a designer ottoman. Violet sometimes wondered if they did indeed grow up in the same household. But, as ever, she couldn't wait to catch up with her sister later. Perhaps she could do it at the end of this stocktake. Hopefully. But you couldn't finish without starting, could you? Time to get going.

Violet drained her tea and placed the empty mug on the table. She picked up a large pad of paper and walked back into the main area of the shop. She surveyed the mass of wools. Where to begin? Merino, cashmere, alpaca, cotton, mohair, organic, acrylic, novelty, polyester... gosh, so many different types. So much more to stocktake than back in the day. Maybe Betsy was better off thousands of miles away. Still, at least the satisfaction of getting it done would be ginormous. She just needed to crack on.

Maybe she'd just give Sheena a quick ring to see if she was on her way. Two sets of hands would make for much lighter work. Violet had a faint suspicion that maybe last night's sherry had stopped her mentioning it to Sheena after all.

Chapter 4

Feeling the crunch of the gravel underneath his boots as he approached the front door of Burrow House, Noah Wheeler couldn't help but smile. He was always beyond ecstatic to be at home and not running around with his job. So, another contract working for Sir Buster at Burrow Hall was joyous, as it was literally on his doorstep. Plus, having worked for Sir Buster before, he knew the job would be a pleasurable one. And one which meant no time away from his wife Pearl. His precious Pearl.

His work as a landscape gardener kept him highly busy. And after twenty-five years in business, it had taken him pretty much all over the world. Highlights of his career had included being one of the team creating a garden of tranquillity for one of Monte Carlo's most high-end hotels. Although how anybody could find anything even resembling tranquillity in that rich boy's playground was beyond Noah. He'd also been part of a highly talented collective that had created an exotic and colourful garden for one of Barbados's six-star health spas. It was during that visit that London born-and-bred Noah had met and fallen in love with Pearl, who had been working there as a receptionist and masseuse. After a hard day of creating the exotic, a massage was high on the agenda and Pearl's hands had worked wonders. As had her smile, which could light up any room, and her friendly banter which had won Noah over before his first knotted ball of sinew had loosened.

By the time Noah had left Barbados six weeks later, he and Pearl had become inseparable. For a while, they contacted each other daily by any means possible, but their separation soon became unbearable, and Pearl made the decision to leave her native Barbados for life with Noah in London. They married and lived at Noah's house in Crouch End. It was the house where they raised their two children, twin boys Reuben and Alistair, a house they had extended to cater for their growing family, a house that Noah naturally created the most idyllic outdoor space for. They had lived there for twenty-plus years, watching their boys grow and eventually flying the nest. It was the most perfect of times in their beautiful family home.

Noah had never been a big one for riches or the trappings of wealth. He had never been a fan of the glitz and the glam that his occupation had allowed him to experience. Fancy hotels and health spas and shiny casinos were okay if you liked that sort of thing, but Noah really wasn't fussed. His jackpot in life was the smile on Pearl's face greeting him when he was lucky enough to wake up in his own bed, or the comfort of snuggling up on the sofa together with their boys on film night, buckets of popcorn and Pearl's famous pumpkin fritters ready to go. That was what life was about.

When the boys left home, it was just him and Pearl, and most often Pearl on her own if Noah was away with work. She was the queen of an empty castle. Their house was magnificent and roomy, but it no longer continued to be a family home. The noise of the kids and the laughter of the family that made it such a special, magical place was missing.

Noah had had the idea in the back of his head for a while that maybe he and Pearl should move. Downsize to somewhere outside of London. It was when Noah was offered a contract at Burrow Hall, landscaping some of the lawns for Sir Buster Burniston, that the idea started to germinate. As soon as he drove into the village of Rooney-at-Burrow, it was as if he felt a huge weight lifting off his shoulders. Suddenly, all of the rigours of the rat race and the five thousand miles per hour speed of hectic life in the big city seemed to be magnified in size but minimised in importance. The bluest of skies and the greenest of fields that he viewed in the picturesque rural village seemed to be a much more attractive proposition to come back to after a hard day at work. And as he drove his way up to the top of Rooney Mound and parked his car outside the splendour of Burrow Hall, he was certain that he had experienced an epiphany. Something was telling him that this was to be the place where he and Pearl were meant to live. Why live in a massive empty house when they could have views like this?

When Sir Buster breezed outside to greet him with the heartiest of handshakes and the heftiest of slaps on the back, the deal was sealed. Most of the clients that Noah had experienced in the big cities were so busy thinking about what financial benefit was around the next corner that they barely bothered to even offer the merest of pleasantries to the here and now. Within two minutes of meeting Sir Buster, he'd been offered a cup of tea ('or something stronger, if it's too early, dear fellow' – it was only 1 p.m. after all), told he could spend what he needed to on the lawns and been requested to tell the Burrow Hall chef exactly what he fancied eating while he worked. Oh, and that he was more than welcome to stay in any room he liked if he wanted to sleep over if that made things easier. Sir Buster was one of the friendliest clients he had ever met.

Noah didn't even have to convince him of his plans for landscaping some of the acres of land around the Hall. 'You did some work for an old rugby pal of mine at his place in Somerset. He was elated and recommended you, so just make me as happy as you did him.'

Noah had spent four weeks on the job at Sir Buster's. During his first night staying there, he had phoned Pearl to tell her about how beautiful the village was. She had sounded more than keen when he'd suggested a potential move. Anything that meant she could spend more time with her love, Noah, was a superb idea as far as she was concerned.

At the end of the first week, Noah had returned to their Crouch End home and brought Pearl back to Rooney-at-Burrow to spend the weekend at Burrow Hall. It had been Sir Buster's idea. Noah had mentioned that he was thinking of asking his wife about potential relocation over dinner with Sir Buster. Sir Buster's response had been emphatic.

'Bring her here for the weekend. Be my guest. Whatever you're looking for, I'm sure you'd both be very happy here. It's a wonderful place to live. Friendly and unspoilt. Everyone will know your business, it's that kind of village life closeness, but people will always have your back. If you ever need your dog walked or your car pulled from a ditch, then this is the place to be. Everyone will go out of their way to help you. I'll hook you up with Margaret Millsop. She's the best person to speak to and she owns some properties here, so she might be able to point you in the right direction.'

It was really that easy. Noah and Pearl, who fell in love with the village the first moment she saw it too, met with Margaret and found her just as friendly as Sir Buster. In fact, everybody they met was. They spoke to more friendly faces in one weekend in the village than they had done back home in months.

Margaret had suggested they rent one of the cottages she owned in the village while they looked for a bigger property. Take a six-month lease while they looked for their rural dream home. As soon as they had moved in, Pearl told Noah that they needed to look no further. She loved the cottage. It was small, but it was perfectly sized for them. Garden front and back, rose bushes around the doorway, a vegetable patch and a shed and hanging baskets decorating the walls nearly all the way to the neatly trimmed thatched roof. It was idyllic.

Noah and Pearl rented out their London property for a small fortune and asked Margaret if she would consider a long-term let. After an initial trail period of three months to see if both sides were happy – in reality, they had both decided they were after about a day and a half – Margaret had said the Wheelers were welcome to be her tenants for as long as they liked. As she'd told Violet the night they moved in, 'they're a lovely couple... that garden will never see a weed while he's there and she is definitely someone who knows the worth of a duster.' Margaret had based this on seeing Pearl carry a huge box of cleaning products into the house. Margaret liked things nice and tidy, and it would appear she had a kindred spirit in Pearl.

Three years on and Pearl and Noah still adored every inch of their rented cottage. They loved village life and for Noah, every moment he could spend at home, even when working, was a blessing. Which was why the offer of another job from Sir Buster was highly appreciated.

Noah knocked on the wooden front door of Burrow Hall and waited for an answer. He checked his watch. Just after 10 a.m. on Saturday morning. Just as he and Sir

Buster had planned.

The door opened with a creak, which, had it been dark, would have sounded haunted-house ominous. As it was, it merely sounded like it needed a squirt of WD40. Noah was greeted by Herbert, the Burrow Hall butler and one of the two members of staff who lived full-time with Sir Buster at the house. The other was Mrs Turner, the live-in chef. Her food was renowned as some of the best in the village. Anyone who had dined at Burrow Hall with Sir Buster over the last few years, or indeed when his wife Fiona had been alive, would have agreed. Pearl and Noah still talked about Mrs T's heaven-sent moussaka with mouth-watering enthusiasm. And her plum flapjacks were always the talk of the annual fayre. Both Mrs Turner and Herbert had been working for Sir Buster and his wife for decades.

Herbert's round, hamster-like face seemed flustered as he greeted Noah with a smile. 'Morning, sir, how are you?' He definitely seemed a little short of breath.

'Morning, Herbert, you okay? Are you all puffed out?' asked Noah.

'Sorry, sir, I was polishing the banister knobs at the top of the main stairs. They take quite a buffing. And I ran down the stairs when I heard the door. Not always wise at my age.'

Noah had never asked but guessed that Herbert could have easily retired a few years ago had he wished to. His domed cheeks were definitely stained with overexertion.

Herbert wiped away a bead of perspiration that threatened to run down his forehead with the duster he was carrying in his hand. 'You're here to see Sir Buster. He said to expect you.'

'Yes, he's asked me about landscaping some of the woodland around the lake. Wants to make it less overgrown or something. He's taking me down there this morning. I feel honoured. Not everyone gets to visit the Burniston private lake.'

'He's already there, sir. He left at the crack of dawn to go fishing. He had Mrs Turner make him up a packed breakfast to take with him. The sun was just poking its head above the horizon. I was up early too. I love the long light days. I like to have an early morning walk myself. It clears the brain. Sir Buster was in a chipper mood as ever. He's convinced the trout are easier to catch first thing as if they've just woken up and might still be a bit sluggish. If he's caught a load, I dare say you and your wife will be having trout for tea.'

'Fingers crossed, eh? Pearl's fried fish in breadcrumbs with her Caribbean seasoning is joyous. So, shall I go on down and meet him at the lake?'

'That's best, sir. You know the way?'

'Of course,' replied Noah. 'Pearl and I walked every inch of this estate when Sir Buster let us stay here. Thank you. I'll see you later.'

Herbert nodded. 'You too, sir. I'll get back to polishing that staircase. Have a good day.' He shut the door with another creak.

The walk down to the lake took about twenty minutes. It was at the far corner of the Hall grounds and surrounded by woodland. The early-morning sun warmed Noah's face happily as he walked across the lawns and entered into the more shaded yet still sun-dappled shelter of the woodlands. The canopy of trees overhead intermittently let shafts of light pierce the landscape. Noah couldn't help but smile as he caught glimpses of wildlife around him. Was that a chaffinch he saw flitting around or maybe a wood warbler? He wasn't sure either way, but the bird looked and sounded happy and that was all that mattered. Apparently, there were grass snakes to be seen. Noah never had, but he liked the idea. The nearest the family used to get to nature when they lived in London was the odd urban fox riffling through their wheelie bins. One of the reasons Noah had always wanted to be a landscape gardener was that he loved being outdoors. Apart from his time spent away from home, it really was his ideal profession.

The woodland started to become less dense as he approached the area where the lake was. By the time the lake came into full view, just a few trees dotted the landscape. He scanned his eyes around to locate Sir Buster. There was no immediate sign.

'Right, where are you, you old buzzard?' Noah asked himself. He placed his hands to his temple to stare out across the lake. The glare of the sun was already beginning to bounce off the glassy surface, making it a little difficult to focus. He squinted his eyes at a spot on the far side of the lake. What looked like a cool box and a picnic chair had been set up by the side of the water. Was that a blanket on the floor too? Yes, it appeared it was. He should have brought his binoculars. That must be Sir Buster's chosen spot. No sign of Sir Buster, though. Maybe he had nipped into the woods for a much-needed toilet break. Noah knew that he would need one if he'd been down here for five hours already.

It took Noah a few minutes, but he soon approached the blanketed area. The sound of a radio filled the air. Jazz music. The tinkly upbeat sound of a saxophone and piano hit his ears. He recognised the tunes but wasn't sure why. Nevertheless, it instantly brought a smile. The sun on his face, the music in his ears. The combination made for a wonderful Saturday morning.

A voice on the radio spoke at the end of the song. 'Good morning, you're listening to The Joy of Jazz FM, that was the maestro John Coltrane with "My Favourite Things", his interpretation of the song made famous by

The Sound of Music.'

Of course, that was where Noah recognised the song from. *The Sound of Music* was one of Pearl's favourite films. He and she had enjoyed themselves singing it with the twins on many occasions in the past.

Noah stood by the water's edge and waited for Sir Buster to return. It was then that he noticed the shape in the water. About twenty or thirty feet out from where he was standing. Face down. A body wearing those rubber long welly boot things that fishermen wear. A pair of jeans and a brown checked shirt. A cap and a fishing rod appeared to be floating alongside the body. It was a large body. How had he not seen it before? Maybe the glare of the sun? Maybe the dull colour of the clothing had made it blend in with the water. He cursed himself for not having spotted it sooner.

Noah felt all colour drain from his face and any sense of happiness vanish from his heart as he stared at the body. There was no doubting who it was. His hands began to shake as he reached for his phone to ring the police.

The cheery voice on the radio continued. 'I hope you're having the most amazing Saturday morning and that life is treating you well. Here's another classic slice of jazz that I know you're going to just adore on this most beautiful of mornings.'

His intro segued into the opening bars of 'What A Wonderful World'.

It seemed life was not treating Sir Buster well this beautiful Saturday morning at all. And that his world was very far from wonderful.

Chapter 5

Violet had just been bagging up a couple of balls of brightly coloured double-knit for Margaret Millsop at Brewer's Loop when Pearl Wheeler came bounding into the shop at both the speed and force of an SAS member. Her arrival made Sheena, who was busying herself up a ladder rearranging a selection of quilting books, nearly lose her balance and tumble to the floor. Luckily, she managed to grab one of the heavier tomes to steady herself as Pearl rushed up to the counter.

'Pearl, as I live and breathe, what on earth necessitates this kind of commotion on a Saturday morning. You nearly took the shop door off its hinges,' stated Violet. She turned back to Margaret and handed her the bag of wool. 'That'll make for a lovely cardigan will that, Margaret.'

Margaret's eyes were on Pearl too. 'You're all out of puff. What is going on?'

Pearl placed her hands on the counter and tried to catch her breath. 'I know, I've run all the way from the cottage to tell you.' It was only down the road, but Pearl would happily admit that she wasn't as fit as she once was. 'I'm glad you're here too, Margaret, as you were next on my list to contact.'

Sheena, now successfully back on terra firma, joined the three ladies at the counter.

Pearl took a couple of deep breaths to regain her composure. 'You'll never guess what's happened. Noah just phoned me. He's totally distraught. Honestly, I thought the poor love wasn't going to be able to get his words out. He was in such a state. He could barely bring himself to say it.'

'He's not the only one failing to get to the point, Pearl,' piped up Margaret. 'It must run in the family. What has happened? It had better not be anything to do with the fayre. Two weeks today and so far so good on the organisation front, although my marrow is not as big as I'd like it to be. But that's by the by. There's always time for a last-minute spurt. If anything has upset the apple cart now for the fayre, I'll be livid.'

'Shush, Margaret, let her talk…' said Violet.

'Noah found him face down in the lake, dead as can be. He was out fishing, and Noah had gone to meet him to discuss the lawns. He's doing some work up at the Hall. Or at least he was. I guess he won't bother now.' Pearl hesitated a second before turning to Margaret. 'Actually, maybe the fayre won't happen now. Seeing as it's on the grounds.'

Even though Pearl had not said it aloud, the penny had already dropped for all three of the women and none of them dared to air their thoughts.

Before they had a chance to do so, the door of the shop burst open once more, yet again endangering the hinges. This time it was Jimmy Coates, his ample frame filling the doorway. He was wearing a pair of jeans, a white T-shirt and a pair of wellies. All were splattered with mud.

'Oh my God, you guys, I was mucking out, but I had

to come and tell you. Sir Buster's dead. Face down in his own lake.'

'I was just about to say that,' said Pearl, somewhat vexed that her news had been stolen. 'Noah found him. How did you know?'

'This village knows when someone upgrades their telephone or suffers a runny nose in a matter of seconds, so news of a death is going to rocket onto the gossip grapevine like wildfire. Can you believe it? Sir Buster dead.'

Sheena burst into tears, unable to hold back her sadness. 'I was only talking to him yesterday. How can he be dead?'

Violet rolled into action and pulled up a box of tissues from under the counter, passing them to Sheena. 'There you go, dear, mop those tears. Right, Jimmy, come on in, shut that door and turn the sign to closed. Everybody out the back. I'll put the kettle on. I want to hear every detail of what we know so far. Although maybe a tot of something stronger might be in order, given the circumstances. Oh, and wipe your feet please, Jimmy, you're filthy and I don't want this floor mucked up. It's freshly mopped this morning.'

Jimmy closed the door, turned the sign and the five of them went through to the back room. As Violet grabbed both the gin and the teabags, she couldn't help but consider how many crafting kits she'd counted in the stocktake that specialised in sympathy cards. She'd probably be selling a few more of those than usual over the next few days.

Chapter 6

'So did I look impressive pulling the body out of the water. It took quite some dragging, I can tell you. I'm pleased I had that second bacon roll this morning. Gave me a bit of much-needed energy.'

Sergeant Samuel Pollett puffed out his chest and patted his belly at the same time. Maybe the second bacon roll wasn't the best idea, given the half a stone of extra weight that he was carrying around his midriff. But when his wife, Rita, was on an early shift at the corner shop and it was his decision alone as to whether he should plump for a bowl of muesli that looked fit for a guinea pig, or the rather juicy and tantalisingly succulent rashers of Coates' Farm bacon that were sitting in the fridge, there was really no choice. That decision was a good one. Muesli really had no valid place in life as far as he was concerned. Maybe his decision to dive in for a second helping of the bacon was not such a wise one. Had he have known he'd be pulling a dead body of rather mammoth proportions from Burrow Hall lake in under two hours' time, he might have thought again. The unsmoked rashers had definitely lay heavy in his stomach as he'd waded out to retrieve poor Sir Buster. Not that WPC Paula Horton, his good friend, colleague and often underling, needed to know that.

The two officers were standing in the tiny kitchen at Rooney-at-Burrow's rather compact police station. They were enjoying their first cup of much-needed tea after a morning of strenuous policing. And even though both of them were highly sorry to see that poor Sir Buster Burniston had passed away, they were both rather unapologetically thrilled that the morning had given them something meatier to deal with than a lost dog or a newly scratched expletive on the bench opposite the duck pond. Kids would be kids after all. Perhaps the real crime was that the last juvenile defacer hadn't even managed to spell the expletive correctly. Samuel planned to bring it up with their head teacher the next time he went to the village school to talk about the dangers of drugs and road safety.

'You looked highly impressive,' lied Paula. Let him have his moment, he'd been waiting a long time for this, she thought. His moment of true importance. She knew better than to remind him that she too had waded into the lake to help bring poor Sir Buster's body back to dry land. Or that Sarge Pollett's face had turned the colour of a slab of back bacon when he was trying to remove Sir Buster's seventeen stone body from the lake. She guessed seventeen stone. It was a hobby of Paula's. Trying to guess people's weight. She normally did it at Jazzercise to take her mind off the pain of the actual workout. Samuel Pollett was definitely weighing in at thirteen stone, she guessed right now, but she'd have said twelve at the start of the year. She did have an added advantage when it came to guessing Sir Buster's as she'd had to be rather hands-on. He was a two-person job. Something that Samuel seemed to have conveniently forgotten.

'I felt like I was in one of those fancy detective shows me and Rita love watching.' He dunked a biscuit into his tea as he spoke. He left it there a little too long and as he pulled it out, a sizable chunk of it belly-flopped back into the brown liquid. 'A mysterious body found in the lake on a cold misty morning. A stranger on the shore stunned by what they see. A phone call to the brutally handsome and enigmatic police officer who swoops in to solve the murder. A crime is unravelled, a murderer revealed, and a village can rest easy. All in a morning's work.'

WPC Horton nearly spat out her own biscuit as Samuel finished his poetic telling of their previous few hours. Okay, he'd had his moment now. That was done with. 'All right there, Taggart, wind your neck in. I'll translate, shall I. Noah Wheeler finds Sir Buster face down in his private lake on a warm August morning, phones you in hysterics, and you ring me saying we need to get up to Burrow Hall. When we do, it takes both of us to remove him from the lake and sadly it's too late for Sir Buster. He is indeed dead. There was no murder wound or bloody stab mark and no evidence of foul play. Just an old man who'd keeled over whilst out fishing in his own lake. He'd not even caught anything, poor man. The only sign of food was his half-eaten sandwiches in the cool box. Mind you, he had some appetite, I'll give him that. There was enough food to feed the entire village in that cool box. Seems you're not the only one with a love of gastronomy.'

It was now Paula's turn to pat her belly. She smiled as she did so. 'As for brutally handsome and enigmatic. Well, if knocking forty-five and thinning a bit on top with a touch of middle-age spread makes you Magnum PI, then I'm one of Charlie's Angels. But you do have a certain something obviously, because Rita adores you. And it did feel worthy to be doing some kind of police work other than tracking down a stolen bicycle or finding out who graffitied the side of the bus stop. So, job well done.'

'Bit harsh… I don't have middle-age spread, thank you.' He picked up a biscuit and placed it whole into his mouth in defiance.

'It's such a shame about Sir Buster, though. Everybody loved him. But he was a good old age, I suppose. Seventy something. I guess it was his heart. Just gave up,' Paula remarked.

'That's what Dr Roberts said.' Sergeant Pollett had

phoned him from the side of the lake to come and check that Sir Buster was indeed dead. They knew he was, of course, what with him being face down in the water and not breathing, but they had to do these things correctly. Samuel had seen that enough times on the TV. Then someone had come to take the body away.

'It's all so sad. Noah must be in a right state. I'm surprised he didn't wade in to try to pull Sir Buster out. He must have known he was dead and been paralysed with shock. The whole village will be in a state of shock, to be honest. Two weeks before the fayre as well,' said Paula, finishing her brew. 'We should still have it as a mark of respect. A memorial to Sir Buster. He'd have liked that, I'm sure.'

'That's up to Margaret, I guess, and whoever gets the Hall in the will,' guessed Samuel.

'He has kids, doesn't he?' asked Paula.

'He does indeed. A son and a daughter. I remember them being quite bratty when they were younger, but I've not seen sight nor sound of them for donkey's years. I wonder if we'll hear from them now that poor Sir Buster's dead.'

'We're bound to. There is nothing like a death to bring out all the weirdness and dysfunctions of a family. Especially when I'm guessing there will be a pretty sizable slab of money to consider in the will.'

'Aren't you clever with your deductions. Although you'll never be one of Charlie's Angels, you're not glam enough,' smirked Samuel. 'And you're too old. What are you now, thirty-eight?'

'I'm thirty-four, you cheeky—'

Paula's words fell short as Samuel's phone rang. He put down his mug and picked up his phone.

'Talking of dysfunctional families, look who's ringing. I knew it wouldn't be long.' He clicked the phone on. 'Hi, Aunty Violet. How are you?'

Paula smiled. She loved Violet and spent many hours discussing village affairs with her either in the back room of Brewer's Loop over a packet of Bakewell tarts or when Violet spontaneously dropped into the police station. Samuel said they gossiped; Paula saw it much more as an exchange of intriguing and potentially useful information about village life.

Samuel held the phone away from his ear. The cause was easy for Paula to hear. Violet Brewer was in full flow.

'It's about the terrible news about Sir Buster. Such a loss. I'll be speaking to your mum in Australia later and she'll want to know everything, as do I, to be fair. I hear you were the first police officer on the scene. No surprise, seeing as you're virtually the only one around here for miles. I hope you took that lovely WPC Horton with you. She's always such a switched-on girl.'

Paula grinned and took a mock bow of thanks. Samuel merely smirked again.

There was no stopping Violet. 'I'm in my flat above the shop. I've shut up for the day. Your daughter's been very upset. She loved Sir Buster. You realise she may have been one of the last people to see him alive. I've sent her to the corner shop to be with her mother. I suspect she'll shut up shop too as a mark of respect. Mind you, people will be wanting tea and milk, no doubt, as there's a lot of things to discuss. Like the cause of death for one? What was it?'

Violet finally drew breath. The phone fell silent as she

waited for a response.

'That's police business, Aunty Violet.'

'And I've seen you naked in the bath as a five-year-old playing with your rubber duck, so I think we can drop any ideas of importance, don't you, dear? Plus, I'll find out from Dr Roberts anyway. So, you may as well cut out the middleman.'

Paula tried to stifle a laugh at the mention of Samuel naked playing with his rubber ducks.

Samuel, turning a deep shade of crimson, blustered on. 'They think it was his heart.'

He waited for Violet's response, but for a few seconds one didn't come.

'I knew you were going to say that. And I'd put good money on that being poppycock. That man was as strong as an ox and fitter than most men half his age. You never saw him with a paunch, did you? He looked after himself. And don't think I've not noticed yours creeping on recently, Samuel. You know what they say about little pickers...'

Another smirk and stifled laugh from Paula.

Samuel didn't have time to answer before Violet launched again. 'Right, I'm putting the kettle on. Can you come over now? Tell me everything. Bring WPC Horton with you too. And stop in at Rita's if she's still open and grab some Bakewell tarts. I'm all out.'

Samuel knew his aunt well enough to know that it was pointless to argue and caved in. 'Okay, we'll be over now.' He ended the call. 'She's incorrigible. I guess you heard all of that. She doesn't think it was his heart.'

'Every word. And maybe it wasn't.'

'C'mon, let's go. And what do they say by the way?'

'Who?' asked Paula.

'The people who talk about little pickers.'

'That they wear bigger knickers,' laughed Paula. 'Talking of which, Sarge…' She pointed down to his legs. From the waist down, all he was wearing was his boxer shorts.

When they had finished dragging the dead body of Sir Buster out of the lake, their uniforms had been soaked. WPC Horton had nipped home and changed into her spare uniform as soon as she could. Samuel, meanwhile, had tried to change at the station, but his spare pair of trousers was in the wash. They were currently placed over a wall at the back of the station drying in the summer sun.

'Oh yeah, could you get them for me... please?' asked Samuel with more than a dose of childish pleading. He was already regretting his choice of Superman logo boxers he'd slipped on that morning but was very thankful that at least today wasn't one of those days when he'd decided to wear his virtually threadbare pair of Bart Simpson 'Don't Have A Cow, Man!' boxers that Sheena had given him for Christmas nearly a decade earlier.

Of course, Paula did go and fetch the trousers. She'd do anything for Samuel Pollett. He may have been her boss, but primarily he was her friend and somebody she loved working with. And not everybody could say that about the people they worked with, could they?

WPC Horton left her boss standing in his Superman boxers as she went to fetch his trousers, desperately trying to rid the image of him playing with a rubber duck in the bath from her mind.

Chapter 7

Stephanie Brooks was in a state of shock as she took the bags of crisps from the ripped cardboard box on the floor behind the bar and placed them in a rather more presentable bowl alongside the till. They needed to be displayed as they were intended to tempt the customers of The Six Pennies into buying the new flavour she'd been sent. Pickled pork, they were called. Meaty with a hint of vinegar. How they'd stand up against smoky bacon or prawn cocktail remained to be seen. She didn't hold out a lot of hope. She'd just offered one to the elderly gentleman she'd served a pint of lager to. Not one of the village regulars, thankfully, as the look on his face when she'd offered him a bag was far from pleasant. She doubted he'd ever come back given his reaction. Maybe he was Jewish?

Not that the flavouring of her bar snacks or the customer's reaction to them was the reason for her shock. No, it was due to the news that had swept through the village that poor Sir Buster had gone to meet his maker. He may have been seventy-one, but it still felt that he had so much more living to do. Didn't they say that the good died young? Well, Sir Buster definitely had a streak of the deliciously bad about him, which meant that he should have stayed around for quite a while yet. Not a horrible kind of bad, of course. Oh no, just that streak of bluster and cheeky, lovable rogue that made him so popular with everyone in the village.

His death would be a huge loss for the village. And for Steph. Whenever Sir Buster was in the pub, he was always the centre of attention. He had been just a few nights before, regaling everyone with tales of immature pranks and toilet humour from his days at boarding school. He always had a smile on his face and a story to share. Steph had never forgotten the time he'd made her blush the colour of the village postbox by telling her about his first ever experience with a girlfriend. Things hadn't gone quite to plan and the house alarm had somehow gone off during his first attempt at seduction. She could still hear his words now. 'I had to bloody run off with my britches around my ankles and the alarm ringing in my ears as the girl thought her parents had set off the alarm deliberately to alert the police. Talk about a blessed passion killer.'

But at least Sir Buster had lived every moment to the fullest, right to the very last. That was the way anyone should live their life. To the max. Not spend their life doing mundane things. Like unpacking boxes full of pickled pork crisps. Steph had experienced more interesting days with more interesting chores.

But it was a chore that needed to be done, and if one person plumped for pickled pork as their chosen snack after opening time, then it was a job well done, Steph tried to convince herself as she flattened the empty crisp box and took it out through the rear of the bar, out the back door and into the back yard of The Six Pennies where the recycling bins were placed.

It was there that she found her husband, Phill. On his knees, overalls on, painting a bench for the beer garden in the summer sunshine. No wonder she'd hardly seen him over the last few hours. Now she knew where he'd been hiding. Out the back with a brush in one hand and a pot of paint in the other. Another lick of paint for the good of their pride and joy, The Six Pennies.

Now in his late forties, as was she, Phill and Steph had been together as man and wife for eighteen years. Solid, dependable, liked by all, Phill was one of life's nice people. He always had been, but sometimes Steph longed for him to have a little something more. A bit of an edge maybe. To not be so... er, nice. Not that Steph didn't thank her lucky stars for what they had achieved as a couple. No kids, that hadn't happened, but their babies were the string of pubs they had run together for nearly two decades.

Phill loved each and every one of them, as did she in her own way, but whereas Phill would find a huge amount of excitement in printing up a new pub menu or organising a karaoke night or a local DJ to entertain beer drinkers with an 'Oops Upside Your Head' or a 'Macarena', Steph sometimes found that her heart just wasn't one hundred per cent in it. In fact, more often than not these days.

Phill could literally wax lyrical about the joys of stocking scampi fries and pork scratchings as opposed to dry roasted peanuts, whereas Steph couldn't really give a monkey's if they started selling devilled kidneys and meringue nests behind the bar, which given the pickled pork crisps may not have been such a fanciful idea.

But, having said that, there were moments when being behind the bar in a pub was the best position in the world. A beautiful fusion of pride and enjoyment. Two nights ago, with Sheena singing like an angel on stage and Sir Buster making Steph laugh until her sides ached was one of them. She sighed. He would be missed. By her. By Phill. By the village. By the very brickwork of The Six Pennies itself.

Steph opened the lid of the recycling wheelie bin and popped the flattened cardboard inside, which roused Phill from his painting.

'Have you tried them yet? The suppliers said they've been very successful at some of the pubs up north. Pickled pork could be the new prawn cocktail, you mark my words,' stated Phill, one eye on Steph and one on the bench he was working on. Steph wasn't convinced, but what did she know.

'I've not had the pleasure of them as yet?' Steph hoped she didn't come across as sarcastically as she sounded in her own mind. 'I offered them to someone, but he ran off...'

'Where do you stand on beef jerky?' asked Phill, apropos of nothing.

'Ummm… I'm not sure really. Why?'

'The supplier was trying to convince me that it would have worked as a bar snack in any of our bars over the years. I said that maybe it might have worked with some of your younger clientele, but I can't see it being a hit here in Rooney-at-Burrow. I think you and I know what makes for a popular snack item, don't we?'

'I guess we do,' said Steph, non-committally.

Ignoring her vague response, Phill continued with both the conversation and his painting. 'That's why we're such a good team. We always have been. We know what makes a good pub. It's why The Prince Regent in Cockermouth worked. And The Raised Stag in Melton

Mowbray. And The Six Pennies here. How long has it been now? A decade here? And still going strong. Because we know the right things to make a pub successful. Decent folk, great entertainment – I hear that people still talk about that sensational ventriloquist in Cockermouth – and the right mix of bar snacks and food on the menu. Plus, the best landlord and landlady that any pub could want. We're the perfect team you and I, Stephanie. We always have been. The perfect combination. Like steak and kidney. Or cheese and pickle. Loved by all. And I love you.' Phill looked up from where he was painting directly into Steph's eyes. 'I really do, you know. I love you more than ever.'

Steph smiled. He didn't say it very often, but when he did, her husband always delivered it with affection. If sometimes with a slightly iffy comparison. At least it wasn't pork and pickle. But it was always nice to hear.

'I love you too, Phill.' She fell quiet for a second. 'I can't stop thinking about Sir Buster. It's so sad. We should organise a night here to celebrate his life. Like a kind of memorial but not at all sombre. Nice and cheery. The kind of night he loved here. Maybe next weekend?'

'That's a lovely idea. I've been thinking about him ever since you told me that he'd died. It's why I'm painting this bench. He loved to sit in the beer garden, didn't he? So, I thought I'd give this a revamp. Strip and sand it back, give it a fresh lick of paint and get a plaque engraved for it. Kind of a memory for years to come of one of our greatest customers. Sir Buster Burniston, friend and customer, blah, blah, blah…' He bit his bottom lip in thought. 'Does that sound like a nice idea. I thought it was.'

Steph could feel her heart becoming warmer in her chest. 'I think that's a genuinely nice idea. He'd love that. You could unveil it on the night. Right at the end, as some kind of grand finale.'

'Great idea. Right, I'd better crack on. I'll hide the bench away when I'm finished, up by the shed so that no one sees it before the night itself.' Phill returned his full attention to the bench. He stretched his arms out, trying to crack his bones back into place from where he'd been bent over. They were sore. One in particular. It had been for a while now. Just by his shoulder. Dr Roberts had prescribed some smelly gel thing to put on it. Which he had been doing. He just wasn't sure it was working. He'd go and see Dr Roberts again if it persisted. The joys of old age, he thought to himself, despite not yet being fifty.

Steph wandered back inside the pub. The bench was a very nice idea indeed. But then Phill was a nice man, wasn't he. So very, incredibly nice. Maybe they were the perfect combination, but it just wasn't always easy for her to see it clearly.

Back in the bar, Steph opened a packet of the pickled pork crisps and popped one in her mouth. She wasn't keen. The elderly customer had been right. She wasn't convinced that pork and vinegar were a perfect combination at all. Only time would tell.

Chapter 8

'Another Bakewell, dear?'

Violet offered the plate of cakes to WPC Paula Horton. There was actually only one left, and it looked a little lost on the commemorative royal wedding plate on which she has originally arranged the packet of six. All that remained was the one solitary almond delight, a doily covering most of the prince and princess and a few stray crumbs.

'It seems such a shame to leave just one. Hardly worth putting back in the packet. And you've only eaten one, anyway. A strong policewoman like you needs to keep your stamina up, especially now that we have a mystery on our very own village doorstep.' Violet turned her gaze to her nephew, Samuel, and raised her eyebrows. 'I assume that's why you've already had three of them. Keeping your stamina up, are we?'

Samuel ignored her dig. Paula declined the offer of the last Bakewell tart with a shake of her head, so just to spite his aunt, Samuel reached across and grabbed the cake and took a large bite. Well, they were incredibly moreish.

'Well, I guess it won't be going back into the packet after all, will it?' smiled Violet as she placed the now-empty plate back on the table in front of her. She had been discussing the details of the discovery of Sir Buster's body with the two police officers for the last thirty minutes. But despite chewing over every morsel that was offered up, Violet was still not satisfied. 'So, let me get this straight…'

Samuel sighed heavily through a mouthful of cake. He knew what was coming. Again.

'So, Noah Wheeler called you at about 10.30 this morning to say that he had found Sir Buster's body in the lake. You two made your way up there just before 11 a.m. and retrieved the body from the lake. You took a statement from Noah and then called Dr Roberts to come and give poor Sir Buster a final once-over to make sure he was dead. He gave his opinion and then the coroner came to take the body away. That's correct, yes?'

'Like we've told you twice already.' Samuel knew that there was no point stopping his aunt once she was in full flow. She would want to be word-perfect when she reported it back to his mum, Betsy, in Australia later.

'And Dr Roberts' opinion was that Sir Buster had died from a heart attack?'

'That was his initial thought,' offered Paula. 'Given Sir Buster's age and the fact that he was found face down in the water. He'd been fishing stood in the lake, suffered a heart attack, keeled over and drowned.'

'How do you know he was fishing in the lake itself, and not on the side?' quizzed Violet.

Paula answered, 'He was wearing those long welly boot things that go right the way up your legs. If he'd just been fishing on the side, he wouldn't have had to wear them to keep dry, would he? Not in this weather. It's glorious out there today.' She pointed out the window of Violet's flat.

'Good point,' remarked Violet.

'Which I was about to say,' said Samuel, keen to show

off his investigative skills. He was the officer in charge of this case after all.

'Course you were, dear,' said Violet, reaching over to squeeze him on the knee.

'Plus, if he'd have fallen over on dry land it's unlikely he'd have rolled into the water as the land there is fairly flat on the banks of the lake.' WPC Horton was on a roll herself.

'Another valid point,' noted Violet.

'I thought that too,' said Samuel to no one in particular.

'What about the time of death then? Were you able to pinpoint that?'

'Well, we interviewed Herbert, the butler at Burrow Hall…' started Paula.

Samuel cleared his throat and coughed with an air of interruption. It obviously worked, as Paula stopped mid-sentence.

He spoke. 'Er, thanks, WPC Horton, I think I can take it from here, if you don't mind.' He coughed again, the crumbs from his fourth Bakewell tickly in his throat still.

Violet winked at Paula and smiled. They both knew that Samuel needed to have his moment in the spotlight. It was hardly *Prime Suspect*, but Violet knew that in her nephew's mind, every scene was playing out like one of his favourite cop dramas. He'd watched them ever since he was a kid. They were the very reason he wanted to be a police officer in the first place. And seeing as there weren't that many episodes focussing on everyday village crimes like who nicked a pitchfork from the local allotment, this was probably the closest Sergeant Samuel Pollett was ever going to get to a meaty crime, even if there was no crime at this point. But there was a dead body, and that was definitely a few rungs up on the intrigue ladder from a missing garden implement.

'Under my instructions, WPC Horton and I went up to Burrow Hall to inform Herbert, the butler, and Mrs Turner, the housekeeper, of our findings. As you can imagine, both of them were deeply upset and distressed at what we had to tell them.'

Violet nodded her understanding.

Samuel continued. 'We gathered them together to break the news. Herbert told us that Sir Buster had left Burrow Hall at about five that morning to go fishing. Mrs Turner said that she'd made him some low-fat egg mayonnaise sandwiches, his favourite apparently, as instructed the night before, and packed some fruit and yoghurts for him with a flask of tea and sent him on his way.'

Violet couldn't help but interject. 'He was always a healthy eater that man. Good hearty snacks. I could never tempt him with a piece of shortbread or a Jammie Dodger when he popped in for tea here. He was always semi-skimmed in his brew, you know. And he never touched one of his late wife's crumbles ever. That's a crime in itself. They were delicious. I still salivate over the taste now and she's been six foot under for ten years. Sir Buster has always been so good with his food. Loved his beer but careful on the calories front. Hangover from his sporting days, I guess. Mrs Turner is a wonder. She creates the most amazing healthy fare for him.'

Samuel coughed again. 'As I was saying...'

'Sorry, dear, do continue.'

'So, if Herbert saw him head off down to the lake at about five in the morning and Noah found him just about ten, then there's a five-hour window for time of death. I guess the coroner will be able to work out exactly how long Sir Buster might have been in the water for. He'll report back to me as chief officer on the case, of course.'

Was that a swelling of her boss's chest Paula just witnessed? She knew it was. She raised her hand excitedly. 'But Sir Buster had eaten some of his sandwiches, I know that because I looked in the cool box. There was so much food in there, Violet, honestly, it was fuller than the shelves at Rita's. But there was a screwed-up ball of cling film there with some breadcrumbs inside, so he'd obviously eaten them at some point. I think there was some more sarnies in there too. Logic says that he probably didn't eat them straight away when he got to the lake. You never do, do you? So, let's say he didn't have them until about eight. That narrows down the window a bit. I'm totally guessing, but personally I can't eat in the morning until I've had at least two mugs of coffee.'

'I think we'll leave that to the coroner, don't you, Paula. We both know that good police procedure should not involve guesswork.' Samuel's words were patronising but never malicious. He just liked to have the final word, which, of course, he was never going to have when Violet was nearby.

True to form as ever, Violet ignored Samuel's tone. 'I think you're right, Paula. You normally are. I suspect Sir Buster would have been straight into the lake fishing. Otherwise, why get up so early. Did you inspect the flask? Had he drunk much of it?'

'About a third. It was still warm,' Paula confirmed.

'That's flasks for you. I'd never be without one on our crafting expeditions with Margaret. Marvellous things. Hot tea wherever you may be. And, believe you me, keeping the shop stocked can be thirsty work.' Violet raised her chin and pondered what Samuel and Paula had told her. 'Did either Herbert or Mrs Turner say whether Sir Buster had been feeling peaky at all. Under the weather, out of breath, anything like that. Not that I've ever known the man to have so much as a runny nose in all the years I've had the pleasure. I'm sure his records at Dr Roberts' surgery barely amount to more than a couple of sheets of A4.' She made a mental note to get Dr Roberts round as soon as possible. Maybe she could fake a fever to create a sense of urgency to get him to visit.

'No, both of them said that he was as fighting fit as ever,' remarked Samuel. Paula nodded in agreement.

'Interesting. And as I thought. Sheena was saying earlier how she was having a job to keep up with him yesterday when he was out golfing. And she's a third of his age. You must catch up with your daughter, by the way, Samuel. She'll be needing a hug.' Violet contemplated all that she had heard. 'So, what happens, now? Will there be a major investigation? I suppose we'll all be being interviewed, will we? Last time we spoke to him. Where we were at the time of death. How fascinating will that be? You two will be very busy over the next few days, I dare say. You'll be feeling very important, dear nephew. Perhaps you can shift some of those excess calories when you're running here, there and everywhere.' Violet let out a slight ripple of laughter as she pointed once again to the empty plate on the table between them. Paula gave a small titter too.

'I think you're going to be highly disappointed, Aunt Violet,' replied Samuel. 'Sir Buster was a man of mature years who lived life to the fullest and, just as Dr Roberts suggested, it looks like he had a heart attack and sadly died while out fishing. I'm sure the coroner will say exactly the same. It's an open-and-shut case pretty much.'

If Samuel thought that he was going to have the final word for once, then yet again he was wrong.

'Oh no, dear, there's definitely something more to this than meets the eye. Sir Buster Burniston may have been around for a while, but he was as strong as can be. I refuse to believe that his heart simply gave up. Call it female intuition, the ramblings of a silly woman, or some kind of gory gut feeling, but there's foul play involved somewhere, so I suggest you start investigating. I certainly would be if I was you. Who benefits from his death, for one?' Violet paused before finishing. 'There's definitely something fishy going on. No pun intended. I'm not alone in thinking this. Margaret, Pearl, Jimmy and Sheena all feel the same. We were discussing it earlier over a calming gin. Something fishy at Sir Buster's private lake. You mark my words.'

Was there more to it than simple old age and a heart attack? The wannabe heroic telly detective inside Sergeant Samuel Pollett hoped that maybe his aunt was right.

He also hoped that she wasn't dishing out gin to his daughter on a Saturday morning.

Chapter 9

'You and your crafting pals may think that there's foul play involved, but that's still no excuse for you sitting your muddy bits and pieces down on that chair. The finest pink velvet upholstery and hooped solid brass legs are not a winning mix when splattered with pig muck. It's the height of in vogue Art Deco furniture, Jimmy. I have influencers in Abu Dhabi who would literally murder their grandmother for that right now.'

Jimmy was in no mood to discuss the décor desires of some person he'd neither heard of nor cared about thousands of miles away. There were more important matters close at hand to discuss. 'Don't worry, honey, I'll use the Fairy Liquid and Febreze on it later, it'll wash out good as new.'

Jimmy Coates was used to the flowery rants of his interior designer boyfriend, Bailey Frazer-Ferguson. They were a common occurrence when he was at home on the farm. Which was the last place you would normally expect a man like Bailey to indeed call home. With a degree in fashion and design from a top London University under his belt and an ever-busying, highly lucrative interior design business keeping him very much in demand from those with money and taste – but rarely the two together – he was the epitome of the successful dandy. Eccentric, kooky, flamboyant and as colourful as a room full of peacocks. The male ones, of course. He usually had more colours going on in one frilly-cuffed shirt than Jimmy had in his entire wardrobe.

But that was the professional Bailey. Rants about opulence and texture, the animated energy flow of a house and the symbolism of what you hung on your walls. Important stuff, right? Bailey seemed to think so. But Jimmy loved him as 'his Bailey', which came with all of the above plus the biggest heart he'd ever met in a man and the knowledge that even if all of the fancy stuff was taken away and they lived in a corrugated iron pig pen together they would still be deeply in love. Not that the pig pen thing would ever happen. Both of them were far too successful in their own polar-opposite ways.

Jimmy and Bailey were now in their early fifties and doing very nicely, thank you, in their different fields – one with pigs and sheep in and one that would have to be feng-shui'ed to within an inch of its life and probably contain some supposedly iconic and weird award-winning piece of artwork that consisted of two broken bits of pizza box, a dead beetle and an antimacassar. Bailey had taken him to many an art exhibition where he'd had to fawn over some famous artist who might as well have been exhibiting one of Jimmy's old muck shovels, covered in said muck, for all of the artistry that their own unique projects contained. But Jimmy would smile sweetly and say the right things because it was important to Bailey and Bailey was important to Jimmy. Indeed, Bailey was his true love. A decade together said so.

They'd met through a dating site. One where you had to actually write about yourself and not just send a picture of some body part. They were both charmingly nervy on their first date, not knowing what to expect, but despite their different backgrounds, they seemed to gel instantly. Ten years later and they were still gelling nicely. Ten years in which Bailey had turned the interior of Coates Farm into a showcase of style that you would normally find at some Kensington hotel. Bailey would change at least one room every six months. So far, in their relationship history, Coates Farm, which was as rustic and bare-brick basic as it could be pre-Bailey, had been treated to stark metalwork, luxury jungle, museum minimalism, train hub chic and a homage to Russian history, to name but five 'looks'. As long as Jimmy had somewhere comfy to park his backside at the end of a busy day farming, he was happy. Which was why stark metalwork and museum minimalism were themes that had to be very short-lived. Thankfully, Bailey's current fad of Art Deco opulence was much more posterior-friendly when it came to hours of cross-stitching, crosswords or diving into his latest psychological thriller book. All of the things that kept Jimmy occupied when his man was away with work, which sadly was too often for his liking. But such was life. Yes, thankfully velvet was comfy... even with mud on it.

Jimmy shifted in his seat. 'I'm not sure you should be joking about murder, Bailey,' he said, referencing his quip about his clients in Abu Dhabi. 'Violet definitely thinks that Sir Buster didn't just drop down dead. Nobody has actually mentioned the "M" word. But we all think it's highly likely that there might be somebody else involved. Think of all the money that's wrapped up in Burrow Hall and the lands. I know how much this place is worth, or at least I did when it was just a farmhouse, so imagine how much Burrow Hall could be sold for if Sir Buster's family decides to sell.'

Bailey sat himself down on the equally pink and velvet chaise longue alongside the chair where Jimmy was perched. 'It is a huge property. I would have killed to get my hands on that place and give it a makeover.'

'Ooooh, suspect number one!' cooed Jimmy, pointing an accusatory yet jokey finger at his boyfriend. 'Don't let Violet hear you saying that, or she'll be taking down your particulars.'

'Very funny. I'm of the belief that Sir Buster died of natural causes. When your time is up, it's up. End of. It's all very sad but very understandable. He was knocking on. But seeing as we are on the subject of his family, who's set to gain?'

'I would imagine his kids.'

'I didn't even know he had any.' Bailey seemed genuinely surprised.

'You should actually try talking to the villagers a little more when you're here. There's a lot you don't know. You're normally too busy with those clients you work with. Those people off the telly. Whoever they are.' The last person that Jimmy could remember Bailey working with was some ex-kids TV presenter who now hosted a bizarre TV show interviewing prisoners after he himself had been charged with embezzlement.

Bailey huffed. 'Just because I prefer to get my gossip from the gossip columns and from the mouths of the stars themselves rather than from over the fence in the local pub beer garden doesn't mean I don't care about village life. You know I love it here. I love the charm of the village.

And everyone loves me. Go on, admit it.'

It was true, they did. Bailey did bring a certain celebrity flare to Rooney-at-Burrow which the younger villagers seemed to love. Jimmy would often jot down the name of the latest celebrity that Bailey was furnishing so that he could name-drop it to a very easily pleased Sheena at their weekly C.R.A.B. meetings. She had once became nigh on catatonic when he'd mentioned the name of some YouTuber who had made a fortune and amassed millions of followers through doing something creative with hair extensions.

'Didn't Sir Buster ever mention his family to you. Or was he too busy swinging you around the dance floor?' There was a saucy slice of sarcasm in Jimmy's words.

'Oh,' Bailey tutted. 'That old chestnut. Just because I got a little bit drunk at the New Year's Eve bash at Burrow Hall and ended up insisting that Sir Buster try to Argentine Tango with me. I think I was a bit giddy, wasn't I, and thought I knew the steps as I'd been working with that total Adonis from *Strictly*. I didn't have a clue. Neither did Sir Buster, but he was more than happy to twirl me around at high speed. He was extremely energetic. In fact, he was much less knackered at the end of it than I was. Maybe you and the gang are right. His heart must be fairly robust.'

An air of silence and sadness fell over Bailey for a moment. Jimmy noticed it immediately.

'You liked him as much as the rest of us, didn't you? He will be missed by everyone in the village.'

'I did,' contemplated Bailey. 'He was very sweet. And very handsome. Let's be honest. Major Daddy vibes going on there. But I will miss our chats. We used to talk about my veganism all the time. He didn't get it totally, but he was always into healthy eating, so we had long chats about food. He always found it most odd that a vegan would be sharing their life with a farmer, but as I told him, you can't choose who you fall in love with, can you. And heaven knows I've tried to convince you about plant protein agriculture. I'll win you over one day.'

'Old habits die hard,' said Jimmy. He was open to change; he just hadn't convinced himself how as yet.

'Now, who's talking about death,' Bailey reprimanded.

'Anyhow, who are Sir Buster's kids. I've certainly never seen them around here.'

'Boy and a girl. All grown up now. Both of them were your average teenagers, from what I remember. Mardy and mopey and sticking two fingers up to the world. Sir Buster and his wife shipped them off to boarding school and we didn't see much of them again. I think the last time I saw them was at their mother's funeral.'

'Well, they'll be back,' remarked Bailey. 'Where there's a will, there's always a way home. Especially a will with lots of zeroes.'

Jimmy was just about to agree with his boyfriend, when Oscar, one of the two farmhands that worked at Coates Farm, strode into the room. Oscar and his girlfriend, Hannah, she of Jazzercise fame, were invaluable as far as Jimmy was concerned and had both worked on the farm for nearly a decade. They had been teenagers when they'd started and now, in their mid-twenties, had become experts about farm life. Jimmy knew he could trust them with anything.

'Sorry to interrupt, fellas. But there's a problem with

the chicken coop,' said Oscar.

Jimmy and Bailey were both listening but neither of them could stop themselves from momentarily staring at what Oscar was wearing. Topless from the waist up and showing off a considerably chiselled body, he was sporting tight knee-length denim shorts. On any normal pair of legs, they would probably be roomy, but Oscar had thighs that most Greek gods would envy. Jimmy and Bailey had discussed them frequently as natural wonders of the world. And the shorts showed them to perfection. The two of them sat there now stunned into appreciative silence.

Their concentration was only broken when Bailey's mobile phone sounded. Staring at the screen, he answered it with haste. 'Darling, girl, how is Abu Dhabi...' It was obviously a work call.

Jimmy's daydreaming snapped back into the here and now as well. He used to have a body like Oscar's back in the day. Well, nearly. Maybe a few fry-ups heavier. Working on the farm was definitely a strenuous workout. And getting older was definitely a bit of a bugger.

'So, what's the problem with the chicken coop...?'

As Oscar told him, Bailey's animated voice on the phone filled the air around Jimmy as he spoke to his client. 'Yes, darling, I loved your Instagram post about the quad biking. Yes, you looked fabulous in your bikini, you always do. Have you made a decision on the new apartment? You *would* like me to furnish it for you? Oh that's marvellous. I was thinking Art Deco opulence. How do you feel about pink velvet? I have just the thing.'

Before he had to hear any more about chenille and pelmets or whatever was coming next, Jimmy blew a kiss at his boyfriend and went to follow Oscar out of the room to go and fix the chicken coop. Apparently, a fox had managed to get in and had killed off two of Jimmy's prize hens. The bugger. He'd have to tell Violet and co that, indeed, there was a killer on the loose in Rooney-at-Burrow. But this one had four legs and a big brush.

Just before he disappeared, Bailey waved at him frantically. He spoke to the person on the phone. 'Just hold a tick will you, doll…' Bailey placed his hand over the phone and turned to Jimmy. He pointed urgently at the pink velvet chair as he did so. He mouthed two words quite vehemently before returning to his call. 'Fairy. Liquid.'

Jimmy smiled and left the room.

Chapter 10

It appeared to be a rather hectic morning for Violet's sister, Betsy, at her home in Willow's Spit, Australia. She definitely seemed a tad red-faced when she appeared on the screen of Violet's laptop for one of their regular FaceTime calls. In her kitchen, guessed Violet, who was tucked up in her bed, steaming mug of relaxing cocoa in hand, at the end of what had been a most unconventional day for her too.

'Sorry if I'm flustered, Violet, I've only been out of bed half an hour and it's been quite a morning already, what with one thing and another. You're lucky I've had chance to do my hair. Mind you, I've run out of that edelweiss face cream that I adore so had to run to the store. I was sure I had a spare, but no. And poor Rod's already out the back cleaning up by the pool as some wombat has been gnawing at the fence near the deep end and made a whacking great big hole and a right mess. We've not even sat down for breakfast properly yet.'

Violet loved to hear about life in Willow's Spit, but talk of pool cleaning and wombats made her happy that she lived a much simpler life in Rooney-at-Burrow. Mopping shop floors and counting balls of wool seemed much less arduous than tidying up after a rampaging rodent. Were wombats rodents? She assumed so. Finding the odd mouse nibble mark on your skirting in the shop was one thing but dealing with a huge hole in your garden fence panels was quite another. The price you paid for having a fancy house with a pool, she supposed.

'Well, I suggest you make a brew and sit down, dear sister, because I have got some serious village news to share with you. You'll never guess who's died.'

'Died!' screamed Betsy, shoving her face towards the screen, virtually filling it. 'Who? Oh my God, hang on, let me tell Rod.'

Betsy placed the phone she was on down on the

kitchen table. When she was expecting a call, she would often set up her laptop too, but Violet had called her on the fly, so phone it was.

Violet stared at the screen and sipped her cocoa. All she could see was Betsy's kitchen ceiling and a couple of in-built spotlights. She attempted to name the colour of the ceiling in her mind as she listened to her sister shouting to Rod out the back: 'I'm going to speak to Violet for a while. I'm shutting the back door because of the banging. I can't have that going on while I talk. Violet said someone's died.' Violet plumped for buttermilk. Maybe biscuit. She was still deciding when her sister returned to the phone, her face replacing the ceiling, whatever colour it was.

'Rod's been banging away with a hammer to fix the fence, so I've shut the door.'

'So I heard.'

'So, Violet, tell me, who's died? Is it somebody we really like?'

Betsy listened to Violet's every word as her sister explained about the events of the day and the death of Sir

Buster Burniston. Betsy said nothing but, in between listening and boiling the kettle for her morning coffee, let out the odd gasp of surprise or tut of sympathetic disappointment as Violet divulged every detail she had photographically remembered from her conversations with Samuel, Paula and Team C.R.A.B. throughout the day.

Betsy was just stirring her freshly poured coffee as Violet concluded her story. She was shocked by what she heard. 'Well, blow me. Poor Sir Buster, I thought he'd outlive us all. Always thought he was built like a prize bull and was as healthy as one. Is he still as fussy with his food as he's always been? And is Samuel sure it's his heart.'

'Yes, he is… er, was… on the food front, and no, of course not, regarding the heart. You know what your son is like, Betsy. He's got nothing to really base that on at the moment other than a hunch and an inconclusive suggestion from Dr Roberts, who I shall be tracking down in the morning for a subtle and medically investigative village chat, let me tell you.'

'I bet Samuel is loving this, isn't he? Finally, he gets something more exciting to do than just trying to deduce who forgot to use a poo bag for their daily dog walk on the village green.'

'It's definitely given him a pumped-up sense of importance, that's for sure. Doubtless he'll be screaming "book 'em, Danno" to poor WPC Horton and leaping across car bonnets outside the wool shop thinking he's Starsky – or was it Hutch? – like one of those telly cops he's always been obsessed with. He'll be growing a moustache like Hercule Poirot before you know it and speaking all continental.'

Violet and Betsy both giggled at the thought.

'Tell him to ring me, if he's not too busy solving a murder, of course. And Sheena too. I bet she's taken this hard, hasn't she? Such a lovely girl and she really liked Sir Buster. She's been working for him, hasn't she?'

Violet set down her now empty cocoa mug on the bedside table and pulled the duvet up over her. Despite it being a summer's night, there was still a slight chill in the air. And she always thought that at her age she could never be too careful when it came to chills. Maybe the chill had settled on her with her sister's use of the word 'murder'.

Violet dragged the laptop slightly closer towards her and opened her eyes widely as she prepared to answer Betsy's question. Betsy moved the screen of her phone closer to her own face too as if in anticipation of a juicy secret that her sister was about to divulge. The siblings knew each other inside out and Betsy could almost hear the cogs of Violet's mind whirring into action as she pensively starred into the lens.

Violet began: 'Well, yes, Sheena has been working for Sir Buster. In fact, she was with him yesterday. Said he looked as strong as ever and there were definitely no signs of any kind of health issues. In fact, she said she could barely keep up with him as he strode off across the Hall lawns playing golf. He's always had quite a stride on him that one, especially if there's a sport involved.'

'Or a pretty woman...' offered Betsy, her eyebrows raising as she spoke.

'Quite.' Violet paused for a moment before continuing. 'Sheena was telling me that Sir Buster had been talking about his kids. You must remember them as much as I do. What were they called – Alexi wasn't it, the boy? And then there was Belinda, the girl. Only about a year between them. I don't really remember them being particularly likable, to be honest.'

Betsy felt an air of indignation rush over her. 'You're right. That Belinda was a snotty-nosed little thing. Always a right little sassy-pants, thinking she could lord it over everyone in the village even though she was only a teenager. Do you remember when she complained to her own mother, dear Fiona, about her booking a brass band for the annual fayre instead of some DJ that she thought was supposed to be trendy? Apparently one of her school friends had booked him for some event and he was "amazing". And also cost six figures, if I remember Fiona telling me right. Told her poor mum that she was "ruining her life" and "making her uncool". There is nothing uncool about grown men and women playing trombones and a euphonium. Their "Yes Sir, I Can Boogie" was a triumph, I can tell you.'

A smile spread across Violet's face in recollection. 'Oh, it was, wasn't it? And their "Dancing Queen".'

Betsy persisted, plainly enjoying riding her high horse

for the moment. 'And that Alexi was a proper pain in the backside too. Weren't the brass band the same year that Alexi upturned the prize marrow table and tried to run off with the raffle takings. Just because he wasn't the centre of attention for once. Fiona and Buster were quite right in sending them off to boarding school. A good stiff bit of authority was what they both needed. So, yes, I do remember them. Just not fondly.'

'Well…' Violet was keen to get to the point, 'Sheena was telling me about how Sir Buster never sees the kids anymore except for Christmas cards and their requests for him to sell Burrow Hall.'

'Typical kids. I barely get a phone call from Samuel these days,' piped up Betsy.

A slight gritting of teeth from Violet about the needless interruption. 'Quite. Well, who is most likely to benefit from Sir Buster dropping down dead? Surely the two children. Not that they're kids now, of course.'

'Well, there's bound to be a will.'

'So, they're bound to come out of the woodwork, aren't they? To claim their inheritance,' Violet remarked.

'Probably driving into the village as we speak. Or flying. Where do they live now?'

'No idea. Maybe abroad. I seem to remember Sir Buster perhaps mentioning them in passing down at The Six Pennies once in a while, but you know me, nights out in the pub are the only times I can't remember everything that's said.'

'Especially if you've had a sherry or two. You've always been the same. You can remember every detail and then that final sherry tips you over the edge into blurriness. You were the same at mine and Rod's wedding. One minute you were sensibly discussing table decorations with the caterers and the next you were swinging yourself dangerously around the dance floor to "Holding Out for A Hero".'

'Yes, yes, dear. But that's just it. My blurred memory after one too many sherries is what's making me think about poor Sir Buster. I'm sure when I was at the bar with him the other night at Sheena's singing performance – she is phenomenal by the way, you should be so proud – that he mentioned "not giving in to threats" and that someone was "giving him grief". I was a little fuzzy and I couldn't really hear everything he said over Sheena's Cher. She can get quite loud when she's Shoop Shooping. Sir Buster was laughing, as he always does, but I can't shift a feeling that maybe he was a little more worried about something than he let on. I should have asked more, but Stephanie came back with the drinks and I headed back to Pearl and Margaret. They send their love by the way.'

'Send mine back,' stated Betsy automatically. 'So, you think there might be more to this than meets the eye?' Her voice was layered with intrigue.

Violet was adamant. 'Yes, I do. The two children obviously want him to sell the house, he's as strong as a pit pony despite his age and he's always been super healthy. Plus, he mentioned the word "threats" in the pub. I'm not saying anything fishy is going on, or indeed has been, but it just all seems a little convenient that poor Sir Buster has now dropped down dead during a supposedly relaxing morning's fishing at his lake.'

'So, you do think Samuel might be investigating a murder?' Betsy's face fell aghast.

'Well…' Violet stopped to consider her words. The chill returned across her body and she pulled the duvet further up under her chin. 'I don't know as yet, but I am saying that the clues are potentially there and I that I really wish that I'd not had a little too much to drink the other night. Maybe things would be a little clearer if I'd stayed off the sherry. Even if it was jolly nice.'

'So, Sir Buster might've been murdered…' A dramatic if silent dah daaaaah hung in the air at the mere suggestion.

'It's a possibility, Betsy, it's a possibility.'

'I hope not. Samuel will never phone me if it is. He'll be way too full of his own importance. So, what are you going to do?'

'Not too sure, but I have an inkling. I'll let you know.'

Betsy's stare of astonishment was interrupted as the sound of the kitchen door opening came from behind her. Her husband, Rod, a vision of wholesome ruddiness and still in good shape for a man approaching sixty, appeared on Violet's screen. His thick head of hair, peppered with grey but still lustrous in his waves, looked unusually dishevelled.

'G'day, Violet. How are you? So, who's copped it?' he asked, his accent as rich and as thick as his hair.

Betsy was up off her seat in a flash, clamping her palm to her face. 'It's Sir Buster, but never mind that. What the hell have you got there?' Her words were slightly muffled under her hand.

Rod was holding a dustpan in his hands. Piled inside it were small, unattractive brown cubes of heaven knew what. Violet could see from the way Betsy was reacting that whatever they were, they obviously smelt as horrid as they looked.

Rod smiled. 'Oh, that's just wombat poo. You can tell by the shape. The little bugger left us a pile of presents poolside. I'm just taking them through to the bins out the front.'

'Rod! This is the kitchen. We cook in here. Get it out... now.'

'Time for me to sign off, Betsy,' smiled Violet a little unnerved. 'I'll report back soon with more information.' She waved at a harassed Betsy and a grinning Rod and clicked the screen to darkness.

Placing her laptop alongside her mug on the bedside table, she switched the lamp off and lay down to sleep, her head full of Sir Buster's demise.

Well, that and wombat poo.

Yes, Violet was very pleased that she didn't live in Willow's Spit.

Chapter 11

As a traditional cosy UK village Sunday lunch, Pearl Wheeler's Bajan chicken and potato roti delights would not normally be many people's first choice. But there was nothing traditional about this particular Sunday, the day after the discovery of Sir Buster's lifeless body.

Despite the absence of tradition, the entire lunch was a delicious hotch-potch of various tastes, all prepared and lovingly packed into plastic snap-tight containers and then transported to the bowling-green-sized back garden of Margaret Millsop's cottage. It was there that Team C.R.A.B. were now sitting on one of Margaret's many lovingly handmade quilts enjoying their picnic-style Sunday lunch. Naturally, it wasn't just the taste of Pearl's heavily spiced roti treats – was that the hint of a Scotch bonnet pepper Violet could feel on her tastebuds? – that was on the tip of everyone's tongue. It was the subject of potential murder.

'So, having all slept on it, are we now all in agreement that perhaps there is more to Sir Buster's death than others might think?' asked Margaret, dipping her roti into a ramakin of Jimmy's marrow chutney. She had been delighted when he'd turned up for the lunch with his offering – a rather splendid and huge pork pie and a sizable jar of his famed chutney. It was only Margaret who seemed to care for it, so it was always gratefully received. A dollop of the chutney detached itself from the roti as she moved it to her mouth and fell onto the quilt.

'The more I think about it, the more I think we're right,' said Violet, swallowing a mouthful of cloudy lemonade to try to alleviate the spiciness of the roti. It had been supplied by Sheena and bought at Rita's, alongside a bottle of dandelion and burdock, two bags of salad and a six-pack of cheesy puffs. Sheena could sing beautifully, but her skills at homemade cooking were non-existent. But when your mother ran the corner shop, you didn't really need to worry too much, did you? Violet pointed to the molehill of chutney that had landed on the quilt and pointed it out to Margaret. 'That'll stain this beautiful quilt, Margaret. Surely, you've got a picnic blanket we can use instead. The craftsmanship is sublime. You really are very skilled.' She ran her finger along the stitching between two of the quilt's panels.

'Oh, this old thing,' said Margaret, dismissing the suggestion with her hand. 'I've made a good half-dozen since this one.' It was true, she had. Margaret had made enough quilts to cover her entire garden if she cared to. And that of Pearl and Noah's cottage too, to be fair. 'It'll wash out.'

'I told Noah that you think it might be murder,' offered Pearl, guiding the discussion back on track. 'But he was having none of it. He says that Sir Buster looked as peaceful as a sleeping kitten when he found him. No sign of pain on his face.'

'He was face down in the water, Pearl,' stated Jimmy, adjusting the sunglasses he was wearing as he spoke. The August sun overhead was blissful on the skin but was making Jimmy squint as he chomped down on his cheese and tomato roll. It was an offering from Violet. She had turned up with a large container packed to the brim with bread rolls. Some tomato, some pickle and some ham, all accompanied by thick crumbly slices of strong-tasting cheese.

'I know, but Noah said he looked peaceful when they flipped him over,' said Pearl. 'He's trying to get some rest right now. He didn't have the best of nights. Kept waking up saying he could see dead people floating around the room. He was having nightmares. Poor chap. It's not every day you find a dead body when you head off to work to talk about digging up somebody's hedgerow, is it?'

'Well, I don't think it was his heart,' Sheena piped up. 'I'm no expert. I can barely follow *Casualty* half the time, but Sir Buster was in great shape right up until his death. I'm with Great Aunty Violet, though. This all needs investigating. We could leave it to my dad, but....'

She left the sentence hanging as her fellow members of Team C.R.A.B. considered the possibility of her father, Sergeant Pollett's, involvement and was busy poking a breadstick into a pot of taramasalata.

It was Margaret who replied first. She'd been responsible for supplying the breadsticks and the dip. 'As much as I adore your father, I suspect this may be a little beyond his normal call of duties. Don't tell him I said that...'

'I won't,' smiled Sheena, mouth full of breadstick.

'I'm glad you like that by the way.' Margaret pointed at the taramasalata. 'It's the real stuff, not the horrid shop-bought alternative. I first tried it when I went to Greece on that five-star holiday to spend some of cheating ex-husband's money and now I always make it fresh. It's divine, isn't it.'

Sheena nodded, fully aware that she would never be able to tell the difference.

'Let's be fair to nephew Samuel,' said Violet. 'He has no reason to suspect foul play. Old man goes fishing, has heart attack, dies. End of story. As much as I am sure dear Samuel would love to have a meaty murder case on his hands, there is nothing apart from the daft ramblings of this craft group to say otherwise. Even if every bone in my body tells me we're right. So, let's do what we can to dig a little deeper.'

'How can we do that?' asked Jimmy.

'Well,' pondered Violet, 'why don't you try to find out as much as you can about Sir Buster's son. You can find out all sorts on Google these days, can't you. Ask discreetly around the village too. See if anyone knows what he's up to. Where he lives? Married, kids, et cetera. And, Pearl, you could do the same with Belinda, Sir Buster's daughter. I have a feeling she got married, so her name will have changed. See what you can unearth?' Violet's gaze turned to Sheena. 'I'm sure Sir Buster talked about threats, so see if you can do some digging up at Burrow Hall. As for you and me, Margaret, I think we should do a double-pronged investigative attack on Dr Roberts. Try to get some information out of him about Sir Buster's health. We'll invite him for tea and cake.' She stopped mid-flow and turned to Pearl. 'Actually, Pearl, could you make another tray of your delicious roti bites. I'm sure Dr Roberts would adore them, especially as he's the only other person apart from you, Margaret, who actually likes Jimmy's marrow chutney.' Pearl nodded as Violet pointed at the ramakin. 'No offence, Jimmy.'

'None taken,' he smiled. 'It's an acquired taste.'

'Yes,' said Violet. 'A little supper date with Dr Roberts and your chutney, Margaret, and we might be able to loosen his lips about patient confidentiality.'

'Can he talk about him freely now he's dead, none of this patient confidentiality malarkey?' asked Margaret.

'I'll guess we'll find out,' winked Violet, happy in her administering of the tasks.

It was a couple of seconds later that Sergeant Samuel Pollett walked into the back garden of the cottage. The five people sat on the quilt all stared up at him as he arrived.

'Hey, Dad, what are you doing here? Working on a Sunday?' questioned Sheena.

He smiled a little awkwardly. 'I hope you don't mind me letting myself in through the side gate, Margaret. The wife said that Sheena and you all were here. And, FYI, Sheena, it's Sergeant Pollett when I'm in uniform, and I think you'll find that even on a Sunday a police officer has to work when there's a massive case on the go. No rest and all that.'

'So, this is a massive case, nephew Sam— Sorry, Sergeant Pollett,' grinned Violet, baiting his attempt at pomposity.

'Well, actually, it's not, to be honest. I think it's pretty done and dusted now. I've heard back about Sir Buster's body and it seems just like we said. He was out fishing at his lake, and it looks like his heart gave up. He keeled over in the water and that was that.'

'So, no further investigation?' asked Violet.

'Apparently not, case closed,' sighed Samuel.

All five of those seated could almost feel the disappointment in Samuel's sigh. It was clear that he would have loved the death to be shrouded in intrigue and mystery.

'So that's that, then? What a pity. And we were thinking that it might have been so much more. Oh well, we were wrong, can't be helped.' Violet's words were rushed, clipped and dripping in efficiency. They also seemed completely out of character. 'Don't let us keep you if you're working, dear nephew. We were just about to discuss some exciting new card ideas for the group. There's some fabulous new layered stamps we're dying to try, and some fresh new découpage sheets, aren't there, team?'

Something in Violet's tone told them all just to nod silently and agree.

Feeling a little awkward and not really knowing what to say, Sergeant Pollett made his excuses and went to leave the garden.

Violet shouted after him as he disappeared out of sight. 'And make sure you phone your mother. She's been asking about you.'

A hurried cry of 'will do' answered back.

Once they were five again, it was Margaret who spoke first. 'Découpage sheets and layered stamps? Care to explain, Violet Brewer? And I thought you'd be the last person to say this case was closed.'

'Closed? I think not, Margaret. I just wanted rid of my dear nephew as quick as possible. If he's not going to try to find any evidence, then it's definitely up to us to do so. I can feel that something sinister is afoot. I can feel it in my bones. It's a feeling as strong as Sir Buster's heart. Which I am sure was a lot stronger than some people actually seem to think. It's time we swapped découpage for deduction, my friends. Let's see what we can find out. Just don't let dear Samuel know what we're up to.'

'Mum's the word,' smiled Sheena. 'Or should that be dad?'

All five of Team C.R.A.B. laughed.

Chapter 12

Pearl and Jimmy were walking back through the village from their picnic at Margaret's. Pearl, carrying a jumble of plastic food containers under her arm, was just about to step off the kerb outside The Six Pennies pub onto the road crossing when Jimmy, who was standing beside her, suddenly screamed. His scream, rather high-pitched and horror-teen for a man of his build and age, was accompanied by a flinging out of his arm in front of Pearl to stop any chance of her walking into the road, despite the crossing indicating that it should have been safe to do so.

An open-top car, sporty and obviously expensive, shot past them at high speed. The booming of loud music, some kind of rap from what Jimmy could make out, filled the air as it passed. Jimmy had seen, or more so heard, it advancing towards them at breakneck speed as they had stood waiting to cross. He'd assumed, wrongly, it now appeared, that it would slow down and stop. The driver didn't even register the fist-waving farmer and the distraught woman dropping a pile of plastic boxes into the road as the flashy motor sped off into the distance, leaving nothing in its trail except the smell of burning rubber and the dimming sound of the expletive-laden tune.

'What a total idiot? Are you okay, Pearl?' Jimmy put his arm around his friend, who looked stunned and was shaking slightly at the near miss.

Pearl let out a long sigh, suddenly realising that she had obviously been holding her breath for the longest time. 'That was a close shave, indeed. I could have been on my way to see Sir Buster at the Pearly Gates a little quicker than planned,' she stammered. 'Who on earth was driving at that kind of speed? On a Sunday lunchtime too. How can somebody be in such a hurry?'

'I don't know. All I saw is that they were wearing a baseball cap. I don't even know if it was a man or a woman. They must have been going about sixty miles per hour at least. If not more. Hopefully the speed camera will have flashed them, and they'll get some kind of fine. Or hopefully lose their licence.'

'You'll be lucky, that flaming thing hasn't worked for months,' a voice sounded from behind Pearl and Jimmy, who was now bending down to collect the fallen plastic boxes. Any remains of food left inside them from their picnic lunch were broken and in crumbs or in sticky messes.

It was Phill, landlord of The Six Pennies.

'Are you two all right? I heard your scream, Pearl, as I was clearing glasses in the beer garden and thought I had better come out and see what was going on.'

Jimmy didn't bother to mention that it was his lungs that were responsible.

'Did you see the car that zoomed past?' asked Pearl. 'Whoever it was thinks they're the next Formula 1 champion.'

'No, but I heard the din it was playing. A right royal racket. Could barely hear the pub radio out in the garden.'

'It was some young boy racer, no doubt. Or girl,' remarked Jimmy, stacking the boxes back into some kind of easy-to-carry pile. 'They could be halfway to Land's End by now given the speed they were going. Thankfully we're all right, though.'

Phill was still perturbed by the look of open-mouthed terror that seemed to have painted itself across Pearl's features. 'Are you sure you're okay, Pearl? You're as pale as can be.'

'And that's not easy for a woman of my colour, Phill, let me tell you. Things like this just make you realise how it could all be over in a second. Your life flashes before your eyes. One minute you're here and the next, boom, you're meeting your maker. You read about these things in the paper – road accidents and deaths – but you never expect it to happen on your own doorstep. I guess the shock of the entire weekend is kicking in. What with poor Sir Buster too.' She wobbled, a little unsteady on her feet.

Phill took charge of the situation. He put his arms around Pearl to steady her. 'Here you go, Pearl, you hang onto me. Yes, it's been a weekend like no other in Rooney-at-Burrow this one. Dreadful news about Sir Buster. I'm going to have a bench to commemorate him in the beer garden and we're thinking of having a fundraising night in his honour. I can tell you all about that over a drink. C'mon you two, you look like you need one after a shock like that. On the house.'

Even though the offer was much appreciated, Jimmy was keen to turn it down. 'Thanks, Phill, and the ideas about the bench and the fundraiser are wonderful, good for you. I'll pass on the drink, though. I've got to get back as Bailey is heading off to Abu Dhabi late afternoon and I need to take him to the airport. Some fancy telly client of his wants a refit. But I definitely think Pearl could do with something to steady her nerves. Tell you what, Pearl, I'll drop the containers on your doorstep on the way back to the farm. I won't knock just in case Noah is still sleeping.' Jimmy turned to look at Phill and mouthed silently 'he found Sir Buster, you know'. He wasn't really sure why he'd mouthed it silently. And he was sure Phill already knew the details. The entire village did.

'Well, maybe just the one. My nerves are shredded,'

said Pearl softly. She was never one to pass on a free drink, no matter what the circumstances. 'And thanks, Jimmy, that's very kind.'

'I'll bell you later for a catch-up,' he replied.

Jimmy watched as Pearl was escorted by Phill into the pub by her arm. He could hear her words 'flashed before my eyes, it did, Phill, right before my eyes' as they walked away.

Jimmy stood by the crossing again and looked left and right. He then did it a second time just in case. There was nothing coming. There never normally was in Rooney-at-Burrow. But after their close shave with Speedy Gonzales moments earlier, it was wise to double-check.

Ensuring the coast was clear, Jimmy stepped out into the road and headed for home. He had lied about going to the airport. Not about Bailey going to Abu Dhabi, that was true. He'd be away a few days. Jimmy made a mental note to ask Phill and Stephanie at the pub to hold off on the fundraiser until Bailey returned. He wouldn't want to miss that. No, he'd lied because he wasn't taking his boyfriend to the airport. Bailey had ordered a taxi for that.

But Jimmy was keen to return home as he wanted to start sleuthing and to try to find out as much information as he could about the late Sir Buster's errant son, Alexi. He wondered where he was. In what far-flung corner of the globe could he possibly be? The thought thrilled him. He imagined it was what Jonathan and Jennifer Hart must have felt like back in the day on *Hart to Hart*. He loved that show. He'd had posters of Jennifer on his bedroom wall when he was young. Then he'd swapped them for Jonathan as he became slightly older and more conscious of his own hormones.

As Jimmy stepped up onto the kerb on the other side of the road, what he didn't know was that he'd already been a lot closer to Alexi Burniston than he realised. Dangerously close, in fact.

Chapter 13

Alexi Burniston loved the sound of the gravelly pebbles underneath the wheels of his sports car as he spun it into position and parked outside the main doors of Burrow House. He could see a few of them fly off in various directions from underneath the rubber as the car came to a halt.

He removed his baseball cap and let what hair he still had tumble down from where he'd tucked it inside the cap. He felt the heat of the sun overhead on the bald spot that seemed to be getting bigger year by year on the top of his head. He checked it out in the car mirror and considered that a trip to Istanbul for a hair transplant might be in order. He opened his mouth and ran his tongue along his teeth to inspect his reflection further. And maybe a trip to a dental clinic to get his veneers done too. The ones the playboys used.

He could definitely do with some bodywork. What was the point of having a brand-new motor that could go nought to sixty in the click of a finger and a table in the fanciest restaurants if your forty-three-year-old body was beginning to look a little flabby and shabby? Yeah, he'd get his teeth and hair done. The bald spot with a curtain of shoulder-length rocker locks was maybe not the best of looks. In his mind, he pictured himself as some kind of urban, dangerous, streetwise hipster. That cool dude that only danced to the beat of his own drum. The man ladies wanted to be with, and other guys wanted to be. That guy who walked to the front of a nightclub queue. Someone effortlessly edgy. The reality was a little more edge of a mid-life crisis.

Alexi vacated the car and shoved the keys in the back pocket of his overly tight chinos. He'd normally have flung them to someone to park up his pride and joy somewhere safe, but he guessed that his father had never stretched to a valet. Plus, who would even contemplate nicking his car out here in the wilds of nowhere? It was one of the reasons that he'd not been home to Burrow Hall in years. The area wasn't just sleepy, it was comatose. Where was the nearest sushi bar or tanning salon for heaven's sake? And Lord only knew where the nearest nightspot with a VIP area serving decent fizz and gold-diggers would be. No, Burrow Hall, Rooney-at-Burrow and generally anywhere within a twenty-mile radius was not, as they say, giving Alexi chills or serving him life. Well, at least people half his age said that.

Maybe Mrs Turner would know. It had been her that had emailed him to say that his father had died. She had always been Alexi's one constant connection to Burrow Hall. To be honest, the only person he actually liked there. And she was, truth be told, the only person who actually seemed to like him. He hadn't seen her in years, but they had emailed. He'd never given her his mobile number. She was staff after all. He liked to think his phone contacts list was full of movers and shakers, not pensioner bakers.

The door opened and a very excitable Mrs Turner came striding out across the gravel to greet him. She had obviously seen and heard the car pull up. She looked exactly the same as she had done when he'd last seen her a decade earlier at his mother's funeral. Wider than she was tall, hair scraped back off her face, ruddy cheeks. She'd always reminded him of Mrs White on the *Cluedo* playing card from when he was a kid. It was his favourite game when he was younger. There was something about living in a house that actually did have a ballroom and a conservatory and where you could actually find massive candlesticks and hunting daggers hung on the wall that made the game seem even more realistic. There was probably lead piping and a revolver somewhere. Sadly, there was no Miss Scarlett lookalike, only Mrs Turner as a photofit for Mrs White. Alexi smiled as she sort of waddled towards him. Maybe there was a factory somewhere that turned out short, stout, grey-haired ladies who were awesome cooks and always pinched your cheeks.

'Oh, you poor boy, I'm so sorry about your father. It's such a sad time. But it's wonderful to see you again. Look at you! You haven't changed a bit in ten years.'

Alexi knew that sadly this wasn't true. He'd had a full

head of hair last time he'd seen her. And carried less timber.

Mrs Turner hugged him with the crushing strength of a bear for slightly too long to remain comfortable and then, as Alexi, has suspected, squeezed his cheek with a rapid pinch. As ever, it felt out of place at his age, but it wouldn't be Mrs Turner without a powerful clinch and crab-like finger-nip of his face. Old habits would never die.

Unlike his father, who had done exactly that the day before. Alexi was sad. Of course he was. In the same way anyone would be when their father died. But to say that he and his father were close would have been a lie big enough to fill the lake his poor dad had been found face down in. Perhaps there was a little part of his brain that regretted the fact that he'd not really seen his dad properly for about a decade and now the chance to had been removed for good. But communication was a two-way street and Sir Buster had never really made the effort, so it was his loss too, right? Alexi had nothing to feel guilty for in his opinion, but then anyone who knew him would be fully aware that Alexi always considered himself to be in the right. Even when it was clear that he wasn't.

'Hello, Mrs Turner, you've not changed either. Still as hands-on as ever.' Alexi rubbed his cheek with his fingers where she had pinched it. Doubtless, the skin there would be a little rosy in colour. 'It's good to see you again. Even if it is in such sad circumstances. Thanks for letting me know.'

'Oh, dear boy, how could I not.' She linked arms with him as they walked towards the house. 'I'm just glad that you were close enough to get here in reasonable time. I never know where you're going to be. What with you being such a successful businessman jetting all over the world. You could have been in Japan or somewhere equally as exotic for all I knew.'

'That's true, Mrs T, but luckily for once I wasn't. I was in London, so getting here was no issue.' The truth was that Alexi hadn't really been anywhere exotic for far too long, unless you counted his little trip to Lithuania for a spot of blepharoplasty – the removal of the bags under his eyes. 'I see the old pile still looks the same as ever.'

'Oh, nothing changes, Master Alexi, nothing at all. Except your dad not being here now, of course.' She bowed her head, attempting to hide an emotional sniffle.

'Is crusty old Herbert still here scaring visitors to the door with his vampiric looks?' Alexi bared his teeth as if he were Dracula, causing Mrs Turner to grin and blush. 'Oh, and drop the Master Alexi, you know I hate that, I'm not six anymore. It's Alexi.' It was another old habit of Mrs Turner's that failed to disappear.

'Oh, you're a one.' She tutted playfully. 'Yes, Herbert is still here and still a valuable member of the household. It's only him and me really, and a girl from the village, Sheena, lovely girl, who comes in to do some cleaning for extra cash. Although what will happen now Sir Buster has gone is anybody's guess.'

'Well, you don't need to worry about that now, do you? Because I'm here, Mrs Turner. Your little Alexi has come back to sort things out.'

'Not so little now, eh?' The housekeeper patted his belly with her hand and stifled a titter.

Alexi raised his eyebrows. So, she had noticed a

change in him after all. Yes, a bit more bodywork would definitely be in order. Maybe a touch of lipo, or a decent PT if he could be bothered to put in the effort. Probably easier to go down the procedure route. Physical exertion had never been his thing, much to Sir Buster's annoyance.

He smiled without answering.

'Have you been in contact with your sister, Alexi? How is Belinda?' asked Mrs Turner.

'Yes, I've phoned her, she's on her way.' It was a lie, he hadn't, but he did plan to later. She deserved to know, of course. He just wanted to get to Burrow Hall before she did, to get the lie of the land.

'Oh lovely, it'll be nice to see her here too, the pair of you back together again, just like it used to be when your dear mother was alive. Now, come on in and let's get you something to eat. I've made some chocolate chip cookies. Extra thick and chunky. Just how you like them. I could never make them for your father, he wouldn't touch them, but I always remember you loving them. And you obviously still do.' She patted his belly again and they entered into the house. 'It's so nice to have you home,' she said. 'Back where you belong.'

'Yes, indeed I do,' said Alexi, surveying the entrance hall. The size of the house always surprised him every time he visited. Large without being grandiose. Stately without losing its welcome. A lot more appealing than where he currently resided.

'I love Burrow Hall,' said Mrs Turner, leading Alexi towards the kitchen. 'I really don't know what I'd do if I wasn't here. It keeps me busy, and I love it. But thankfully I don't need to worry about that now that you're home, do I.'

Statement of fact or a question searching for an answer. Alexi wasn't sure. But he was looking at Burrow Hall through different eyes. He hadn't lived there for years, but suddenly it felt like home. Not as in sentiment, but as in possession. Surely as the eldest child, it would be his now. Or fifty-fifty with Belinda at worst. Finally, he could get his hands on Burrow Hall. He'd been wanting to for the longest time and had a plan of action all ready and raring to bring to fruition.

He just wouldn't let Mrs Turner know of his plans just yet. He wasn't sure she'd like them. That would come in time. When the moment was right. But for now, it was time for chocolate chip cookies. Extra thick and chunky. Just how Alexi liked them indeed.

Chapter 14

Jeremiah Halliwell had never lived his life on the straight and narrow. The only time he had ever been pure in thought and deed was when he played the Angel Gabriel in his school nativity at the age of five, and that was five and a half decades ago. And even then he had tried to run off with the three wise men's gifts as his tearaway scampish mind had reckoned that gold, frankincense and myrrh must be worth a bob or two. Not that he'd been clever enough to realise that the gifts' were actually made of papier mâché and had no value whatsoever. That fact had not become apparent to Jeremiah until he had tried to swap them with one of his classmates in exchange for the contents of his lunch box.

Jeremiah had left school at the age of thirteen to work

with his dad as a scaffolder. And a brickie. And a plumber. And a chippie. And whatever was required and paid. His dad, 'Hoppo' Halliwell, nicknamed because of his tendency to hop from one job to another, and also from his apparent ease at hopping from one woman's bed to another, taught Jeremiah all he knew. Which was, in a nutshell, how to make money from the misfortune of others. And Jeremiah was a fast learner. If there was scam brewing, then you could guarantee that Jeremiah would be at the heart of it. Nothing was off limits. Theft, joyriding, bribery, deception, even the odd spot of GBH if required. Anything to make money and to make his dad 'Hoppo' proud. Both Jeremiah and his dad had been forced to enjoy a spell or three at Her Majesty's pleasure over the years. In fact, in Jemiah's case, it was seven spells so far. Doubtless an eighth might occur at some point, but seeing as Jeremiah was fast approaching his sixtieth birthday, he hoped that any scams that fell his way at his age would not result in incarceration. He'd done his decent share of time.

To be fair, Jeremiah had tried to keep his nose fairly clean over the last few years. Maybe it was age. Or maybe it was the fact that his once chiselled body was not as strong as it had been. His days of outrunning a cop after mugging an old lady or shimmying up a church wall to steal the slate roof tiles were over. Plus, these days he was a solo act. His dad had hopped his last and died nearly two decades earlier, the result of a rather brutal loss in a bare-knuckle fight with a business rival. Jeremiah's mum was long gone too. Not dead, but she lived up north somewhere. He wasn't really sure where. Perhaps Scotland? Or Skegness? Was that north?

Jeremiah now lived in a rather swanky caravan in a field just outside the village of Darrochdean, which, as the crow flew west, was approximately twenty-five miles from Rooney-at-Burrow. The caravan had been his home for the last twelve years.

The door of Jeremiah's caravan was open and the pungent odour of fried fish emanated from within. It was accompanied by the sizzle of the dish as Jeremiah flipped over the trout he was cooking and watched it splash in the oil. A spurt of oil landed on the apron he wore, covering the freshly pressed dress shirt underneath.

'This is nearly ready to serve,' he said. 'Why don't you pour us a glass of beer, Sheila, and we'll tuck in?'

He was talking to the woman sitting at table in the dining area of his caravan. Mid-forties, toffee-brown hair and make-up slapped on with a trowel and with the delicacy of a rugby scrum.

'My name's Shona. You should know that from our first date.' She tutted loudly but poured two beers nevertheless.

'Sorry, darling. Names have never been my strong point,' smiled Jeremiah as he brought the fish to the table. Truth be told, he didn't really care what she was called. Their first date had only been memorable as the après-dinner action was the best that he'd experienced in a while. And that was worth a second date. And by having it at the caravan, they wouldn't have far to roam once the fish was eaten.

'Wow, that looks rather fabulous. You didn't get that at my Lidl did you?' smirked the woman. It was where they had first met when Jeremiah had popped in for a four-pack of beers and been served at her checkout.

'No, this is freshly caught from the Burniston Estate over in Rooney-at-Burrow. Well, freshly poached...'

'Poached. Like you do with eggs?' asked the woman in all seriousness. 'I'm normally a fried kind of woman. Or scrambled. Depending on my mood.'

Jeremiah untied his apron and tossed it onto the kitchen counter as he slid into place alongside the woman at the table. She was not the sharpest tool, but as he'd already discovered, her talents lay beyond her brain. He couldn't be bothered to correct her mistake.

He lifted his beer glass and pushed it towards her. 'Cheers, Siobhan.'

'I said it's Shona.' For a second, a sweep of deep annoyance stained her face. But it passed as soon as it came and she picked up her glass and chinked it against his. Free booze and food were not to be sniffed at even if her date couldn't get her name right. She smiled widely, revealing a set of uneven and off-white teeth.

The night would doubtless be ending as Jeremiah hoped. And in the morning he intended to put a freshly hatched little scam into action. When he was sneakily poaching fish at Sir Buster's private lake, it wasn't just the size of the trout that had caught his eye. Oh no. He'd spotted something that could possibly result in a prize even more delicious and tasty than the pilfered fish he and whatever her name was were about to tuck into.

Chapter 15

After the unexpected events of the weekend in Rooney-at-Burrow, Monday morning seemed horribly mundane and lacking in any sort of adventure in comparison.

Well, that was certainly how it felt for Sergeant Samuel Pollett as he opened up the door to the police station with a turn of a key and hefty push. For some reason, it was sticking a little and needed a bit of extra coaxing. Changes of the season perhaps? Did wooden doors expand in the summer? Or contract? He added trying to sort it out to the list of important jobs in his mind that needed doing. So far, the list amounted to one. That. And it was obvious that the word 'important' was totally surplus to requirements and was most certainly overselling the job in question.

He walked behind the front desk and flicked the light switch on. The bulb hanging over his head crackled into action, somewhat reticently, it seemed. Maybe it possessed an air of Monday morning about it as well.

Still, being a police officer was always a joy and he had to remember that, even on days like today when it already seemed beyond humdrum and he hadn't even actually done anything. The village needed him. He was there to make sure that law and order always came out on top. That justice was always victorious and that good triumphed over evil. It was his duty. He was sure that the villagers would need him more than ever today. They would definitely still be in a state of shock after the horrible news about Sir Buster. There was bound to have been tears. Sir Buster was very much loved. Maybe a cursory visit from their local caring police officer would be a wise and comforting idea.

Samuel sat down at his desk, opened the jotter that lay there and contemplated a list of those who would need to see the friendly face of the law today. That face being his. It was his job to put them at ease, to let them know that there was nothing to worry about. Aftershock was a human thing too, wasn't it? Or did that just happen with earthquakes?

Samuel chewed the end of his pencil as he mulled over the question. Not finding an answer he began to write down some names. He started with Aunty Violet and Margaret. He was fully aware that neither woman would need comforting and were both far more robust and ready to deal with anything in life than he could ever be. But if he timed his rounds correctly today, he could try to orchestrate a visit to the wool shop mid-morning and Margaret's mid-afternoon. That would give Violet ample opportunity to have been to Rita's to buy more cakes. Samuel's wife often joked that she could always tell when it reached 10.30 a.m. in the shop, even when she had no means of telling the time, as Violet, or Sheena if she was working at Brewer's Loop, would nip in on their first brew break of the day for something sticky and calorie-laden. So, cakes and a comforting chat with Aunty Violet at the wool shop late morning seemed like a cunning plot to fill his belly as well as fulfil his lawful duty as the local constabulary. Margaret's late afternoon was also a wise move as he would be peckish again by then and Margaret's biscuit barrel was always full to the lid. Plus, she often favoured a garibaldi, which Samuel adored and Rita would never entertain as a snack option after a customer had called them squashed fly biscuits. Even the mention of them now turned her stomach and if a customer bought some in the shop, she'd have to hold her breath until they were safely packed away in a bag for life for fear of gagging.

The next name Samuel wrote down was Pearl. Samuel should definitely try to visit her and Noah at some point too. Noah was bound to still be highly affected by finding the body on Saturday morning. Maybe he'd need counselling or professional help. Samuel had seen that many times on the crime shows he watched. Awful flashbacks to the discovery of the mutated corpse. A person unable to concentrate on their life because of constantly replaying the moment they stumbled across a crime of atrocious proportions. For all Samuel knew, Noah could be riddled with the terrors of what he'd seen. And poor Pearl would need some advice too, as Samuel was sure it must be appalling for her to witness her husband's demons as he recalled the goriness of forty-eight hours earlier. He'd be sure to google some helpline numbers before popping round.

He was just thinking that perhaps his Monday was shaping up nicely after all and pondering who to write next when WPC Paula Horton came bounding in.

'Morning, Sarge, I'm here...' Her arrival was almost singsong, and she gave a girlish twirl before lowering into an exaggerated curtsey. As ever, she was beyond perky. Her arrivals were often animated and highly jolly episodes that always managed to put a smile on Samuel's face. Even on a Monday. For WPC Horton, another day at work was always a good day. Paula loved her job. He had to admit that sometimes he barely managed to put one foot in front of another on a Monday morning, even after two coffees.

Samuel noticed that she had done her hair differently, her shoulder-length blonde mane tied back into some kind of lumpy knotty creation around the back of her head. She normally left it to hang, curving in at her neckline. He sensed there was a name for it, he'd heard it somewhere, but couldn't recall. He'd had the same hairstyle for over three decades after an unfortunate foray with a Mohican in his teens which ended any sense of experimentation. So, as hairstyles went, Samuel wasn't truly up to speed.

Paula noticed the quizzical look on her boss's face as he surveyed her hair. 'I'm trying a chignon. Mr Bublé thinks it looks good. He was purring away when I did it this morning.' Mr Bublé was Paula's ginger tom cat, who lived with her at her cottage. The cottage next door to Noah and Pearl's on Rooney-at-Burrow's village square. The other cottage owned by Margaret Millsop. Paula loved it there. She also loved the fact that Margaret Millsop let her rent it for virtually next to nothing.

Paula had originally grown up in a village about eight miles away but fell in love with Rooney-at-Burrow when she had started working there a few years ago. She used to drive to work every day, but when Margaret bought the two cottages after her financial windfall of a divorce, she had asked Paula if she'd like to rent one. There was no way Paula could afford it on police wages, but Margaret was unconcerned and adamant she should take up her offer. 'Dear girl, you're a village police officer and if ever I was in need of your services in the middle of the night, I would prefer you to be living on my doorstep as opposed to in some village where it would take you at least an hour to come to my aid given some of the roads around here.' When Paula had reminded her that Sergeant Pollett only lived a few doors down from her, Margaret had still been determined. 'But you're a female officer and what if the crime was of a personal delicate nature? Something that I wouldn't be overly keen on sharing with my best friend's nephew. Sometimes talking to a woman can be so much easier.' Margaret had sealed the deal with, 'Plus, your ginger tom will get to see you so much more and he is just adorable.' She and Paula had often cooed over videos on her phone of Mr Bublé, named after Paula's favourite crooner of course, playing with scrunched-up balls of tin foil.

Paula and Mr Bublé had moved in, and she still considered it to be the best move she had ever made. Noah and Pearl as neighbours, the easiest landlady ever living across the village square, her boss and his family just over the duck pond too and a mere seven-minute walk past the wool shop and Rita's to get to the police station. It also meant she could nip home and feed Mr Bublé if she had the chance. The portly puss spent his days sitting quite contentedly in Paula's front garden watching the world go by and unsuccessfully attempting to ensnare a sparrow.

Paula placed a paper bag she'd been carrying next to Samuel on the desk and perched her behind on the wooden corner. 'Apparently chignons are big again, so I thought I'd give it a whirl. Talking of which, there's a couple of cinnamon ones in there if you fancy some breakfast. I picked them up at Rita's on the way in.'

The thought definitely appealed to Samuel – it had been at least an hour since his bacon sandwich. He opened up the bag and peered inside. They looked too good to refuse and it would be a good while before cake at Violet's, wouldn't it?

'You deserve it after the weekend you've had. You should spoil yourself,' Paula encouraged.

The truth was that Paula spoiled him all the time.

Hardly a week went by without some kind of delicious offering. Paula had a genuine affection for her boss and, more often than not, she showed it in sugar. Which was his sweet spot after all. Sergeant Pollett's appetite wasn't complaining even if his waistline was.

Paula spotted the names on the jotter. 'What are they for?'

'I'm thinking of checking in on people today, just to make sure they're okay after the weekend. Nerves might be in shreds. People aren't used to this kind of thing happening, not like you and me. We're trained to deal with death. It's in our blood.'

Paula smiled inwardly. The only death she and Samuel had dealt with lately, before the tragedy of Sir Buster, was the mysterious discovery of one of the ducks, stone-cold dead, at the village pond. Paula had feared that Mr Bublé had attempted to attack something larger than a sparrow but given his complete lack of hunting skill and his reluctance to wander too far from his stretched-out position in the cottage garden had decided that he wasn't the culprit.

After an investigation from the local vet, it was discovered the poor bird had quacked its last, due to someone feeding it avocado, which was apparently highly toxic to ducks. Who knew? Paula and Samuel had questioned everyone in the village about who might have done it. There was quite the scandal. No one had seen anything. And, of course, there was no CCTV in the village. It was a full five days before a very sheepish Sir Buster and Phill from The Six Pennies had come into the police station to confess that they had drunkenly stumbled down to the village duck pond just after sunrise following a mammoth poker lock-in at the pub to feed the ducks the remains of the previous evening's pub buffet. Which included quite a collection of left-over chicken and avocado sandwiches. Both men were mortified when they had heard about the duck's death.

Samuel and Paula should have rapped their knuckles for both their stupidity with the feathered friends and also for breaking the law with a lock-in, but maybe there were certain things in village life that had to be overlooked once in a while. Samuel had suggested that maybe Sir Buster and Phill should pay for a new duck for the pond and perhaps consider a generous donation to a bird charity. In return, he and WPC Horton would turn a blind eye and keep their dastardly duck secret safe. A suitable solution for all.

So, maybe the weekend's events weren't the first mysterious death in the village, but they were certainly the one that every villager was thinking about on this particular Monday.

'That's a nice idea. I would leave Pearl for a while, though. I just saw her in Rita's. Buying paracetamol. She says she has a hangover. Apparently, she had quite a scare outside the pub yesterday, nearly got hit by a car, and so she ended up having a drink with Phill and Stephanie to steady her nerves. One drink became quite a few apparently. She was a little fuzzy by the time she stumbled home yesterday evening. Bless her.'

'Phill didn't hold another lock-in, I hope,' remarked Samuel. 'We all know what happened last time.'

'I can safely say no ducks were harmed after this round of drinking,' confirmed Paula, taking a cinnamon swirl from the bag and biting into it. 'Only Pearl's brain.' WPC Horton was just about to take another bite of the swirl when she stopped herself. 'Oh yeah, I forgot. Rita said that I had to tell you that a woman came into the shop first thing this morning looking for some fancy muesli and she thought she recognised her from somewhere, but Rita wasn't sure where. And then, this woman's mobile goes off and she answers it saying *hello, Belinda Flatt speaking*, so Rita thinks about the first name and then the penny drops. It was Belinda, Sir Buster's daughter. She's back in the village already, it seems.'

Samuel knew it wouldn't be too long. He expected Alexi to turn up at any moment too. 'I've not seen her in years. What did Rita say she was like?'

WPC Horton replied, 'Rita wasn't keen. Apparently, Belinda got all snooty when she suggested Rice Krispies instead of muesli.'

Samuel smiled. Monday had just become a little more interesting.

Chapter 16

Sheena was more than a little startled when she bumped into a rather bleary-eyed man shuffling his way out of the entrance of Burrow Hall wearing nothing more than a black silk dressing gown and a pair of equally black corduroy open-back slippers. There was a breeze in the air, despite the time of year, and she had a sneaking suspicion that the man in question was not wearing anything underneath the robe. One haphazard gust and she would probably witness something that she'd never be able to unsee.

If he was startled to see her too, he didn't show it. 'Oh hello, morning. Is it morning?' He checked his wrist, but there was no watch to look at. 'I don't suppose you know where they keep the pills in this place, do you? My head is banging, and I'm buggered if I can find Mrs Turner. I was going to see if I had any in my glove compartment.' He pointed at the car parked out on the gravel. Sheena had wondered who it belonged to when she'd been walking towards the Hall moments earlier. 'Nice motor, eh?' commented the man. He smoothed down the hair that was randomly sticking out from the side of his head with a flamboyant gesture. If it was meant to impress, it didn't.

'Er, yeah,' offered Sheena before adding, 'if you like that sort of thing.' She checked her own watch. 'And it's afternoon. Just after one. I'm Sheena. I work here. I clean and tidy and generally help out. I think Mrs Turner might have a medicine box somewhere or you could ask Herbert. He knows everything. If not, I can try to find something for you.'

'Thanks, I dived a little too eagerly into dear old Daddy's supply of whisky last night in his study and my head is paying for it this morning.' He scratched his head and corrected himself. 'Er, afternoon. Thought I might as well toast the old boy.'

Which was just what Alexi had done. Having

demolished a plateful of Mrs Turner's homemade cookies, he had then made her give him a refresher tour of the Hall. It had been a while after all. Having found Sir Buster's decanter of Oban whisky in the study, Alexi had spent the rest of the evening topping up his glass as he wandered from room to room making a list of anything he wanted to keep or, more to the point, that would be worth a fair few bob that maybe he should hide away before Belinda turned up to try to bag dibs on what was equally likely to be hers. As he drank more whisky, the list had become less choosy. By the time he'd stumbled to bed in the wee small hours of Monday morning, he had pretty much decided that he would try to sell as much as possible behind Belinda's back. That included everything from a fairly raggedy decades-old stag's head that hung pride of place above Sir Buster's study fireplace right through to the crystal glass Alexi was drinking from that he placed on his bedside table as he slipped, rather sozzled, between the sheets for his first night at Burrow Hall in about a decade.

Alexi moved towards the car, the hem of his dressing gown flapping as he did so. Sheena determinedly kept her gaze at eye level.

'I've got to find something to stop the steel drums playing in my head. Nice to meet you then. See you inside, no doubt. Or are you just collecting your stuff now that the old man doesn't need you anymore? I suppose I could keep you on if you fancy still whipping a vacuum around the place. I guess it's only right now that I'm lord of the manor, as it were.' He mulled the notion over in his head, letting it bounce around for good measure. 'Yeah, I like the sound of that. Lord of the manor.' He played with the words, giving them their own unnecessary swagger.

'So, you are…?' Sheena left the sentence mid-air, even though she'd guessed who he was after his 'dear old Daddy' comment earlier.

'Oh sorry. I kinda guessed you might know who I am. Alexi Burniston. Sir Buster's son and heir.' He moved back towards her to shake her hand. 'Nice to meet you.'

'You too.' She left a gap before adding, 'Sorry about your father, by the way. I was very fond of him. He'll be really missed by everyone in the village. We had some fabulous nights in the village pub together. He was always the life and soul.' She meant it, despite the words being drenched in cliché.

'I heard that Dad had an eye for the ladies. Can't say I blame him.' Alexi let his own gaze move rather lecherously up and down Sheena's T-shirt and jeans combo. 'The apple didn't fall far from the tree after all.'

Cringing within, much more for him than for herself, Sheena smiled as best she could, he was potentially her new employer after all, and let the awkwardly inappropriate and obliviously cocky comment and sleazy stare slip by.

'I sing at the pub sometimes and your dad would always come and watch. The entire village does.'

'I bet they do. And I bet Daddy had a front seat.' Alexi continued to stare.

Sheena couldn't resist. 'Oh, and I'm twenty and my dad is the local police sergeant.'

Alexi coughed slightly and moved his eyes off her. Was he blushing slightly? Sheena thought so. She felt a glow of satisfaction pass through her. Nothing thrilled her more than knocking a leery man off his pedestal.

'Er, you may want to start cleaning in the study. I may have looked in a few drawers and cupboards last night and not really put everything away.' He winked, and then added, 'I blame the whisky for my lack of tidiness.'

Sheena was tempted to say that she blamed his laziness for it, but wisely bit her tongue.

'Yeah, I will. I came up to see if I can help at all. Poor Herbert and Mrs Turner must be in a right state about Sir Buster too, and I guess it's all hands on deck at times like this. I'll go and make a start. Nice to meet you…' Sheena had turned to walk through the entrance into Burrow Hall, when she stopped herself and turned back to Alexi. '…Lord of the manor.' It was always wise to keep on side with the potential new boss, even if he did appear to have a sleazy streak. But nothing she couldn't handle.

Sheena was just about to depart when another voice cut through the air. It was female and damning.

'Lord. Of. The. Manor?' The words were spat. Separate and questioningly mocking. 'Not looking that you won't ever be. And I suspect Daddy will have left this' – she circled her fingers in the air in the direction of

Burrow Hall – 'to both of us. At least he had better have done.'

Alexi said nothing, shock stunning him into silence.

The woman continued. 'And Jesus, Alexi, you've let yourself go, haven't you? I would have thought all of those years living in the Caribbean, or wherever you were, would have least put some decent colour on your skin. Or is white, balding and pasty the new golden brown? And what in the name of fashion are you wearing. Should any man in his forties be wearing black silk? I think not. It would have taken about five thousand poor silkworms to create that beautiful garment and yet you manage to wear it with all the style and finesse of a seagull rummaging through a wheelie bin.'

Sheena was loving this woman already. She was obviously very capable of handling the male of the species too. She guessed it was Alexi's sister, judging from her daddy comment too.

Clarification followed. Firstly, from Alexi.

'Oh, hi, sis, I was just about to phone you,' he sneered.

It then came from Mrs Turner, who was standing

alongside the woman. They had both just appeared from another gravelled area around the side of the Hall. 'Sheena, I'd like you to meet Belinda Flatt. This is Sir Buster's daughter and Alexi's sister. I assume you two have met?' The housekeeper gestured to Sheena and Alexi. Sheena nodded that she had. 'Belinda, this is Sheena, lovely girl who helps with the cleaning and helps out at events here at the Hall. Your father was extremely fond of her. Loved her like a daughter.'

'A granddaughter, I hope, given that she looks about fifteen. Maybe he treats them better than he did his own kids. Buries poor mother and then sends us off without so much as a cheery goodbye. This place was never the same without her.'

Sheena could sense that it wasn't just Alexi who received the pointed barb at the end of Belinda's tongue. She merely raised her hand, waved and said 'hi'.

'Hello. Good afternoon.' Belinda's words were brusque and uninterested. She oscillated her attention back to her brother. 'So, you were going to phone me. When would that have been? After you'd searched the entire house for things to get your thieving hands on, no doubt.'

Alexi, still silent, merely looked down, both scolded and caught out, and kicked the gravel with his corduroy slipper.

There was no stemming Belinda. 'Luckily, Herbert phoned me. I arrived this morning. I've had Mrs Turner take me around the grounds for the last few hours. There's quite some land – I'd forgotten just how much. And the private lake. Some beautiful grasslands and woodlands out there too. I'm sure I spotted a hawfinch and they're in such rarity these days. Remarkably unspoilt habitat. So lovely to see. So very green and verdant. I just wish Daddy had popped some solar panels on this monstrosity of a house to make it greener too. And please tell me that he's been using energy-efficient light bulbs in every room. Or mere candlelight. And do you have recycling bins in the kitchens, Mrs Turner?'

Alexi decided it was time to stem. His headache was not subsiding any time soon. 'Why don't you come on in, Belinda, and give it the once-over yourself. I think you'll find it's as energy-efficient as your four-by-four and the little utilitarian apartment in Dubai that you nip off to with increasing regularity. So not at all. Where is your four-by-four by the way, or have you traded it in for a car that runs on compost and mends the planet every time you turn on the ignition?'

Belinda spoke from behind clenched teeth. 'You stupid boy, Alexi.'

He merely smirked, knowing he was right.

Aware that she hadn't answered his question, she added. 'The Merc's around the corner and Dubai is fine. We were there last week, actually.'

'See any hawfinches at The Burj, did we?' asked Alexi sarcastically. 'Or taking a drink at The Atlantis pool?'

Belinda ignored the question. 'Right then, Mrs Turner, a green tea, if you please, and I'd like you to show me the insides of your kitchen cupboards too please. I don't know what Daddy liked to eat, but if I'm here for a while I'd like to believe that you're well stocked organically.'

She strode past her brother, Mrs Turner in tow, and marched into the house. She passed Sheena too as she did so.

Belinda turned back, just as Sheena had done earlier, her words unfinished. She stared directly at Alexi again. 'And can you tie that kimono wannabe of yours a little tighter please. I'm getting quite an eyeful. And nobody wants to see that. Nobody is, I bet. I assume you're still single and that no woman has lost leave of her senses long enough to contemplate even looking in your direction.'

Belinda did not wait for an answer and walked off, Mrs Turner behind her, leaving Alexi to fiddle with his hemline and contemplate the disaster that was indeed his love life. His sister riled him massively, but sadly she was often correct.

Sheena kept her eyes straight out in front her again as Alexi walked past her and followed his sister into the house, still fiddling with his robe. It was clear that Alexi Burniston and Belinda Flatt may have been related to each other, but that they were definitely abrasive chalk and a very organic cheese.

Sheena followed Alexi into Burrow Hall and made her way to the study to see what kind of mess he had left there.

Chapter 17

Jeremiah had forced his date to leave his caravan as soon as the first smear of light hit the early-morning sky. The night had been fun, but once her welcome was outlived, she needed to go. Besides Sheila or Shona or Shandy or whatever her name was had an early shift back at Lidl, so it was pretty easy to send her on her way. And that suited Jeremiah just fine.

He had bigger fish to fry than the one he had dished up the night before. And from what he'd been reading in the local paper, he reckoned he could be onto a nice little earner. He'd spent two hours in bed with the paper when his date had left. It was yesterday's paper, but it housed the story he needed to read. As well as poring over the story that interested him time and time again, Jeremiah was also working out just how he could put his latest seed of a scam into complete germination mode. By the time he had risen out of bed, the sheets of the local paper spread across the bedsheets, he knew exactly what he planned to do.

He showered and dressed himself. Jeans and a T-shirt. He looked in his caravan mirror and styled his long ginger locks and goatee beard into place. He may have been knocking sixty, but his hair, both on his head and on his chin, was still richly red and showed only the merest hint of grey. His face, though, bore the lines of a man approaching his seventh decade on earth.

The caravan mirror was stained and old. He rubbed it with the palm of his hand to try to get a clearer view of what he was doing. Nothing changed. Maybe this new opportunity had come at exactly the right time. A lot of his caravan was beyond help when it came to both cleanliness and usefulness. A midsummer spring clean was definitely in order.

Jeremiah tucked his hair under a baseball cap and grabbed what he needed before leaving the caravan, a smile planted itself firmly on his face. He slammed the caravan door behind him and climbed into his car. That was another thing in his life that needed a bit of an upgrade. The thought of a tidy new motor that didn't stall at every opportunity pleased him.

The engine started with a splutter and the radio in the car burst into life. The song playing was a track by the Spice Girls. Jeremiah immediately tutted and flicked the button for another station. 'You can shut right up!'

He had nothing against the Spice Girls, but when his own name was Halliwell, he had ginger hair and he used to shorten his first name to Jerry, there were moments when he could happily have throttled a certain pop star who had been the bane of his life for the last few decades. If he had been given a pound for every person that had asked if a certain Spice was his sister, daughter, niece or whatever, then he would have never had to contemplate a moneymaking scam again. The girl band were replaced with a twangy burst of country and western.

Jeremiah paused in thought for a moment before putting the car into gear. He needed to make sure that he had everything he needed and that his plan was ready for take-off. He reckoned it was. He put the car into first gear and drove towards the gate at the corner of his field. The raspy tones of Wille Nelson's 'Always On My Mind' sounded from the radio. Jeremiah sang along. There was one thing always on Jeremiah's mind and that was making money.

He drove out of the field and onto the open road. He knew where he was going. No satnav needed. He was heading towards Rooney-at-Burrow. He knew the route. He'd already been there once in recent days.

Chapter 18

Belinda Flatt was definitely a tour de force. There was no doubting that. But she was also a complete dichotomy, with a rather canyon-esque-sized gulf of contradiction running through her entire being.

To the world, she was the ever-supportive wife of conservationist Rupert Flatt, following her husband around the world as he brushed shoulders with the high and mighty in the World Wildlife Fund and applauding his every word as he spoke of yet another feathered friend's potential brush with extinction at The Royal Society for The Protection of Birds. Rupert was the go-to man if a snow leopard needed saving or a quote was required on *BBC Breakfast* about reducing your carbon footprint. His spirit of adventure and his zest to try to save the planet were incredible and one of the many reasons a young, ready-to-change-the-world Belinda had fallen in love with him when he'd been speaking at a protest rally in London to ban the hunting of some furry woodland creature over twenty years ago. He was inspirational and Belinda had immediately fallen under his spell when their eyes had met across a protesting crowd. Cupid's work was done. Together they would indeed create a new future. Not just for them but for everyone.

Their courtship was whirlwind quick and within six months they were married on a beach in Costa Rica where they'd both been volunteering saving turtles. Belinda was nineteen years of age, Rupert nine years older. The phone call back to Burrow Hall to tell her parents that she was a married woman was a difficult one. Especially as she was married to a man that neither of them had ever met. Sir Buster was fuming, Fiona less so. She understood that affairs of the heart were a curious thing. But she was highly disappointed to have not been at her daughter's side on what should have been one of the proudest days of her life. Belinda had housed a streak of regret ever since but continually attempted to bury it.

For a few years, all was rosy. Or at least very green. Rupert and Belinda had navigated their way around the planet, the new kids on the conservation block. They worked side by side, relentlessly adventurous and blissfully happy at the changes they were endeavouring to make on mother earth.

But then things had swung from Mother Nature to motherhood. Belinda became pregnant and, despite her best efforts to try to deal with her ever-expanding waistline in Namibian mud huts and mosquito-riddled jungles, her terrible morning sickness and need for an afternoon nap to rest her swollen ankles meant that she was becoming much less useful in trying to save the planet when she couldn't even save herself from constantly throwing up.

Belinda had returned home to the UK. Rupert didn't. A fact she didn't mind at first, seeing as he would be saving some scaly beast from being wiped out of existence in Tanzania or helping lay water pipes for a village in Swaziland, as it was back then. His work was vital, and the need of the villagers was much greater than that of her ankles.

Her parents had wanted her to come back to Burrow Hall so that they could look after her. The beating heart of a family and the wholesome meals of Mrs Turner would be just what she needed. But Belinda's morals had said otherwise. Such a big house for so few people. It was a scandal. An energy-eating, non-eco-friendly scandal. It went against everything Belinda believed in. Belinda had moved into a rather small yet characterful flat in London instead and told her parents she would be having a natural drug-free home birth, with one of her conservationist friends acting as midwife. She knew that Rupert would be by her side, holding her hand and guiding her through the magic and beauty of a journey into creating a new life. The soundtrack in the room would be of birdsong or whales at play.

Sage Elm Buster Flatt was born at one of London's top private medical clinics six months later. Belinda was full of enough painkillers and stress-busting drugs to stock a street full of chemists and neither her eco pal nor Rupert were present. Apparently, Rupert, who had actually only been home twice during the entire pregnancy, thought that trying to build a safe habitat for Angolan meerkats was more important than witnessing his own son's birth. It was mum Fiona, who'd held Belinda's hand as she'd pushed a baby the size of a bowling ball into the world. The soundtrack was the skin-ripping screams of pain and a vocabulary a football crowd would find explicit as Sage (burning sage was said to expel negativity from the world) Elm (symbolising sturdiness. Not difficult at ten pounds ten ounces) Buster (had to be done to keep grandad sweet) Flatt uttered his first cry.

Belinda had caved in. All of her wishes to be natural, eco-friendly, tree-huggingly correct as a first-time mum had gone out of the window. It had been too hard and too painful. For a few days, private was the new green.

And that was where Belinda's dichotomy had begun, if she ever thought about it. Raising Sage as an eco-child was fine when she was able to be alongside her husband. And as Sage grew up, she often was. They travelled the world as a family. But on the occasions where Rupert, whose conversationalist star seemed to be shining bigger and brighter as the years progressed, was away for months on end and Belinda would find herself at home looking after Sage, her moral high ground always began to wobble Jenga-style. Healthy vegetarian meals were replaced with a quick trip to a fast-food chain. A yelling Sage, distraught about his broken wooden toy, would find it substituted for a plastic one as that was all the shop had in. Needs must when a child is bawling.

Belinda had to appear to be the perfect eco-wife. And for most of the time she was. But when she slipped, she slipped badly. Because sometimes comfort won over caring. Practicality over ecology. She just tried to keep those things a secret from Rupert. She had never told him about the private ward for Sage's birth, or about buying her first fuel-guzzling four-by-four for the school run. It was much more spacious for the shopping too. When Rupert started earning big bucks for his work, he would send some money home. As much as she wanted to spend it on a totally biodegradable lifestyle, sometimes it just wasn't practical or convenient. It was much more convenient when Rupert was back by her side.

It wasn't that Rupert was a bad father. Far from it. Sage knew he was loved and he adored his father. When he saw him, that was. No, Rupert wasn't a rubbish dad, he was just a very absent one most of the time. And these days he was more absent than ever with his work. As was Sage.

Despite the fact that the two of them were hardly in the same time zone for much of Sage's childhood, now that Sage was all grown up – twenty-one next birthday – he had turned into a chip off the old eco-block. In fact, he was currently down under with his father working with whales at the Whitsunday Islands. Whether this was because he saw himself as the successor to his father's eco-crown or because the Whitsundays had some of the best coral diving in the world, Belinda wasn't sure, but either way, she was home alone more often than Macaulay Culkin these days.

Well, one of her homes. Belinda had insisted, about a decade ago, that she wanted a little bolthole away from London. Away from the UK. Somewhere to disappear to. It was just after her mother had died and she didn't want to be around anything that reminded her of her mum's passing. And that included her dad, Sir Buster. It was also about the time that Sage was set to start boarding school. So, the time for her to escape had never been better. Rupert was always away anyway. He'd flown home for Fiona's funeral, stayed a couple of days and then flew back off to Outer Somewhere.

Belinda had toyed with the idea of buying a project. Maybe a shack in some leafy glade where she could live a healthy, zen-like existence with nature. But then a friend of hers had just returned from Dubai, where she had snapped up a luxury apartment in a new-build high-rise near the marina. Apparently, there were about four left on sale. It was something that Belinda would never have contemplated in a million years, but the photos looked fabulous. There were comforts galore and it was both affordable and fully furnished. Maybe it was the madness of having just lost her mother, but she'd bought one. In her own name. Outright.

It was another thing that she didn't share with Rupert. Not for a good three years anyway. When he found out, he hit the roof. Dubai was the last place he would ever consider going. Unless it was to save some rare sand beetle or something. He still hadn't been there ten years on. Belinda knew he never would, and, in truth, she didn't care. In fact, she was pleased. It was her bolthole and she loved it there. Yes, she cursed herself inwardly every time she drove her four-by-four to the airport and then caught a huge plane to Dubai. But she soon forgot about any inner conflict when she revelled in the playland's many opulences. She'd loved every visit.

To be honest, it had become her most pleasurable of jaunts these days. She hardly ever went on a conservation trip. Not at the front line anyway. But she would play the ever-supportive wife when required. It wasn't that she had fallen out of love with conservation at all. She had total respect for it. She always would and would do everything she could to stay green. Just it was more a case of when it suited her these days. No, she hadn't fallen out of love with the idea of conservation. She had just fallen out of love with the conservationist. That had happened about a decade ago too.

She'd been merrily enjoying her latest break away from Rupert when she'd found out about her father. She'd headed to Burrow Hall straight away. Despite the awful circumstances, it felt inexplicably comforting in a way to be back.

Belinda watched from an upstairs window at Burrow Hall as her brother Alexi got into his car and sped off across the gravel outside her family home. He was dressed now mercifully, that dreadful kimono nowhere to be seen. Where he was going, she neither knew nor cared. Well, maybe she was curious a bit. He was bound to be up to something. He always was.

She'd lied to him earlier about the entire family being in Dubai last week. It had been just her as ever. Alexi was one of the only people, aside from Rupert and Sage, who knew about her Dubai bolthole. She'd idiotically told him about it in a moment of vulnerability. She wished she never had. He held it against her rouletting green principals at every opportunity. Which was another reason why she hardly ever saw him.

She'd spoken to Rupert and Sage earlier that day.

Apparently, it might be hard for them to get back for the funeral from down under. Belinda didn't really mind. She missed Sage, but he hardly knew his grandfather, to be honest, and was a sombre funeral worth travelling thousands of miles for? Probably not.

Sage didn't really know Burrow Hall. But he might like it here. Once she'd made it a little greener, of course. She had plans for it. Big plans. Big green plans, in fact. She'd had her eyes on the place for years. It could be quite the project. But one that would need to exclude Alexi.

She watched as her brother's car sped off out of sight. She guessed he'd be back again later. The thought displeased her.

Chapter 19

Margaret Millsop fidgeted slightly in the squishy armchair she was sitting in and looked down at the two hexagons of fabric she was stitching together for her latest project and smiled. The fabric shapes were yellow and black in colour and stripy with a selection of bee motifs dotted across them. An open-topped basket sitting at her feet contained a pile of the same patterned fabric hexagons.

She stared across at Violet, who was sitting opposite her in another equally squishy armchair, both of them in the front room of Violet's flat above Brewer's Loop. Violet was dealing with an embroidery pattern of a wombat that she had found during the shop stocktake a few days earlier. She'd obviously ordered it in at some point and had forgotten about it. It was part of an Australia-themed triple set containing a kangaroo and a koala bear. She'd ordered it in as a gift for Betsy. The pattern was stretched out across an embroidery hoop which Violet was happily attacking with a needle and thread. An air of contentment swirled around both of the women, hanging somehow in the air.

'I knew he'd cave in and talk. How can any man resist that marrow chutney? It's a taste sensation,' said Margaret.

Violet stopped her attack on the wombat. 'I think it was more likely to be Pearl's roti bits that put him in such a talkative mood, don't you think? They taste incredible, even with that wretched chutney on them. How you can stomach it is beyond me.'

'Jimmy's giving me twenty jars of it for the village fayre. And they'll be beautifully displayed on this once I've finished it.' Margaret pointed to the fabric shapes. 'It'll make a lovely tablecloth.'

'Wouldn't that be better for jars of honey given the design?' queried Violet rather cheekily. She knew that the question would provoke a snappy response from her best friend.

'You get back to your blessed wombat, Violet Brewer. And when your shop starts selling fabric with marrows on it, I'll make a tablecloth from that, all right?' She let out a slight giggle.

The two women returned to the matter in hand. To the chutney-loving man in question, Rooney-at-Burrow's resident medic, Dr Roberts. Thanks to his sheer love of Pearl's roti bites and Jimmy's marrow chutney, he had happily polished off a plateful when he had been with the two ladies earlier that day. He hadn't really wanted to see either of them after a busy day at surgery (if two verrucas, a deep red allergy rash and an ingrowing toenail counted as busy), but the temptation of roti bites, marrow chutney and a glass or two of rhubarb gin seemed to be able to banish any air of fatigue. They were, indeed, just what the doctor ordered, to make him push his malaise to one side.

'I knew that there was nothing wrong with Sir Buster's heart,' cooed Violet, smug that her hunch had seemingly been proved right.

'That is what Dr Roberts said, I must admit,' echoed Margaret.

The doc had only left about an hour ago, having feasted on enough treats to loosen his lips sufficiently.

'His exact words, Margaret, were that Sir Buster had never been prescribed any kind of heart medicine and that his heart had not seen a day's trouble in its entire life.' Violet had played the words over and over in her brain ever since Dr Roberts had left them to an evening of crafting.

'Until now, he said.'

Violet had conveniently forgotten those two words.

'Why would a man as healthy as Sir Buster suddenly have a heart attack?'

'Er… his age.'

Violet was not to be beaten, even though she knew what Margaret was saying was perfectly true. Something was niggling at her insides. Nipping away at her like one of the trout in Sir Buster's lake.

Margaret continued, 'Dr Roberts, who is a man who can be trusted in my books because of his love of marrow chutney, said that the most likely explanation for Sir Buster's demise was that he had a heart attack, fell into the lake and drowned. It does seem more than likely, bless his soul.' Margaret reached for her glass of rhubarb gin on the top of the nest of tables alongside her and raised it towards the ceiling. 'May the poor man rest in peace.'

Violet did the same before replying. 'Likely is one thing, but definite is quite another. Do you think top police officers are happy with a likely?'

'Well, Samuel seems to be…'

'I said *top* police officers, Margaret. There is a difference. Do you think the officers working on the Jack the Ripper murders were working on a likely? They needed a definite to catch him.'

'I actually don't think they ever found out who really did it, did they? So, there was no definite?'

An air of fluster wrapped itself around Violet. 'Oh, you know what I mean. Maybe that's not the best example. But I need to be definite about Sir Buster to let him rest in peace in my mind.'

'So, what happens now? Even though Dr Roberts is ninety-nine per cent certain that it could possibly be most likely a heart attack.' She was aware how blurred that sounded. 'You're still not satisfied.'

'Are you, Margaret, are you?' Violet pinned the words in the air, leaving them for further rumination.

'Well, I guess not. But I'm not sure what we can do about it really. We've exhausted every avenue.'

'Well, that, Margaret, is one of two big reasons why you and I are completely different in our make-up. I think we have got other avenues to explore. I've just got to work out where exactly in the village they are. We need to try to find some kind of evidence.'

Margaret nodded, half in agreement, half in exasperated confusion.

Silence took centre stage for a second. It was Margaret who broke it.

'So, what's the other reason you and I are completely different?'

'You liking that blessed chutney. It tastes like a spoonful of—'

Violet's words were cut short as the telephone sitting alongside her began to ring. Violet answered it.

'Oh, hello dear, how are you… you sound out of breath.' For the next couple of minutes, the only words

Violet said were a questioning 'really?', pondering exclamations of 'aha', a smattering of 'oh my' and 'well I never' and eventually a rather strange yet congratulatory 'bravo'. Her face throughout seemed to contort itself into every possible emotion from intrigue to dismay.

Margaret, who could hear a voice at the other end of the phone but couldn't quite make out who it belonged to or what they were saying, was on tenterhooks as her friend hung up. 'Who was that? Your face was a picture.'

'That was Sheena. You'll never guess what she found up at Burrow Hall. It appears that we may have our evidence to suggest that someone was out to get Sir Buster.'

'You mean…?' Margaret raised her eyebrows curiously.

Violet nodded. 'Yes, it appears that someone wanted our dear friend as dead as the stag that hangs on his study wall.' She was tempted to add 'I told you so' but resisted.

She unravelled the story of what Sheena had just told her to an open-mouthed Margaret. It was only when she'd finished that they both returned to their crafting, their minds buzzing with possibilities.

Violet looked at her wombat. Somehow whilst stitching the creature's dark nose into place, she had managed to repeat a few stitches too many, giving it the appearance of a rather large black eye instead. Betsy would never stand for that. She started unpicking the nose and made a note to FaceTime Betsy later with the latest revelations.

Chapter 20

Sheena was standing in the doorway of St Charlotte's Church on the outskirts of Burrow Hall's grounds. She didn't really know why she had decided to come there to break the news to Violet about her find, but it seemed like the most sensible choice. She knew it well for one. Indeed, it had been the backdrop for all of her many victories in the Ravishing Rooney Queen pageant, so it seemed somehow comforting. She couldn't go home, after all, as her father might be there, and she wanted to tell Violet about her discovery before Sergeant Pollett got hold of it and gave his opinion. Also, St Charlotte's was the quickest place she could run to once she had stashed her findings into a carrier bag and run off across the lawns. It was that or the forest around the private lake, but seeing as that was still pretty fresh as a crime scene, she had no real desire to go there. Plus, it was heading towards mid-evening and she didn't want to be anywhere, as the day dipped into dark, that a dead body had been just a few days earlier.

It had been quite a day. First the meeting of Alexi Burniston and his sleazeball ways. Then the hurricane that was Belinda Flatt blowing into the village. Sheena had been more than content to get away from both of them to go and tidy around the Hall. And when she said tidy, she absolutely one hundred per cent meant snooping around to try to find some kind of clues for the Team C.R.A.B. investigations.

Despite Alexi's advice about starting in the study with his boozy mess from the night before, she had chosen instead to head upstairs to have a sneaky peak around the bedrooms. Primarily, Sir Buster's bedroom. Belinda and Mrs Turner were busy in the kitchen, Alexi was still rooting around his car and Herbert the butler was nowhere to be seen. Probably out shopping.

She had found nothing despite a thorough going-over of Sir Buster's room, including a rummage through every drawer, cupboard and wardrobe and even a shimmy under his bed to see if anything menacing lurked there. Nothing did except for an old pair of slippers that looked like they may have been hiding in their dark and forgotten corner since Sir Buster's wife had died. The dust piled upon them suggested they hadn't been worn for the longest of times.

It was when Sheena had heard Alexi coming back up the stairs that she'd decided that descending to the lower floor might be a good idea. Like people on a weather clock, as he'd meandered upstairs, she'd sneaked past him unseen and made her way downstairs to the study and to the scene of Alexi's excess.

Alexi wasn't lying. Sheena had entered into the study and gasped slightly. She had never seen it in such a state. Drawers hanging open, papers strewn everywhere. Pictures on the wall slightly skew-whiff. Sheena had let out a sigh. Okay, this would take some cleaning. But a thorough clean meant a thorough snoop.

She began by straightening the pictures on the wall. It was funny. Sheena had been cleaning and working at the Hall for nearly three years now and even though she had cleaned the study countless times, she had never really taken much notice of the portraits on the wall. Most of them appeared to be individuals from the history of the Burniston family.

Sheena had smiled as she moved around the room straightening the portraits. Quite why Alexi had moved them in the first place was a mystery. Loterina Burniston from the late 1800s. Tobias Burniston and his wife Davinia from 1824. Sheena had inwardly thanked her lucky stars that she hadn't been around back then. Lacy bonnets, tight ringleted hair, a mass of pearly jewellery pieces. Blimey, the women in those days must have spent half the time intricately fiddling their hair into place and the other half deciding what accessories to go for. On a good day, Sheena could exit the shower, dry her hair, pick her outfit and head out of the door in under ten minutes. Maybe that would have been longer if she'd have had a portrait to pose for.

She had moved across to a framed photograph hanging over Sir Buster's desk. Well, what she could see of his desk under the mass of papers that fanned out across it. On one corner of the desk sat an ashtray. Three cigarette stubs lay bent and crushed inside it.

'Whisky, fire and paper. Well, that was a super safe combination, Alexi,' she'd remarked to herself as she took the scene in.

The photograph hanging above the desk was again, she'd guessed, a family portrait. Black and white, a group of people all posed stiffly together. Not one of them was smiling. Sheena had been reminded of a story that she'd read online about photos back then. Sometimes a photo would be taken after a family member had actually died. It was a posterity thing. If the body was to stand up in the photo, a special frame to hold it up would be built and sometimes eyes would actually be painted on to make it look like the person was still living. Sheena thought it was as creepy as heck. She had studied the photograph on the wall to see if anyone looked somewhat glazed in the eye area. As far as she could work out, all of them appeared to still be in the land of the living, though none of them looked particularly happy about it.

Sheena had spent the next hour or so tidying the study.

Picking up all of the papers strewn across the desk and those that had fallen onto the floor. She had scanned her eyes across each and every one. She knew that Great-aunty Violet would want a blow-by-blow account later of each and every thing she had looked at. Unfortunately, they all appeared to be dull business letters about the general running of Burrow Hall. A few seemed to be requests from charities, others were quotes for possible work on the house, and one of the letters was from a film company asking to use Burrow Hall as a location. Seeing as the date on the letter was at least a year old, Sheena guessed that, sadly, it had never happened. She couldn't help but wonder what it would have been and whether she would have had the chance to bump into a Hollywood superstar or at least someone who had brushed up against a Kardashian. Sheena would have loved that.

Sheena had arranged the papers as best she could and placed them back into the desk drawers. Sir Buster seemed to be lacking any kind of filing system, so she had just ordered them as neatly as possible. She'd vacuumed the floor, which appeared to contain a liberal sprinkling of cigarette ash and what she thought looked like biscuit crumbs. She had wiped up any spillages on the bar area in one corner of the study. Alexi appeared to be of the belief that you didn't refill a glass, you merely poured a drink into a fresh one. Unless he had held some kind of party with his mates, which Sheena was sure Mrs Turner would have informed her about had that been the case, Alexi was simply a messy individual. She felt sorry for his cleaner back home if they had to deal with this on a regular basis. Or maybe he didn't have one and just lived his life walking around in a sea of ash and crumb debris up to his eyeballs. But surely someone with a hideously expensive car like his and just plain hideous silk dressing robes could afford a cleaner. Sheena wondered what he did for a job. He obviously had a bob or two. She would have to ask Mrs Turner.

Sheena had been just about to leave the study, finally spotless, when she'd noticed a book lying on the floor under the sofa. She hadn't spotted it before, but then she wouldn't have been able to see it from certain angles. There had been papers laying across the sofa too, so maybe

Alexi had been looking at the book at the same time as the papers and then drunkenly dropped it. Seemed likely.

She had walked across to the sofa, got down on her hands and knees and reached underneath for the book. She had pulled it out. It was a thick, leather-bound copy of Robert Louis Stevenson's *The Strange Case of Dr. Jekyll and Mr. Hyde*. It was Sir Buster's favourite book. He'd told her about it once. Even tried to persuade Sheena to read it. Her mind had flashed back to him telling her that it was 'a bloody glorious read' and that 'everyone has a bit of Jekyll and Hyde in them'. She'd considered reading it, but never did as she had been midway through a juicy tell-all autobiography about one of her favourite TV stars at the time. A seemingly wholesome TV presenter who was actually up to all sorts of debauchery behind closed doors. Maybe Sir Buster had been right that everyone had a bit of Jekyll and Hyde in them after all.

She had sat down on the sofa with the book and opened it to have a look at the first chapter. She'd give a quick skim over the first few pages and then maybe read the whole of it if she liked what she read. She thought that

Sir Buster would like that and the thought of making him happy even though he was no longer around pleased her.

As she was about to read, she'd noticed a bookmark sticking slightly out of the novel roughly about halfway through. She'd flicked to the page and smiled. She had immediately recognised the bookmark as one that Margaret had made for Sir Buster. It had a cross-stitch of his name running vertically from top to bottom. Sheena had one exactly the same. Margaret had crafted a batch of them during a Team C.R.A.B. meeting just before Christmas one year and gave personalised ones to half of the village as festive gifts. Margaret would be pleased to know that Sir Buster had placed it inside his favourite book.

The bookmark wasn't the only thing held in those pages, however. An envelope sat there too. It was torn open at the top and had the words 'Sir Buster Burniston' printed on it. Unable to stop herself, a curious Sheena had opened the envelope and pulled out the sheets of paper that lay inside.

There were three different sheets. They had all been

folded together. All three of them contained a message that had been cut out from magazine and newspaper letters. Sheena had gasped as she read the words on the sheets.

I KNOW WHAT YOU'VE BEEN DOING,

STOP IT NOW

I'VE WARNED YOU. STOP BEFORE IT'S TOO

LATE

THIS IS YOUR FINAL WARNING.

ENOUGH IS ENOUGH

Sheena had no idea what it meant, but she knew that whoever had sent these to Sir Buster had not been a happy individual. She also knew that Sir Buster had obviously been up to something. Maybe something bad enough to get him killed.

Sheena could feel her heart pounding inside her chest. She had placed the three sheets back into the envelope. She guessed that they hadn't all been sent at once.

She needed to tell Violet.

She had shut the book and held it tightly in her hands as she'd left the study, made her way towards the entrance and out into the early-evening air. Luckily, she didn't bump into anyone from the household as she did so.

Excitement washing over her, Sheena had run as fast as she could in the direction of St Charlotte's Church. She was out of breath by the time she arrived. She was still somewhat breathy now as she dialled Great-aunty Violet to excitedly tell her what she had found.

Chapter 21

Phill Brooks pinned the poster he'd been working on in pride of place behind the bar at The Six Pennies. He stood back and admired his handiwork.

'Well, if I say so myself, that's a job well done. That should grab people's attention and get them in on the night.'

He read the words on the poster to check the spelling. '

MEMORIAL FOR SIR BUSTER. COME AND

CELEBRATE THE LIFE OF ONE OF OUR

GREATEST VILLAGERS WITH AN EVENING OF

SONGS, MEMORIES AND GOOD FOOD. £10 EACH.

ALL MONIES RAISED TO GO TO THE RSPB.'

The four corners of the poster were decorated with illustrations of fish and ducks that Phill had chosen. He was pleased to see everything was spelt correctly. His first attempt had unfortunately said 'wife' instead of 'life', 'thongs' instead of 'songs' and called the deceased man 'Sir Butter'. Phill wasn't always the most computer-savvy of people.

'So, what do you think, Steph?' He turned to his wife, who was flicking through the day's edition of the local newspaper sitting on the other side of the bar. She held a glass of Pinot Grigio blush in her hand and sipped at it, a little lost in sadness as she read the paper. Unsurprisingly, it was Sir Buster's death that still filled the front page.

She looked up to survey her husband's work. It was hardly a work of art, but it said what needed to be said, she guessed, and a memorial night for Sir Buster was a wonderful idea.

'Yes, it's great, dear. Have you asked Sheena about singing yet?'

'No, but I'm sure she will. She liked the old fella.'

'As did we all.' Steph raised her glass and took another sip of her wine. A puzzled haze embossed over her as she looked at the four corners of the poster. 'Do you not think fish are a little inappropriate given that Sir Buster died of a heart attack in his lake? And why the ducks?'

'The ducks are a private joke, plus they tie in with the bird charity. Sir Buster would approve, I'm sure. As for the fish, I thought it would be an homage to something that he loved doing. I was going to put rugby balls as well, but I wanted to stick with living things for the design. I thought balls would spoil it.'

'I guess so,' said Steph, not really sure if she agreed or not.

Phill looked at her, worry written across his face. 'Do you really think that it's inappropriate? I could always change it. Hang on, let's ask the troops.'

Phill shouted across to Pearl and Jimmy, who were sitting together at a table on the far side of the bar. It was early evening and seeing as both of their other halves were away with work – Bailey in Abu Dhabi and Noah, now a little less traumatised than he had been two days earlier, dining with a potential client in London – the pair had decided to come to the pub and eat there. Pearl didn't feel like cooking after she'd whipped up another batch of roti bites for Violet and Margaret's attack on Dr Roberts. Plus, she and Jimmy had lots to discuss.

'Oi, Jimmy. Pearl. We're having a memorial night for Sir Buster. To raise a bit of money and toast the old boy. I've made a poster. I think it's smashing, but the wife thinks the fish might be a little inappropriate given the circumstances of his demise. I can change it. What do you think?' Phill held his hands aloft in a questioning manner.

Jimmy and Pearl both stared across at the poster.

'Well, I think the memorial night is a lovely idea,' cooed Pearl. 'We need to send Sir Buster off in good fashion. It's what he would have wanted. A right good old knees-up. And I think he'd be chuckling in his grave about the fish. He loved his fishing, so the fact that he died doing something that he loved has to be a good thing, right? So, I say keep it.'

'Yep, me too,' agreed Jimmy. 'Why the ducks though?'

'Private joke.' Phill chuckled. 'Do you think Sheena will mind singing? I should have asked her first really before printing up the poster. Mind you, I don't say who's singing songs. If she says no, I'll have to get you two up

211

there. Tonight, ladies and gentlemen, Pearl Wheeler and Jimmy Coates are Ike and Tina Turner.' Phill laughed again, evidently amusing himself with the notion.

'That's never going to happen,' smirked Jimmy. 'But I'm sure it won't need to as I'm certain Sheena will be more than happy to sing. She can pick out some of Sir Buster's favourites. You'd better check that the date doesn't clash with the funeral though.'

'I suppose I had better check with Sir Buster's family,' smiled Phill. 'The kids will be organising that, I suppose.'

'You could ask Belinda Flatt – Sir Buster's daughter. She's back in the village,' nodded Pearl. 'Sergeant Pollett and WPC Horton told me that when they popped round to check up on me earlier. To see how I was doing. They said it was to do with the trauma, but I think they'd heard that you got me a little tiddled yesterday, Phill Brooks. You and that wife of yours.' Pearl pointed good-naturedly across at Steph, who was still immersed in both her glass of wine and the local paper. 'I was quite the giddy goose when I got home.'

Phill grinned. 'That'll be why you're on the mineral

water tonight then, Pearl. I thought you Caribbean types would be able to drink all day long. All those tropical cocktails in the sunshine. I thought you'd be used to it.'

Pearl raised her eyebrows. 'Phill Brooks, I've not actually lived in Barbados for over two decades, so my days of drinking Caribbean cocktails in the sunshine, as you say, are long gone, unless you count the odd tin of Malibu Pina Colada in my back garden. And besides, I was in shock yesterday after my near-death experience. I blame you for taking advantage of a poor shocked woman.'

Phill winked and then grabbed two packets of crisps from behind the bar. He walked over to Pearl and Jimmy at their table, passing Steph as he went. As he did so, he slapped her playfully on the bottom.

'You hear that, Steph. I'm being accused of taking advantage of another woman. What d'you think of that, eh? Wahey! I swear that Pearl is flirting with me.'

Steph looked up from the paper and stared across at Pearl and Jimmy. 'Pearl, if you want him, you can have him. But I don't think you really do, do you?' she deadpanned.

'You're too much woman for me, Pearl,' laughed Phill, causing her to screech with merriment.

He arrived at the table and dropped the two packets of crisps down in front of Pearl and Jimmy. 'Here you go, you two. Try these on the house. New flavour. Pickled pork. The supplier thinks they're going to be big. Steph wasn't sure about them. I think they show potential. Dive on in. It'll soak up all of that mineral water, Pearl.' Phill returned to the bar. As he passed Steph again, he placed his hands on her shoulders and planted a kiss on the back of her head. 'You weren't keen on them, love, were you? You thought they were a bit basic. I'm off to empty the ashtrays outside.'

Steph didn't answer. Today was a day where she was finding the entire pub a bit basic. And that included Phill. She flipped a page of the newspaper and checked out her horoscope to see what delights might be around the corner.

Over at their table, Jimmy and Pearl tried a couple of the porky crisps, decided they weren't the best and carried on with their conversation.

'So now that Belinda is back in the village, what were you able to find out about her?' asked Jimmy.

Pearl swallowed a mouthful of mineral water to try to remove the taste of the crisps and began. 'Well, I didn't realise that Sir Buster's daughter was married to Rupert Flatt, the conservationist. I love him when he pops up on the morning telly explaining how to recycle my rubbish properly or telling a tale about saving some tiger in Bangladesh. Well, when I heard her say her name in the village store and then Rita told me who it was, I did some googling about her. She seems like the model wife. One child, name of Sage—'

'They should have had another called Onion,' quipped Jimmy.

Pearl smiled and continued. 'Both him and his mother have been very complimentary about all of the work that Rupert does around the world. There are lots of photos from years gone by of the two of them, Rupert and Belinda, in various parts of the world, but it appears that in more recent times Belinda is more of a stay-at-home type while Rupert does all of his work. She pops up with him at events, but ask me what she actually does for a living and I've no idea. I couldn't see that she actually has a job, other than being wife and mother. Which is a darned good job in my eyes, seeing as it's the one I do.' Pearl guffawed, her laugh hearty and joyous. 'She does write the odd magazine article about all things green though, so she obviously still cares greatly about it.'

'Interesting,' said Jimmy, taking a swig on his beer. 'It sounds like she was a lot easier to find out about than the son, Alexi. There was hardly anything online about him. I was hoping he'd have his own Wikipedia page, but he doesn't.'

'Could you find anything at all?' asked Pearl.

'Not really. There's stuff written about Sir Buster and Fiona and that they had two children. There are pictures of when Alexi was young. But as far as I can gather, once he went off to boarding school, it's pretty much a blur after that. It's literally like he disappeared. I wish I'd asked more when Sir Buster was alive. But I suppose we didn't really have any reason to then, did we?'

'Maybe Mrs Turner and Herbert up at Burrow Hall

know more about him. They've both known the children since they were born,' offered Pearl.

'Good call. Maybe one of Team C.R.A.B. needs to do a bit of digging.'

'Violet gets on well with Mrs Turner, I think. Doesn't she come into Brewer's Loop for her wool. She likes to knit, if I remember. I seem to recall Violet saying that she would have liked to have been in the craft group had she not been so busy with Sir Buster's needs.'

'That does ring a bell,' replied Jimmy before draining the last of his beer. 'Right then, Pearl, I had better get back as I want to check on the chickens. A fox killed off two of them quite horrifically and the others seem to have been finding it hard to settle ever since.'

'Well, a death is going to do that, isn't it? Look at us. I shan't be able to rest properly until I know that Sir Buster's death wasn't anything more than an unfortunate heart attack. You know that there might have been' – Pearl looked around the pub and lowered her voice to a whisper to finish the sentence – 'foul play.'

'Agreed. Are you calling it a night too?'

'Yes, I've got some Christmas card sets I've been making that I want to have ready to sell at the village fayre. Margaret is determined that it should go ahead if possible. Not long now.'

'Til Christmas? It's August, Pearl!'

'No, til the fayre, you fool. Plus, it's always good to get your Christmas things sorted early. Saves you running around like a headless chicken come the twenty-fourth of December.'

'Talking of which. My clucky friends await. Let's go.'

The two of them stood up and walked towards the bar. Just as they were saying farewell to Phill and Steph, a car screeched into The Six Pennies car park, loud music blaring from its stereo. As it did so, they both looked out of the window in the direction of the awful noise. It was the same open-top sporty number that had nearly sent Pearl flying the day before.

Pearl clenched her teeth together. 'Well, will you look who it is. Only that stupid idiot who almost knocked me off my feet yesterday. I shall enjoy giving the driver a piece of my mind.'

Alexi Burniston pulled the key from the ignition and tossed it into the air before catching it again. He was in a good mood. Much better than he had been earlier with his whisky hangover and his unexpected crossing of swords with his sister. He'd call her his least favourite sister, but that was kind of superfluous when you merely had one.

But this afternoon had been a good one. He'd spent most of it talking to housing development companies who he was considering working with in the very near future. Well, once Burrow Hall was his. There was a lot of land there that could be built on. Demolish the church, dig up the forest, maybe even knock down the Hall itself. There would be room for a lot of luxury developments. Commuter-belt buyers with cash to splash. Cash that would come in very handy indeed.

Yep, there was no way he was just going to keep Burrow Hall as it was. What was it to him except a whole heap of dusty old memories? And not many of those were particularly happy ones, to be honest. But if things worked out right, then the future could look very rosy indeed.

Now that the hangover had worn off, another drink

was in order. And the village pub seemed a much better proposition than going home to drink alone, or worse still with Belinda. And perhaps that pretty young thing he'd met this morning would be at the pub too. Didn't she say she sang there? What was her name again? It momentarily escaped him. Women's names often did.

When he walked into the pub and looked around, he could see that sadly she wasn't there. Her loss for now. What he found instead was a woman sitting rather glumly at the bar, a seemingly distant man behind it and a large farmer type who appeared to be holding back a rather agitated-looking woman. Alexi wondered whether the pub would liven up later on. He hoped so, as this was hardly going to keep him entertained during his stay.

Pearl was just about to launch into a tirade of abuse about his driving skills when the man spoke.

'Doing a night for Dad, eh?' He pointed to the poster on the wall. 'Count me in, especially if it's that cracking young woman doing the singing. Don't suppose she's on tonight, is she?'

Alexi threw his keys down on the bar and sat down.

All eyes were on him.

It was Phill who spoke first to break the brewing silence in the air. 'Your dad was Sir Buster? So that must mean that you're—'

'Alexi Burniston,' boomed Pearl, allowing a huge smile to paint itself across where her clenched teeth and anger had been just a second ago. 'Welcome to the village. I'm Pearl Wheeler. This is local farmer Jimmy Coates, and this is the landlady of this fine establishment, Stephanie Brooks. Welcome back to Rooney-at-Burrow and can we all say how sorry we are about your dear dad. We all loved him greatly. He was quite the character.'

'Was he?' said Alexi, before deciding that it was better to turn his reply on its head. 'Er, yeah… he was.'

The others murmured their condolences at Alexi.

'Thanks for that. Shall we drink to him. I'll have a whisky please, landlady.'

'I'm… I'm afraid I've got to fly. Chickens to sort on the farm,' stammered Jimmy. 'But I'm sure Pearl would love to stay and toast Sir Buster with you, wouldn't you, Pearl?'

Jimmy pushed Pearl towards the bar with a coaxing shove like a sacrificial lamb.

Alexi spoke before she could. 'You're the farmer. I kind of remember your family from when I was young. Vaguely. Big farm not far from the village square?'

'That's the one.'

Alexi turned to Pearl. 'I don't remember you, though. You're obviously not born and bred here then.'

Pearl was finding it very hard to see any likable qualities in Alexi Burniston, but for the sake of investigation, she kept the smile branded onto her face. 'No, I'm originally from Barbados actually, I moved here a few years ago. It's such a charming... British... village.' Pearl could feel her teeth re-clenching.

'Barbados. Now we're talking. I lived there for a while. Great place. Fabulous people and soooo laid-back.' Alexi knocked his whisky back.

A light bulb illuminated in Pearl's head. 'Maybe a drink to Sir Buster is an excellent idea. Right, Jimmy, off you pop to look after your chickens. I'll catch up with you soon.' She waved Jimmy away with a polite yet definitive flicking of her fingers.

'Oh yeah, suppose I had better be going. Nice to meet you, Alexi.'

Alexi nodded, not even looking at Jimmy, as the farmer wandered out of the pub. Jimmy knew Pearl was up to something and couldn't wait to hear what it was.

'Right then, Alexi, another whisky for you? And I think I'll join you. Shall we retire to a table? Two whiskies, Phill, please. We'll be sitting over there.' She pointed to the table she and Jimmy had just vacated.

Lured by whisky, Alexi got down from his stool at the bar and followed Pearl to the table. A free drink was a free drink after all.

Pearl smiled as the drinks arrived. She wouldn't mention that Alexi had nearly killed her yesterday. That could wait. As could her Christmas cards. There were more important things to deal with.

'So, Alexi, whereabouts in Barbados were you? Tell me everything.' Pearl did her best to keep smiling and banish any temptation to clench her teeth again.

Chapter 22

The day had not gone as smoothly as Jeremiah Halliwell had planned. How could the one person that he needed to see in a small village manage to escape him all day? He'd looked everywhere. His head was bursting with possibilities, but nothing could start taking shape until he had found that certain someone. He'd wandered through the square and sat by the duck pond for a while, scanning every passer-by. He'd pulled his baseball cap down over his forehead as far as he could, trying to remain as anonymous as possible. He wasn't really sure why.

He'd spent the best part of twenty minutes stroking a rather contended ginger cat on the wall outside a cottage near the square. The cat, whose fur was exactly the same colour as Jeremiah's hair, had purred loudly as Jeremiah ran his hand down his back. Jeremiah was not normally a cat kind of guy, the only pet he'd ever owned was a black rat, but there was something very endearing about the fulsome feline. Jeremiah had only stopped when he saw a female police office heading into the square and walking in his direction. Shuffling away from the puss, he was pleased when the uniformed woman passed him and began to stroke the still purring cat herself. Jeremiah had been pretty certain that he himself had been the reason for her approach so was more than relieved when she'd sailed past him.

He'd walked past the local farm at least four or five times in search of his prey and even found himself skulking in the window of the local wool shop looking out onto the street, twiddling with balls of wool that he had absolutely no idea what to do with. The woman behind the counter had asked him about something called macramé, at least that was what he thought she'd said, and he'd panicked and scuttled from the shop.

He'd even spent over half an hour in the village pub, seeing if he could find the person he needed to see there.

Maybe they would go in for a drink? It was a hot day after all. The pub hadn't been busy and it had been hard to try to remain inconspicuous so he'd left after just one drink. Plus, he was being offered strange flavour crisps by the landlady again. That was twice in a week. He was hoping that after today he wouldn't have to step foot inside the pub again. Not that he had anything against pubs, but he preferred his a little more lively.

It was early evening by the time Jeremiah was ready to call it a day. He had tried his best to find the person he wanted all over the village, but somehow they weren't there. Maybe they weren't from Rooney-at-Burrow after all. Maybe his cunning plan was as dead in the water as Sir Buster had been at the weekend.

It was just as he was about to climb into his car and head back to his caravan in Darrochdean that finally a frisson of excitement surged through Jeremiah's body. The person he was looking for had finally come into vision. He was pretty sure it was them. They looked slightly different. Less hassled, he guessed. But he was fairly certain he had found the right person. Where they had been hiding all day was anyone's guess.

He looked around. Most of the village high street was surprisingly deserted. The moment was perfect. Fate was on his side. Chancer's luck was with him. He slid his hand into his trouser pocket to make sure he had what was needed and approached his quarry.

They looked a little startled as he drew near, but smiled nevertheless, the reaction voluntary if not sincere. Before they could speak, Jeremiah began to talk.

'Don't say a word. Just listen to what I have to say. I saw you at the lake on Saturday. That morning with Sir Buster. I was there, fishing. Illegally as it happens, but that's how I roll. I'd had a tip-off from a mate that his Lordship's lake was rammed with trout. A good poaching opportunity. They weren't wrong. But me nicking a few fish is nothing compared with you, is it? I saw what you did. I saw it all. It's amazing what you can catch sight of when you're skulking in the bushes. I know you killed him.' Jeremiah passed over an envelope that he had withdrawn from his pocket. 'I won't tell a soul, though. As long as you do what it says in here. And don't go getting the police involved. I think you've got way more to lose than me, right? I think murder trumps a bit of poaching any day.'

The person in front of Jeremiah took the envelope and remained silent. Not a single word fell from their lips. Lips that hung open in disbelief. And horror. A bit like one of the illegal fish that Jeremiah had been poaching.

They were still hanging open as Jeremiah returned to his car and drove off, his scheming work done for now.

As Jeremiah passed the 'Welcome to Rooney-at-Burrow' signpost at the edge of the village, the person he had seen at the lake on Saturday morning began to tear open the envelope and read the contents. Jeremiah's plan had been in set in motion and he couldn't help feeling thrilled.

Chapter 23

'So, Sheena popped in on the way back from Burrow Hall and gave me this book…' said Violet, once more tucked up in bed as she FaceTimed Betsy in Australia.

'Oh, hang on, Vi, Rod's shouting like crazy from the shower. Apparently, there's no towel in there. Hang on will you, he's in a rush as he's off to the film set this morning again and it's a good two hours from Willow's Spit.'

Betsy stood up and scuttled off, disappearing from Violet's screen, leaving just the garden seat she had been sitting on and a backdrop of a patched-up fence. Violet assumed this must have been where the wombat debacle had occurred. Why Betsy was sitting outside around their pool at this time of the year was beyond. Wasn't it supposed to be winter in Australia right now? It was a question she asked her sister when she returned to her screen a few minutes later, having furnished her actor husband with something fluffy to dry himself with.

'Violet, it may be winter here, but it's still incredibly mild. When you've spent nearly every Christmas Eve for decades singing carols in Rooney-at-Burrow's village square when it's minus four and you can hardly feel your fingers underneath your mittens, then a little breeze around the pool in the morning is nothing in comparison. Now, what's this book that Sheena has given you?'

Violet filled her sister in on the latest news about Sheena's discovery of the three threatening notes hidden away inside the copy of *Jekyll and Hyde*. As Violet unravelled the latest revelations, Betsy sat wide-mouthed, taking in every juicy morsel.

It was only when Violet had finished that a highly contemplative Betsy, who was letting every word of the story spiral around her brain with huge excitement, began to ask questions. 'It does look possible that someone was gunning for Sir Buster after all. How utterly horrid. But do you think that maybe it's just a coincidence and that the notes were meant to scare him a little?'

'Well, it could be a coincidence, but I tend to favour the notion that it is more likely to be conspiracy. Someone has been conspiring to frighten the life out of poor Sir Buster with these notes. I can imagine he just dismissed them as nonsense. He'd have called them poppycock, no doubt. But that doesn't take away from the fact that somebody sent them and that their tone was threatening.'

'Well, who are the most likely suspects? Surely it's got to be Alexi and Belinda now that they're back in the village?' Violet had already retold the tale of Sheena's meeting of both of Sir Buster's children. 'They're the ones set to gain the most, surely? When is the reading of the will?'

'No news as yet,' replied Violet. 'Although I may take a trip to Burrow Hall tomorrow to do a bit of snooping around. See what information I can gain. All under the guise of paying my respects and offering my condolences, of course.' Violet pinned a thought in her brain to perhaps make one of her summer berry drizzle cakes first thing in the morning to take with her. It would add sincerity. Plus, it tasted wondrous.

'That Alexi sounds like a right piece of work,' remarked Betsy. 'What do we know about him? Apart from a fleeting glance at Fiona's funeral, I really can't remember much about him.'

'Well, Jimmy has been trying to dig up some information about him online and hit a brick wall. There was nothing really to go on, but then he and Pearl were at The Six Pennies tonight and who should come wandering in but Alexi. And with a very cocky swagger in his manner apparently for someone whose father is barely five minutes deceased. So Pearl decided to corner him for a chat. Jimmy phoned me earlier to suggest that we meet up tomorrow to discuss what Pearl found out.' It suddenly dawned on Violet that maybe her Tuesday was going to be a very busy day. 'I may have to ask Sheena to look after the shop for me tomorrow. I may be otherwise engaged.'

'And Belinda, she's married to this conversationalist?'

'No, dear, she's married to a conservationist. A tad different. He's very popular apparently. I'd never heard of him, but no surprise there. She's quite opinionated apparently. Rita in the corner shop wasn't keen on her and if anyone can judge someone's character, it's someone who sees what we put in our shopping baskets. Always highly telling, if you ask me. And Sheena said it was clear that Belinda and Alexi are far from close. In fact, they don't seem to like each other very much at all. They were snipping away at each other like crazy.'

'So do we think one of them could be behind the letters?' queried Betsy.

'Well, that was my first thought too,' offered Violet. 'But then I looked at the envelope. There's no franking mark on it, or stamp, or anything like that – it's just got Sir Buster's name printed in ink – so I'm thinking it must have been hand-delivered. If it did come from Alexi or Belinda, then surely they would have had to post it from somewhere. I know there's only one envelope, but I'm assuming the other two were the same. Sir Buster must have thrown those. I'm thinking the third one must have come quite recently, as I'm sure Sir Buster was talking about "not giving in to threats" the other night at the pub.

My memory is definitely recalling that he said something. Didn't I say to you? I'm sure that's what I heard him say. Even with Sheena mid-Cher.'

'We don't have a clue where either of them has been recently, though, do we. Surely it would be very easy for them to hand-deliver the letters in person. No one in the village has seen them for years, so it would be a piece of cake to just pop a note through the door. Stick a woolly hat on him or get her to tie her hair back and nobody would recognise them. Or the notes could have been sent with flowers or a gift. Here's some stargazer lilies and a threat. You can have anything delivered these days, can't you. There's a woman three doors down from us who gets all of her meals delivered in individual sachets. Seems very lazy to me. But each to their own.'

'Indeed. Sheena was saying that apparently Sir Buster had been telling her the day before he died that both Alexi and Belinda had been telling him to sell the Hall for years. Apparently, it was pretty much the only contact he had from them these days. Isn't that dreadful. Again, I think some digging needs to be done there.'

'So, who else could be sending the notes?' pondered Betsy. 'The tone of them, I KNOW WHAT YOU'VE BEEN DOING, STOP IT NOW, doesn't really tally in with the idea of his two children wanting him to sell the Hall. It suggests that Sir Buster had been doing something that somebody didn't like. What d'you think that could be? An affair? Dodgy money dealings? International spy?' Betsy couldn't help herself from smiling at the thought of all three.

'Have you been watching too much James Bond with Rod?' asked Violet. 'I hardly think Sir Buster was an international spy. Dodgy money affairs maybe. I know he liked a game of poker back in the day with Margaret's ex-husband and I think the odd night of poker still goes on at The Six Pennies sometimes. I think Jimmy and Bailey went to one of them and said that Sir Buster played a mean game. Maybe he owes someone a lot of money and didn't pay up.'

'What about an affair? We all know Sir Buster had an eye for the ladies.'

'He was the biggest flirt around. He could charm

anybody. But I think we'd have known if he'd been having an affair. The village gossip grapevine would have seen that particular titbit of information rocket around the village square and the pub straight away. And Sheena told me that Sir Buster had been telling her how no woman he had met since Fiona could ever compare to her. So even if he was having a bit of fun now and again, it doesn't seem like there has been anything serious. And, like I say, we'd have known. Nothing gets past me and Margaret.'

'Unless you've had a sherry or two,' smirked Betsy.

Violet was about to say 'touché' when their conversation was interrupted by the dashingly handsome Rod, rubbing his mop of thick hair with a towel in one hand and trying to eat a slice of toast with the other.

'G'day, Violet, how's tricks?' he offered in between mouthfuls.

'Oh, hello Rod, how are you? Everything is very good, thank you. I hear you're off to the film set.'

'I am, I must dash. I've got a busy day ahead. Big scenes today for me as it'll be the first time that my character confronts the killer.'

'Oh, how wonderful,' said Betsy. 'Will it be a gory one? Gallons of fake blood and limbs everywhere?'

'No, I think the blood comes later,' said Rod.

Violet widened her eyes, a little spooked by their conversation. 'Betsy, you never cease to shock me. Blood and limbs? What kind of thigs do you like watching, for heaven's sake.'

It was Rod who answered. 'She's obsessed, Vi. You know that. She's thrilled I'm playing a cop in a horror movie. She loves being spooked silly. Gotta say, I'm loving it too. My character is Peter Beacham, a cop who comes out of retirement to try to track down a deranged chef who's killing people with all kinds of kitchen gadgets. I'm getting to do things that my character in *Kookaburra Heights* has never had the chance to do.'

If Violet remembered rightly, Rod's character in Australia's third-most popular soap opera was a cheery and much-loved handyman whose height of danger was potentially falling off a ladder whilst trimming a hedge. Yet somehow, as soaps tended to, he had experienced many a sensationalist storyline. She knew the soap was

237

shown on one of the many UK channels Sheena had told her about, but she could never remember when it was on.

'It sounds ghastly, Rod, but I'm pleased it's giving you something different to do.' She said it with love, although his words flooded her mind with images that meant she would never be able to watch that nice chef on *This Morning* with a blender in the same way again or indeed watch anybody wielding a cleaver on *Bake Off*. 'Have you given up the soap opera, then?'

'No, I'm on a six-week break to make the film. My character is visiting his long-lost sister in New Zealand. I'm back on set in about two weeks. Talking of which, I had better go. I'm due on the film set in about three hours and I need to get cracking. Maniac kitchen killers wait for no man. See ya, Vi.' Rod threw the towel over the back of the chair Betsy was sitting on and leant down to kiss her on the cheek. 'Love you, wifey.' And with that he was gone.

'He seems very happy, Betsy. What an odd way to spend your days, though. Surrounded by blood.'

'Says the woman trying to solve what she thinks might

be a murder. But, yes, Rod is very happy. So am I. I love a horror film, as you know, and the producers think this could become quite the franchise if it's successful. It could open Rod up to even more types of fan events. They're such good money-makers.'

'How lovely,' smiled Violet, not really sure what Betsy meant. 'I'll look out for the movie. What's it called?'

'*Cheese Wire*. Apparently, it's the killer's favourite tool to use.'

'Oh.' It was all Violet could say. She had never had any intention of watching it anyway, but even if she had, the title would have definitely put her off. Cheese wire was only good for one thing and that was slicing a good chunk of Cheddar to pop on your ploughman's.

Before Violet's imagination could run away with her, Betsy returned to the subject of Sir Buster.

'So, you've got a busy day tomorrow. I had better let you sleep. Make sure you contact me again as soon as you have any more information. Things seem to be hotting up, don't they? Are you going to give the book to Samuel in the morning? He's still not phoned by the way.' Betsy shrugged, unsurprised.

'I suppose I should, shouldn't I? It is evidence, I guess. But maybe I should do a little more digging around first. What do you think?'

Betsy knew that Violet was merely looking for validation even though she had already made up her mind. 'I think you should do what you think you need to do.'

'Am I being stupid, Betsy? Do you think there's nothing more to Buster's death than simply a heart attack? Am I just being a silly old woman?'

'Do I think that potentially there's foul play going on and that perhaps there is more to Sir Buster's death than just a failing ticker?' She thought for a moment. To Violet, it felt like a lifetime. 'Yes. Yes, I do. And if anyone is going to find out what it is, then it will more than likely be someone with a massive amount of tenacity. And that, dear sister, is you.'

It was what Violet needed to hear.

Ending the conversation, Violet went to turn the light off. Before she did, she looked at the notes again. The letters cut out from magazines and newspapers. It was all very playground. Who would do something like that?

She scanned her eyes across the final note. Just like the others, it was a mixture of typefaces. There was nothing there that screamed local paper. That would be too obvious, but there was something familiar about some of the letters. Especially the W in WARNING. That definitely twanged a nerve in Violet's brain. Big yellow W on a purple background. She stared at it, but nothing came.

The notes slipped back in their envelope inside the book, Violet turned off the light. As she drifted off to sleep, her head was full of thoughts of what and who could possibly be behind the threats. She was determined to find out. She just prayed there were no cheese wires involved.

Chapter 24

Despite any disturbing forethoughts that she may dream about cheese-wire killers on the rampage, Violet had slept incredibly well and was fully refreshed and ready for action when she woke up at 5 a.m. the next morning.

By the time it came for her to open up Brewer's Loop at 9 a.m., she had already made a rather spectacular summer berry drizzle cake which she would take to Burrow Hall later to pay her respects, and she had also summoned Team C.R.A.B. to a meeting in the back room at 9.30 a.m. But for once it was the potential of killing and not the potential of quilling that needed to be discussed.

Bang on nine thirty, Violet, Margaret, Jimmy and Pearl were all sitting around the table in the shop. Sheena, who had dutifully agreed to look after the shop for the day, hovered in the doorway between the back room and the shop itself just in case anybody should come in and need serving.

Siting pride of place on the table, sandwiched between four mugs of steaming tea, stood the copy of *Dr. Jekyll and Mr. Hyde* and alongside that the three notes. They had all been passed round for each of Team C.R.A.B. to look at.

Margaret had mentioned that perhaps them all touching the notes wasn't the best idea, seeing as their fingerprints would now be all over them. Unfortunately, she hadn't mentioned this until after they had all pawed them. Violet had apparently thought of this too but had dismissed it, realising that both she and Sheena already had their fingerprints all over the pages. When it came to being overly careful with the evidence, maybe that horse had already bolted. She'd ask WPC Horton at a later date if any kind of test could be done. She'd try to keep Samuel out of the loop for now, if possible. Although, to be honest, Violet guessed that if she herself had been the threatening scoundrel behind the notes that perhaps she would have worn rubber gloves when preparing the letters and putting them into an envelope. That would be the sensible option.

'Well, this definitely opens a can of worms,' said Jimmy. 'There's no doubting now that somebody had it in for Sir Buster. The main question is why?'

The would-be sleuths had already discussed the possibilities that Betsy had thrown into the ring the night before. Of the three – spying, love or cash – they had decided that the best bet was that maybe that Sir Buster did indeed owe somebody from a poker dispute. It was Jimmy who could shed the most light on this.

'Even though it may be the most likely of those three options, I still don't believe for a second that a poker debt is worth killing for. Not even worth threatening for, unless it was a substantial debt. On the few occasions that Bailey and I have been at one of the poker nights at the pub, the betting has been pretty minimal. Out of all of us, it's probably Sir Buster that had the most money anyway, so he would be able to pay his debt if there was one.' Jimmy turned to Sheena who was still standing in the doorway. 'And, by the way, your dad must never hear about those poker nights. He'd have my guts for garters. They were all during illegal lock-ins.'

Sheena said nothing, but just smiled, raised her fingers to her lips, made a zipping motion and then pretended to throw away an imaginary key.

Margaret pointed at the farmer. 'Jimmy Coates, are you as green as the fields your sheep graze in? Do you really think that Sergeant Pollett doesn't know about them? He may not always be as sharp as a poky tool, but I think he turns a blind eye to those. He'd have to arrest half the village. Those poker nights have been going on for years. It was what caused the demise of my marriage after all.'

'Maybe somebody with less money feels a bit aggrieved that Sir Buster and his supposed riches didn't care to cough up,' suggested Violet. 'Who normally goes to these poker nights and how much money are we talking?'

'Not a lot. Maybe a couple of hundred quid. I think the most I've ever seen owed was about five hundred. And that was to Sir Buster, if I remember rightly. It was ages ago,' replied Jimmy.

'You do remember rightly; it was my louse of an ex that had to pay him the money.' Margaret's words were coated with a glaze of acidity.

'Oh yeah, it was, wasn't it? Well, your husband used to go, Margaret. I think Dr Roberts has been to a few. Obviously Phill joins in, then there's me and Bailey. Hannah and Oscar from the farm have been once or twice recently. I think even Noah came once, didn't he?' Jimmy looked over to Pearl.

'He did. But he won't again as he came back a hundred and fifty pounds lighter. I told him what a silly game it is. Well, it is if you lose.' It was clear to see who wore the trousers in the Wheeler household.

'Maybe Sir Buster was part of another poker group. Something a little more serious. Was he a better player than the rest of you?' asked Violet.

'Hell yes. He knew his poker,' answered Jimmy. 'Most of us didn't stand a chance, to be fair. But then he had been playing it for a good few years more than all of us.'

'Did he have poker nights up at the Hall, Sheena? Did you ever work there when he was having one or clear up after one?'

Sheena shook her head. 'If he did, then I certainly never saw them. I could ask Mrs Turner and Herbert for you if you like.'

'Don't worry about that, dear, I can ask myself. I'm heading up there later with my drizzle cake. I'll be asking some questions, fear not. I'll report back. Now, let's talk about Alexi Burniston. I understand that you had a rather detailed chat with him yesterday, Pearl. Well done. How marvellous that you could grab the bull by the horns.' Violet clapped her hands twice in quick succession in appreciation.

All eyes fell on Pearl.

Pearl placed her mug of tea on the table, cleared her throat with a little cough and began to talk. 'Well, let me start by saying that Alexi Burniston is not, and never will be, my cup of tea. That man has such an inflated opinion of himself, he could float sky-high like a balloon. He's so full of hot air, he'd give helium a run for its money. But, naturally, I didn't let my total dislike of him show on my face when he told me all about himself. I was as poker-faced as my Noah should have been at your card games, Jimmy, let me tell you.'

The three others sitting around the table all wriggled in their seats in anticipation as they took in every syllable of Pearl's words.

'So, when I mentioned to Alexi that I am from Barbados and was born there, he got all excited and started saying that he used to love it there because the people are so friendly. It turns out that Sir Buster's son lived there for a decade or so, on and off.'

'How come he's so pasty now then?' barked Sheena from the doorway. 'He doesn't look like he's seen the sun in years.'

'He left there a long while ago. Apparently, he first went there in his twenties. He didn't tell me the exact date, but he was saying that he'd finished his education and had *bummed around*, his words not mine, for a bit before deciding that the UK had nothing worthwhile to offer him, so he decided to get on a plane and go somewhere tropical and exciting. He also said, and I quote him again, that he wanted somewhere like him, that *woke up when the sun went down.'*

'That's why he's pasty, Sheena, he's a vampire,' sniggered Jimmy. Both he and Sheena giggled.

Pearl continued, 'According to Alexi, he spent many years on the island raising funding for housing that needed to be built there. He also helped out with a lot of charitable causes. He told me he was very instrumental in giving a lot of *my people* a roof over their head. He actually pointed at me when he said it. Silly boy. He said he spent years going from place to place across the island, *making a difference.* He said it was his job and his aim to make life better for people.'

'Well, that seems jolly nice...' said Violet with a smile.

'If you believe a word he says,' lip-smacked Pearl.

'And I'm assuming you don't.' Violet's tone took a serious 180.

'Well, I was not brought up to doubt a person's word without letting them prove themselves, so I kept asking him for the names of the charities he'd been involved with and also the names of the places where houses had been built from the funding he said he'd helped to raise. He just kept saying it was a long time ago and that he'd forgotten, but that he could sleep easy at night knowing that he'd made a difference to people thousands of miles away. In *my homeland*.' She pointed at herself again.

'If it was a long time ago, then maybe he had forgotten. Sometimes I get to the front of the queue in Rita's and forget the very thing that I went in there to buy. And that happened only last week,' said Margaret.

'Like I say, innocent until proven otherwise, so I thought I'd play a little game with him. Just to test the water.'

'What kind of game?' asked Violet. She was thoroughly enjoying Pearl's revelations and also her evident vitriol about Sir Buster's son.

'Well, I bought him another whisky from the bar. I pretended I was onto the vodka, but really I was on a still water. I needed to keep myself together so that I could remember every word. And then, when I got back to the table, I started to play. You know that game we sometimes play when we're together, guessing whether ink colours are true or false. You know they always have bizarre names like shabby shutters and rusty hinge or worn lipstick and frayed burlap and sometimes we make ones up like burnished bruise or aching squirrel to try to catch each other out. Well, I thought I'd play that with Alexi.'

'You made him guess crafty ink colours?' said Jimmy with layers of bemusement.

'No, not inks. I named some places in Barbados to see if they rang a bell with him or not. I asked him about Brighton and Cambridge and Bath and Hastings and all sorts of places.'

'Is everywhere in Barbados named after somewhere here?' asked Sheena.

'No, it's not, but remind me to give you a history lesson of Barbados in our next crafting session, young lady. So, then I threw in some bogus names as well, like Edinburgh and Swansea, and he sits there and says that they rang a bell and he thinks he did do some charitable work there. I even told him that I loved the famous statue of Saint Aloysius The Ninth who sits in the middle of Swansea's picturesque village square and he said he remembered that well. Interesting, seeing as it's completely made up from the depths of my imagination. I even invented a few charities that he seemed to remember an involvement with. I think he's full of the stuff you shovel up on your farm, Jimmy.'

Violet tapped her fingers on her chin in contemplation of Alexi's deceit. 'Interesting. So, if he's lying about that, then he could be lying about anything. Do we know why he's not been back to the village since his mother's funeral and what he's been up to over here. And where did he actually get the funding from that he says he managed to procure?'

'That was my next point of questioning. When I asked him where the money came from, he said that it was always good to come from a minted family, so it would appear that he got the funds from Sir Buster and his wife. But I don't think he spent it on housing projects for *my people*. I can't be certain as I've not been there for years, but the majority of my family are still there, so some investigation into Alexi Burniston's claims are definitely on the cards. You can leave that with me. I shall send a photo of him to my uncle, who knows pretty much everyone on the island. I snapped one when I was at the bar getting his whisky.' Pearl held up her phone to show the others. Sure enough, a photo of Alexi filled the screen. 'I'm not sure how much he's changed over the years, but it might jog a few memories.'

'Nice work, Pearl,' said Margaret. 'So, what else did he say. What about his time in the UK? What does he do now?'

'According to him, a bit of this, a bit of that. He said he works with a lot of influencers, people from reality shows, and here's another of his sanctimonious quotes, *trendy movers and shakers that I would never have heard of.* He named a few, and he was right, I hadn't, but that's not the point. He said he organised deals for them, appearances, sponsorships. Apparently, he is quite the thing on the scene.'

Jimmy looked sceptical. 'Well, I'll be asking Bailey about that. I'm thinking he might be able to shed some light on it. I'll contact him later. He'll know whether it's BS or not.'

'BS?' queried Pearl.

'Er… whether he's lying,' replied Jimmy.

'So, how was it left?' asked Violet. 'Any more to tell.'

'Well, we left The Six Pennies together. He was a little wobbly on his feet. I suggested he didn't drive, but he was having none of it. Said he was more than fine. He even offered me a lift home. I declined, seeing as he was half-cut and the cottage is only five minutes away. That is quite some motor he has. He must have some money from somewhere. And another thing. He opened the glove compartment while I was bidding him farewell as he wanted some chewing gum or something. Now, I may not have been around it for years, but I spent enough of my teen years in Barbados to recognise a bag of weed when I see it. He's obviously got enough money to buy a lot of that when he needs to. His glove compartment was virtually filled with it.'

Jimmy gasped at Pearl's revelation. The level of intrigue and drama in the normally sleepy Rooney-at-Burrow was getting higher by the day. In more ways than one.

Chapter 25

Nothing would stop Violet Brewer when she was on a mission. She was determined, and some would say reckless. Which sometimes meant that if she wanted something that wasn't easily going to fall into her lap, then she would have to position herself at the most strategically advantageous place to make sure that it could happen. She had always been the same. Even if it meant taking things to the extreme and pushing her uncontrolled nature to the max.

Like the time a teenage Violet was determined to meet the drummer of her favourite band, Coconut Ice. She'd had posters of them plastered all over her bedroom wall, but it was the drummer in particular, Keith, that she was obsessed with. He was butter-wouldn't-melt handsome with a glorious eyebrow-skimming blond fringe and a set of teeth so luminously shiny that they could have been spotted from outer space. When she heard that the band were playing in a local town near Rooney-at-Burrow, a thirteen-year-old Violet was steadfast that she would meet her idol. But when she asked her parents, sadly there was no way that her folks were letting her go. She was far too young, in their opinion. Violet didn't mind missing the concert, that would probably mean staying up way too late anyway. Besides, she could listen to Coconut Ice all day long on her records and tapes. But meeting Keith in the flesh was a dream that she had to make happen. So, she needed to hatch a plot to turn her dream into a reality. And one that meant that her parents had no idea what she was up to. She asked Betsy, who had no interest in Coconut Ice – she loved another group, some ear-splitting combo called Dead Skunk or something, that Violet thought were awful – to cover for her and say that she was at a friend's house for tea. Betsy agreed on the proviso that she would do the same for her, come the time. Violet would have agreed to anything to meet Keith and thanked her lucky stars that Betsy hadn't been more ruthless and insisted on her doing all of the washing-up duties for a year or something equally as tedious.

Violet had read in her Ice fanzine that the band always turned up to concerts in their tour bus and sometimes would stop to chat to fans before going into the venue. Keith had even said in an interview on Saturday morning telly that they always liked to arrive two hours before a gig at least. Piecing the clues together, which wasn't overly hard, Violet took two buses and a taxi to the venue, using pocket money she had saved up for weeks before and carrying her Polaroid camera and a banner written out in glittery letters – maybe her first venture into craft, looking back – to make sure she was positioned at the stage door two hours before the gig was due to start.

Sure enough, as predicted the tour bus pulled up pretty much on time. Violet wasn't the only fan there, but she guessed she might be the youngest. There was a group of about twenty, most of them around seventeen. As the band descended the tour bus steps, the fans pushed towards the group, thrusting poor Violet out of the way.

For a second, Violet was crushed, both mentally and physically. The band, including her heart-throb, Keith, started to sign autographs and pose for photos. Violet didn't stand a chance of getting near them with the older girls around. And when the band started to be ushered into the venue by one of their crew, Violet feared that she had missed her chance for good. She had to act fast to make sure that her attempts to meet him were not in vain. She needed to do something drastic.

Without thinking, a teenage Violet pulled herself clumsily yet successfully onto the top of a postbox near the stage-door entrance and began singing at the top of her voice. She sang one of her favourite Coconut Ice songs, pretty tunelessly to be fair, but maybe that was even better for her plight of getting noticed. Above the tearful sobs of the fans present suddenly Violet stood out. She was not in tears shoving autograph books and cameras into their faces, she was stood precariously on top of a postbox, caterwauling with her glittery banner, two sheets of A4 taped together and stuck onto kitchen roll tubes so it could unfurl like a scroll, held aloft above her head. It read

KEITH, YOU ICED GEM in marker-pen-outlined letters filled with glitter. It was basic but effective. Violet was hugely proud of it too as Iced Gems were one of her favourite snacks.

All of the crowd gathered turned around to see where the din was coming from. Including the band. Seizing the moment, Violet caught Keith's eye as he spied her banner and waved her Polaroid camera at him. As she did so, she began to wobble and, before she knew it, she had tumbled off the postbox and fallen onto the grass below. How she didn't break any bones, she would never know, but sadly her banner ripped as one of the kitchen roll tubes squished itself out of position and tore into her glittery letters. Luckily, her camera was still in one piece.

Violet looked up from her position on the grass to see a group of about five girls gathered in front of her. As she let her dizzy eyes focus, she saw her hero, Keith, pushing between them and bending down to be by her side.

'Let me through, girls, let me through. Stand back and give us space. Are you okay, sweetheart?'

Keith was so close, she could literally feel his breath. It

was the moment she had waited for.

'I think my ankle may be a little sore. And my banner is not looking too good, but apart from that, yes…' Violet could feel herself getting breathy between the words with excitement at being in such close proximity to the divine drummer.

Keith held out his hand to help her up. It felt like electricity when he did.

Violet put her weight onto her ankle. It thankfully didn't hurt.

'Nice banner, by the way,' said Keith. 'I always love it when I see my name!'

'You're the best, Keith, that's why.'

'Look, I've got to get inside to soundcheck with the rest of the band, but I just wanted to make sure that you're okay.'

Violet was more than okay. This was more one-on-one time than she could ever have imagined.

'Thanks, Keith, can I have a photo with you before you go and will you sign my banner, even if it is a bit battered.'

Keith took Violet's Polaroid camera and gave it to one

of the girls in the gathered group, who begrudgingly took a photo. Keith wasn't her favourite, she was more into Darren the lead singer, but he'd gone inside with the rest of the band.

Keith signed Violet's banner and even waited to see that the Polaroid developed properly and signed that too before leaving Violet with a hug and a cheery wave.

Another cab ride and two buses later, Violet was back home from 'her friend's' where she had supposedly had her tea. Betsy had covered well; her folks were none the wiser and her signed banner and prized Polaroid with Keith were stashed away in a box under Violet's bed.

Her ankle was a little sore when she went to bed that night, but sometimes it was worth going to extremes to make sure you got what you wanted.

It was this gung-ho attitude that Violet possessed that kicked into action once again that morning. She was about to leave Brewer's Loop to head up to Burrow Hall. With her summer berry drizzle cake all boxed up in Tupperware under one arm and a foldaway brolly in the other – it may be summer but the lady on the BBC had said to potentially expect the odd shower – Violet pulled open the door of the shop and turned to say goodbye to Sheena behind the counter.

'Thank you for looking after the shop, dear. I'll be back in a while. Any worries, then ring me. And I'll let you know what I find out from Mrs Turner. I might see if I can accidentally bump into either of Sir Buster's children as well.'

'Well, now's your chance.' Sheena pointed outside the shop. 'That's Belinda Flatt right there.'

Violet gazed out in the direction Sheena was pointing. Sure enough, there was a well-dressed woman, a paper bag full of shopping in her arms, just about to cross the street. Her four-by-four was parked opposite the wool shop and she had obviously just been to Rita's a few doors up. A box of Rice Krispies stuck out the top of her bag.

'She looks hassled,' noted Violet.

'I may have only met her once, but that seems to be her go-to face. She obviously has resting-hassle-face,' remarked Sheena. 'Perhaps now isn't the best time to try to grab her.'

'Oh, there's no time like the present, Sheena, believe you me. You always need to strike while the iron is hot.'

With that, Violet was out of the door.

Belinda was obviously hassled, and her overfilled paper bag beginning to tear as she navigated her way across the village high street did nothing to aid her annoyance. Neither did dropping her car keys as she tried to deftly take them out of her trouser pocket as she balanced the bag on the car, aiming to open the boot. Violet watched her face turn redder and redder with each mishap. Maybe she should offer to help.

'Bloody hell,' said Belinda, loud enough to be heard on the other side of the street.

Maybe not, thought Violet.

'Morning, Violet. I hope you're good this morning. Because someone is in a bad mood, aren't they?' It was WPC Horton who joined Violet on the pavement. She had been doing her village rounds and had seen Belinda crossing the road.

'Morning, dear. That, Paula, is Belinda Flatt. Sir Buster's daughter.'

'I'd never have guessed. I heard she was more of a fancy muesli kind of woman.' WPC Horton tipped her head in the direction of the box of Rice Krispies that had now fallen from the paper bag into the gutter by the back of the car. 'So, she's back.'

'Yes, we have a full house of Burniston children as Alexi is back in the village too. There's a funeral to be arranged and a will reading to take place. Do we have any news on either of those yet?'

Violet began to walk up the pavement away from the wool shop towards Rita's, keeping an eye on Belinda at the four-by-four as she did so. WPC Horton automatically followed.

'Nothing as yet, but Phill and Steph are holding a memorial night at The Six Pennies, which will be lovely. Sheena's going to sing apparently. It'll be a fitting way to send off Sir Buster, but there's no news on the funeral itself or the reading of the will.'

Violet held the box containing the drizzle cake up for the police officer to see. 'I was on my way up to Burrow Hall to pay my respects. I was going to give this to Mrs

Turner too. She and Herbert must be so upset about Sir Buster. They've both worked up there at the Hall for the longest time. I was going to ask them if there was any news.'

'Oh, that cake looks lovely.' WPC Horton licked her lips hungrily.

'But I'm guessing the person most in the know would be Belinda, right?'

'I guess so. She'd be organising things, I guess.'

'I guess so too.' Violet could feel a cyclone of thoughts blowing into action inside her brain.

'Right, I must go, I can see Mr Bublé needs feeding. Or more so hear that he does.'

It was true. WPC Horton's chunky kitty cat was sitting on the wall outside the cottage, mewing so loudly that both Paula and Violet could hear him from where they stood outside Rita's.

Violet had wanted to ask WPC Horton about fingerprint tests, but now wasn't the time. Mr Bublé was evidently ravenous and also Belinda Flatt was finally climbing into the front seat of her car, the shopping, including the overboard Rice Krispies, now safely packed away in the boot. She slammed the door shut, turned the key in the ignition and revved the car into action. Yanking it into gear, she pulled the four-by-four out into the street to drive off.

'See you later, dear,' said Violet, as WPC Horton headed inside her cottage.

Taking a deep breath, Violet crossed her fingers on the hand she was carrying the brolly with and stepped out directly into the path of Belinda's huge Mercedes. Violet threw both the Tupperware box and the brolly into the air and let out a frail yet audible scream as the sound of screeching brakes filled the air.

Yes, sometimes it was worth talking things to the extreme and being reckless to be in the right position to get exactly what you really wanted. Even if sacrifices had to be made. Violet had always believed that.

Both the cake box and Violet landed on the hard surface of the street at the same time.

Chapter 26

Hannah and Oscar were the kind of couple in Rooney-at-Burrow that on paper should be ridiculously easy to dislike. Both young, in their mid-twenties, good-looking and ridiculously fit. They were pretty much perfect. And everyone liked them. They were the poster couple for living the good life in the clean country air.

Not that it smelt particularly clean at the moment. Farm air never did. There was nothing delightfully fragrant about standing in a pen with more than its fair share of sheep poo on the floor. Both of them, who had been working on Coates Farm since they were teenagers, were currently ensconced in giving a much-needed pedicure to some of the woollier members of the Coates Farm family. Sheep needed their hooves trimming every six to ten weeks on average and today was the day that some of them were booked into the farmyard salon to get their pedi done by the perfect pair.

Hannah was undertaking the job in the usual combo of wellies, T-shirt and jean shorts, Oscar just the wellies and jeans. Clothing on his upper body often seemed to be superfluous to Oscar, not that anyone had cause for complaint. The warmth of the August day was bringing a healthy glow of sweat to both of them. Satisfied with the taloned results of the woolly creature he had just been snipping, Oscar let it go. He smiled as he watched it trot off merrily to the other side of the pen, ready to be let back out to freedom in the fields. Hannah finished her 'client' too and her happy customer joined Oscar's.

Hannah reached down to grab two water bottles. She passed one to her boyfriend. Sheep hoof trimming was thirsty work.

'Are you two okay for drinks? I'll get some fresh ones if you need them.'

It was Jimmy speaking, walking up to the side of the pen where the two sheep were under starter's orders, waiting for the gate to open. When Jimmy did so, they bounded off happily, their freshly treated nails gambolling merrily across the lush grass.

'Hang on two seconds, love.' Jimmy was now talking to the screen of his phone, which he carried in his hand. 'I'm just saying hi to Hannah and Oscar.'

He held the phone around to face Hannah and Oscar. Hannah was drinking from her bottle, whereas a topless Oscar was merrily tipping his over his head and shaking his hair in order to cool down. It was pure Diet Coke ad.

Bailey was on the screen sitting in his hotel room in Abu Dhabi. Or rather on the balcony of his hotel room. He was wearing some kind of bright green diaphanous kaftan and sunglasses and evidently enjoying the Arabian Peninsula sunshine.

'Cheers, Bailey,' said Hannah, raising her bottle.

Oscar gave a pearly white smile and waved.

'Well, don't you two look all lovely and... er... rustic,' said Bailey from behind his shades.

'Right, guys, I'll fetch you some more water. I think you may have used all of yours, Oscar, somehow,' said

Jimmy, watching it cascade down his tanned skin.

He returned his attention to Bailey on the screen. They had been talking for a good thirty minutes already, with Jimmy bringing his interior designer boyfriend up to date on the goings-on in the village. Including Pearl's chat with Alexi Burniston about his supposed current occupation.

Back inside the farmhouse, Jimmy placed his phone down on the huge designer kitchen table Bailey had lovingly imported from Morocco and rested it against a vase of flowers – the vase was hand-blown in Murano apparently – so that he could look into the screen. He sat down at the table.

'Did you see those thighs, Jimmy? And that chest and those biceps. It's like he actually has legs for arms, they're that thick.' Bailey practically swooned.

'Will you stop objectifying Oscar. But yes, of course I did,' smirked Jimmy.

'Would it help if I said Hannah looked incredibly gorgeous too. Who knew that sheep poop could be such a workable fashion model accessory on both a man and a woman? We should shoot a calendar with those two to raise money for a charity. Hannah could sell it at her Jazzercise group too.'

'I don't really think they're into that kind of thing, are they?' said Jimmy, although the idea pleased him. 'But we're not here to talk about a blessed calendar. Have you ever heard of Alexi Burniston before? Did you recognise him?' Jimmy had WhatsApped Pearl's photo of Alexi to Bailey during their conversation.

'No, I don't think I've ever seen him before, but he does look as shifty as hell. If I was a reality star or a pop wannabe, I'm not sure I'd want somebody like that guiding my career. He looks a touch unsavoury to me, but I guess we should never judge a book by its cover, should we? Look at me, a flamboyant fabulous vegan hanging out with telly stars. Yet behind the scenes, I'm totally in love with a carnivorous farmer who wouldn't know a *Housewife Of...* if she fell on him while he was milking the cows. So maybe he is what he says he is.'

Jimmy felt a smile migrate across his face. 'Totally in love with me, eh? Even if I don't have thighs like Oscar?'

'Dear Jimmy, you could add my thighs to yours and they still wouldn't be anywhere near the size of his. But I love you whatever size you are.' There was a slight pause before Bailey felt obliged to backtrack a little. 'But, for the record, you do have very good thighs. Years of farming have assured that. They're just not as supersize as Oscar's. Nobody's are.'

Jimmy's smile diminished somewhat without disappearing. 'So, can you try to find out about Alexi? See if any of your contacts know anything about him. From what Pearl said, I'm not sure if he's our guy when it comes to being potentially responsible for his dad's death. But there is definitely something underhand about him. And he is a right sleazeball.'

'I'll be on a flight tomorrow for nearly eight hours heading home with Tanya. She'll know him if he is who he says he is. She knows everybody. Like, *everybody*. And if he is a sleazeball, he'll have probably tried it on with her. Most have. And failed.'

Jimmy didn't know much about Tanya, but he did know that she had been part of some reality show about her family's jewellery business that had been a smash hit and that she had then been given her own spin-off series. He knew she was minted, that she loved employing Bailey to find her pretty things for her houses around the world and that whenever Jimmy mentioned her to Sheena, the reply would always be 'oh my God, I love here, she's amazing, and so beautiful'. Jimmy also knew that a lot of that beauty was paid for in Harley Street as he'd met her once and her face appeared waxier than a box of candles. But he guessed there were a thousand versions of beautiful, depending on who was looking.

'That's great you're coming home already. Let me know what time you land and I'll come meet you at the airport. Has it been a successful trip?'

'Tanya loves the pink velvet. She wants one of the rooms over here kitted out in it and also one of her bedrooms back home in the UK. I'm thrilled.' He placed his hands in the air and rubbed his thumbs and forefingers together and sang, 'We're in the money...' a grin coating his face. 'I know loads of antiques markets and shops that always have plenty of olde-worlde furniture up for grabs, so I'll have her kitted out in no time.'

'And you think she might be able to shed some light on Alexi?'

'If she knows him, then definitely. Darling, believe you me, eight hours of endless champagne in first-class and Tanya's lips will be freer flowing than the Limpopo. So, I may be a little tiddled myself when I land. She drinks like a fish. Sorry in advance.'

'No change there!' smirked Jimmy.

'Right, dear heart, I must go. Tanya wants to try this new eatery. All experimental food and innovative drinks. It sounds fabulous. Loving you. See you tomorrow. I'll let you know the time. Give my love to everyone. Bye for now.'

'Love you too. And you'll be back in time for—' Jimmy's words came to an abrupt halt as the screen turned to black. He was about to add '...Sir Buster's memorial night at The Six Pennies', but Bailey had already terminated the call. He'd tell him tomorrow when he landed. He wouldn't want to miss the night.

Jimmy's stomach started to rumble. Maybe a little

something to eat?

He went to the fridge and opened it. Two cold sausages lay on a plate on the middle shelf. He picked one up and grabbed a jar of Piccalilli. It was half full. A jar of marrow chutney sat unopened bedside it. Jimmy dipped the cold sausage into the Piccalilli and bit into it.

He may not have been in Abu Dhabi at some fancy restaurant – sorry, eatery – with a famous telly socialite, but he could still be just as experimental with his food.

Chapter 27

There was never a jar of unopened marrow chutney at Margaret Millsop's cottage. It was almost impossible that a jar of it would even reach her fridge before Margaret had opened it and stuck an apostle teaspoon into it to scoop out a delicious mound of the muddy brown joyfulness. But Margaret was fully aware that she was pretty much alone in her love of it. Other than Dr Roberts, it was a delight that most seemed to turn their noses up at. They didn't know what they were missing out on.

Margaret couldn't really remember where her love of marrows had actually started. She had loved them for as long as she could recall. She wasn't even that sure what it was about the earthy beauties that she actually loved. The taste was no more than an elaborate courgette really. They weren't actually that tasty. But something about them always brought a smile to her tastebuds. Whether they be stuffed with pungent cheese, baked into a delicious tea cake or blended with garlic for an appetising soup.

Her ex-husband had hated them. She'd tried to tempt him on many an occasion, back in the happier days of their union, but he had never succumbed. She should have seen the clues there and then. They were never going to be compatible for life. How could she love a man with a roving eye and an utter dislike of marrow? Looking back, it was clear to see that the marriage was doomed.

But even though the light had certainly dimmed on her marriage, her love of her favourite vegetable would burn bright forever. And being able to organise the annual Rooney-at-Burrow village fayre, and more specifically the prize marrow contest, was very much a highlight of Margaret's year.

But it had occurred to her that perhaps in the light of Sir Buster's death that maybe this year's contest was in jeopardy. There could be no contest without the fayre, and Margaret needed to know that whoever was now dealing with Sir Buster's affairs was still willing for the fayre to happen at St Charlotte's Church on the Burrow Hall estate. And there was also the matter of Sir Buster's edible entry into the contest itself.

Margaret had liked Sir Buster for many reasons. He was jolly, he was eternally friendly, he adored the spirit of the village and he always produced the most incredible crop of marrows. Which is why he had won the annual marrow contest on many an occasion. His last time, if Margaret remembered correctly, and she knew she did, was three years ago. She'd come second that year and Jimmy was third. Two years ago, she herself had won, Phill had romped in at second place and Sir Buster had slumped to third. Last year, it was Jimmy who bagged first prize, Phill again in second and Sir Buster was third. Her own crop last year was not her finest vintage. She had not tended to it as meticulously as she knew she should have. She had taken her eye off the ball – or off the marrow, as it were – and tumbled to a lowly sixth position, which wouldn't have been too disastrous if there hadn't been only seven entrants.

Which was why Margaret had been particularly diligent this year about coaxing her crop of marrows to the biggest size possible. She was sure she would be back in the top three and hopefully maybe even coming out as marrow supremo for the year, or Mrs Marrow, if you will, by grabbing pole position.

Margaret had spent the early part of the afternoon tending to her crop in her back garden. There was something about the soil in the area that marrows seemed to thrive on. And her marrows were thriving indeed. One of them in particular was growing to a remarkably good size. Margaret had inwardly commended herself on what had obviously been her extraordinarily good planting techniques this year. Sheltered position, full sun, planting in a bucket with drainage. She had left nothing to chance. Prize marrows were a serious business. Especially for those who wanted to regain their crown.

Other people's marrows were always wrapped in secrecy before the fayre. Phill and Steph kept theirs hidden away at the bottom of the pub garden and Jimmy was most militant about making sure than no one saw what he was offering up prior to the day of the village fayre itself. Pearl and Noah often attempted to grow something impressive too, but the culinary curiosity of Pearl usually meant that she had picked any prizeworthy specimen and turned it into a curry or an equally spicy marrow-based treat before the big day itself, much to Noah's allotment annoyance but not his food-loving fulfilment.

A thought suddenly struck Margaret as she lovingly moved the position of her prize vegetable to make sure that it was indeed getting full access to the August sun's rays and not missing out on any inch-adding chances of growth. She had considered the fact that now that Sir Buster was dead it was improbable that anyone was actually tending to his prize crop. With less than a fortnight to go to the actual contest itself, should it happen (and Margaret was determined that it would), it would be a crime of its own for his marrows not to receive the genuine green-fingered TLC they would need for the final sprint. Maybe Herbert was looking after them. But Margaret doubted it. He'd be too busy with the rest of the Burrow Hall affairs. And Margaret was certain that Sir

Buster never employed a gardener to actually look after his marrows. She knew that he would never trust them to anybody else, for fear of things not being executed properly. And she was sure that Belinda and Alexi would not want to get their fingers dirty.

Margaret decided that it was up to her, as a fellow marrow devotee, to make sure that Sir Buster's marrow-loving tenderness would not have gone to waste. Plus, there was the fact that Sheena had mentioned to her in the back room of Brewer's Loop earlier that day that Sir Buster had said the 'luck of the marrow gods was definitely on his side' and her inner curiosity to see exactly how girthy his crop were was picking at her soul like a crochet hook.

It was mid to late afternoon by the time Margaret found herself wandering towards the allotment that Sir Buster adored at the far reaches of the Burrow Hall grounds. She was a little out of breath given the half-hour uphill climb it had taken to get there from the village and her skin tingled slightly from the heat. But good sturdy footwear and a lashing of SPF had made sure that she reached her destination in one piece and as comfortably as possible.

It was clear as soon as she arrived that perhaps the allotment had been neglected for a day or two. The soil between the rows of veg was parched and a little cracked in places from the baking of the summer sun. Margaret guessed that unlike most of the Hall's grounds, perhaps there were no inbuilt sprinklers on the allotment that could be turned on and off. The soil and plants were definitely in need of a drink. She made a note to grab a hose from the allotment shed before leaving to give everything a good drenching. It was what the produce, and indeed Sir Buster, would have wanted.

Margaret walked up and down the rows of vegetables until she came to a spot where she began to see the familiar clues to a marrow grower. The buckets with holes for drainage where marrows had been planted. A smattering of smaller courgette-sized offerings that no doubt longed to grow bigger, yet somehow Mother Nature had decreed otherwise. She smiled at the cosy familiarity of it all.

Her smile rapidly vanished, however, as Margaret's eyes moved to the spot where Sir Buster's crop of this year's prize-grabbing marrows should have been. Instead of finding a display of hearty, mouth-watering excellence, she found a squishy mess of marrow, pulverised into oblivion where someone had decided to pound it, or perhaps them – it was hard to tell how many there had originally been – into a puddle of gooey nothingness. Her first thought was that an animal had obviously been here, hungry for food. But that notion passed as quickly as it came. Nothing around had been disturbed and she was more than sure that squished marrow was not top of any potential scavenger's list of food preferences. Plus, if they had squished the marrows, it really didn't look like they'd downed so much as a mouthful. No, this wasn't the work of a four-legged beast. It was definitely a two-footed one that had done this.

Margaret could feel tears pricking at her eyes at the scandalous misjustice of it all. How could anyone be so disrespectful? Was it plain heartlessness or could it be sabotage? Either way, she would have to clear it up. Or maybe it should be left as evidence. She really wasn't sure. She'd tell Sergeant Pollett and WPC Horton and let them decide. But she wouldn't let the other vegetables around the carnage suffer too. They still needed a good watering.

Margaret made her way to the shed at the corner of the allotment. She pulled at the handle on the wooden door. It opened with a rusty creak. Inside, it was like any garden shed that Margaret had ever found herself in. Full of plastic flowerpots and tubs, paints and treatments, slug pellet bottles, weedkillers, a radio on the windowsill. Standard shed fodder. A group of garden tools leant against one of the wooden walls, a coiled hose curled up at their base like an obedient dog.

Margaret felt a chill cross her flesh, unexpected given the stifling heat within the shed, as she spied two more objects. One was a gun leant against one of the walls. She recognised it as Sir Buster's. And, also, as the gun that had been instrumental in the death of his dear wife, Fiona, a decade before. Margaret shuddered at the memory and tried to push that day from her mind. Such a loss.

The other object she spied was a pair of wellington boots. There was nothing unusual about that. Most sheds would have one, if not more pairs of boots, inside them. Indeed, Margaret reckoned she had at least two pairs in hers, maybe three. One pair was her cheating ex's. The decision to throw them out on her return to her cottage later streaked across her thoughts.

What was unusual about the pair of wellington boots Margaret was staring at now was that the soles of both of them were covered in the same gooey mess that she had witnessed outside. Unless there was a scavenger that had suddenly taken to walking on hind legs and wearing boots, then the destruction of the marrows was definitely a human action.

But why would somebody do that? It seemed so pointless. And needless. Unless somebody really hated Sir Buster?

It suddenly occurred to Margaret that perhaps marrow growing was more serious than even she had ever realised. But serious enough for somebody to kill for? Surely not. But those boots were evidence indeed that something horrible and underhand had been going on. And coupled with the threatening notes, it really did seem that somebody had a huge problem with the late Sir Buster. Perhaps a problem big enough to squash him just like the marrows.

Margaret pulled her mobile phone out of her bag and scrolled through to Sergeant Pollett's number. It was listed as 'Samuel' in her phone, of course.

She stopped herself. She'd leave it five minutes. The evidence would still be there then. The vegetables needed watering first. They were in dire need of a drink. As was she. She reached into her bag again and pulled out a small hip flask. She opened it and took a swig. It was always with her just for moments such as this. A trusty tot of whisky always did the trick in emergencies.

She picked up the hose and walked out of the shed. She'd water the vegetables and give them a good soaking. Try to save their poor little lives. Then she'd phone Sergeant Pollett. Or, actually, she'd phone Violet first. She should definitely know about the massacre of Sir Buster's marrows.

Chapter 28

'Oh my gosh, I am so sorry. I didn't see you were about to cross the road. Seeing as there's not actually a crossing here. That's a bit further up by the pub.'

Belinda Flatt pointed her forefinger up the village high street in the direction of The Six Pennies. She wasn't entirely sure whether she should be gushing with her apology to the woman, who, as far as she could make out, had just stepped out in front of her four-by-four without so much as a 'look left or right'. But the woman was older than her and maybe a little frail and Belinda had only just missed her with the front bumper of her large car by administering a rather nifty swerve. She was sure she'd heard her shopping tip over in the back of the car. She prayed that her free-range eggs were still in one piece.

'Oh, I am so sorry, my dear, the fault was entirely mine. My mind seems to drift a little the older I get and sometimes I don't seem to think before putting one foot in front of the other.'

'Are you sure you're okay? There's nothing broken is there? You seemed to go down with quite a tumble. Er… actually you seemed to start falling before I even reached you. Unless I'm mistaken.'

'Shock can be a funny thing. It plays with your mind, dear. Yes, I'm okay. Nothing broken, although I think my summer drizzle cake may be more of an Eton mess now, unfortunately.' She looked down at the Tupperware box, which, despite still remaining tightly closed, now housed a cake that was smeared and squidged around all four of its interior sides. 'I'm Violet Brewer by the way. I own Brewer's Loop, the wool and craft shop. And you are?'

Violet held out her hand. As she did so, she wobbled slightly and went to fall back down to the ground. She had only just been helped up by Belinda and a panicked WPC Horton minutes earlier. The fact that Violet was mercifully as steady as she had ever been on her feet was of no consequence. A little wobble was just highly necessary to convey her apparent frailty. She grabbed onto Belinda's shoulder as she went to faux fall.

'Oh, I'm so sorry, dear, maybe the shock has got to me too. Maybe I do need a sit-down, or a strong coffee perhaps...'

'Oh my. Are you sure I shouldn't get that policewoman back? Or maybe we should phone an ambulance? And I'm Belinda by the way. Sir Buster's daughter.' She was more than a little flustered and couldn't stop herself ruminating on the notion that the last thing she needed right now was an old lady's broken hip on her conscience.

'I'm sure that won't be necessary,' said Violet. She had already sent a reluctant and slightly confused WPC Paula Horton on her way with a silent mouthing of 'I'm fine. Now leave me alone with her' and an urgent dismissal with a waggling of her fingers.

Violet needed Belinda Flatt to believe that she was as vulnerable and frail as a lady of her age could be. And thanks to her well-placed wobble, it seemed to be working.

'I'm sure WPC Horton has important police work to

do. Now… I can't believe you're Belinda, Sir Buster and Fiona's daughter. I am so sorry to hear about your father.' She steadied herself in Belinda's hold as she offered her condolences. 'Gosh, the last time I saw you was probably your mother's funeral. That was…'

'Ten years ago.'

'Well, I didn't see a lot of you that day, but you look younger now than you did back then. You must tell an old lady your secret.' Violet's words came with extra syrupy helpings. She gave another wobble. 'Gosh, I do need a coffee to steady myself, don't I?'

'Oh, bless you. Look, let me park the car again and can I take you for a coffee somewhere? Is that little café on the village square opposite the duck pond still there? Maybe a coffee and a cake to make up for me demolishing the one you had with you might be a good way of apologising.'

Violet grinned internally. Job done. 'Oh, it's still there, dear. And that would be lovely, if you don't mind. Only if you have the time. I'm so sorry to ruin your day. You must be so busy planning the funeral and arranging about the will reading, there's always so much to think about at these sad moments. I don't want to take up your precious time.'

'No, don't be silly. It'll be my pleasure. It's me that's ruined something after all. Your cake.' Although a little niggle inside Belinda made her think that she'd seen the woman throwing the cake box and umbrella into the air herself. But that would be ridiculous, right? The thought passed, replaced by a moment of vanity. 'And do you really think that I look no older than ten years ago? Really?'

A 'frail' Violet was still enthusing about how marvellous Belinda looked when they walked into Burrow Bites, the village's café, about five minutes later. Indeed, Belinda was still blushing with the unexpected and much-needed praise when their two mugs of coffee and two pecan caramel brownies subsequently arrived.

'Well, these are absolutely delightful,' gushed Violet, taking a bite into the brownie. 'I was so fond of both your mother and indeed your poor father. How are the funeral plans coming along for Sir Buster?'

Belinda took a bite from her brownie too, agreed about the taste and then began to talk. There was something about the old lady, maybe about the same age that her mother would have been, to be honest, that made her very easy to talk to. She had an air of innocent simplicity about her. She didn't really remember seeing her at her mother's funeral. But then she didn't remember much about that day, apart from her rage at her mother's passing.

Before she knew it, Belinda Flatt had literally told the woman her life story. It felt somewhat cathartic. Perhaps she'd been bottling things up lately.

This pleased an inquisitive Violet greatly. Two mugs of coffee and an almond macaron each later – well, talking things over was both thirsty and hungry work – Violet knew that the funeral would probably be 'next week', date TBC, and that the reading of the will would be 'the day after tomorrow at noon' as Belinda had spoken to the solicitor earlier that day.

More importantly, thanks to a very loquacious Belinda feeling that she could strangely confide in a woman that she had only run into by virtually running her over barely ninety minutes earlier, Violet also learnt that Belinda had always hated her father living on his own in such a big house after Fiona's death. Apparently, it wasn't very green and 'a bloody waste of space'. She also soaked up the fact that Belinda blamed her father for Fiona's death for having a gun in the house in the first place. 'A gun should never be used to shoot a living thing, Violet, especially when that happens to be your mother,' she had said with a horrid hybrid of sarcasm and serious critique.

Violet also discovered that Belinda was not a fan of her brother, Alexi, as he was 'a waste of space who had sponged off the family for years' and that she 'prayed he didn't get Burrow Hall in the will'. Belinda was equally forthcoming about her feelings for her husband, Rupert. Or maybe that should be her lack of feelings. It appeared that 'it's very hard to stay in love with someone when they're tree hugging on the other side of the world and you've not had so much as a decent hug for the last five years'. Indeed, Belinda apparently wondered 'why I'm still with him. I admire his work, but I'm not sure I admire the man anymore'.

She was, however, very complimentary about their son, Sage. Well, in the most part. 'I adore Sage, I do. But now he's a million miles away from me too, suddenly all pally with his father. Not that I resent that, of course. No, I don't resent that at all. It's natural for a boy to want to see his father, especially when he's not seen a lot of him for years. No decent mother could resent that, could they.' It was more of a questioning search for validation than a statement. Violet had said nothing in return. She had merely sat there, innocent and naïve in her macaron-nibbling, dropping the odd word to goad a remarkably willing Belinda Flatt to spill her emotions. Violet guessed that sometimes it was indeed easier to talk to someone who was almost a stranger.

Conversation exhausted, Belinda had paid up and made her excuses to drive off to a nearby retail outlet. She had enjoyed her chat with Violet and felt in a better mood than she had done all day. Shopping could only raise that good mood even higher. She would need a new outfit for the reading of the will, and one for the funeral, of course. And maybe one for the memorial night at The Six Pennies that Violet had mentioned just before Belinda left to go shopping. She needed to look good, and she loved a retail outlet. The shopping near Rooney-at-Burrow wouldn't be as good as in Dubai though, no doubt. They had some fabulous malls in Dubai. One even had a ski slope in. How mad was that?

As Belinda had climbed into her four-by-four and headed off to the retail outlet she realised how horrified her younger self would have been about having a ski slope in a shopping mall. She had changed a lot lately. Sometimes she hardly recognised herself.

She'd use the joint account bank card to pay for her purchases. Why not? Might as well while she could. Something told her that might be changing soon too.

By the time Margaret rang Violet on her mobile to tell her about her discovery of the squashed marrows, Violet was alone in the café.

Chapter 29

Jeremiah Halliwell sat himself down on the bench near the edge of the riverbank. He checked his watch. It was ten to the hour. Ten minutes until hopefully a rather unexpected windfall came his way.

He scanned his eyes around. Apart from the gentle hum of an advancing boat coming down the river towards where he was sitting, hardly a sound dented the air. It was calm, tranquil and serene. The perfect spot for a dose of blackmail.

The sun was strong yet still comfortable against his skin. It was late afternoon and there were only the merest traces of wispy clouds decorating the sky, their whiteness layered across the blue. It was only now that he could feel just how hot the sun actually was. The area leading to the spot he had picked for his rewarding rendezvous was mostly shaded by trees and dense woodland. He hoped that the person he was meeting would be able to find it okay. He was sure that they would have no problem. Jeremiah had spelt it out clearly enough in his instructions. Park up, take the path through the woods and out into the clearing by the river, turn to the left and meet me on the bench near the riverbank, 6 p.m. Bring the money.

He had picked a place roughly equidistant between Rooney-at-Burrow and his own caravan in Darrochdean. It was a secluded spot he had brought ladies over the years for a spot of late-night necking. He knew it would be quiet, it always pretty much was. He couldn't even remember how he'd first come across it. That didn't matter now. Nothing really mattered now, because in just under ten minutes, he should hopefully be £50,000 richer. That was what he had asked the person to bring. In cash. Once the cash was handed over, the person would never hear from Jeremiah again. That was what he had told them in the letter. He hadn't decided whether that was true yet. He might need further payments.

What could £50K get you these days? He could use it to modernise the caravan a bit, maybe take a holiday, perhaps even buy a new car or perhaps a boat. How much did they even cost? He looked at the one advancing down the river towards where he sat. Somebody seemed to be having a party. He could hear the dull throb of music coming from onboard now dusting the air, mingling with the sound of the engine.

Maybe £50K was underselling himself. If somebody had told him last week when he'd been sat outside his caravan with his mate talking about the chances of poaching some fish from some posh fella's private lake that a windfall of £50K was coming his way, Jeremiah would have been cock-a-hoop. But now he couldn't help but think that he'd sold himself short.

In truth, he'd had a lucky break. Not only had he managed to land a few decent trout from the lake early on that Saturday morning, but he'd also managed to stay hidden and undetected when he'd seen the man, who he now knew as Sir Buster, starting to fish. He'd seen another figure arrive and what had taken place. Even from his hidden vantage point in the bushes, it had been clear to see what had occurred. And when he'd read the story in the papers suddenly things had slotted into place. Heart attack? Nah, this had been far more cold-blooded. He'd witnessed it all.

Jeremiah had been lucky not to be seen. But the person meeting him had been much unluckier to be seen. Much unluckier. To the tune of £50,000. For now. Jeremiah sometimes thought that he was born lucky.

He checked his watch again. Five to six. He tipped his head back and looked out from under the brim of his baseball cap at the sky again. A sound of a bird flying overhead filled his ears. It was the last sound he ever heard.

He felt something wrap itself around his throat, a pressure against his skin. He wanted to struggle, he wanted to try to stop the pain he suddenly felt. He wanted to stop his eyes from closing to black and to nothingness. But he couldn't. His luck had run out. For good.

It was just turning six o'clock when the boat that had been furthering down the river passed the spot where Jeremiah Halliwell still sat. His eyes were closed, his head tilted forward. His face was hidden by the baseball cap. To the group of revellers dancing on the deck of the boat that went past, he looked just like a person asleep in the early-evening heat. They waved to him as they danced. He never waved back. They were dancing to a Spice Girls song. For the first time in the longest while, Jeremiah Halliwell wasn't irked and riled by hearing the girl band. But only because he was dead.

Chapter 30

Alexi starred at his phone. The day after tomorrow at noon, the text said on his screen from his sister. That was when the reading of the will would be taking place. At least now Alexi knew. He had been wondering about it. And typical that Belinda had organised it. Annoyingly efficient as ever. Not that Alexi had even thought about trying to help with any kind of organisation. He'd been way too busy trying to look after number one. As for the will reading, the sooner, the better, as far as he was concerned. If all went to plan, then that would mean finally he could get his hands on Burrow Hall and turn it into a financial jackpot. And hopefully a jackpot for one. Him.

He'd been looking for the will that first night at his

family home. That's why he'd turned the place pretty much upside down. But no amount of drawer-emptying or whisky-drinking had enabled him to find the all-important document. No surprise, really. Who kept a will at home? Unless there was a safe. And it appeared that daddy dearest didn't have one. Alexi had asked Herbert, who had told him that Sir Buster had never wanted one as he had 'nothing to hide away'. Typical trusting nice guy. Alexi was rapidly learning from everyone in the village that his father was a hugely likable, well-respected and trusted member of village life. Or at least he had been before face-planting in his own lake.

Alexi had spent most of this evening, on and off, sitting in The Six Pennies beer garden. He was trying to keep out of Belinda's way. A text from her was one thing, but the chance of bumping into her and her acid tongue was another. Alexi had forgotten just how much he disliked his sister when she was in full flow. He was supposed to be the big brother, but yet she always seemed to lord it over him. If he was honest, she actually scared him a bit. Not that he would ever admit that. Hence his reasoning for the sanctuary of The Six Pennies garden. Plus, he was hoping that Sheena girl might come in, in need of refreshment.

'You've been a busy man,' said Steph, coming over with his latest drink. She placed it, a whisky sour, on the table. She could count on two hands the number of times she'd made one of these in The Six Pennies over the years. It was not your average drink, but she loved the fact it made a change from the lager and sherry drinkers of the village. Not together, of course. 'You seem to have been glued to that every time I come out.' She pointed at his phone. She couldn't help but read the message on the screen as it was still illuminated. 'So it's the will reading in two days. Gosh.' The words dropped from her lips before she had a chance to stop them. 'Sorry, I didn't mean to pry.'

'No worries. Yes, it's the will reading. Pretty straightforward, I imagine. A down-the-middle split with me and Belinda. She's my sister.' He crossed his fingers as he said it, pleading inside that it wouldn't be an even split. If he was really wishful, he hoped there wouldn't be a split at all. He returned to the subject of his being on the phone. 'The wheels of industry constantly need oiling to run smoothly. I need to keep ahead of my game to make sure my clients are happy bunnies. One wrong word from me and a million-pound sponsorship deal for the hottest TV star in the land could be in deep water. You know what I'm saying.'

Steph didn't exactly, but she knew she loved the idea. 'Pearl said that you were some kind of flashy telly star type, or at least you look after them. Anyone I know?'

Steph was sure she could smell weed in the air. She knew that smell from her college days. Which now seemed like Jurassic times, they were that long ago. The ashtray of butts on the grass that she spied next to Alexi proved that she was right, but she chose to ignore it. Alexi was outside and he was doing no harm.

Alexi answered, happy to know that someone was interested in his favourite subject. Himself. 'I can't tell you that. I'd have to change the names to protect the guilty, you know what I'm saying.' He offered a wink.

Again, Steph didn't really, but she continued her line

of questioning. 'Have you ever been to any of those fancy London clubs with your clients? And those swanky bars that you always see them going to on reality chows?' Almost unaware that she was doing so, Steph sat down opposite Alexi, waiting expectantly for the answer. She hoped it would be as exciting as she had imagined. It was.

'Babe. I've got platinum membership cards to them all.' Alexi tapped the top of his wallet which lay on the table.

Steph let out a little gasp of exhilaration. The fact he had called her babe didn't go unnoticed either. She felt her skin colour a shade deeper. 'Oh my word, you must know everyone in, like, Knightsbridge or Hoxton or wherever the people you hang out with hang out.' Steph shifted excitedly in her seat. This was the most exciting conversation she'd had since... she couldn't remember when.

'Hey, they hang out with *me*, babe...' The sentence lingered in the air like a cheesily bad smell, but Steph was eating it up.

'You must find village life so slow in comparison. I bet

you're glad you'll not be here for that long.'

Phill was walking past their table and had heard Alexi both calling Steph babe and also her comment about the village.

'There's nothing wrong with village life, I think you'll find,' smiled Phill with a two-handed two-finger point at his wife as he sauntered past. 'I'm going back in to serve, *babe.*' He emphasised the last word with a grin and a wink and left his wife alone with Alexi. A fact a very shallow Alexi liked. A captive female audience. Alexi starred directly at Steph. She wasn't as enticing as Sheena, but beggars couldn't be choosers.

'Those bars and clubs in London open their doors for me and my clients. Sure, I know every glitzy, ritzy one of them. Drinks on the house. It's about who you know and what you stand for. I would never bring them to a place like this' – he circled his finger in the air to indicate The Six Pennies – 'no offence. It's just a little provincial. But I gotta say that rural village life and local pubs aren't without their more interesting features.' Alexi gazed at Steph meaningfully.

'No offence taken,' she said as Alexi reached forward and placed his hand on her leg. She gasped again but let it rest there. Somehow, alongside the talk of glamourous London nightspots and free drinks with countless stars that she was bound to have read about in celebrity magazines, Alexi unashamedly touching her leg while her husband served drinks less than fifty feet away didn't seem as crass and as foolhardy as it would to anybody else.

Alexi spotted the glint of adventure in her eyes and pounced on it. 'Care to join me for a smoke. He picked up the ashtray.

Steph knew that he didn't mean a quick drag on a cheap roll-up or a crafty pack of ten. And she didn't mind. She was feeling daring, playful even, and God, it had been years since she'd experienced anything like it.

He rolled a joint, passed it to her and lit it. Steph inhaled deeply as the feel of the weed hit the back of her throat. It took her back to her wild and free college days. She'd have been worthy of hanging out with the London crowd back then. She wouldn't have just been drinking in the bars and clubs, she would have been behind the bar.

Serving, Owning. Living. Loving. Doing anything except wondering whether Pickled Pork crisps were a goer in a rustic village and regretting the fact that Alexi's hand was no longer on her leg.

Alexi took the joint from her and enjoyed a toke too. He liked Steph. She seemed cool. Because she obviously thought that he was and that was what mattered. Even though he'd been lying to her. He hadn't been making any lucrative deals for clients that afternoon. What he had been doing was finding out just how many luxury homes could be built on the land left by the Burrow Hall estate. The answer was a lot. According to those in the know, the acres there could mean that scores of luxury flats could be erected. And that would mean millions in rent alone for the person in charge. He hoped that the day after tomorrow it would be him. Finally, the house could be his.

Both Steph and Alexi looked at each other and smiled. He put his hand back on her leg. She left it there again. It felt good to live dangerously and think of life beyond the fences of The Six Pennies beer garden.

Chapter 31

Violet had left the café as soon as she had hung up on the phone call from Margaret about the annihilated marrows. In the time she had walked back around to Brewer's Loop and told a very confused Sheena that she might be a little longer than planned, asked her to try to rescue the mess of a drizzle cake that was still inside the box and explained that she was off to see about some squashed vegetables, WPC Paula Horton had also been phoned about the incident. Margaret had called Sergeant Pollett and told him, to his minor annoyance, that she had also spoken to Violet and told her to come and see the destruction. Samuel Pollett had phoned WPC Horton to join him and the others.

Paula Horton saw Violet going into her wool shop and

was standing outside waiting for her when she vacated the shop. At first vexing to Violet, this pleased her when she found out that Paula knew about the marrows and could indeed save Violet a half-hour walk by offering a lift in her car. As an upshot, all four of them – Violet, Margaret, Sergeant Pollett and WPC Horton – were all standing marrow-side within forty minutes of the initial shocking phone call.

'Well, I think this proves somebody had it in for poor Sir Buster, don't you?' said Violet, shaking her head as she surveyed the allotment carnage in front of her.

'D'you think?' said WPC Horton. 'This could have just been some hooligans passing by.'

'I do think you ladies could be letting your imaginations run away with you a bit,' offered Sergeant Pollett. He was talking to Violet and Margaret, although, in truth, he didn't think WPC Horton was any closer to the mark, as hooligans passing by was as likely as him getting a phone call from a Hollywood legend asking him to be their new bodyguard. 'The poor man had a heart attack, and somebody squashed his marrows. That's all this is. It's not CSI Ground Force! Maybe he did it himself before he died because they weren't big enough for the fayre this year. A bit of self-sabotage. Or perhaps Alexi or Belinda have done it in a rage. It sounds like they both have quirky personalities.'

'Quirky personalities make you line up the food tins in your kitchen cupboards to within a millimetre of each other, or change your toilet roll if the sheets are dangling in the wrong direction, Samuel. They do not make you slip on a pair of wellington boots and jump up and down on a prize marrow until it looks like a dropped pizza.' It was Margaret who submitted her opinions.

'Very well said, Margaret,' agreed Violet. 'I'm quirky as charged on both counts there, but there's no way you would ever see me jumping up and down on a large root vegetable. I'm not sure my ankles would stand for it.' Violet turned her attention to the two police officers. 'I do understand what you're saying, Samuel, it's hardly a smoking gun or a bloodstained hammer, I get that, but it does show that somebody might have had some kind of grudge to bear with Sir Buster.'

'But Sir Buster wasn't shot or bludgeoned to death, he had a heart attack. So, this is hardly evidence, is it?' lobbed back Samuel.

But Violet wasn't deterred. 'And as for hooligans, Paula, I really don't think that even the densest of hooligans would venture all this way to slip on a pair of wellies, do their worst and then put the wellies back in the shed. It's not very juvenile behaviour is it. I suggest that this was calculated and that it was definitely a deliberate act of destruction. One that was performed with rage and a certain amount of hatred. As for self-sabotage. Well, I know it's highly unlikely that you can estimate the time of death of a marrow like you can with a human, but I suspect we can definitely say that this was done after poor Sir Buster's demise. But quite why I can't begin to fathom.'

'How do we know that it was done after his death?' asked Paula. 'We don't know the last known sighting of prize marrow. Or how big it was.'

'It was big enough for Sir Buster to tell Sheena that he thought he had this year's contest in the bag the day before he died. And Sir Buster wasn't one to blow his own trumpet for no good reason,' said Margaret.

'Well, I'm not convinced, but I guess we could ask Herbert and Mrs Turner if they had seen the aforementioned prize marrow recently. And Belinda and Alexi while we're at it. But that seems a little vulgar, talking marrows while they're planning funerals and suchlike.' Samuel scratched his head.

'The funeral is next week at the earliest. The reading of the will is at noon the day after tomorrow and if you're going to ask Belinda now, don't bother as she's out shopping.'

Samuel raised his eyebrows at Violet's news. 'And how do you know all that?'

'She ran into me earlier and we had a good chat. Not the happiest of women, I must say. There's quirky and then there's downright gloomy. I'd suggest she may be straying into the latter.'

'What about the boots? Judging from the gooey mess on the wellingtons, I'd say that from the colour of the marrow that's left and the consistency, it's been there about two or three days. Enough time for it to start to rot and attract the flies. That would make it… well, the day that Sir Buster died.' Margaret couldn't help but feel a little smug that finally her love of her favourite food had come in handy. She'd seen enough rotting marrows in her time to know exactly how discoloured they could become and approximately the time it took.

'Oh bravo, Margaret,' praised Violet, registering that it was indeed an ingenious if somewhat vague course of resolve. 'I suggest that Samuel and Paula remove the wellingtons as evidence and perhaps fingerprint test them to see if it's just Sir Buster's prints on there. If it is, then so be it. But there might be others. You can't slip on a pair of wellies without touching them really, can you?'

Exasperated, defeated and actually contemplating that maybe there was more motive to the marrow crushing than just a silly prank, Sergeant Pollett asked WPC Horton to go and bag up the wellingtons. She willingly did so.

'There's a gun in the shed, Sarge,' remarked WPC Horton on her return. 'Should I bag that up too?'

'What for, no one's been shot?'

'But it's a dangerous weapon, isn't it?'

'We know it's there, that'll do for now. Now, I suggest you two ladies head back home and I'm going to make some enquiries at the Hall. See if I can speak to Alexi or either Mrs Turner or Herbert about the last time they saw the marrows or if they have any idea when they was crushed.' Sergeant Pollett could hear how ludicrous it sounded, but he said it anyway. 'Or if they can think of anybody that would want to kill Sir Buster because of his prize-winning vegetables.' He tutted, before adding, 'WPC Horton, can you get the boots fingerprinted and kindly drop these two off on your way back to the station.'

She nodded and the three ladies headed to her car. They had just cleared the grounds of the Hall when Violet said, 'That gun was probably the one that killed poor Fiona, you know.'

'So?' asked Margaret.

WPC Horton stared at them both in the seat in the rear-view mirror.

'Well, I happen to know that Belinda does blame her father for her mother's death and, well, it wouldn't be unimaginable for Belinda to have wandered to the allotment and seen the gun in the shed. Suddenly, all of those horrid memories come flooding back and in an incandescent rage she stamps on the marrows as she knows they were so dear to her father. He could have won the competition posthumously. Now we will never know.'

'Do you think I should get the gun fingerprinted too?' asked WPC Horton to the two ladies, fully aware of the sudden role reversal.

'Oh, I would, dear, yes,' said Violet.

'And the book with the nasty death threats too,' added Margaret. 'Get them all done.'

WPC Horton pulled the car over to the side of the road leading into the village and slammed on the brakes. She turned round to face the two ladies. 'Excuse me? Nasty death threats?'

'Oh, I thought you might have said...' Margaret's words petered away to silence.

'No, I hadn't got round to mentioning that just yet,' said Violet, her cheeks rouging at the admission.

'Well, I think now is the time, don't you?' said the policewoman.

'It's getting late,' remarked Violet, looking at her watch. 'Sheena will be wondering where we are. How about you come around to the shop tomorrow morning at nine and I'll explain everything. But don't tell Samuel for now. He'll just think we're being silly.'

Even though it went against everything she had ever been taught in police training, something inside WPC Paula Horton's head agreed to show up the next morning and turn a blind eye to the new evidence until then. Violet could twist her around her little finger, and she knew it.

'Okay, just this once,' she agreed.

As she dropped Violet and Margaret off outside the wool shop, she told the women she would see them in the morning.

'And this had better be good, ladies.' She tried to sound stern but ruined it with a chirpy 'cheerio' as she disappeared home to feed Mr Bublé.

'What a day!' said Margaret.

'Oh, there's more to tell, Margaret. Gather the Team C.R.A.B. troops for nine in the morning too. They'll want to hear about the marrows and everything I've learnt from

Belinda. See you in the morning, dear. What a day indeed.'

Chapter 32

There must have been a real sense of keenness in the air the next morning as everyone except Violet was already sitting at the table in the back room at Brewer's Loop by 8.50 a.m. Sheena had let them in using her set of keys when she had turned up at 8.45 to find Jimmy, Pearl and WPC Horton all gathered eagerly outside the front door. Margaret had appeared a couple of minutes later, snacks in hand.

They were all drinking tea and diving into a plate of garibaldi that Margaret had brought along from her famed forever-full biscuit barrel by the time Violet arrived at a minute after nine. Pearl was flicking through a craft magazine.

Violet made her excuses. 'Sorry I'm a little tardy,

everyone. I can't fib, I was busy watching a lovely segment on the breakfast news about a woman in Chipping Sodbury who has been making a crochet zoo for an animal charity in her area. She's spent months making everything from tigers and penguins through to meerkats. Glorious makes, they are. But, apparently, she can't manage orangutans or sloths for love nor money, so she was putting out an appeal for people to help. I was thinking we could try to make something at our next craft session.'

The entire table, including WPC Horton, nodded merrily. The policewoman didn't even craft but loved the idea of a crochet orang-utan. She toyed momentarily with the idea of asking one of the group to make her a mini crochet Mr Bublé at some point. She decided she'd ask when she wasn't on official police business. As it was, she'd not slept overly well, worried that she was making the wrong decision about not having pressed Violet and Margaret about the death threat evidence when they had revealed it to her the night before. Sergeant Pollett would definitely tear her off a strip if he knew. As such, WPC Horton was keen to take control of the meeting. She needed to present herself with an air of gravitas.

'Well, that's lovely… about the zoo thing… but I have to tell you that you've all done a really bad thing in concealing the evidence about the threats. It could be really important.'

'Oh, we're sure it is, dear Paula,' said Violet. 'But let's come onto that in a minute. We must let everyone know about the latest development with Sir Buster's marrows.' She narrowed her eyes at Paula. 'You do look a little tired, Paula. Is that Samuel working you too hard? Or Mr Bublé keeping you up all night?'

So much for gravitas. Paula admitted defeat and took a sip of tea, sitting back to let the others guide the meeting.

Jimmy, Pearl and Sheena sat open-mouthed as they listened to Violet and Margaret's revelations about what had happened to Sir Buster's prize vegetables. They took in every word. Then Violet filled them in about her conversation in the café with Belinda Flatt and how she had revealed her true feelings towards her father, brother and indeed her husband.

'Oh my. The husband always seems so lovely when he

pops up on the TV,' chipped in Pearl. 'Doing all that good work and giving tips on being eco-friendly. I like him a lot. There's a lot of dislike going on there with her. Too much if you ask me. Sounds like she can't be trusted. I wouldn't be surprised if she's behind the marrows.'

'But what does she gain from that?' asked Jimmy. 'It's not like she was going to enter her own marrows into the competition, was she?' He paused in contemplation before adding, 'Or was she?'

'That's doubtful, but we can ask her. I know Samuel went to the Hall after we left him last night. Maybe he managed to catch up with Belinda,' speculated Violet.

'I can ask him when I head to the station straight after this. With the newly produced evidence. Which is where, by the way?' WPC Horton was growing a little impatient.

'In a moment, Paula, in a moment.' Violet returned to Jimmy's question. 'What Belinda gains from that is immense satisfaction. It's what I call the bubble-wrap effect. What do you do when you have some bubble wrap?'

'You pop the bubbles.' The answer came en masse from around the table.

'Exactly. You can't help yourself. You do it for the satisfaction of it. The bubbles are pretty much useless after they're popped. But the satisfaction of destroying each and every bubble is too great to resist. Maybe Belinda felt the same about the marrows. She's blamed her father for her mother's death and living his non-green life in that big house and she sees his marrows and views them as a representation of him and decides to bash the life out of them. You can see how that might be highly satisfying.'

'Have you fingerprinted the boots yet, Paula?' asked Margaret.

'No. I'll get that done today. Plus, I'm going to collect the gun and have that fingerprinted too. And the new evidence of course. So, can we discuss—'

'I think it was her. Definitely,' said Pearl, not meaning to interrupt WPC Horton, but doing so, nevertheless. 'I'm not saying she has anything to do with the threats and Sir Buster's death, but I think she's a shoo-in for the marrow bashing.'

'It does seem likely. I mean, let's be honest, would somebody kill another person just because they are rivals in a marrow contest? That's lunacy,' remarked Jimmy.

'They don't even taste that nice,' said Sheena, before trying to fend off a filthy look from Margaret. 'I know Sir Buster told me he thought he was going to win, but no vegetable is worth killing for.'

'Where was his stiffest competition coming from this year?' asked Jimmy. 'I know that everyone's entries are always swathed in secrecy every year, but word still gets around the village.'

'Yours is supposedly quite a whopper this year, Jimmy?' said Pearl. She felt herself blush at her choice of words and pretended to concentrate on the magazine in front of her.

'I could be a winner this year, but I really don't care if I come first or fifth. Believe you me, there are many times that I have said that I would kill for a burger or a bacon sandwich, but I have never literally wanted to kill because of a marrow. So no, not guilty on that front.' Jimmy laughed, a little nervously, considering the jokey accusation.

'I'm the same,' offered Margaret. 'I could win, and I want to, of course, but not enough to take down a rival.

All's fair in love and with marrows.'

'Well, Noah and I are in the clear because his weren't that big and I picked them to use for some fritters. He wasn't happy about it, but at least it gives us an alibi.' Pearl giggled. 'You must all come and try them next time I make them. They were delicious.'

'There's Phill and Steph,' said Sheena. 'They've mentioned a few times that their entry for this year's fayre has been coming along very nicely. But again, there's no way they would kill for the prize, or try to nobble somebody else's entry. Phill's literally one of the sweetest men you could ever meet, and Steph and I are always talking about how lovely Sir Buster is. Er... was,' Sheena blustered to a close.

'So, we're no clearer on all that then,' said Violet.

Silence floated in the room for a second or two.

It stayed until WPC Horton let out a small cough. 'So, about this new evidence. The threats? These seem so much more important than a few squashed marrows. Not that they're not important, of course, but... well, you get my drift. Can I please see them?'

Paula pulled her gloves from her pocket and slipped them over her hands. It was common practice if she was going to be handling evidence.

Sadly, Violet didn't do the same as she took the copy of *Jekyll and Hyde* from her bag, flicked the pages to the one with the envelope, pulled out the three notes and spread them on the table.

Paula watched in horror as she did so. 'Violet! Your fingerprints will be all over them now.' The police officer's voice was soaked with exasperation.

'Oh sorry, but they were before, dear. We've all handled them, haven't we?' Violet scanned her eyes around the table and watched as Jimmy, Pearl, Sheena and Margaret all raised their hands to say they had been hands-on with the book.

WPC Horton let out a sigh. She would have the book and notes fingerprint tested anyway, but she suspected the results would come back with more names than a phone book. She let her eyes take in the cut-out magazine letters on each of the three notes.

I KNOW WHAT YOU'VE BEEN DOING,

STOP IT NOW

I'VE WARNED YOU. STOP BEFORE IT'S TOO LATE

THIS IS YOUR FINAL WARNING.

ENOUGH IS ENOUGH

'Wow. Well, there's no doubting that somebody must have had some beef with Sir Buster. When did you get these?' The police officer stood up as she spoke to lean across and stare at the letters a little closer.

'A few days ago.' Sheena filled WPC Horton on the story of how she had come to find the book under the sofa in Sir Buster's study.

'And you didn't think that maybe you should be showing this to Sergeant Pollett? The officer in charge of this case.'

'Well, we just thought that he might dismiss it as nonsense and our imaginations running away with us again,' said Sheena. 'You know what Dad can be like?'

It seemed reason enough.

'Well, between this and the marrows, perhaps we could make a few more investigations. I will need to take it with me. I'm not happy about you all keeping evidence from us. And Sergeant Pollett will be livid.'

Violet smiled. 'Does he really need to know that we've had it a few days already? Can't you just say that lovely Sheena found it whilst tidying and decided to borrow it as she was going to read the book as it's such a classic and when she opened it, she found the notes and then reported it straight away. I mean, after all, if we were to present Samuel with the *total* truth, he would question why you didn't take it from us last night, Paula, when Margaret and I first told you.' Violet was still smiling. 'It would be such a shame for Sheena to get into any unnecessary trouble.'

WPC Horton looked on unsure.

'Oh, go on, Paula. We meant no harm. Another garibaldi, dear?' Violet offered the plate to Paula.

'Please?' added Sheena.

Paula stared at her friends around the table. And then she caved.

'Okay, just this once.' She was fully aware that she had already said that the night before. 'But if any more evidence turns up unexpectedly, then you're all to tell

Sergeant Pollett and I immediately. Is that absolutely clear?'

'Crystal' said Jimmy.

The others nodded eagerly to show their equally eager commitment in sharing anything else that came their way.

WPC Horton was in the process of carefully folding up the notes and placing them inside the book when suddenly Pearl leapt up from where she was sitting. She was holding the craft magazine that she had been reading in her hand.

'Hang on a minute, WPC Horton. Let me have a look at that third message.'

Paula placed it unfolded again on the table.

'Oh my,' Pearl exclaimed, looking at the words THIS IS YOUR FINAL WARNING. ENOUGH IS ENOUGH, 'will you look at the W.'

It was the big yellow W on the purple background. It was the letter that had rung a bell with Violet a couple of evenings before. A fact she was quick to share.

'It's so distinctive that, isn't it? The yellow on the purple. I recognise it from somewhere. I was trying to wrack my brains about it after FaceTiming Betsy the other night, but I'll be beggared if I can think of where I've seen it.'

'I know exactly where it was,' said Pearl. She held the craft magazine aloft and pointed to the competition page where you had a chance to 'WIN A LIMITED-EDITION DIE-CUTTING MACHINE'. The typeface was yellow letters on a purple background and was identical to the letter on the note. It had clearly been cut out from the page of a copy of that magazine.

The whole table stared wide-eyed.

'Oh, my word, so it is. It's the W from WIN,' said Margaret. 'Well, you know what this means, don't you?'

'That whoever sent that note had this magazine,' said Jimmy.

'Which means that they, or someone in their house, is most likely into crafting,' added Pearl.

'They could have bought it in this very shop,' said Violet.

Reflection hung heavy in the air as everyone gathered thought about what that could possibly mean. The person who sent the note might have been into crafting. And the biggest crafters in the village were sitting in that very room right now.

Surely it couldn't be one of them, could it?

Awkward smiles momentarily filled the room.

Not one of their own. Surely? That would be ridiculous, right?

Chapter 33

Sheena was walking out of Burrow Bites café with a brown paper bag containing a BLT sandwich in her hand a couple of hours later when she ran straight into her dad. The look on his face was not a particularly happy one. Placation may be in order.

'Hi there, Dad. You look good in your uniform, as ever. Really trim.' It was her best pacifying tactic. Normally, it would be greeted by a smile from ear to ear and a response of 'guess your old dad doesn't scrub up too badly, does he?' and an evident delight that his little paunch weight worries seemed to be in order. Today, though, no such luck.

'Can I talk to you, Sheena?'

'Sure thing, Dad.'

Sheena followed her dad to a bench near the duck pond in the village square. The wood was a little hot against the skin on her legs as she sat down. It was a glorious August day and the sun shone directly above them, its reflection rippling on the surface of the pond as two ducks swam towards them, the promise of a lunchtime titbit from a tell-tale paper bag always too appetising to resist.

'So, WPC Horton has filled me in on everything that you and your crafting friends have been up to. And I can't say I'm happy, Sheena.'

'Oh…' Sheena left it there as she opened up her paper bag and took out her sandwich. The two ducks both quacked expectantly in front of her. She wondered just how much of the actual truth WPC Horton had divulged. She remained silent.

'I appreciate your desire to read good books, but you should never take something from somebody's house. Especially the house of someone who had just died.'

Sheena took a bite and inwardly sighed. So, thankfully, it appeared WPC Horton had told the requested version of what had happened.

'You should have asked Herbert or Mrs Turner if you wanted to borrow something. And you clearly didn't, did you?'

'No, sorry, Dad.' Sheena played along, knowing she was getting off lightly.

'And now it turns out that there is evidence inside the book that signals that somebody had it in for Sir Buster all along. This makes a big difference, Sheena. Imagine if you had just shoved that book in a cupboard in your room and left it there for a few months before reading it. Those notes would have stayed hidden away.'

'Yeah, sorry, Dad, I didn't think.' Sheena picked off a small piece of bread from her sandwich and threw it to the ducks. The one with the quickest reaction pecked his head forward and gobbled it down. Feeling a little sorry for the other, Sheena picked off another piece and threw it in the direction of the bird who missed out. The bread disappeared in the time it took the other duck to quack disgruntledly.

He placed his hand on Sheena's leg. 'You're a good

girl, Sheena. Your mum and I are very proud of you – we always have been. You really liked working at Sir Buster's, didn't you?'

'Yes, I did. I still do. I'm hoping that whoever takes over the Hall will let me stay on. It won't be the same without Sir Buster, though. I know he was a bit of a rogue and said inappropriate things at times, but he was totally harmless and I really enjoyed our chats. I think he liked the fact that I brought a bit of youthful spirit to the house. I don't suppose Mrs Turner and Herbert were always the chattiest of people. Maybe Sir Buster felt that he could really open up to me. I am genuinely going to miss him a lot. I'll bawl my eyes out during the funeral, no doubt.'

'It's been confirmed by the way. I spoke to Mrs Turner last night after Margaret phoned me about the marrows. Apparently, it's next Thursday. Two days before the fayre. It'll be a sad day indeed.'

'Is the fayre definitely happening then? It would be such a shame if it didn't.'

'Well, Margaret is full steam ahead with the organisation and as far as Mrs Turner and Herbert are concerned, it should still be happening. Not that they know much about anything, really. I suppose they're worried about their jobs too.'

'Did they know anything about the marrows?' asked Sheena.

'You know I can't discuss police business with you, Sheena.'

'We're talking about marrows, Dad.' Sheena's face was deadpan.

'Well, okay, fair enough. No, neither of them had seen the marrows since Sir Buster had died and even though Herbert was cursing himself for not going up to Sir Buster's allotment to water the stuff up there, he was certain that Sir Buster would have mentioned had he known that they had been trampled. Apparently, he was definitely thinking he would win this year as he had produced his best crop in ages.'

'That's what he told me,' said Sheena. 'I hope he never knew that someone trampled them. I can't believe somebody would kill Sir Buster, I know we don't know yet whether it was murder or not, but it really pains me to think that somebody could even send him those threatening notes. That's so horrid too. He must have been scared about it. Even with all of his "big man, nothing can upset me" attitude. He said to Violet at the pub that he would never give in to threats. Or at least she thinks he did. She can't clearly remember. You know Aunty Violet and the sherry.'

'Sir Buster talked to you a lot, didn't he? Can I ask you a few questions?'

'So now I'm good enough to discuss police business with, eh?' Sheena grinned. 'Yeah, of course. Ask away, we talked about a lot.'

'Okay, so, given the wording of those notes, it looks like Sir Buster had obviously done something to upset somebody. Do you have any clue who that might be?'

'No, not at all. As far as I was aware, everybody liked Sir Buster.'

'Do you think he could have been having an affair with someone?'

'Well, I wouldn't blame him if he did because he'd been on his own for years, but even though he was a real ladies' man and used to flirt with anyone, I don't think he was. I think there may have been the odd fling here and there, but you should have heard the way he talked about his ex-wife, Dad. He really put her on a pedestal. I don't think he ever stopped loving her.'

'Did he ever talk about his kids to you? Alexi and Belinda?'

Sheena threw another piece of bread down for the ducks. 'No, not a massive amount. The most I found out really was during that chat I had with him the day before he died. He said that they were both ungrateful and that they had sent Christmas cards and letters telling him to sell the Hall and that was that.'

'Did he say why they wanted him to sell the Hall?'

'No, he didn't. He was keener to speak about his wife. I vaguely remember her. I was about ten when she died, wasn't I? Apparently, Belinda still blames her dad for her death.'

'Yes, WPC Horton mentioned that your Aunt Violet had conducted a rather deep and revealing conversation with Sir Buster's daughter. I'm thinking that maybe I need do to the same.'

'You have to hand it to Aunty Vi. She has a great way of finding out what's going on.'

'Yes, she does. She's persistent, I'll give her that.' Samuel raised his eyebrows and gave a small sigh. 'What about gambling. We all know that Sir Buster loved a game of poker. Did you ever see any poker games at the Hall?'

'No, and again I think I would have heard about it if there had been. Mrs Turner loves a gossip, and she would have doubtless catered for any such games. Apart from the odd dodgy lock-in at the pub, which we know Sir Buster liked, I don't know when else he played poker. You do know about those lock-ins, don't you?' She looked at her dad and paused as the mistake hit her. 'Oh hell, have I just landed Phill and Steph in trouble? I'm singing there for the memorial night. They'll murder me if I've let the cat out of the bag about their after-hours nights.' She realised her clunky turn of phrase as soon as she said it. Maybe now wasn't the time to joke about being murdered. Luckily, her dad was smiling.

'Don't worry. I don't *officially* know about the lock-ins,

but between you, me and the ducks, let's just say that I am fully aware of what goes on. There's no avocado in that sandwich by the way is there?'

'Er no, it's a BLT… why?' queried Sheena.

'No matter.'

'I'm going to sing all of Sir Buster's favourites for his memorial night. The ones that he gave his biggest cheers for. Shirley Bassey, The Carpenters, Cher. I'm dreading it, as I want it to be perfect for him, but I am so excited about it at the same time. He was such a special person and I want to do him proud.'

Samuel could feel his throat drying up with emotion. 'Who replaced my little girl with a fabulously mature and respectful grown-up woman? We really are so incredibly proud of you. Come here. I love you so much.'

Samuel put his arms out and pulled his daughter towards him in the biggest hug he could give. She really was amazing. He held her close and kissed the top of her head. He could feel tears threatening in his eyes.

'You're crushing my sandwich, Dad.'

'Oh, sorry.' He loosened his grip. He could have stayed

like that for hours, but not if it meant spoiling his daughter's lunch.

'I love you too.'

Sheena's mobile phone ringing interrupted the family love fest. She didn't recognise the number but answered it anyway.

The call lasted about a minute. Sheena ended it with the words, 'Okay, I'll be there, thanks for letting me know.'

Her dad was keen to quiz her when she came off the phone. 'Everything okay?'

'I'm not sure,' replied Sheena. 'That was about the will reading tomorrow. I've been requested to attend. Burrow Hall, midday.'

'Blimey,' responded her dad, not really sure what to say.

'I know. Dad, why on earth would they want me there?'

Chapter 34

'That might be a great way for the killer in *Cheese Wire* to bump somebody off. He could smash them over the head with a whacking great big marrow. And then, of course, Detective Peter Beacham could come to the rescue.'

'Oh, my gallant knight in shining armour.'

Violet was FaceTiming Betsy and Rod in Willow's Spit. She watched as her sister leant over to kiss her actor husband. It was late evening in Australia, heading towards midday in the UK, and Violet had filled in her family down under on the latest news from Rooney-at-Burrow.

'I thought you said that the killer in your creepy horror film only murdered people with kitchen implements, not garden vegetables, Rod?' asked Violet.

'Fair point. Maybe somebody should get mangled in a

blender making a marrow smoothie.'

Violet was fully aware that Rod seemed to be enjoying his new grisly role a lot more than she considered any man should. He and Violet's sister were both wearing T-shirts with the name of the film emblazoned across it. They had offered to send one to Violet, but she had politely declined. She'd stick to Marks & Spencer for her clothing, thank you.

Both Rod and Betsy had a ginormous plate of barbecued shrimp and fries on their plates in front of them, which they had been heartily diving into throughout the call. Violet had caught them mid BBQ and offered to call them back, but Betsy was more than happy to sit and chat and eat at the same time.

'You two have the most incredible appetites. How are you not both the size of Tasmania, given the amount you eat? That is down your way, isn't it?'

'Sure is,' replied Rod. 'I burn those excess calories off very easily with my daily early-morning swim. Well, that and my *playtime* with this one.' Rod slapped his wife softly on the back and guffawed. Betsy did too, identical in volume, if a good few octaves higher.

Violet guessed that obviously they were having wine with their meal. Quite a lot. Her sister was not normally this giggly. Actually, to be fair, since meeting Rod and moving down under, she was. Violet ignored what Rod was hinting at.

'We love our food. Especially when it tastes this good,' said Betsy.

'Sir Buster had a massive appetite too, didn't he? Although he was very careful with what he ate. Paula Horton was telling me about all of the food he had in his cool box the morning he went fishing and sadly died. He only got to eat his sandwiches, bless him, everything else in there seemed to be untouched. Loads of it apparently. Gosh, I do hate wasted food. Such a pity. Mind you, hardly the most serious issue that day, given that Sir Buster went to meet his maker. I hope Mrs Turner gave the leftovers to the birds or something. I shall have to ask her. I'm heading up to Burrow Hall after our chat. I was supposed to go yesterday, of course, but well, I bumped into Belinda Flatt and that was that, as you well know. I'm hoping I might be able to have a chat with them all up there – Mrs Turner, Herbert, Alexi, if he's there, and maybe even a coffee with Belinda again if she's in the mood. I think Samuel has already had a chat with Mrs Turner and Herbert, but I'm not always sure he asks the right questions.'

Betsy nodded. 'He's always been like that. I remember when he was at school. His report always said he was an inquisitive boy, but if he showed more interest in asking about spelling and less about what the teacher's car and favourite TV show was, he would have been much higher up in his class. Sometimes I do wonder how he managed to become a policeman.'

'I'm glad he has WPC Horton by his side. Anyway, tomorrow is the will reading, so it will be interesting to see what comes of that. I wonder if both Alexi and Belinda will be happy with the outcome. I can't imagine they will be, as they don't really seem to like each other a huge deal. I got the impression yesterday that Belinda would like to keep it so that her son, Sage, can get to experience it. Odd name. Nice, but odd.'

'And what about Alexi?' asked Betsy, before tucking into yet another barbecued shrimp. A smear of sauce left itself on her chin as she attempted to manoeuvre it into her mouth.

'I would imagine that somebody like him would like to turn it into a casino or a nightclub or a house of ill repute. Something sleazy, that is for sure. I have everything crossed that he doesn't gain total control of it. He is the eldest, after all. That can happen. Heaven forbid.'

Violet was just about to let her sister know about the saucy smear on her chin when Rod, who had briefly vanished to collect a bottle of wine – Violet was right, she knew they'd been drinking – returned into view. He obviously spotted the smear too.

'Well, look at you, Betsy, somebody hasn't quite finished their shrimp, have they?' He bent across and licked the smear from his wife's chin. 'There you go, nice and clean now, you mucky pup.'

Cue more guffawing.

Violet decided that it was time to make her excuses and run. Promising to phone Betsy and Rod again with any news from the will reading, she ended the call. She had no wish to witness any more potential face licking from her brother-in-law.

And besides, she needed to make her originally planned trip to Burrow Hall. She had questions that needed answering. Violet's brain seemed to be smeared with a mass of different pesky niggles.

Chapter 35

Seeing as the summer drizzle cake that Violet had made to pay her condolences at Burrow Hall had taken such an unfortunate tumble, she knew that she had to come up with an alternative. She could not turn up empty-handed to offer commiserations. Could you imagine? 'Oh hello, I'm so sorry to hear about Sir Buster, now stick the kettle on and crack open the Mr Kipling.' No, that would never do.

But she certainly didn't want to spend a couple of hours whipping up a new one. There was no time today. So, a Plan B needed organising. And it was B for Burrow Bites café. Violet had gone straight to the café after her FaceTime with Betsy and Rod and bought an entire carrot cake. It was a pricy alternative, but needs must when the devil drives and today the devil was driving her all the way to convenience and not cookery.

As she left the café, cake all wrapped up, she spied Sheena and Samuel on the bench near the duck pond hugging each other. She would have gone to say hello, but it seemed to be a special moment that did not warrant interruption. Besides, she needed to whip back to the shop, remove the cake from its branded bag and place it into a Tupperware container to take to Burrow Hall. It may have been convenient, but she preferred to let people think she had been busy baking every last crumb of the carroty goodness nevertheless.

She was nearly at the door of Burrow Hall, a good brisk if somewhat clammy walk later, when her phone beeped. It was a message from Sheena telling her about the request for her to attend the reading of the will the next day. This pleased Violet greatly as she has been plumbing the depths of her mind to try to find out how she could possibly have someone on the inside to hear every minute detail of Sir Buster's last will and testament. Fortune had played directly into her hands with the news about Sheena.

Violet knocked on the door, not really knowing who would open it. Would it be Belinda? Alexi? Herbert? As it happened, it was Mrs Turner.

'Oh, hello, Mrs Turner. It's Violet from the wool shop. I just wanted to come round and see how you are. Isn't this business with Sir Buster so dreadfully sad. It must be so hard for you; you've worked here for the longest time. He was such a good man.'

'Oh, hello, dear, thank you so much.' Mrs Turner liked Violet. Because she owned the wool shop. And Mrs Turner liked the wool shop because it sold her favourite DK wool. The wool that she favoured when she was having a bit of quality me-time away from cooking and the general running of Burrow Hall. Knitting time was her time and having the best wool shop for miles around virtually on her doorstep had always pleased Mrs Turner.

'I baked a cake to offer my condolences. It was the least I could do. It's carrot, a bit like the one they do at the café in the square. I thought it might come in handy with the procession of people that are likely to be trooping through. Isn't it always the way in the aftermath of such a sad event? How are you? You must be shattered.'

It was true, she had hardly had time to draw breath over the last few days. 'It's a full house at the moment. What with the children being back. All grown up now, of course.'

'Yes, I saw Belinda yesterday. Lovely girl. I'm yet to have bumped into Alexi, though. Is he about at all?'

'I think so, I heard him barking orders at someone down his phone earlier in his room. And there's a funny smell up there that seems to follow him around. I'll attack it with the sandalwood and jasmine Glade later. Why don't you come on in?'

'Well, if you're sure you're not too busy with all of the stress going on.'

'I'm due a break, to be honest. I've been making sure we have enough food and drink in for the reading of the will tomorrow. Tea, coffee, wine, et cetera. Some sandwiches. What do you actually serve at the reading of a will? Mind you, who's going to serve it anyway is beyond me. I've been told that I've got to be there for the reading.

Actually listening to what's going on.' There was a blend of shock and excitement in her expression.

'Well, you are an valued employee. Perhaps you're mentioned. I would suggest Sheena could help out, but she's been told to be at the reading as well. I'd be more than happy to help myself if you wish. I tell you what, if you're due a break, why don't we sit down together and have a cup of tea and a slice of a carrot cake and you can tell me what needs doing tomorrow. That way, you won't have to worry. Mind you, I'm not sure my cake will be anywhere near as delicious as your famed plum flapjacks. They're the talk of the fayre every year.' Violet felt delighted at the way the conversation was going.

'Oh, you are too kind. They are gorgeous, though, and I say that knowing they're made by my own fair hands. Seems a trifle conceited. Not that Sir Buster would ever eat them. A tad too calorific for him. Yes, a brew would be lovely. Are you sure you don't mind helping out tomorrow?'

'Of course, I don't. It would be my pleasure. I was a huge friend of Sir Buster as you know, and dear Fiona back in the day, so I would be more than happy to help.'

Plus, it would mean a second pair of ears to try to soak up every legal word and potentially vital information. Violet couldn't help but smile as she followed Mrs Turner to the kitchen for a cup of tea and some cake. She liked Mrs Turner too. She'd slip in a couple of extra balls of wool for free next time she came into the shop.

Alexi had seen the old woman approach the house. He'd caught a glimpse of her as she neared the door. He was standing by his bedroom window smoking a joint and talking on the phone. Well, shouting. Well, maybe not shouting but definitely with a raised tone. It was what he did when the bank phoned him. He couldn't help it. It was automatic. He would hear the word 'bank' and his temperature and his decibels would go through the roof. What was the point of having a personal bank manager if they were only ever going to deliver grim news to him? She'd loved him when he'd had money in his account. So, she could love him now, quite frankly. When the balance had lots of zeros, she was always on hand with friendly advice. Now that it contained only zeros, or minuses, she wasn't so amenable.

Today's call had been about another seemingly needless spend on his account. Overdraft this, declined payment that. She needed to change the record. It was not what he needed to hear right now. So, the latest payment on his car hadn't gone through. And the rent was due on his flat. So what? He'd ignored the letters. And the final bills. Red had never suited him as a colour. And why was it that important that his credit card was maxed out to way beyond its limit? He could look online for that information if he needed to. He didn't have to listen to it from some officious woman on the phone. Sticking her nose into his affairs.

He took a deep drag on his joint and blew as much of the smoke cloud out of the window as possible. He needed to calm down. And the weed was the only way he knew how. It had been for the longest time. Strangely that seemed to be the one thing that Alexi could always find the money for. There was always money to be found for essentials. But he was onto his last bag. When that was gone, that was it. Unless… Hopefully, he was less than twenty-four hours away from being told he was back in the money. Burrow Hall would be his. He could use that as a bargaining tool and as collateral should anyone say that he needed to cough up. Because he did owe some people money. In fact, he owed some of them a lot. Like a hell of a lot. He'd escaped them. For now. But if they did find out where he was, then he'd be royally screwed. One funeral in the family was enough for the moment. Anyway, he'd changed since then. In many ways.

Tomorrow, things would be different. Much. But for now, as Simply Red had prophetically sung, money was indeed too tight to mention. So why the intrusive woman on the phone had picked now to start talking about it quite so verbosely was beyond him. If it was too tight to mention, then the best bet was not to mention it at all, right? He'd only picked up the phone as he thought it might be one of the housing companies calling.

He took another deep pull on the joint. He should block her number.

Roll on tomorrow.

Violet had to admit that she would have been very hard-pushed to make such a delicious carrot cake. It was moist without being waterlogged and light without being crumbly. And it was the perfect accompaniment to a pot of tea, under cosy, served at the kitchen table of Burrow Hall in a bone-china cup. Tea tasted different when it was presented like that. Even when 'downstairs', which is essentially where they were right now. She had seen enough of *Downton Abbey* to know that. Violet didn't know what it was about housekeepers, bone china and a knitted cosy, but it appeared to be the perfect trinity for success when it came to serving a flawless brew. She would do her best to emulate Mrs Turner when she served 'upstairs' tomorrow.

'So, who is coming tomorrow then, so I know how many to expect?' Violet asked Mrs Turner.

'The person reading the will, me, Herbert, Sheena, Master Alexi and Miss Belinda. That's it, I imagine, unless anybody else turns up unexpectedly. Can't imagine they will. So, a plate of sandwiches and a round of teas will be all that's required. I'll show you where the bar is as well, in case anyone wants anything stronger. But at least if you're sorting it, then I can relax a little. I've never been to a will reading before, which is surprising given the number of funerals I've been to at my age. I don't know what I shall wear.'

'Something befitting both the hot weather and the sombre nature of the occasion. Not an easy mix, but I'm sure you'll manage. I'll come early, maybe get Margaret to help out too with slicing the bread for the sandwiches, if that's okay.' Violet smiled inwardly, pleased with herself for thinking on her feet and getting another member of Team C.R.A.B. involved.

'Yes, of course. Many hands make light work and all that. I've bought enough food in to feed a battalion. A lot of it is veggie as Belinda likes to be green. Well, green with the odd meat pasty as far as I can work out. I found a wrapper in her bedroom bin. I suppose they are irresistible at times. But I know she'll want it all just so for tomorrow.'

'Where is Belinda today? Is she upstairs too?' enquired Violet, sipping on her tea.

'No, she's shopping, I think. She went yesterday. She was out for ages. She came back with loads of clothes, but I think I heard her moaning to Herbert this morning that she would have to pop out again as she still didn't think she had the right outfit. I guess she was panicking about what to wear tomorrow too.'

Violet returned to the subject of food. 'I suppose you're used to buying a lot of food. Sir Buster had such a wonderful appetite, didn't he? I hear his chiller was absolutely rammed with goodies the morning he went fishing.'

'Only healthy stuff, though. There was no chance of me trying to get Sir Buster to eat anything that wasn't steeped in nutrition and low in calories. He's always been the same. He was a bit of a nightmare with the kids when they were younger. He would never let them eat the Easter eggs from the village egg hunt. Mrs Burniston would have to sneak the eggs to their bedrooms afterwards and tell them to eat them without their dad's knowledge.' She tutted. 'That's not right is it, kids should be allowed to have a bit of chocolate now and again. And he would never let me cook a decent fry-up for them. Don't get me wrong, Sir Buster was a great dad, always lots of fun to be around, but he was a stickler for health and nutrition. I suppose that came from his sporty days.'

'It must be a hard habit to break if you're used to treating your body like a temple, I suppose. You don't get to represent your country at sports from a diet of burger and chips.'

'No, he was always very healthy on the food front until the day he died. He may not have been the easiest man to cook for sometimes, but he was always appreciative of a good, healthily balanced meal. I do love to see a good appetite on a man.'

'So, no KitKat Chunkys and a packet of Wotsits for Sir Buster's packed lunch when he went fishing? I must admit, I do love a cheesy puff myself, very moreish,' commented Violet.

'Oh, heaven's above, no. I knew exactly what he would want. Apples, bananas, natural yoghurt, a muesli bar, a packet of protein balls – ridiculous things they are, if you ask me, but he loved them – and his favourite low-fat egg mayonnaise sandwiches and a flask of tea. He'd asked me to prepare it the night before as he said he would be up and out at about 5 a.m., but I'm a light sleeper and I knew I'd be up anyway, so I made some tea and a fresh batch of egg mayo sandwiches that morning. I was literally foil wrapping them as he was walking out the door. Foil keeps them so much fresher than cling film. That makes food so sweaty, I find. Horrid stuff.' She almost shuddered at the thought of it. 'He normally spent all day down at his lake when he went fishing. He'd be there with his radio on, listening to music and having a lovely time. It was his personal happy place. I think that's why he kept it private. It's so sad that he's gone, but if you're going to die, then the lake is a beautiful setting.'

'His poor heart just gave up. So unexpected,' coaxed Violet.

'I know. Seems so odd, given the fact that he was such a strong and healthy man, but what is it they say about the Lord and his mysterious ways.'

'Quite, you never know what's around the corner. You need to be grateful for every day. What you do think is around the corner for you now, Mrs Turner? You've worked here at Burrow Hall for years. Both you and Herbert could happily retire, couldn't you?'

'That all depends on the reading of the will. I'd like to stay on and work for whoever is in charge of the Hall next. I could stop tomorrow, but you become engrained, don't you? I've been the housekeeper here for so long now that I really can't imagine doing anything else. I'd like to think there's a good few years left in me yet. Mind you, I'd have said the same about Sir Buster. In fact, I'd have put money on it.' Mrs Turner picked up another slice of carrot cake and nibbled at the edge. 'You just never can tell, can you?'

Chapter 36

Sergeant Samuel Pollett was just polishing off a sneaky cheese and onion slice he'd grabbed from Rita's for lunch at his work desk when the phone sounded. He picked it up just as WPC Horton wandered into the office and waved at him with a half-smile. He screwed the white paper bag his slice had been in into a little ball and threw it into the bin as swiftly as he could.

Paula sat down at her own desk with an loud and slightly peeved sigh. He was of the opinion that both of them were finding it a little bit strange and somewhat dull dealing with things like squashed marrows after the excitement of Sir Buster's body being discovered at the weekend. May he rest in peace. Sergeant Pollett was more than aware that none of his favourite crime series from when he was younger had groundbreakingly dramatic and high-tension episodes featuring crimes against root vegetables.

'Hello, Sergeant Pollett, Rooney-at-Burrow, how can I help you?'

Paula watched with intrigue as Sergeant Pollett reacted to whomever was speaking to at the end of the phone. She normally didn't listen to his conversations, having learnt to white-noise them into the background if they didn't sound at all appetising, but when this one started with Sergeant Pollett's rather expressive reaction of 'bloody hell, where?' she knew that something juicy was being discussed. Her ears pricked up immediately.

She couldn't wait to grill him when he came off the phone five minutes and a lot of scribbling in his desk pad later. His face was flushed, his cheeks alive with colour. His face was a mixture of concern and excitement.

'Well, that sounded interesting?' she enquired.

'It was. That was Sergeant Sheridan over in Darrochdean. She thought we should know they've found a body hanging in a tree in a wooded area between there

363

and here. About fifteen miles away.'

'Blimey, a suicide? That's always so sad. But what's that got to do with us?'

'Because there was a note attached to the man apologising for killing Sir Buster.'

WPC Horton could feel a wash of coldness run through her body. It was now her turn to utter a 'bloody hell'. She felt her mouth drop open and her eyebrows raise in disbelief. 'Who was it?'

'Some shady character called Jeremiah Halliwell. Bit of a petty criminal over the years. Lives in a caravan in Darrochdean. Well, lived…'

'What did the note say? Why did he kill Sir Buster?'

Sergeant Pollett scanned his notepad. 'It said: I'M SORRY FOR KILLING SIR BUSTER. FORGIVE ME.'

'So Violet was right after all? She's a canny old thing, isn't she? What was the motive?'

'Nobody knows as yet. Sergeant Sheridan is phoning from the crime scene. She wants me to come over and see for myself. She said there's something odd about the message.'

'Oh my gosh, let's go now. And what's so weird about the suicide note?'

'It's made up from letters cut from magazines and newspapers. Just like the ones Sheena found in Sir Buster's book.'

'Flipping heck. So you think this Jeremiah fella was the one threatening Sir Buster?'

'I don't know, but I've watched enough crime dramas over the years to know that somebody writing a suicide note is highly unlikely to spend time cutting out letters and gluing them onto a piece of paper. It seems needlessly elaborate. Something just doesn't make sense. Let's get over there now.'

Sergeant Pollett and WPC Horton were in their police car, siren on and driving past the 'Welcome to Rooney-at-Burrow' sign, leaving the village behind them, in less than two minutes. Sergeant Pollett always loved the sound of the siren. It made him feel like a ten-year-old in front of the TV again. And the fact that he was on his way to uncover a mystery rather than a marrow definitely added to his excitement.

Chapter 37

Pearl was still thinking about the fact that one of the letters on the threatening notes had come from a crafting magazine. Maybe more. Despite the connection, she refused to believe that anyone who knew the joy of decent découpage and the hypnotic beauty of heat embossing would be embroiled in any kind of dastardly dealings in an attempt to terrorise an old man. Like a bad glue, it just didn't stick. And there was no way that anyone connected with Team C.R.A.B. would be involved. Was there?

Pearl tried to push the thought from her mind as she waited for her call to connect. She checked her watch. It would be mid-morning in Barbados. Her uncle Josh was expecting her call. It had been a couple of days since she had sent him her phone snap of Alexi Burniston to see if anyone recognised him. Uncle Josh would definitely have news for her by now, she knew that. He was like a human Google. If ever you needed any answers about anything, especially if had something to do with his Caribbean home, then Josh was your man. He always knew someone who knew someone who knew someone. He was that kind of laid-back, affable, loved-by-all guy. He was also Pearl's favourite uncle. A feeling that seemed to be mutual as he picked up the phone.

'Hey, my favourite niece. When are you coming back to see us over here in the sunshine? Bring those twins and that man of yours. Barbados needs to see that beautiful winning smile that only you can bring.'

His flattery always made Pearl blush. She let out a girly giggle. You could be having the worst, incredibly bothersome, most middle-aged day ever and two seconds with Uncle Josh and you would feel like a carefree teenager again. She adored him.

'Hopefully soon, Uncle Josh, hopefully soon. How are you?'

'The Caribbean sun is shining, beer is chilling for later

and I've got some money in my pocket, so I'm as good as good can be right now. Plus, I'm speaking to you, Pearl, so life is sweet.'

It sounded heavenly. Sometimes Pearl missed the easy-going vibes of her home country. 'Oh, I miss that sun, believe you me. I'll have a word with Noah and see when we can get ourselves booked onto a flight and come visit. It's long overdue.'

'The beach party welcome is waiting...'

As much as she would've loved to have fantasised on that idea, Pearl was keen to get down to business. 'So, tell me, Josh, did you recognise the photo I sent you of Alexi Burniston. Reckons he lived in Barbados and did lots of great charitable work for *our people* yet hasn't got a clue about anything on the island.' She was still reeling from Alexi's expert knowledge on the fictitious Saint Aloysius The Ninth.

'There was definitely something highly suspicious about him when I saw the photo. It's not the clearest of photos, is it, but I sat and studied it and then it came to me. I know that face. It's a bit older than the last time I saw it, and certainly a lot less tanned, but it's definitely him.'

'Who?' Pearl could feel a flutter of excitement butterfly through her at Josh's news. She couldn't wait to tell the others. Whatever it may be.

'Well, he has quite the history. He called himself Alex Brown when he was here. We're talking many years ago now when he first came here. I didn't know him at first. I only knew him when he came to Freights Bay in Oistins.'

'Such a lovely beach.' It was always one of Pearl's favourites. And she loved Oistins as it was the home of the famed Barbados Fish-Fry. Some of the best catches on the island ended up being dished up to locals and tourists at the fishing village's famous market. The nostalgic thought jogged her into the here and now and the fact that there was some fish in the freezer that she should defrost for Noah's supper when he got home later.

Uncle Josh continued with his revelations. 'Alex Brown was a total con man. If there was a dollar to be made in an underhand way, then he would do it. He was notorious for tempting holidaymakers into parting with their cash. He had worked his way around the island over the course of a few years, moving from area to area. He worked most of the surfing areas and the tourist spots as that was where the big-money potential lay – Dover Beach, Sand Bank, Surfer's Point, Long Beach. You name it – he worked them all.'

'How, what did he do?' Pearl was eager for more.

'At first, he just conned tourists into giving him money for non-existent excursions. He'd hang around at beach bars, outside hotels and at coach stops, spotting susceptible tourists and telling them about luxury private trips that weren't advertised by the average travel agent or excursion shop. He'd inform them about special hidden things that most tourists would never hear about – sunken treasure ships, special breweries for extra-strong Bajan drinks, jeep rides to lost villages. He would basically make stuff up.'

'Lost villages? And people really believed him?' asked Pearl. Surely, they could have seen straight through him as quickly as she did. Two minutes in The Six Pennies and she could tell he was full of BS. Jimmy had eventually taught Pearl what that actually meant after her confusion before. She didn't like the phrase, but it seemed extremely fitting for Alexi, she had to admit.

'He had a talent for picking the right people. Mostly elderly and rich or young and up for adventure off the beaten track. Thrill-seekers wanting something different to tell the folks back home. They'd cough up a deposit and arrange a time to be picked up at their hotel for a secret trip. And, of course, he'd take their money and never show up. He could keep doing it as most tourists would only be in town a few days and not be able to track him down. He obviously had the gift of the gab as he made a pretty penny.'

'How do you know all of this?' asked Pearl.

'I shared his photo in a lot of WhatsApp groups here in Barbados and also on a few of the local Facebook pages. Technology has made the island a much smaller place. I'm in constant contact with people all over the island now – bar owners, hotel workers, et cetera. It's part of my job.'

Indeed, the reason that Josh was so well connected these days was that he had his own recruitment agency. If there were jobs to be filled, then he would know a very likely candidate or two. Josh's reputation stretched right across the island.

'So, lots of people remembered him?'

He nodded. 'Once one did, that seemed to get the ball rolling and jog people's memories. Some knew him much more than others. Alex was not stupid. He would go on a tourist spree and then lay low for a while. Or change his appearance a bit – dye his hair, shave it or weave some dreads. That's how he looked when I knew him. Which is why I struggled at first with the photo. He would spend a lot of his time chilling on the beach or getting stoned. He was a big one for that. But there were people in every hot spot on the island who remember him. He was pretty creepy and sleazy. A total tourist pest.'

'But what about the housing projects and the charities that he said he worked on?' Pearl asked, although she had her suspicions.

'Completely made up. Apparently, he used to brag to people, normally when he was stoned, about how his rich folks would send him money to help out as he told them he was working for charities doing good for...'

Both Josh and Pearl said, *'Our people'* in unison.

'You got it,' echoed Josh. 'He had money coming in from his gullible folks, but apparently that stopped when they began asking too many questions about the housing projects and Alex couldn't give them any evidence as it was all tosh. But he must have made enough from trusting and naïve tourists to keep his weed habit alight as he had turned into a total stoner by the time he had worked his way to Freights Bay when I knew him.'

'That's probably why he can't remember the names of places and believed in my phony Saint Aloysius The Ninth,' remarked Pearl. 'His brain is probably more mashed than marrow chutney.'

'And he's still smoking now, you say?' asked Josh.

'Oh yes, the bag in his glove compartment was very hefty indeed.' Pearl had filled her uncle in on her dealings with Alexi when she had sent the photo.

'Doing it on the beach in paradise is one thing, but driving around with it in your car is quite another. That's not going to end well,' Josh commented.

Pearl drummed her fingers on the table she was sitting

at in her cottage dining room. 'Precisely. So, basically, Alexi Burniston is Alex Brown, a rather pathetic and small-fry con man?'

'Hold your horses, Pearl. He was small-fry, but here's where things become really interesting. And somewhat alarming.'

Pearl stopped drumming to listen fully.

'It appears that one of his last con jobs on the island was a lot more serious than just ripping off a tourist with their holiday cash. Your man had moved on from when I knew him to a beach area across the south side of the island. He was doing the same tricks for a while, conning visitors, usual stuff. But then he became friendly with one of the bar owners there, a guy called Vin Sutton, who rather foolishly seemed to take a shine to Alex and think that he was harmless. He just saw that Alex could charm the tourists and thought that he would be good PR for the bar. So, he employed him a few days a week as one of those people who butter you up and then bring you to a bar to spend your money. It worked for both of them. Alex got free drinks, a cash-in-hand job and still lots of time to try to con tourists on the side. He was onto a nice little earner. And Vin got backsides on seats.'

'Then what happened?' Pearl pressed, knowing the story was only just beginning.

'Alex got mighty greedy. The bar started doing really well, becoming one of the most popular around, and Vin was adamant that part of the success was due to his friendship with Alex. So, he suggested they go into business together and open another bar. Vin was making good money and Alex was still bragging about his dad sending him cash, whether that was true or not, but I suspect not, so Vin thought that Alex was good for a fifty/fifty stake if they tried to buy a bar together. Alex agreed and suggested that he himself would find a place as he was good at spotting a bargain and could talk a prospective seller into a fantastic price. A few days pass and Alex comes back to Vin and tells him he has found a bar and that the seller had agreed a much lower selling price if they pay in cash. Vin went to see the bar and it's basically an empty building. But it had potential and Vin saw that. They both met with the owner and a cash price was agreed. Later at the bar, Alex tells Vin that he'll do the deal alone with the guy as he set it up and that if Vin gave him his half of the cash, he'd get his own from the bank on the way to go and pay the man. Vin trusted Alex, gave him the cash and guess what?'

'What?' Pearl already knew the answer.

'He never saw Alex again. Him and Vin's money gone for good.'

'But what about the new bar?'

'The building was never for sale. It was just an empty space Alex spotted. The supposed seller was someone Alex had bunged a wad of dollars to in order say what Vin needed to hear. The whole thing was a set-up.'

A gasp escaped from Pearl. 'And this Vin Sutton never saw Alex again or got his money back?'

'Not until you sent that photo through, Pearl, you little beauty. He saw it in one of the WhatsApp groups. Vin lost everything back then. The money he gave Alex was about 150,000 Barbadian dollars. That's about £50,000. It wiped Vin's business out at the time. Ruined him. But that was nearly a decade ago. Vin is a strong man, a good man, he fought back and now he owns a few bars on the island, through hard graft and a bit of good luck. But what Alex, or Alexi did, could have ruined Vin for good. The cheating scumbag fled the island with his cash. We're a trusting breed us Barbadians, you know that, nice and laid-back. But not about this. People were looking for Alex Brown, but they should have been looking for Alexi Burniston.'

'Blimey, Vin must be fuming.'

'Oh, he is, Pearl, he is, and he wants his money back. If this Alexi has a flashy car and a weed habit, then he must have money. Plus, it sounds like he might be even more minted now his dad is dead. So, yeah, Vin Sutton does want his money back, and he wants it back now. With added interest, to the tune of £100,000.'

'Wow. I don't blame him, though.'

'Vin's a tough businessman these days. He's had to battle to get where he is today. He's successful now, but no thanks to this Alexi. I've spoken to Vin and I have his bank details and he says that Alexi can transfer the money. If he does and he does it soon, then they're good. It's that or the alternative. Which I don't think Alexi will want.

Now that Vin knows where the scumbag is, he gets on a plane to come visit and persuade him face to face. And I am totally certain that Alexi would not want that. It's up to him. But Vin wants paying either way and he won't be taking no for an answer.'

Pearl gulped. She knew what was coming next. She listened to the voice of her uncle.

'And, Pearl, I hate to say it, but you're going to have to be the one to tell Alexi Burniston that he needs to transfer the money as soon as possible. Or else.'

For once, Pearl knew that even laid-back Uncle Josh and his Caribbean cool was being deadly serious. And somehow, she'd ended up being pulled in to play the messenger.

Chapter 38

If Alexi's ears were already burning, then they should have been volcanically hot by the time that Bailey Frazer-Ferguson, interior designer to the stars, and Tanya Lumley-West, socialite and narcissistic reality star, landed back in the UK after their eight-hour flight from Abu Dhabi. To the constant soundtrack of two chinking champagne glasses, they had discussed him during practically every air mile.

Having cleared customs and deposited a very tipsy Tanya into her chauffeur-driven Jaguar, Bailey had reunited with Jimmy, who had chosen to arrive at the airport in the old Ford Escort van that they used for errands on the farm.

He was apologetic about this choice. 'I'm sorry about

the van, I couldn't find the keys to the car and I was so worried about being late to meet you after washing the tractor down. I'm sure your cases will survive being rammed in between all that crap in the back.'

The couple were just turning onto the motorway beyond the airport grounds in the van and were heading for home. Bailey chose not to look around at what the crap might be potentially staining his Gucci suitcases, but he was sure he had spotted a tractor tyre and some kind of pump from a milking machine back there. Thankfully, an afternoon of much fizz drinking at 30,000 feet made you more tranquil and less analytical than normal.

Bailey didn't really care where he was sitting or what his cases were up to now that he was back with Jimmy again. Even if Jimmy's jeans were splattered with mud and his T-shirt was far from ironed. He leant across to kiss Jimmy on the cheek. It was, as ever, a joy to be back home.

'Get out of it, will you, I'm trying to drive. Lord knows this van is temperamental enough as it is without you slobbering all over me.' Jimmy was joking about the slobber, if not about the van. It was exceedingly old and prone to fall apart at any moment, but for now,' like a comfy pair of battered old slippers, it still did the job.

'I'm just pleased to see you, you big chunk of farming loveliness.' Bailey grinned. He was a little sozzled himself but thankfully still able to string his words together.

'Chunk? I've been called better,' smiled Jimmy.

Bailey reached his hand across to rest it on Jimmy's leg. He began to try to pick off a fleck of mud on his jeans with his nails without thinking.

'So, Tanya was full of information about Alexi Burniston,' he began.

'So is Sir Buster's eldest exactly who he says he is?'

'Well, he is known to lots of reality stars and low-listers, but for all the wrong reasons. Don't ever tell Tanya that I used the term low-listers, by the way. She'd never buy a moleskin lampshade or an objet d'art from me again.'

'Like I would. So, what did she say?'

'He's been on the scene for a few years and was kind of popular with a lot of people to begin with because he used to flash the cash and supply them with a good time.' Bailey showed what he meant by good time by putting his thumb and forefinger to his lips and pretending to drag. 'He would always be in the clubs buying people drinks and saying that he should manage them. A few took him up on it and that went well for a while.'

'There's a but coming, isn't there?' asked Jimmy, the van kangarooing a little as he changed gear.

'There sure is. He made a few dodgy choices for his clients when it came to sponsorship deals and partnerships online. Pairing people with diet pills that didn't work and contained all sorts of horrid stuff tested on animals or with a clothing company that had very blatant links to sweatshops in the Far East. Let's just say he didn't have a lot of integrity when it came to what he pushed upon his clients.'

'But surely any manager would do the same. Isn't it the nature of the business? Not that I profess to know anything about it. But I do get the impression that half of your clients would do an Instagram post for the devil himself if it meant they could filter themselves to look like a shop dummy and then get paid a small fortune. Integrity isn't really in the job description, is it?'

Bailey knew Jimmy had a point. 'But it's a trust issue too between manager and client, isn't it? Once that trust goes, it can never be repaired and Alexi didn't just break that trust, he smashed it into oblivion with a battering ram.'

'How come?'

'He left his clients high and dry when it came to advising them when the inevitable backlash came from the press. There would be all of these online trolls giving his clients real grief about supporting something hideous and instead of coming up with a quote and a plan of action to pacify the whole thing and make it blow over, suddenly he would be uncontactable and not taking calls or returning messages. Tanya said that one of her friends from *Seduction Central* was duped into promoting a fake tan product that contained some kind of ingredient that ended up giving you the worst headaches and nausea. Like, proper poorly. But it didn't happen until a few days after you'd put the fake tan on and it had soaked into your system. You'd be deep brown and then, boom, literally as sick as a dog. Throwing your guts up for days.'

'That sounds horrid. Um… I've got to ask…'

'Yeah, I know. It's a dating show, a group of singletons put in a house together looking for love. It was massive two summers ago.' Bailey knew Jimmy inside out and knew straight away that *Seduction Central* would not be on his radar. He was also fully aware that it was one of Sheena's favourite things to watch. She would love to know that gossip. 'So, Alexi would leave them hanging and then suddenly get back in touch two weeks or so later when the storm had passed, saying that he had family issues, or his phone had broken or whatever. Making excuses as to why he hadn't helped them.'

'So, he's a complete coward. Couldn't they just dump him?' The van spluttered again as Jimmy took the slip road off the motorway. 'Come on, old boy, don't give up on us, now.' He was talking to the vehicle and not his boyfriend.

'As a client, you're normally tied down for at least a year with your contract and there's always all sorts of small print meaning that your choices are as limited and as controlling as possible. Especially if Alexi wrote it in the first place. So, their hands were tied.'

'It all sounds horribly one-sided,' said Jimmy. 'I'm so glad I'm just a farmer. The only thing controlling me is Mother Nature.'

'But it gets worse. It then turns out that this girl from *Seduction Central* decided to try to speak to the company behind the fake tan product and ended up in a blazing row with this wide boy who runs it who tells her that she should be glad to have pocketed the £100,000 for it and just shut up.'

'A hundred. Thousand. Pounds!' Jimmy separated the words with a pause to underscore his total disbelief at the amount. 'Blimey, I think I'd consider going the colour of a Duroc and suffering some sickness for that kind of money.'

Jimmy could see from the puzzled look on Bailey's face that it was now his time to explain.

'A Duroc is a breed of pig. Really deep brown in colour. Always well built. Very muscly.'

'They sound divine,' laughed Bailey, before returning to his story. 'Well, that kind of money is not what Tanya's mate thought she was getting, because Alexi had told her that the company were paying her £50,000. And, of course, let's remember that he would be taking his own twenty per cent out that too. So out of a £100,000 deal, Tanya's mate saw £30,000 of it and Alexi pocketed the rest. It turns out that your man Alexi Burniston did it with lots of deals. It all started to come out of the woodwork. So, as soon as they could, all his clients pretty much dumped him.'

Jimmy clicked the indicators and went to steer the van into a side road. Just as they were about to turn, a police car sped past them, siren shrieking. Jimmy was pretty positive that it was Samuel Pollett at the wheel but wasn't completely sure and chose to ignore it.

A sign on the verge said that Rooney-at-Burrow was fifteen miles away. It was the part of their journey where two lanes were now to become a luxury. Nearly all of the homeward stetch from here on in was single lane. For a moment, the van's engine cut out. Silence filled the air inside the vehicle before somehow the motor coughed back into life again. Jimmy shifted in his seat nervously.

'So, what does he do now?' asked Jimmy.

'That's anybody's guess. Tanya said this was about

eighteen months ago and when he stopped managing the celebs, he just disappeared. He never popped up in the bars or clubs or anything. He had a house that he lived at in London, but none of his clients had been there, so they had no idea how to contact him. And his telephone number stopped working too. He must have changed it. He vanished into thin air with all of their money. But the word in Tanya's world is that apparently he's spent all of the money now and is flat out broke. Someone who knew someone else had heard something. You know how the grapevine works. If that's true, then I imagine that he will be gagging to get his hands on whatever Sir Buster has left him in the will.'

'I bet. What a lowlife. A right nasty piece of work.' Jimmy had no sooner finished the sentence than the engine of the van cut out again. This time, despite furious pedal pressing and key turning, the welcome growl of the engine didn't return. The van glided to a halt, slap bang in the middle of a single-lane country road, blocking it completely. 'Oh, well that's a bugger.'

Jimmy tried to start the engine again, His attempts

were in vain. As he did so, a small cloud of steam started to escape from underneath the bonnet at the front of the van.

'Oh, well that is definitely not a good sign. We had better push the van to the side of the road to try to make it as passable as possible if anyone needs to get through.'

'Excuse me?' snipped Bailey, a little sassier than he'd meant to. 'Like where? We are the road. We fill it. And besides, I'm not dressed to push a van, Jimmy. This Prada turtleneck and fleece pants combo screams first-class air travel and not shoving a clapped-out van into a brambly hedge. Why don't we just give Oscar a ring and see if he can come and tow us home in the truck, darling. I'm sure he won't mind.'

'I'll just give it a little push. It might help a bit,' said Jimmy. 'C'mon let's get out.'

Bailey was a little too fuzzy-headed to disagree and the two of them did so. Bailey stood by the van as Jimmy attempted to push it. As Jimmy bent over at the back of the vehicle and pushed the car all of two inches, making diddly-squat difference for anyone who would indeed try to pass them, Bailey couldn't help but feel his heart fill with love.

With his mud-splattered jeans and his un-ironed T-shirt, once again Bailey was reminded of how much he adored Jimmy.

The drive home had been a journey of learning. Jimmy had learnt about one of the most popular reality TV shows of recent times and Bailey had definitely learnt a new pig breed. And as he stood in designer clothes next to an overgrown hedge, he had learnt yet again that opposites really do attract. He and Jimmy proved that every day.

Jimmy had also learnt that perhaps it was time to trade in the van, but more importantly that Alexi Burniston may not be the flashy success he was pretending to be. Which could prove to be very interesting indeed.

Chapter 39

Samuel Pollett had never had to watch the dead body of a man being lowered from a tree before. And for all his macho bravado at times and his chest-puffing about how much he loved the excitement of his job, it was not an easy thing to watch. Even though he had been informed that Jeremiah Halliwell was not the most savoury of characters, he couldn't help but think that he was somebody's son, somebody's friend, maybe somebody's dad. Seeing a life at an end, even when it was somebody who was already advancing in years – nearly sixty, he'd been told – was not a pleasant thing to witness. And he'd now seen it twice in a few short days. Samuel may have loved his job, but sights like this would never be easy for the sergeant.

He and WPC Horton had spent most of the afternoon

speaking to Sergeant Sheridan about the find. According to her, a dog walker had found the body hanging from a tree late that morning. A length of rope had been used by Jeremiah to tie around his neck and then attach to a thick branch. She believed that he must have climbed up the tree himself so that he could jump off and that his body had been there since the day before, although time of death could not be pinpointed as yet. Severe burn marks around the neck confirmed that Jeremiah's death was caused by the tightening of the rope. His car was found at a nearby car park. The suicide note confessing to Sir Buster's death was attached with a safety pin to Jeremiah's T-shirt.

It was the suicide note that Samuel was keen to discuss with WPC Horton when they were alone in their squad car after the other officers from Darrochdean had left and the body of Jeremiah Halliwell had been removed. Even though their work at the crime scene was finished and the case appeared cut and dry, something was not sitting easy with Sergeant Pollett.

'Why would somebody who was going to kill

themselves spend time creating that note? Going to the effort of cutting out all of those letters and sticking them to a piece of paper if they were just going to then pin it onto their outfit and then kill themself? It doesn't ring true.'

'I couldn't agree more, Sarge,' said WPC Horton, who had found the afternoon just as confusing and as disturbing as her boss. 'It does seem a bit fruitless. And a bit show-offy. He could have just shoved a handwritten note in his pocket and we would have found it. Bodies will always be searched. But the actual skill and attention to detail of putting it together and then pinning it right in the middle of his T-shirt so that it was centre stage seems dreadfully...' She searched for the right word. She plumped for 'cinematic'.

'And why come all of this way?' remarked Samuel. 'He lives only a few miles from here. He could have killed himself in the comfort of his caravan. Or I'm sure there are trees closer to him than here if he was really set on hanging himself.'

WPC Horton nodded. 'Maybe he liked this spot.

Maybe he'd been here before. It's off the beaten track, so maybe he didn't want to be disturbed.'

'Good point, Horton. But it doesn't seem to gel in my mind. The man was a petty criminal. It was easy to police-check him. He's got a list of offences as long as your arm. In and out of jail for all sorts over the years, mostly low-rent stuff. Fights and theft. So murdering someone seems a little dramatic for this stage of his life. And why Sir Buster of all people? Did they actually know each other, or was it a random killing? I've never seen him before and I'd never heard Sir Buster mentioning him.'

'It's weird, but when I saw his face, I felt like I recognised it from somewhere. But I can't think where. That ginger goatee seemed familiar. I was thinking maybe I had come across him through work, but I don't think so,' WPC Horton mused.

Sergeant Pollett scratched his chin. 'He just doesn't seem like the kind of person who would orchestrate such an elaborate death and go to the trouble of creating the notes. It doesn't suit his character.'

Both police officers were thinking exactly the same

thing, but until now had been unable to actually say it. Their conversation suddenly began to ricochet back and forth.

WPC Horton began. 'Maybe he didn't create the notes'

'And someone else did.'

'Because they wanted to frame him.'

'And make it look like case closed.'

'When, in fact, somebody did kill Sir Buster for some reason.'

'And that person is still very much alive.'

'So this isn't a suicide?'

No, it might be a murder. In fact it might be two...'

'Poor Sir Buster...'

'Maybe Aunty Violet was right after all.'

Both officers shared a moment of contemplative silence before Paula Horton let out a spooked scream. It made a shocked Sergeant Pollett do the same. It wasn't due to their potential conclusions, it was due to Paula's phone sounding rather loudly in her lap and scaring her from her thoughts. She looked at the screen.

'Talk of the devil. Her ears must be burning. It's Violet. Shall I…' She looked to her boss for approval and he nodded. 'Hello, Violet, what can I do for you?'

'I'm phoning about the fingerprints. Any revelations as yet?'

'Not on that front no, but…' WPC Horton looked at her boss again, seeking his approval to tell Violet what they had both found. She pulled her ear away from the phone and mouthed to Samuel, 'Should I tell her?'

He mouthed back that she should as word would no doubt be in the papers the next day. Plus he was interested in his aunt's take on things to see if she would share the same doubts as he and WPC Horton.

For the next few minutes, Paula shared every detail of the day's events to a highly attentive Violet. Having finished recapping, she ended by asking, 'So what do you think?' Paula then clicked her phone to speaker and rested it on the dashboard between her and Sergeant Pollett.

Violet was adamant. 'It's all too convenient and way too blatant. This man, Jeremiah, does not sound like someone who wants to be in the spotlight. He sounds like the shady type to skulk in the sidelines. Not that I really want to speak ill of the dead, of course, but I don't think he would come up with such a flamboyant plot as to write all of these notes and scare Sir Buster. And then why kill him? What does he gain? What's the motive? It doesn't make sense. I suppose the police will be searching his caravan top to bottom, so maybe some evidence will appear, but I definitely think somebody else is behind the notes and that this is a ploy to frame this petty criminal into taking the rap – is that the phrase you police types use? – for the death. If he knew Sir Buster, surely one of us in the village would know of him or have seen him over the years. What does he looks like?'

Paula answered. 'He's approaching sixty, he's got long ginger hair and a ginger goatee beard. Speckles of grey in it, though, and he was wearing—'

'A baseball cap?' interrupted Violet.

'How on earth do you know that, Aunty Violet?' asked Samuel, genuinely perplexed at his aunt's apparent clairvoyant ways.

'Because, dear boy, I've seen him. He was skulking in

Brewer's Loop earlier in the week, fingering two balls of wool in my window. Looked very shady.'

'Oh my God,' piped up Paula. 'He was the man stroking Mr Bublé outside my cottage. I know I'd seen his face before. When he was alive, that is.'

'So why was he in Rooney-at-Burrow?' asked Samuel. 'Sir Buster was dead by then. Unless he came to see Alexi or Belinda, of course – maybe he knows the family.'

'I think that's a possibility, but I think whoever he came to see could well be the person behind the notes. Now all four of them.' Violet paused for a second to let the cogs of her mind whir a little more. 'Can I ask about the latest note. The cuttings…'

Paula knew exactly what Violet was going to ask and this time it was her turn to interrupt. 'One of the letters was from the crafting magazine. I recognised the yellow and purple colour combo for the typeface again.'

'Well,' said Violet. 'There you have it. He didn't get the magazine from my shop when I saw him, and I'll ask Sheena if she has ever seen him, but I doubt if she will have. Unless our petty criminal picked up the delights of crochet and needlepoint when he was at her Majesty's pleasure or the police find bags of découpage at his caravan and Jeremiah had a subscription to a craft magazine, I think we can guess that he didn't put the note together. There's not another shop around here for miles that sells that magazine.'

'So if he didn't, then who did?' asked Samuel.

'Someone who lives a little closer to home and, it seems, although it pains me to say it, may have an interest in crafting. Or at least someone in their household may do.'

The three of them remained silent for a few seconds.

It was Violet who continued the conversation. 'Now, why don't you both pop in here on the way home and show me that latest note. I'll put the kettle on and I think I've got some Battenberg in the cupboard that needs eating, Samuel.'

Resistance was, as ever, futile. And the Battenberg sounded mouth-wateringly enticing. 'We'll see you in a bit, Aunty Vi. But there's something I need to do here first. We'll be over in a couple of hours. See you then.'

Violet rang off.

'Something else to do? What's that?' asked Paula.

Samuel Pollett opened the squad car door and turned to WPC Horton. 'It's just a feeling, but come with me... and wear your gloves.'

Chapter 40

Stephanie Brooks waved at the truck passing in front of The Six Pennies as she shut the front door for the night. It was towing a van behind it. Three figures waved back – Jimmy, Bailey and Oscar.

Steph checked her watch. It was 9.30 p.m. She and Phill had decided to shut up early. Apart from a few devout regulars and the usual bit of passing trade heading through Rooney-at-Burrow for whatever reason, it had been the most uneventful of nights at The Six Pennies. Pearl and Noah Wheeler had popped in for a gin and tonic and a pint of bitter. Dr Roberts had treated himself to a lager top. Belinda Flatt had popped in too at one point. Not for a drink, strangely, but merely just to check the details for her father's memorial night. Even though it was not 'her kind of thing', as she told Steph and Phill, she said she would be there to raise a glass to her late father. It was the kind of night that Stephanie Brooks found utterly crushing. No glitz, no glamour, no excitement. Just an overwhelming sense of local banality.

Her husband, Phill, of course, was of exactly the opposite opinion. To him, an evening like the one they had just experienced meant that it was easy, friendly, simple, cosy and typifying of life in the village. Ordinary people coming to the heart of the village community, the local pub, to enjoy a moment of joy and perhaps a moment of escape from their working day. To be amongst their own. To him, it was bliss.

It was a point he was keen to make to his wife as he passed her a cup of tea as they sat outside in the beer garden, illuminated only by the lamps dotted around the outdoor area now that the sun was beginning to marginally fade.

'How lovely to be shutting up early. We will be crawling into bed before midnight for once. Lovely to see Sir Buster's daughter too. She seemed nice. It seems that everyone is looking forward to the memorial night. I reckon we'll do a roaring trade on bar snacks, come the weekend.'

Steph was not convinced – well, not about Belinda anyway. As for the popularity of the bar snacks, that remained to be seen on the night itself. 'I thought she was a little bit aloof. A bit stuck-up. She didn't even have a drink.'

'No, but it was good to meet her and have a quick chat.'

As ever, Steph could always trust Phill to see the pleasant side of things. That edge that Steph was looking for in life sadly lacking again. A little bit of her would have loved Phill to turn around and say 'yeah, she was a right cow, wasn't she', to flavour his conversation with something other than sweetener, but then, that wouldn't be Phill, would it? The eternal nice guy.

Steph hated the fact that deep down she was unhappy with their village life. Especially as she knew that was what Phill adored. But she knew that they would never be on the same page about that one. Not now. It was too late.

Steph couldn't help herself anymore. Every time she served a pint of lager or reached for a packet of dry roasted, all she could think about was how she would much rather be serving a cocktail and a sharing platter. Nothing against Pearl, or Violet, Margaret, Jimmy or any of them, but she longed to be discussing designer boutiques and chi-chi nightspots, not wool shops and tell-tale liver spots. She didn't dislike their lives; she just didn't want it to be hers anymore.

'How's your shoulder ache doing?' said Steph, attempting to take her mind off her malaise.

'It's not too bad tonight, to be honest,' answered Phill, stretching out his arm and windmilling it slowly to evaluate his pain. 'It was hurting like hell earlier when I was finishing off Sir Buster's bench. That's been quite a job. Between stripping the old paint off, sanding it all back, mixing up the new paint and applying, it has kept me busy. The plaque should be back tomorrow. I hope the engraving looks good. I'll get it screwed on tomorrow night and then it'll be ready. I can finally get that little lot put away back in the shed.' He pointed across to the bench on the far side of the beer garden, or more so to the tools and pots of paints, paint thinners, brushes and general DIY paraphernalia that lay on the grass alongside it. 'I should have put them away already and not left them out while we have customers. Bad landlord.' He play-slapped his own wrist and smiled.

'I don't think you needed to worry too much tonight. It's been so quiet. Don't you ever want things to be a little more exciting?' asked Steph.

'Exciting. In what way? Installing a bouncy castle out here for the kids or something?'

Steph wasn't sure if he was being sarcastic or not, but he was looking at her in earnestness. She guessed not.

'No, just more customers and more excitement and serving drinks somewhere more happening and vibrant. You know when I was talking to Alexi, Sir Buster's son, yesterday when he was here, he was telling me all about the London clubs and bars that he goes to with all of those celebrity types and their neon strip lighting and fancy menus. Don't you ever think that could have been us? We could have been running a place like that. That we *should* be.'

'Not at all, although you know I'd run anything with you by my side. Even a marathon,' he joked before turning more serious. 'Those London bars are just overly priced, watered-down drinks and impersonal bar staff who don't give a stuff about the clientele. As for the celebrities. Our celebrities are the caring village doctor, the cheery farmer, the law-abiding bobby, the lady running the craft shop and the local landlady.' He cupped her face tenderly with his hand as he said the last one. 'Those are the real celebrities. Not the fancy fella off the telly or the influencer off Twitter or Insta-whatever it is.'

His words were sweet, but somehow, even though she didn't want to, Steph found them empty, hollow and a little sad.

Phill drained his tea and placed his cup on the table. 'Right, I'm going to put that stuff away back in the shed now while I think about it. And I'll check on our marrow too. It's coming along a treat. I think we could be in with a chance this year. If the fayre goes ahead, that is.'

Steph groaned internally as a wave of recognition hit

her that she had become the kind of woman who entered marrows into village fayre contests. She endeavoured to park it. 'It's looking likely. Oh, and Pearl mentioned that apparently someone trampled all over Sir Buster's marrows out of spite as his were almost guaranteed to win this year. How dreadful is that? Who would do such a thing?'

'Really?' Phill looked genuinely shocked. 'That's horrible. The poor bloke is barely cold in his grave.'

'He's not in his grave yet. Pearl also said that the funeral is next week. I'll get some flowers sorted and ask if they need a hand with the food or anything. It's the least we can do.'

'See, now that's what makes you a real celebrity. Always thinking about others. You wouldn't get that from the people in those fancy bars. Right, I'll get this stuff away and then how about you and I think about an early night. I've got a Peter James with my name on it. Well, actually it's his name on it, but you know what I mean. I can't wait to dive in.' Phill laughed as he headed off to tidy up the tools and the other equipment.

Thinking about others. How ironic, mused Steph. All

she had done lately was think about herself and how increasingly glum and jaded she was becoming with everything. And those feelings had magnified since she'd had her conversation with Alexi. That exciting conversation. One of the most exciting she'd had in a while. The weed. Alexi's hand on her leg. It was all such a thrilling change from what had become her norm. Her each and every day.

She sighed. She wanted to be happy, she really did. Tomorrow was another day. A brand new one. She prayed it would give her some answers.

But for now, she'd clear up the teacups and contemplate an early night and a read. Maybe a magazine about those celebrities in the fancy bars. Right now, that was Steph's only answer.

Chapter 41

The sun was beginning to descend as Sergeant Pollett and WPC Horton knocked on Violet's front door. She had virtually thrown it open before Samuel had even finished his series of two swift knocks.

Violet was flushed with expectancy. 'Oh do come in, I've been waiting for you to arrive. I saw you coming from the window, so I flew down the stairs.'

'You need to be a bit careful at your age, Aunty Violet. Stairs can be pretty treacherous,' warned Samuel. His voice came across as weary as he felt – a fact not unnoticed by Violet.

'Blimey, you two look exhausted. I'll give you an extra slice of Battenberg each as you both look like you could do with a good sugar rush. Come on in.'

'It's been a pretty major day, Violet,' said Paula as she and Samuel followed Violet back up the stairs. 'We've been at the crime scene for quite a few hours. At first with Sergeant Sheridan and her team from Darrochdean and then on our own this evening.'

'Bless the pair of you, but you did sign up to be a policeman for the adventure, didn't you, Samuel? And I dare say you didn't enrol just so you could help old ladies across the road, Paula, did you?'

'No, I enjoy my work as well you know, Aunty Vi. But seeing that man dangling from the tree was not nice to witness at all. His face was not a pretty sight. Not that you need to know that, of course,' Samuel added.

'Oh but I do, dear,' said Violet. 'I wish to know every detail as it seems that you finally agree with me. That there was something dodgy behind Sir Buster's death.'

'Well, I... er... have to admit that... er...' Samuel stumbled over his words. He left the sentence open.

'Sergeant Sheridan thinks it's a suicide, of course. But then why wouldn't she. It seems a pretty open-and-shut case to her,' said Paula.

'But she wasn't the one pulling poor Sir Buster out of his own lake a few days ago, was she? She might not realise the connection between the two bodies. Apart from the fact she must think that Jeremiah killed Sir Buster, of course.' Violet was now in the kitchen slicing into a pink and yellow slab of Battenberg as the kettle boiled. The two police officers were standing in the kitchen doorway. 'We do still think there's a further hidden connection, don't we? I know I do.'

'Oh, we know there is more to this than Jeremiah simply killing Sir Buster. We're certain of it. I don't believe it for a second. Neither will Sergeant Sheridan when I show her what we found. She doesn't know about the other notes and she wasn't there when WPC Horton and I spend an extra hour or so scouring the area for clues.'

Violet's eye lit up at her nephew's words. 'You found something? What was it?' She started to pour water from the kettle into a teapot and piled a tray with three mugs and a plate of Battenberg slices. She added the full teapot to the tray and motioned for the others to relocate to the front room. 'Let's get settled and you can show me the note that was pinned to this Jeremiah's chest and whatever it is you've found at the crime scene.'

Sitting himself down, Samuel did his usual thing of puffing out his chest a little as the Battenberg was passed his way. 'You know we're not supposed to share any evidence with civilians, don't you?' Samuel's words were more for his own benefit than anybody else's.

'And you know you could have said no to the Battenberg and gone straight home, but you didn't, so let's not split hairs.'

Paula couldn't help but smile at Violet's clipped reply.

'So, where is the note?' continued Violet.

'It's being treated as evidence, but I do have a photo of it on my phone,' said Samuel. He located the photo and passed the phone to his aunty.

As she bit into her Battenberg she studied the photo and the letters that had been cut out to spell out the words I'M SORRY FOR KILLING SIR BUSTER. FORGIVE ME on the note pinned to Jeremiah Halliwell. Placing her fingers on the screen, she zoomed into the letter M of ME. It was the same yellow M on a purple background as the W they had seen on one of the other threatening notes. It had evidently been cut from the same magazine. A crafting magazine. To prove her point, Violet reached down and grabbed a magazine that was lying by her feet. She flicked the pages until she found the page where the letter would have been cut from.

'This is the same magazine. I still had one or two at the shop. It's definitely from here.' Violet pointed at the typeface. 'Identical.'

'So it's more than likely that the same person created all four of the notes?' suggested Samuel, trying to make his question sound more of an intuitive fact.

'I would definitely say so. But the question is who?' asked Violet. 'We can't discount the notion that Jeremiah did have some connection and grudge with Sir Buster that we don't know about and that he is in fact responsible for his death. But that just seems mumbo-jumbo to me.'

'Me too,' agreed Paula, through a mouth full of Battenberg. 'His caravan is being searched tomorrow to see if there's any connection or reason for him killing Sir Buster, but it's far more likely that he has been framed. In fact, we know he has, don't we, Sarge?'

Samuel, also mid slice, swallowed what was in his mouth and puffed out his chest again.

'We do. Because we have this.' He reached into his pocket and pulled out a small clear plastic bag with a piece of paper inside it. The paper had evidently once been screwed up but had now been flattened out.

'Oh what's this?' cooed Violet, tossing the magazine back to the floor and leaning forward excitedly in her seat.

Samuel explained. 'We discovered it in the woodland around the tree where Jeremiah was found. I just had a feeling when we were sat in the squad car talking to you that maybe we hadn't done enough searching around for clues. Sergeant Sheridan's team didn't really look beyond the discovery of the corpse, but I just felt that because of what we knew already about the other notes and the similarity between them that maybe we should look further. So we did...'

'He literally had me on my hands and knees going through the undergrowth,' said Paula, a little miffed.

'No wonder you look pooped, dear girl,' offered Violet.

'Well, you never saw Kojak or Columbo leave a stone unturned in a mystery, did you,' remarked Samuel, 'so why would we?' He handed the clear plastic bag to Violet. 'Leave it in the bag as this is definitely a tasty bit of evidence.'

Violet studied the piece of paper. It was a handwritten note telling someone to meet in a certain spot by a riverbank at 6 p.m. yesterday. It also said that £50,000 should be brought along and that no police should be involved otherwise the recipient's involvement in Sir Buster's death would be disclosed.

'Very interesting,' purred Violet. 'So we are looking at blackmail for sure.'

'Absolutely,' echoed Samuel.

'First off, good work, you two. Help yourself to another slice of Battenberg.' Samuel appeared very pleased with himself. Violet wasn't sure if it was her praise of his professional life or the offer of more Battenberg. 'So, there are two scenarios here, aren't there. Either this Jeremiah Halliwell was being blackmailed because he did kill Sir Buster and the search of his caravan may reveal some kind of motive and he did indeed kill himself and place one of his elaborate notes on his shirt before hanging himself...' Violet bit her bottom lip in contemplation. 'Or...'

There was a moment's silence before she continued.

'Or he was the blackmailer and there is somebody else behind all of this who killed Sir Buster and has now killed Jeremiah too. And decided to frame him at the same time. The dead can't defend themselves, can they? I suggest you get this Sergeant Sheridan to try to find some kind of handwriting from Jeremiah in his caravan to see if he wrote the blackmail note. Or maybe you should offer to help with the search tomorrow, Samuel?'

Samuel tilted his head quizzically. 'Well, I think we all agree that the second scenario seems the most likely, but as yet we don't have a huge amount to go on. We need to know who profits from Sir Buster's death. And we find that out tomorrow at the reading of the will. So, I propose that I accompany Sheena to the will reading – to be honest, I would want to be there with her anyway as she's my daughter – and that perhaps I hold back the fact that we know about this blackmail note for now. We're the only three people who have seen it after all. Let tomorrow's will reading happen and then we see what happens. And more so who profits. I'll ask the police in Darrochdean about a sample of handwriting and see what the search turns up. But I think, for now, that maybe WPC Horton and I need to be the only police officers aware of this blackmail note. If someone is trying to extort money from someone then maybe tomorrow will throw up a few more clues as to whom.'

Paula raised her eyebrows, a mixture of surprise, thrill and respect crossing her features. 'Plus, the fingerprint results will be back tomorrow, so that should give us some more information as well.'

Violet couldn't help but smile. 'So, Samuel, you're withholding evidence in a case, are you? That's not exactly playing by the book, is it?' Her tone was jovial. 'But it's a fabulous idea.' Maybe she and he weren't that different after all. And they obviously both liked Battenberg too, she thought, as they both simultaneously reached forward for another slice.

Chapter 42

Solicitor Jonas Cushing had overseen a lot of will readings in his time, but he knew that this one ranked as one of the most unusual. He had known the Burniston family for a long time. He and Sir Buster had played rugby together back in the day, not that he had ever been as good as the old boy himself. No, whereas Sir Buster had once been part of his national squad, Jonas Cushing had merely contented himself with the odd Sunday morning scrum and tackle at his local rugby club. But that worked for him. Jonas had never had that killer instinct on the field that Sir Buster had possessed. Plus, he'd never been as fit as him either. Whereas Sir Buster had spent a lifetime being beyond careful about the food he ate and the calories he consumed, Jonas Cushing had definitely lived a life where triple-cooked chips and a second portion of steak and kidney pudding were always mandatory. Sir Buster had a healthy appetite, Jonas had a ravenous one.

Indeed, Jonas could feel that he had maybe fastened his braces a little too tight this morning. As he parked his peppermint-coloured Bentley into place on the gravel outside Burrow Hall, he could most certainly feel that they were digging in a little more than normal and maybe splaying themselves a little wider than desired across his bowling ball belly. He knew there was nothing he could do now and hoped that the braces would hold out for the next few hours as he went through Sir Buster's will.

Jonas was sad about Sir Buster. He had always found him the most affable of chaps. They had broken the mould when they made him, that was for sure. He was unique and loved. Which is why Jonas had been more than a little surprised when Sir Buster had phoned him a few weeks earlier to ask him a favour.

The first part of the favour was for the ten-years-retired Jonas to come out of retirement to oversee the reading of his will. For anyone else, Jonas would have declined, but Sir Buster was both personable and persuasive. Plus, there was no way that Jonas could turn Sir Buster down, especially when he had explained why he needed a second part to the favour.

According to Sir Buster, he had a feeling that somebody had it in for him. He hadn't explained why and had merely validated it as 'probably something and nothing' and simply 'an old boy's hunch', but he had informed Jonas that he wished to make some changes to his will. It had been less than a month ago that he and Sir Buster had carried out the necessary legal changes.

Pushing his car door shut, Jonas walked towards the front door of Burrow Hall. He looked at his watch and realised that he had just over two hours until the will reading was due to start. Good, he had given himself ample time to set everything up just as Sir Buster had requested.

An air of melancholy rippled through him as he knocked the door and waited for a reply. How horribly untimely it seemed that the old boy's heart had given out mere weeks after him saying that someone had it in for him. It almost seemed too much of a coincidence. But as he had discovered more and more as he became older, Jonas knew that when your time was up, your time was up. If the heart said no, then it was end of play. Even if you did seem as robust as a bison. It was still a horribly untimely coincidence, though, given what Sir Buster had requested him to do.

The door opened.

Violet Brewer stood there.

'Oh, hello,' said Jonas. There was unmistakable confusion in his voice at seeing her.

'Hello, are you here for the will reading?'

Jonas explained who he was.

'Oh welcome, I'm Violet. I was a great friend of Sir Buster's, do come on in. You were probably expecting Herbert the butler or Mrs Turner the housekeeper. They're both getting ready for the will reading as they've been requested to attend, so myself and my friend Margaret are organising some nibbles and drinks. I normally run the wool and craft shop in the village, but it's all hands on deck at times like this.'

'Of course. My wife likes a bit of that craft stuff. She's forever painting flowers and fancy words on our old garden tools and flowerpots and giving them to friends as gifts. She even makes cards to go with them. There's always bits of paper and all sorts of colourful nonsense all over the house.'

Violet smiled. 'Well, they do say you can't trust a tidy crafter. And I happen to agree. She's sounds like one of us. Now, do come on in. I'll take you through to the study. Is that where you'd like to do the reading?'

Jonas stepped through the door and into Burrow Hall. 'Yes, I think that will do. I'll let you know if not.'

'You're very early,' remarked Violet, looking at her own watch.

'Well, Sir Buster was highly specific about the reading of his will and I need to set a few things up, so it's wise to crack on.'

'I trust you'll have time for a cup of tea, though, and maybe a slice of carrot cake. Or Margaret and I did bring some home-made sticky cherry Bakewell buns with us for elevenses if you prefer. Margaret made them. They're deliciously decadent. Steeped in calories, which is why Sir Buster would never touch them. Silly beggar. Come through to the kitchen.'

Jonas couldn't stop himself. 'Oh, that sounds marvellous. Yes, I can spare ten minutes before diving in. And that doesn't surprise me, Sir Buster missed out on many delicious delights, if you ask me.'

Violet led the way.

'It's so ironic about Sir Buster, isn't it?' she continued. 'He tried to be as healthy as possible and then drops down dead while out fishing. All seems a bit strange to me. I've never met a fitter man, especially for his age. Don't you think so?' Violet was doing some fishing of her own.

'I was very surprised when I heard the news about his death, but then...' He left the words mid-air, which Violet noted. Something told her she could share with Jonas Cushing. And that maybe he would share back.

'But then who knows what's been happening lately to get him upset,' she added, her words découpaged with suggestion. 'Well, actually, *I* do.'

'I have some thoughts of my own on that too,' said Jonas, nodding his head.

Bingo. Violet's fishing had landed a catch.

'Well, Margaret and I would love to hear them over

that cherry Bakewell bun and some tea. It'll do you good. There's no way you can read a will on an empty stomach.'

Jonas's stomach was far from empty, his full English breakfast hadn't been that long ago, but there was always a sugar-coated space ready for a little scrumptious something extra.

Chapter 43

Paula had hardly slept a wink. Despite being exhausted from the activities of the day before, she had spent the night tossing and turning in bed, trying to work out just who could be behind the threats to Sir Buster. Mr Bublé had been so annoyed with her constant wriggling and sighing that for once he had abandoned his favourite cosy night-time spot alongside her and headed to the nearest windowsill to try to get some peace. Like Violet and Sergeant Pollett, Paula was convinced that Jeremiah Halliwell had not killed Sir Buster. Unless he was a long-lost son that nobody knew about. That would be quite the turn-up, if a little Scooby Doo. But Paula was letting her mind consider all possibilities.

Now, the outcomes of the fingerprint tests were back

to occupy her mind even further. The results on the novel, and indeed the notes inside, had come back as she had expected. Sheena, Pearl, Jimmy, Violet and Margaret all had their fingerprints over both the novel itself and each and every one of the three threatening notes. Paula had taken all of their fingerprints before sending the book off for analysis as she has seen first-hand that they had handled everything. The only other fingerprints present belonged to Sir Buster himself.

The results had come back for both the wellington boots and the gun, too. As expected, the only fingerprints on the boots belonged to Sir Buster. If somebody had slipped them on to destroy the potential victory-grabbing marrows, then they had obviously been fully careful about not leaving any incriminating prints.

The same could not be said for the gun, though. Three sets of prints had been found on it. One, of course, was Sir Buster's. The other two, both clearly visible and unsmudged, so they must have been put there since the last time the gun was fully cleaned, belonged to two familiar names. One was Herbert the butler. Paula considered the fact that maybe the butler had moved the gun or handled it in his daily business. But if he had been to the shed recently, then surely somebody who spent their life cleaning, polishing and dusting for a living would have tidied up the mess all over the wellington boots. Unless, of course, he had put it there in the first place.

The police officer's mind wandered further for a moment, contemplating just how much cleaning a butler would have to do. Would that fall under Mrs Turner's remit or was she purely kitchen-based? And didn't Sheena do a lot of a cleaning? Having never had either a housekeeper, butler or a cleaner, and copiously aware that she was probably never likely to, Paula made a note to ask Sheena after the will reading about the split of duties within Burrow Hall. She'd maybe speak to Sheena without letting Sergeant Pollett know.

Even though Sergeant Pollett had pretty much scoffed at the notion that one of Team C.R.A.B. could be behind the notes after the discovery that the W and now an M had been cut from a crafting magazine, Paula knew that she would be letting the consider-every-option investigator in her down if she didn't contemplate every suspect. If there were dirty dealings afoot, and two deaths said there were, then it could easily be that one of the crafty crew who were responsible. And even though Sergeant Pollett would never give the idea a moment's credence, Paula was fully aware that that particular theory had to include Sheena as well. Everyone was guilty until proven innocent, right?

The second set of prints on the gun belonged to Belinda Flatt. It was clear that she had handled the gun since being back in the village. The question, of course, was why? Violet and Margaret's words about Belinda seeing the gun that had killed her mother and flying into an incandescent rage flooded back into Paula's mind. Maybe she was the culprit behind the marrow bashing. And if she was capable of that, then who knew what else she was capable of? Maybe writing threatening notes to her own father... And hanging someone from a tree?

A chill went through Paula as she added Belinda Flatt to the list of people that she would need to speak to as soon as possible. Perhaps if she turned up at Burrow Hall after the will reading, then maybe Sergeant Pollett and she could tackle Belinda Flatt together. And if he was still busy being fatherly-protective over Sheena, then Paula could do it herself.

Paula checked her watch. It was five minutes to midday. The will reading would be about to start.

A frisson of excitement replaced the chill at the thought of her forthcoming interrogations. It was just like the telly dramas that Sergeant Pollett loved so much. She suddenly saw the attraction. And she adored the notion that she would be playing the smart-thinking sidekick considering every possible option.

Chapter 44

Jimmy and Pearl had not stopped gossiping all morning. Or eating. The village was buzzing with the news that a body had been found hanging from a tree and a confession had been written about the apparent murder of Sir Buster Burniston. The story had been front-page news in the local paper that morning, but the details were still sketchy to non-existent about who the body was or as to any kind of motive. It merely said a fifty-nine-year-old-male had been found in woodland about fifteen miles from the home of Sir Buster.

Jimmy and Pearl had both tried to contact Violet, Margaret and Sheena to examine the latest revelations, but all of them left their phones unanswered, although that wasn't so surprising. Jimmy and Pearl were well aware that

Margaret and Violet would be knee-deep in teabags and doilies getting ready with their tasks for the will reading and Sheena was probably biting off her own nails with worries about why she had been summoned to attend.

In truth, everyone else's attendance at the reading was irking them both. 'I really wish we were there right now at that will reading. I would love to know what's going on,' said Jimmy, staring at his watch. 'It's five minutes to kick-off.' He tutted at his annoyance at not being there and picked up the few last crumbs on his plate and put them in his mouth. 'That cake was absolutely delicious, Pearl. Seriously good.'

Pearl and Jimmy were sitting in the back garden at Pearl's cottage. The sun, directly overhead, beat down upon them as they both savoured a hefty slice of Pearl's Bajan pound cake. In fact, Jimmy had already savoured two. Jimmy shifted his chair into the shade of the parasol they were sitting under as he contemplated a third slice.

Pearl read his mind. 'You're welcome to another, Jimmy. It's a pound cake. We normally have them around the Christmas period in Barbados, but when something tastes that good, it's like Christmas every day.'

'A third would be a little piggy, I feel, although, heaven knows, I'm tempted. Maybe you could bag some up for me to take away. I'm sure Hannah and Oscar would love a slice. I'm assuming Bailey can't as it's not vegan.'

'It's not this time, but the next one I make I'll be sure to make it vegan. No man should miss out on that,' grinned Pearl. She pulled her own chair into the sunshine to feel the rays kissing her skin.

Jimmy checked his watch again. Bang on twelve. 'They'll be underway now. Do you think Sir Buster will leave everything to Alexi and Belinda?'

'I hope not. Although maybe then Alexi will have the money to pay back Vin Sutton in Barbados. I am dreading telling him. What if he turns nasty?'

'No chance of that. Let him try,' smirked Jimmy. 'No one messes with one of Team C.R.A.B.'

The pair had enjoyed exchanging their revelations about Sir Buster's son and how it appeared that he wasn't as well off as his car, fancy threads and rather significant weed habit seemed to suggest.

'Well, if he doesn't pay up, then Vin Sutton is getting on a flight and coming over here to confront him face on and Uncle Josh seemed to think that that would be a seriously bad move for Alexi if he did so.'

'Do you think he's a bit of a bruiser? All rippling with muscles and ready to deal out revenge in his own ferocious way. It all sounds fabulously *Goodfellas*.' Jimmy was liking the notion a little more than maybe he should have, letting his brain carry itself away into the realms of fantasy.

'Heaven knows, but if I was owed £100,000, then I guess I'd hardly be asking civilly. Hopefully Alexi will cough up and we won't have to find out.'

Jimmy sat in contemplation for a moment.

'I think Sir Buster is more likely to leave the Hall to Belinda. Although, from what Violet said, it doesn't sound like she and her husband would be turning it into a family home. They hardly see each other. He's busy conservationing – is that a word? – all over the place.'

'What I wouldn't give to be a fly on the wall right now at Burrow Hall,' mused Pearl. 'Especially how everyone thinks that Sir Buster was bumped off. I suppose they will all have seen the paper today?' She paused to imagine what would be if they hadn't. 'Still, at least Sheena is there, and she can tell us everything. And Violet and Margaret are there too sorting out the food, so doubtless both of them will have a glass each jammed up against the study wall so that they don't miss a trick either.'

'They're all there bar us,' said Jimmy, disappointedly. 'Every member of Team C.R.A.B., except us. That hardly seems right, does it?'

'It's not right and it's not fair,' volleyed back Pearl with a smile and a wag of her finger.

Jimmy offered a suggestion. 'I haven't taken a condolence card up to the Hall yet, have you? Saying how sorry we are about Sir Buster.'

'Well, I did buy a lovely paper kit from Violet's that would make the most detailed and découpaged sympathy cards. The kits say it makes sixteen cards, if I remember. Lots of different designs. I'm sure we could make two now if you think we should.' Pearl could feel a plan hatching between them.

'And maybe we could then take them up to the Hall,'

suggested Jimmy.

'Maybe in about an hour, so that maybe we'd run into everyone up there.'

'And maybe hear, hot off the press, what happened at the will reading and see what people are saying about the discovery of this body.'

'And maybe see who's happy and who's not about the outcome.'

'And maybe you could speak to Alexi about the money he owes and suggest that he pays it back.' Jimmy winked at Pearl.

'That's a lot of maybes,' replied Pearl. 'I'm still not sure about the last one, we'll have to see if I'm brave enough.'

'So, shall we?'

Pearl could tell from the way Jimmy asked the question that he had already decided the answer. As had she.

'I'll get the card kit. It's the respectful thing to do, after all.'

Pearl ran inside the cottage to raid her crafting stash, leaving Jimmy to wonder what exactly was going on at Burrow Hall.

Jimmy wasn't the only one wondering. Stephanie and Phill Brooks were engaged in a similar conversation at they prepared the bar for opening time at The Six Pennies. They too had read the shocking story in the morning paper.

'Can you believe they think that somebody actually killed the old boy?' said Phill, flicking the pages of the paper. 'It's a scandal, all right.'

'It's horrible. Truly horrific. Maybe they bumped him off because they thought they'd be getting something tasty in the will today,' offered Steph. She was polishing a pint glass and placing it under the counter as she aired her feelings. 'I wonder what will happen. I reckon if Alexi inherits it, he'll be using it for some kind of development plans. He wants to expand his glitzy empire.' Steph felt a smile spread across her face as she let her mind race into fifth gear about what Alexi might try to achieve. Images of trendy pop stars and social media influencers sashaying up to the bar at The Six Pennies filled her thoughts. The idea of sleepy Rooney-at-Burrow becoming a playground for the rich and famous thrilled her.

'What makes you say that?' replied her husband. 'Mind you, I can't see him settling for a quiet life in the village, living at the Hall. His racy sort never would.'

'Didn't you hear some of the phone calls he's been having when he's been drinking in here. I think he's been talking to people about how much the land would be worth if he was to sell it to housing developers. I'm sure I've heard him mention potential market value and planning permission. Maybe he'll turn it into something a little more modern and bring some fresh blood into the area. God knows this village needs a bit of life pumped into it. It's a little stagnant. And you can't tell me you'd turn down the custom.' She hesitated a second, before adding, 'And what do you mean *his racy sort*?'

Phill looked up from the list he was now making for a trip to the wholesalers. He was as regular as clockwork with his visits. Every Saturday morning early doors. This week would be an extra-special visit as he would be buying surplus in to cater for Sir Buster's memorial night at the weekend, which is why he was already preparing the list two days in advance of his trip. 'You know the type. All flashy and no substance. My late mother used to have a phrase about people like Alexi Burniston. She would say they're *all book under the arm and no breakfast.* Full of themselves. So, intent on looking good and being seen with the right thing that they don't do the normal things in life like having breakfast. He's a prime example of it. He thinks he's a right Jack the lad. He should relish the chance of village life as it might make him realise the important things in life. Talking of which... pickled onions or silver skins for Saturday night?'

'Pickled onions.' Not that she cared. 'Don't you think it would be good to inject a bit of life into Rooney-at-Burrow? It's long overdue. Alexi knows all of the trendy telly types you see in magazines and online. He's managed a lot of them. And he knows the best bars. Where the in-crowd hangs out. He could bring some of that to the village and really put this place on the map.'

'We are on the map, Steph. As a good, honest, decent village boozer. And that's how it should be. I know you'd love something a little more swanky and that life might be more exciting if we were the managers of some Soho nightspot, but I think you'd get bored in a heartbeat. In fact, I know you would. Because the clientele there would be vacuous. A load of bobbleheads. All blah, blah, blah about things that don't matter. You and me together, that's what matters. Letting good honest folk enjoy a great night out at a friendly pub. You're better than some soulless bar with no atmosphere. Now, brown or white baps or half and half?'

'Half and half.' She couldn't be bothered to say any more. It was the first time that Phill had really hinted that he knew how dissatisfied she was with life in the village. But he seemed to know what was best for her. Or thought he did. Right now, Steph felt like she needed more, much more. People like Alexi brought the atmosphere. The danger. And the thought of what might be. He may be a tad flashy, but with Alexi, every word said was electric and exciting. At least with people like him, there was life beyond the village. For a moment, the thought crossed her mind that perhaps the body they had found was Alexi's. No name had been mentioned in the paper. The notion distressed her. She liked Alexi. Or the idea of him. But then she realised that he wasn't a fifty-nine-year-old male and the notion passed.

Steph returned to polishing the pint glasses and placing them on the shelf under the bar. That was just how she felt too. On the shelf and hidden away. It wasn't a nice feeling.

She glanced at the clock behind the bar. It was twelve o'clock precisely.

They'll be starting with the will reading now, she thought to herself and smiled. Change would be good. Sir Buster's death was truly awful, especially now that is was apparently foul play, but wouldn't it be nice if something different could rise from the ashes? Something exciting for the village, something exciting for her.

Chapter 45

The study clock struck twelve. Jonas Cushing fiddled with the remote control in his hand and looked at those gathered before him in the study at Burrow Hall. A sea of faces, the expressions on all of them as varied as could be.

Alexi Burniston slumped, seemingly a little disrespectful, in his chair, impatiently expelling a lungful of air. It was as if the mere thought of waiting to find out what he obviously considered should be rightfully his was irking him somehow. He wore jeans, albeit black ones, and a T-shirt.

Siting along from him – not next to, but along from – was Belinda Flatt. Her expression was a nervy one. She chewed at her bottom lip with her teeth and fiddled with her hair as she waited for proceedings to begin. The dark, fitted suit she was wearing gave her an air of hopeful gravitas that somehow didn't quite succeed. The fact that she was wearing a pair of high heels still with the price ticket attached to one of the soles didn't help in her quest to look as professional as possible.

In the row behind Belinda sat Herbert and Mrs Turner, both of them looking somehow out of place for the occasion. Herbert was wearing a much more formal suit than he normally did in his profession as Sir Buster's butler. Gone was the jet-black suit, tie and suit vest and in its place was a light grey combination of waistcoat and suit with a deep blue tie with tiny pink flecks. His hair, as always, was Brylcreemed into position, not a strand out of place. His face was stern and seemed a little ill at ease, probably due to the fact that his position in the household was for once blurred.

Mrs Turner had let down her grey hair from its usual tight bun to reveal a rather splendid stretch of shoulder-length waves that gave her rotund features a less globular effect. The pretty ditsy-print floral dress she was wearing only added to the unexpected softness of her appearance.

Her face, a little ruddier than normal, suggested that she too felt a little at odds with her surroundings.

Sitting behind Alexi was Sheena and her father, Samuel. Sheena, as ever, looked naturally and effortlessly stunning, her selected combo of black and grey paisley midi dress and ankle boots straddling the two camps of fashion and polite respect beautifully. Her expression was one of bemusement at being there, mixed with sadness at what would be Sir Buster's eternal absence. Her father was out of this uniform for the day and wearing a seemingly identical suit and waistcoat combination to the one that Herbert was wearing. The only difference was that Samuel's tie was a deep shade of shamrock green. Samuel suspected that he and the butler had been last-minute shopping in the same place. There wasn't much in the way of menswear outlets nearby and maybe Herbert had been equally drawn to the fifty per cent off sale sign in the window.

The door to the study was ajar and perched behind it, doing their best to position themselves to be both hidden and yet able to hear every word were Margaret and Violet.

Both women had been discussing the discovery of the body all morning and even though Violet knew that she shouldn't have, she hadn't been able to wait to tell Margaret all about the body's identity and the discovery of the blackmail note that Sergeant Pollett was so far keeping a secret. Shocked at the latest exposés, Margaret was still enjoying every salacious morsel of information, until she heard the sound of footsteps in the study.

It was Margaret who elbowed Violet softly in the ribs and whispered, 'Shush, he's about to start' as Jonas moved to the front of the room with a remote control in his hand.

Quite what Margaret was shushing, Violet had no notion, as she hadn't uttered a word.

Jonas perched himself on the desk at the front of the study. A television was sitting on the desk, a cable running from it to a laptop alongside it. Sheena recognised the television as the smaller portable one that normally sat in Sir Buster's bedroom. He had often told her that he was partial to watching those middle-of-the-night gambling channels that seemed to pop up now and again. 'You can place a bet or two and also they're a bloody good cure for insomnia' was how he described them.

Jonas began to speak.

'Er, thank you, everybody, for coming along today to the reading of the last will and testament of Sir Buster Burniston. I think we'd all agree that whether we were related to him, worked for him, were friends over the years or perhaps a combination of any of those that Sir Buster was a one-off and we will sadly miss his presence in this world.'

'Hear, hear. He was an absolute gent.' It was Herbert talking, unable to stop himself. Sir Buster had always been the best of masters. Aware that maybe he shouldn't interrupt, the butler coughed a little awkwardly and looked into his lap as he sensed his cheeks reddening. A wave of nods circled the room nevertheless in agreement. The wave missed Alexi.

Jonas continued, 'I had known Sir Buster many years and indeed, in my role as a solicitor, had worked for him and his late wife, Fiona, on numerous occasions. I actually retired a few years ago, but I was requested out of retirement as it were by Sir Buster himself only a few weeks back. He was insistent that some changes were made to his will.'

Both Alexi and Belinda's faces suddenly painted themselves with a wash of urgent worry.

Alexi pondered the fact that if the will had been changed, then maybe the natural family order of who was next in line, namely him, might have sailed out of the nearest window. Alexi ditched his slumped position of apparent disinterest and turned it into a stance of bolt uprightness, suddenly hanging off Jonas Cushing's every word. He still, nevertheless, managed to fidget nervously.

Belinda could feel a little bead of sweat beginning to form under her hairline on the back of her neck. Perhaps this reading wasn't going to be as straightforward as she may have thought. Especially after the disclosures in the paper that morning. She had read it in silence over her muesli and discussed it with nobody. She had no notion whether Alexi had even seen it. She neither knew nor cared. Her mind was already full to bursting. The old man definitely had something planned, that was for sure. Belinda couldn't help but wish that her mother was still around to keep things on an even keel. She had always been the sensible one. Never reckless. Not like her father. Always so hot-headed and impulsive.

'What changes has he made?' The words stampeded from Belinda's lips before she could lasso them back in. Maybe some of her father's hot-headedness had been passed on.

'I don't know,' said Jonas. 'All I know is that I was told to carry out the following instructions on the event of Sir Buster's death. I was to gather the list of people he gave me together for his will reading. That's all of you here. Understandably, there were some that couldn't make it, I gather.' He gestured to Belinda, suggesting that her husband and son were also on the list.

Belinda acknowledged the implication, the sweat bead now meandering its wavey way down below her collar.

'He also sent me a video file that I was to play to those gathered. I haven't seen it, but I have had instructions to say that what is contained within is the final wish of Sir Buster Burniston and supersedes all previous wills. So, without further ado, here are the last wishes of Sir Buster

Burniston, may he rest in peace.'

As Jonas Cushing pressed play on the remote control and sat himself down at the back of the study, behind the door Margaret turned to Violet and mouthed, 'OMG'.

At least that's what Violet thought she mouthed. She wasn't too sure.

Both of them shuffled into a position where they could see as much of the television screen as possible though the hinged crack in the door. They watched as the screen went from black and crackled into colour.

Chapter 46

Sir Buster Burniston filled the screen. An audible gasp went up from those watching. He was sitting in the very study where they were all gathered right now. In fact, at the very desk where the television was perched. He began to speak. A voice from beyond the grave.

'Oh right, here we go. Hello to you all. I suppose if you're watching this then I'm guessing I'm dead and that I'm probably looking down on you all from somewhere up there.' He pointed upwards to indicate heaven before laughing. 'Actually, given some of the dodgy things I've done in life, I'm more likely to be dancing around in the flames down there.' He inverted his finger to point downwards. 'Either way, thank you, I've had a great life and it's been a lot of fun.'

Sheena could feel a tear pricking at her eyes watching Sir Buster on the screen, so full of life and energy. She heard a sob and looked down her row of chairs to see Mrs Turner already in full flow. She caught her eye and gave her a sympathetic smile.

'So, you're probably wondering why I am doing this video thing. Well, two reasons. First off, why the hell not. Seems like a fun kind of way to carry on speaking to people after you're dead. Maybe everyone should do it from now on. But, secondly – and the real reason, to be honest – is that I thought it only fair to explain a few things face to face, as it were, about the decisions I've come to in my will about who gets their hands on my money. This way seems a little more personal and hopefully I can answer any questions you might have about my decisions. Not that we can have some kind of Q and A, of course. Me being dead kind of puts a blessed kibosh on that. So, I'm just going to guess what you might be thinking. I suspect I'll have a darned good idea. I'm quite a shrewd old goat – I'm sure Sheena will tell you that from our many chats together.'

Samuel Pollett reached out his hand to take his daughter's in his and squeezed it as Sir Buster mentioned her name. She turned to her father and smiled; her eyes now glossy with tears.

'Right, let me start with this. This has been the reason that I have been doing a lot of thinking and pretty deep soul-searching and have come to a few decisions.'

Sir Buster opened one of the desk drawers and pulled out a book. Through the crack of the door, both Violet and Margaret recognised it as the copy of *The Strange Case of Dr. Jekyll and Mr. Hyde*. Violet couldn't stop herself from quietly saying, 'He was not giving into threats' in a whispered yet proud voice. He had said it to her at The Six Pennies. She knew it.

Sheena and Samuel also recognised the novel as the newly produced evidence. Samuel shifted in his seat a tad uneasily as he thought about the new note that he had kept hidden. Hiding evidence went against every rule in the police handbook even if he knew he was doing it for a perfectly valid reason. Before he could worry too much about it, Sir Buster began speaking once more.

'This is my favourite book. I love it. Jekyll and Hyde. One person, two personalities. One good, one bad. I think everyone has that in them somewhere. Maybe not bad, just a little dark now and again. No one is sweetness and light all of the time. That's too dull. I've seen Mrs Turner's temper when she burns her puddings. That look she gives them is pure venom.' Sir Buster let out a belly laugh. 'I bet you Mrs T is crying now, isn't she? For some daft reason she was very fond of me. Even with all of my strange food habits and the fact I would never take up her offer for some sugary biscuit with my tea. She is, isn't she?'

Sir Buster seemed to pause, expecting everyone gathered to turn around and stare at Mrs Turner, to see if indeed she was crying. They did, and she was. A lot.

'I knew she would be. Marvellous woman. Thank you for everything, Mrs Turner. Anyway, I digress... So, this book, it's not the story I want to talk about, it's these notes that I have kept inside it. There's three of them and they've been sent to me, or hand delivered, I guess, as the envelopes had no stamps or franking marks on them. They've been sent to me over the last six weeks. I've received one note pretty much every fortnight. Jonas can tell you when that was depending on when you're watching this.'

Jonas paused the TV and filled the others in on the time frame of when Sir Buster first contacted him about changing the will. He then pressed play again.

'They're not very nice – in fact, they're a bit threatening. Look.' He held them up one by one for everyone viewing to see. 'This one was first. I KNOW WHAT YOU'VE BEEN DOING, STOP IT NOW. Then this about a fortnight later. I'VE WARNED YOU. STOP BEFORE IT'S TOO LATE. And finally, this. THIS IS YOUR FINAL WARNING. ENOUGH IS ENOUGH. All very amateur with the cut-out letters but still rather flipping horrid, don't you think? Somebody obviously has it in for me. No idea who. Well, I have suspicions, but I'll come on to that.'

Belinda and Alexi both sat watching the screen, their mouths hanging open. Herbert chuntered the words 'disgusting behaviour' to himself and Mrs Turner cried even more. Jonas himself was indeed shocked at the recording's revelations so far. The notes were old news to all the others. Samuel tried to feast his eyes onto everyone to check out their reactions to see if anyone in particular looked especially uncomfortable. In truth, how could anyone appear comfortable given the situation?

Sir Buster put down the book and the notes and next picked up a framed picture. 'Now, I've always tried to be nice to people and I like to think that I'm a pretty good sort. I'd do anything for anyone, within reason, and I suppose in some ways I expect people to do the same for me. An eye for an eye and all that. So, receiving these notes has thrown me a bit. It's made me question the decency of people in the first place. Whoever sent them obviously took the time to look through a pile of papers and magazines, cut and then glue lots of letters into place, like an episode of *Murder She Wrote* or something equally as daft, and deliver them to my door. That's pretty ruthless to begin with, but what gets me the most is that they have chosen to stay anonymous. Doesn't that just show the cowardice of man.' He paused before adding, '… Or woman. Whoever has done this wants to put the willies up me but can't be bothered to tell me what they're getting at. Because, to be honest, I have no idea.'

The cogs of Samuel's police brain were spinning like turbines in a gale. Obviously, Sir Buster had no idea as to why someone might want to threaten him, or indeed kill him.

Sir Buster now held up a framed picture of himself as part of the national rugby team that sat pride of place on his desk. 'When I was playing with this lot, if one of us had a problem with somebody in the team for not doing their bit on the pitch or acting a right idiot, then we would talk man to man, face to face and get things sorted. There was none of this *he said, she said, I know what you did* behind their back nonsense. You bloody got things sorted. Because that's the best way to resolve any issues.'

He put down the framed photo and once more picked up the book and notes. Everyone in the study watched, hardly breathing, as Sir Buster pointed directly down the lens of the camera. His face was stern.

'So, the question is, which one of you sent it? Was it somebody in this room right now? Was it... er...' Sir

Buster let his finger spin around on the screen somewhat dramatically before pointing it off to the left-hand side of the screen. '… *You*?' He overdramatised the last word.

His finger fell on Belinda Flatt, who gasped audibly and gave an indignant cry of 'no it certainly wasn't' at the accusation from beyond the grave.

Sir Buster then swirled his finger back across the screen and pointed it off towards the right-hand side. 'Or… was it *you*?'

This time it pointed at Alexi. He just shrugged and said, 'You reckon, old man?' His tone was extremely dismissive.

Behind the door, Margaret whispered to Violet, 'Gosh, that man really is rather vile, isn't he. I hope he receives nothing in the will.'

Violet shushed her for fear of missing a word of Sir Buster's recording.

Sir Buster let out a huge guffaw. 'That had you, didn't it? The truth is, though, that if you're watching this, then I never found out who sent these notes to me, or if I did, then I took that information to my grave without telling anyone. So, I'm none the wiser about who could be so darned horrid.' He placed the notes back in the book and then put it away in the drawer. 'But these notes have not been without purpose, I guess. Have they scared me? No. I am not one to give into the anonymous threats of others. Never have been, never will be. Like I said, it's a coward's way of trying to frighten someone. But I have learnt something from these notes. When someone threatens you, you immediately wonder what they might do to carry out their threats. Those notes made it sound like the person behind them would do anything to get me to stop whatever I'm supposed to have been doing. You do suddenly become aware of your own mortality. I may be over seventy, but apart from the odd cold or stomach upset recently, I'm as fit as a flea. But I am still an old man, and you never know when your time is up, I guess. It's funny how somebody else's threats can make you evaluate your own life. They have made me look at what is important. And not just what, but *who* is important. Which is where you lot come in.'

Sir Buster pulled another document from one of his

desk drawers and unfolded it. A rumbling of expectation circled around the room as those gathered realised that the moment had come for the will to be read. If indeed that was what the document was.

Sir Buster continued. 'So, this is my brand new last will and testament. The old one is null and void. Gone for good. Jonas has made sure of that for me.'

The solicitor nodded to no one in particular.

'I'll start by saying that the previous will would have been an equal fair-share split of what there is divided between Alexi and Belinda. I changed it to that after dear Fiona died and at the time it seemed like the right and natural thing to do. Those were horrid times. Losing Fiona was a heartache that I would never wish on anyone, especially when it was such a tragic accident that shouldn't have happened.' Sir Buster put the will down on the desk and looked directly down the barrel of the lens again. 'And whilst we're on the subject of Fiona. I know you blame me for her death, Belinda. You always have done. But I think you know deep down that it wasn't my fault. What happened to your mother was just a horrible accident.

Believe you me, if I could replay that day over again and change history, I would. The brightest light went out of my life that day and it was a light that I have never been able to, or indeed wanted to, replace. My hurt was just as great as yours, Belinda. You lost a mother; I lost a wife. My soulmate. And some of your accusations after the event blaming me for her death just added to my pain. But I understood your hurt and anger, so I allowed you to hurt me. We should have sorted that out a long time ago. Now that you're watching this, then I guess it's too late for good, sadly.'

All eyes fell on Belinda. Like Mrs Turner, she too was crying, but unlike the distraught sobs of the housekeeper, Belinda's tears were silent and seemingly detached. Sad yet with no visible emotion other than the wet streaks that decorated her cheeks.

Sir Buster coughed, his air a little flustered. 'Right, where was I? I went a bit off piste there.' He picked up the will again. 'Yes, so I've changed things. I've made what I think is a better will. A fairer one. One that everyone can learn from. I certainly have. Changing this and thinking about what will happen after I am gone has been one of the most cathartic and awakening things I have done in years. Who knew that thinking about your own death would be so bracing?' He gave a little laugh. 'So, let's start with two of the most important people in my life.'

Both Alexi and Belinda, assuming it was them, leant nearer to the screen, as if shortening the gap between them and their late father would prove more rewarding. Both imagined that now would be the moment when one of them would be gifted most, and hopefully all, in their father's will. They assumed wrongly.

'Burrow Hall's faithful butler, Herbert, and the ever-loyal housekeeper, Mrs Turner.'

Alexi and Belinda both huffed and leant back into their seats. In the row behind them, Herbert and Mrs Turner linked hands. Despite the rather starchy nature of their day-to-day employ, they were friends who had their own unique union built from working under the same roof as each other for many decades.

'You two have literally been the glue that has held this house together over the years. I really can't even imagine what me and Fiona would have done without either of you. Your unfaltering dedication has always been appreciated and you've both been there through it all. The highs when the kids came along and the lows when Fiona was taken from us. I personally couldn't have faced any of those challenges without you two by my side.'

The sobs of Mrs Turner formed a soundtrack to Sir Buster's words as he continued to speak.

'I would say that the time has come for both of you to retire and to live your life without having to worry about other people. But I know from the many conversations that we have had in the past that both of you are as stubborn as heck and have always told me that you'd want to work until the day you peg out. Well, that's up to you. You will always have a job in Burrow Hall for as long as it stands. Anyone who says otherwise is going against my wishes in this will.' He gave a penetrating stare down the lens. 'You are the very fabric of this house and always will be. But the option is there to stop at any time if you wish. There is an amount of £350,000 for each of you as a token of appreciation for the work you have done over the years.

Plus, Herbert, I bequeath you my vintage car as I know you have spent many a happy hour cleaning it and tinkering with it and I have always seen the way you look at it with such a covetous eye. To you both, I can only say thank you for everything. And even then, words are not enough.'

Mrs Turner wiped away the tears from her ruddy cheeks as Sir Buster offered his gratitude and smiled. She turned to Herbert, who was also crying, and to Sheena, along the row, who was beaming at her.

'You deserve it,' mouthed Sheena. She meant it. Both Herbert and Mrs Turner had always been unwavering in their line of duty to serve the Burnistons. Plus, they were both incredibly nice people.

Sir Buster paused for a few moments, as if somehow aware that he needed to let the news sink in before continuing.

'There is now the matter of Burrow Hall and the estate. The running of the Hall has always been an easy one. Yes, it's large and the bills are through the roof sometimes, but the money has always been there for it and thanks to a lifetime of shrewd investments from yours truly, the bank balance should be looking healthy for many moons to come. Burrow Hall has always been more than just a family home to me. Yes, it came to me from my father, and to him from his father before that, but I have never found it a... what are the words?'

Sir Buster pulled another two pieces of paper from underneath the desk. He unfolded one.

'Yes, here we are... a letter from you Belinda. One of the maybe two or three times a year I actually hear from you these days. I have never found it a *cavernous waste of energy that could be put to much better use than housing just one person.* Those were the words, Belinda, weren't they? Now, I know that I'm a bit of an old fart when it comes to ecological ways and I dare say that the house needs to be a lot more efficient, but maybe if you'd come to me and taught me how to do the right thing as opposed to the odd letter when you could be bothered, always accusing me of doing the wrong thing, then maybe I would have been a lot more open to change a long time ago. I tried to reach out on many an occasion and incite you, Rupert and Sage to come and stay, but you were always busy, always doing something, rather than coming to see the family home. Because I genuinely believe that you don't see this place as a family home anymore.'

He paused for a moment and uncannily appeared to be looking directly at Belinda. 'To me, these four walls and rooms and hallways are all memories. Memories of when Fiona and I first came to live here after we were married. The excitement on your mother's face when she planted her first rose bushes in the garden, decorated her first Christmas tree in the entrance hall, helping with the first village fayre. She adored this house. She adored this village. I remember when we set up your nursery, Belinda, and painted it like an underwater adventure. We spent days looking in reference books working out how to paint starfish and jellyfish and mermaids. Your mother and I were so proud when we had finished.' A crack of emotion broke his words.

'I loved that nursery,' uttered Belinda, suddenly gripped by the nostalgic beauty of recollection.

'This house is full of happy dinner parties, picnics on

the front lawn, you kids building scarecrows for my allotment. Alexi falling out of a tree down by the lake pretending to be a monkey, Belinda's clown party for her fifth birthday. All of those memories bring such joy to me, so there was never any notion of me selling up and moving out just because I was here on my own. In fact, I was never on my own at all as I always had a head full of memories.'

Sir Buster flipped to the other thing he was holding in his hand. This one appeared to be a card.

'And then there's you, Alexi, our eldest child. What was it you said about this house in my Christmas card the year before last? Oh yes… that I should *downsize and sell up* as I'm *not getting any younger* and that maybe I should *think about giving me some of my inheritance money now as opposed to when you're dead.* All that, and then a quick happy Christmas, Dad. Festive, eh? I didn't really think too much about it at the time. I suppose I've just become immune to all of your demands. I've had decades of you begging for handouts. Christ knows I did it for years when you were living in Barbados. Money for this charity, money for that charity. I never saw what you actually did with it. I thought you'd sorted yourself out for a while as the begging stopped. But then it started again a few years back, didn't it? Telling me to sell up and cough up. Without so much as a *how are you, Dad, what have you been up to, Dad? How's the family home?* Now I'm beginning to question it all.'

Alexi sat silently watching the screen as his father aired his feelings. He shifted uneasily in his seat again and tutted.

Belinda turned to look at him. 'Begging for money in a Christmas card? Really. You're that low?'

'Like you're any better, Miss Cavernous Waste of Energy,' he volleyed back.

Belinda was about to launch another verbal attack but stopped as Sir Buster continued.

He sighed. 'I'm fully aware that I'm rambling on, but I suppose one of the good things about being dead is that no one can stop you when you're in full flow. Unless you've stopped this by now and I doubt that, given as I've not finished. So, Alexi and Belinda, thanks to those threatening notes making me realise that some people really can be unnecessarily nasty, it's made me question whether you two had to be quite so vile and uncaring with your letters to me. We may not have been the closest of families, especially since your mother died, but I think as a family, we're worth much more than those letters, don't you? So, I'm choosing not to leave Burrow Hall to either of you. There's £150,000 for each of you instead. Belinda, you and Rupert seem well off, so you don't need the money. And as for you, Alexi, you've had more than most over the years, so I don't think you have any reason to complain.'

Collective shock erupted from all of those gathered.

'Blimey, that's put the cat amongst the pigeons,' whispered Samuel to his daughter.

Sheena turned her head to look 180 degrees behind her as she was sure she had heard gasps coming from behind the study door. Unable to see anything, she assumed she must have imagined it.

Belinda's face drained of colour as Alexi's anger seemed to turn his a deep shade of aubergine.

'Jesus, we get less than the poxy staff. How does that

work.'

Behind him, a rather amused Samuel chuckled slightly, unable to stop himself.

'But keeping the Burniston name at Burrow Hall is hugely important to me,' continued Sir Buster. 'Which is why I do indeed want to leave it to somebody in the family. Somebody who can hopefully continue to make memories here. Someone who will hopefully see the beauty in it. I leave it to Sage. Well, at least I leave forty-nine per cent of it to Sage. Plus, a lump sum of £100,000. I trust my grandson will bring new life to Burrow Hall. He seems a good lad. I follow him on his social media things, and he seems to have his head screwed on. He can make it as green as he likes, Belinda, so you'll be happy, but there are a few conditions. The village fayre is always to be held on the grounds, the upkeep of St Charlotte's is always to be ensured, the grounds are never to be built on for commercial reason and Burrow Hall is always to be very much part of village life. I don't want that ever to change. I'm sure it's a lot for Sage to take on and I'm not saying he has to live here, I'm sure he doesn't want to, given his wanderlust, but I need to know that Burrow Hall will always be associated with the Burniston name.'

Belinda's face felt tired from the range of emotions she had put it through, or more so her father had, over the duration of his speech. Nostalgia and sadness, mixed with intrigue and surprise, fused with disappointment and anger and now a surge of happiness at the news that her son, Sage, would be receiving Burrow Hall in the will. It meant that indirectly she would be able to hopefully carry out her wishes on the Hall, albeit, it seemed, under the watchful eye of somebody else. Maybe she could live there too. Split her time between greening up Burrow Hall and a little quality R and R at the bolthole in Dubai. Suddenly, the fact that she was being left less than the butler in her father's will didn't sting quite so much. Perhaps she and Sage could make some new family memories in Burrow Hall themselves. At least she still had a direct blood tie to the share in Burrow Hall. Unlike her brother, who, judging from the colour of his face, was about to blow a gasket.

It was a raging Alexi who spoke now. 'Well, if Sage

gets forty-nine per cent, then who on earth gets the rest?'

It was a question that everyone had been thinking and Sir Buster realised that too.

'So, you'll be wanting to know who gets the fifty-one per cent then, won't you?' It was clear that Sir Buster was very much enjoying certain aspects of his will reading from beyond the grave. Almost wallowing in the tension he knew his words would be dishing out to those involved. 'That was an easy decision. I give the fifty-one per cent of Burrow Hall to the village of Rooney-at-Burrow. I bequeath it to the village that has been my family for as long as I can remember. Maybe even more of a family to me in recent times than my actual one. The joy of the annual village fayre was something Fiona adored and now Margaret Millsop has taken it on with such incredible zest. I can happily say that my marrows were often the talk of it. I'd like to think they will still be grown on my allotment after my demise, thank you, and entered into the fayre every year.'

For a moment, Samuel couldn't help but feel sad at the thought of Sir Buster's prize vegetables being vandalised.

Such a banal yet somehow brutal thing. The thought evaporated as Sir Buster continued.

'Then there's the joy of nights down The Six Pennies with Phil and Steph and those lock-ins. Not sure if I should mention them, but hey, I'm dead.' He laughed again at his own morbid humour. 'The village square and the duck pond, Violet and her wool shop. Life in Rooney-at-Burrow is a splendid one. And one that should always be glorious. But I am fully aware that a village can't be in charge of Burrow Hall. So, I must pick someone who I believe will bring a fresh young attitude into the Hall and maybe some new ideas. Nothing too radical, mind you, as I know they will always have the interests of the village at heart as they have family and a history here. You don't get crowned Ravishing Rooney Queen five times on the trot without being a popular member of village life. Plus, she sings like an angel, has worked here at the Hall and knows it very well and also gives me some of the most insightful conversations I've had in the last few years. With great pleasure, I bequeath it to Sheena Pollett. I trust her to do what she wishes with Burrow Hall, but I know that she will do it for the village. The same conditions I set for Sage apply too. Plus, there's a lump sum of £100,000 for you, Sheena, as you deserve it for putting up with me and the ramblings of an old man.'

Now all eyes in the room turned to Sheena. She was sitting in shock, still holding her father's hand. Unable to stop it, a smile swept itself widely across her face. She wasn't sure if it was the thought of the money, the Hall, the trust Sir Buster had put in her or the fact that Sir Buster obviously liked her as much as she liked him. Probably all of the above, but it was the latter that left her with the warmest feeling. He was right, they had enjoyed so many fabulous conversations in her time working there. That was one of the many wonderful things she would miss about him. Her thoughts blended, happiness tinged with sadness.

'Wow.' It was all she could say. She scanned across to look at both Belinda and Alexi, but was unable to fully dissect their expressions. She was also sure she heard more noises coming from behind the door. Everything felt somewhat surreal right now.

Sir Buster's voice sounded from the screen again. 'Well, that's me done, I guess. All of the legalities and the boring bits will be sorted, no doubt, but those are my wishes. I dare say that not everyone is happy, but I am, and I know the future of Burrow Hall will be, so that satisfies me that I've done the right thing. I wish you all well and thank you for happy times. But I must say before I sign off that if one of you did send those threatening notes to me, then I hope that one day justice will come and hit you where it really hurts. Goodbye, everyone. See you on whatever is on the other side.'

Sir Buster bent forward, pushed the button of whatever was recording him, and the screen faded to black.

Alexi was on his feet first. His face was still a deep maroon with frenzy. He stormed towards the study door. 'Well, that was a crock of... what the...' He didn't finish either sentence as he pulled the study door open to reveal Violet and Margaret standing there sheepishly.

As he marched off, Margaret smiled politely as Violet peered in at the people remaining in the study.

'Would anyone like a cup of tea and a sandwich?' she

asked.

Chapter 47

If it hadn't been for Jimmy swiftly grabbing Pearl out of the way at the last second as they walked up to the entrance of Burrow Hall, the angry tornado that was Alexi Burniston would have doubtless knocked her to the floor, sending the crafted card she had made and the bunch of flowers from Rita's tumbling to the gravel.

She and Jimmy had been just about to knock on the front door when it had opened, and a puce-coloured Alexi had come barging through. His anger was visible enough to stain the air.

'What is it with people skulking behind doors in this blessed village?' he questioned, not even a hint of welcoming friendliness daring to cross his face.

'Oh, hello, Mr Burniston. As you know, we were so

sorry to hear about you father. We just thought we'd like to deliver some flowers and cards to convey our condolences.' It was Jimmy who spoke. Pearl seemed to be hyperventilating somewhat at the sight of Alexi Burniston in the flesh again.

Alexi was in no mood for polite banter. 'Oh yeah, whatever. Just leave the cards and flowers on the hall table if you like. And... er... thanks.' His tone was dismissive and unfriendly.

'We've made the cards ourselves,' offered Pearl, as if this would calm his rage. She had no idea as to why it would.

It didn't. 'So... you make cards. Great. Thanks. I really can't talk right now. So, if you'll excuse me... The others are inside if you want to chat about cards to somebody else.' He was going to add 'to someone who actually cares' but stopped himself. He recognised the woman as the one he had enjoyed a drink or two with, or perhaps more, in the pub. He seemed to remember she was fairly pleasant company. And she had kept the drinks coming, so fair play.

'The others?' enquired Jimmy. 'Oh, of course, it's the will reading today, isn't it? Have we called at an inconvenient time? Oh, my word, we both forgot completely, didn't we, Pearl?' He made the words sound overly sincere.

'Completely,' lied Pearl.

'Well, it was a bloody shambles,' snipped Alexi. 'I wish I'd not gone now. Flaming farce.'

Pearl could see that Alexi had the urge to vent. Every egotist needed an audience.

'But surely the will was pretty plain sailing.' Pearl reached out to touch his arm, wanting to appear caring. 'Sir Buster left the Hall and I'm guessing near enough everything to you and your sister, no?'

Pearl was worried that she might have overstepped the mark. Alexi's rapid answer told her that she hadn't.

'Well, you're obviously more sensible than my dead dad, aren't you?' replied Alexi. 'Dad left me and my sister some money, less than the staff as it happened, and has actually left the Hall to my nephew and the girl who cleans this place. Work that logic out. So much for blood being thicker than water.'

Pearl and Jimmy both drew breath in unison.

'He's left it to Sheena?' There was serious disbelief in Jimmy's voice.

'Yep,' he huffed. 'That's her. She gets fifty-one per cent and nephew Sage gets forty-nine. Total lunacy.'

'At least it's still in the family,' Pearl tried to appease.

'I wanted this house. I needed it.' For a split second, there was a vein of sadness that replaced the anger in Alexi's words. Sadness dripped with desperation.

Pearl and Jimmy both knew why. Alexi needed the money. More than he actually knew. Pearl abruptly reminded herself that she had some important news to share with Alexi. It seemed cruel to kick a man when he was down, but that was just timing.

'You look like you could do with a good drink, sunshine,' offered Pearl. 'I know I could after you nearly knocked me flying again. You're making quite a habit of that. At least you weren't in the car this time.'

'No, not for me, cheers. I want to get as far away from here as possible. I want to drive to clear my head. I need to think, so sorry, but no. But feel free to go and drain the old man's bar dry. After all, it won't be me who's paying to restock it, will it.'

Pearl was determined to not let him disappear. She endeavoured to keep the conversation flowing. 'What would you have done with the house? Were you planning to live here?'

Alexi harrumphed. 'In this old place, I think not. Do I look like I'd be happy with village life?' Alexi didn't even have the merest notion of his own rudeness in his response. 'All of this would have gone. This land is worth a lot of dosh and I planned to utilise it to it maximum potential. You could build a huge number of houses on here. Think of all of those affluents who could live here and still work in the big cities. It's low-cost living in the country for all those suited and booted from the city. This place could house more up-and-comings than Wembley Stadium. It's a gold mine. The old man should have got shot of it years ago. Take out the Hall, the church, some of the forest. It could bring in a fortune. Maybe leave the lake for a few waterside properties. It could have been the best new complex in a fifty-mile radius. It could have been so lucrative. And so good. Can you imagine?'

Both Jimmy and Pearl could. And the thought terrified them both. As did the fact that Alexi Burniston seemed oblivious to how it would have affected the village. Shattered the peace of it for good. They glanced at each other in horror.

Jimmy couldn't help but question Alexi, though. 'But all that family history. You grew up here. You wouldn't want to wipe all that out, would you? Literally demolish it?'

'I was a kid here and then I was shipped off to boarding school. I've not exactly spent a lot of my life here. So, it's easy to not see it as a family home. And besides… my family have just left it to the blinking cleaner, so I think my lack of nostalgia is justified, don't you.' Alexi's face was becoming a more violent shade of red again as his anger mounted once more. 'Right. I'm off. Go on in and see the others. Do what you like, I don't care. It's nothing to do with me, is it?'

Pearl was aware that she still needed to try to keep

Alexi sweet and on side as she needed to talk to him about the exposés of his life in Barbados. 'Oh, now, now, don't go off all hot-headed. Why don't you come for one soothing drink with me inside and then you can go off and do what you like for the day. Going for a drive with the wind in your hair will do you the world of good, but don't set off angrily.' She linked her arm into his to try to steer him inside.

Alexi was unwavering. 'No, I need to distance myself from here as soon as possible. For good.' He unlinked his arm from hers.

Pearl couldn't let him disappear. Not yet. Her tone turned more severe.

'No, you need to stay. I need to talk to you.'

'What about?'

She turned to Jimmy and handed him the card and the flowers she was carrying in her hand. He took them. He could see Pearl was plotting and that, as ever, she knew exactly what she was doing. At least she appeared to know. The hyperventilating had stopped.

'About the fact that you owe Vin Sutton a rather

massive amount of money from your time in Barbados and that he wants it back, with interest. And he wants it back now.'

Pearl tucked her arm back into Alexi's. The action was intended to be comforting, but given the words she'd just delivered, to Pearl it felt almost Mafia-like.

Alex's mouth fell open at the mention of Vin's name and his face went from puce to almost void of colour in a matter of seconds.

Jimmy decided it was his moment to say something too. 'And we know what you've been up to back in the UK as I know someone who knows Tanya from that reality programme who's in Abu Dhabi and she knows about the corrupt deal with the woman who was on *Seduction* something or other. The tanning product thing. And that you're broke too.' Jimmy could hear that he was stumbling with his facts slightly and that he'd said 'know' rather too many times. He should really pay more attention to every detail.

Alexi's last smudge of colour disappeared completely from his skin. After the day he had experienced, he was already beaten.

Pearl took her chance. 'Jimmy, you go and see the others, and congratulate Sheena for me. I think Alexi and I need to go and have a serious talk.'

Jimmy walked into Burrow Hall and headed for the study as Pearl led a bewildered and apparently broken Alexi by the arm so that she could fill him on everything he needed to know.

As she entered the entrance hall of Burrow Hall, as ever Pearl couldn't help but be impressed with the grandeur of the space around her. How could anybody in their right mind want to demolish this? But then, it was clear that Alexi Burniston was not in his right mind. And more than likely never would be after what she was about to tell him.

Chapter 48

Despite the fact that Violet and Margaret were actually supposed to be working at Burrow Hall serving tea and sandwiches, all professional etiquette appeared to have gone out of the nearest window after the revelations of the will reading.

While Violet did indeed provide those who wished for an initial, and what turned out to be a final, round of tea and sandwiches – well, as far as she was concerned there was too much fresh news to discuss to constantly interrupt it with endless trips to the kitchen – Margaret had joined Sergeant Pollett and a still beaming Sheena. Having deposited a tray of sandwiches on a table in the corner of the study and telling people to help themselves, Violet had joined them too. Belinda was busy discussing things with

Jonas Cushing near the study desk, and Herbert and Mrs Turner were both in an outwardly stunned state of conversation with each other on the far side of the study.

Jimmy too had infiltrated the group with Sheena and Margaret as Violet sat down.

'Why is everybody from your craft group here?' asked Samuel, directing the question at his daughter. 'Isn't this official family business? And why were you hidden behind the door, Aunt Violet?'

'No time for that now, Samuel. Let's talk about what's happened.'

'Yes, Alexi has just told Pearl and I about you being given this place, Sheena,' said Jimmy. 'Alexi is seriously peeved.'

'Hang on, Pearl's here too?' uttered Samuel, his voice a mixture of being both baffled and not at all surprised.

Jimmy explained what had happened at the entrance to Burrow Hall and brought the group up to speed with the revelations of Alexi's former life in Barbados and also what Bailey had discovered on the flight home from Abu Dhabi. Sheena's eyes seemed to shine even brighter when

Jimmy mentioned Tanya from the telly and the woman from *Seduction Central*.

'So, he's broke,' said Margaret. 'No wonder he stormed out of here in such a stinky huff. He was left £150,000 and now £100,000 of that will be disappearing in an instant. But I can't say I give a stuff. Seeing as he was about to try to demolish this place and turn Rooney-at-Burrow into some kind of yuppie dumping ground.'

Violet nodded. 'I think it seems like Alexi Burniston actually ended up with more than he deserved, but if he's broke and has been apparently for a while, then do we think that maybe he was behind those notes to poor Sir Buster? We saw on the video what Sir Buster thought about them. He may not have been giving into threats, but the notes panicked him, that was for sure.'

'What video?' asked Jimmy.

Violet explained fully to make sure Jimmy was kept in the picture on what had been happening in the study.

It was only when Violet had finished that Jimmy let out a 'good on old Sir Buster'.

'I could imagine Alexi sending those notes. Or

dropping them in here incognito,' offered Samuel, 'but do you think him being broke is reason enough to want Sir Buster dead. And would he actually kill him? Plus, I'm sure everyone is aware of the latest revelations about the body being found not far from along with a confession to killing Sir Buster.'

Before he could continue, Violet butted in, 'Tell them about the confession note. The one pinned to the dead man was made with cut-out letters, just like the ones that Sir Buster found in the book,' cooed Violet, unaware that she had just pretty much told them herself.

A chorus of gasps erupted from the group at the news that there was another note similar to the threatening ones Sheena had found in the book.

Samuel creased his face in annoyance. 'Violet, you shouldn't be telling anyone about that. It only said in the papers there was a confession but not about what the note looked like.' He glanced over to where Belinda was deep in conversation with Jonas Cushing and prayed that she hadn't heard a word of what had been said.

'And you shouldn't be keeping information like that

from the group, so, again, we're equal. Show the others.'

'Yes, show us... hurry,' urged Margaret, desperate to see what the note said.

'And why are you hiding it?' asked Sheena. Her face was more than a tad vexed.

'Because I wanted to see what happened today to discover who would benefit from the will and had the most to gain from Sir Buster dying. If someone did kill him, then there might have been some rather hefty clues given today. Plus, there's another handwritten note that I found too. There's more to all of this than meets the eye, most definitely.'

Was that another puffing out of Samuel's chest? He appeared to be happy at suddenly being the centre of attention again, Violet noted.

'Will you show us the note please?' urged an exasperated Margaret.

'Yes, Dad, come on,' remarked Sheena.

'I'll show you the confession, but I shouldn't really be showing it to anyone connected with the case.' A disapproving stare from Violet directly at him, however, was enough to override any of Samuel's apprehension.

Furtively glancing around the room to see who was looking in their direction, Samuel pulled his phone from his jacket pocket and showed the others a photo he had taken of the confession. All of them immediately noticed the fact that one of the letters was in the same typeface as the competition from the crafting magazine.

It was Jimmy who mentioned it first. 'So, the person who said they killed Sir Buster owned a craft magazine, then? That's a bit weird.'

'I refuse to believe anyone who knows the joy of quilting is capable of ending someone's life,' said Margaret. 'But I suppose everyone is a suspect until proved otherwise.'

'Crafter or not...' added Jimmy.

'Oh my God, Dad, do you think we're all suspects? Is that why you didn't want to show us the note? You suspect it might be one of us that killed poor Sir Buster. Even me?' Sheena's words were half-incredulous, half-accusatory.

'No... er, of course not, but I have to consider... every option, Sheena. It's my duty as an officer of the law.'

Samuel stumbled over his words a little.

'I suppose, but really...' Sheena could see where her dad was coming from but wouldn't entertain the notion that anyone from Team C.R.A.B. was involved in such murky dealings.

Violet leapt to her nephew's defence. 'Samuel is right to consider everyone. Two of those notes have been written using a craft magazine that we all know and have in our homes. Of course we're suspects, but I was doing a lot of tossing and turning over this last night, thinking about the notes and whether it could indeed be one of us, or a crafter that we know. I really can't imagine it is. In fact, every matt and layer of instinct inside me tells me that it's definitely not. And I don't believe that someone would create a note like that to confess to a killing.'

'Seems a bit OTT. And anyway, who was the body with the confession note?' asked Margaret.

'You have to tell us now,' echoed Jimmy.

Samuel knew that he didn't have to, but it was becoming clear that all of the group were sharing what they knew with him now about the case, so perhaps it would be wise to return the favour. He launched into the details of everything that had happened the day before and the grizzly discovery of Jeremiah Halliwell.

He ended his tale by telling them about the handwritten note he had found in the woodland and how he had not shown it to anyone else as yet, apart from WPC Horton and Violet. He was beginning to enjoy wearing the cloak of his own deception.

'So I'm waiting to see what happens when the police search Halliwell's caravan for clues. I've asked for a sample of his handwriting. Hopefully someone will get back to me soon,' Samuel concluded.

'So do you really think that this Jeremiah killed Sir Buster?' asked Sheena.

'No, I don't,' said Samuel.

'Which leaves the question who did?' stated Violet.

'Definitely not a quilter,' remarked Margaret.

For a moment, a contemplative hush rested over the group.

'Well, what about Belinda not forgiving Sir Buster for her mother's death?' asked Violet, careful to lower her voice in case Belinda could hear her. Luckily, she was still engaged with Jonas. 'What do you think of that, Samuel? Is that reason enough to send threatening notes?'

'I can't see Belinda doing that, but it's clear she's got some attitude and that there's no love lost between her and her brother, and indeed her and her late father. She must be gutted she's not been given the house, but at least it's her son that has part ownership in it.'

'I think Belinda had every intention of trying to live here or maybe sell it. She definitely wants to make some money so that she can break away from her husband, in my opinion,' remarked Margaret. 'You said that she wasn't on the best terms with him either, Violet.'

'I did,' mused Violet. 'Belinda Flatt is a woman who doesn't seem to be getting along with a lot of people close to her lately. I think a woman with that much frustration and restless resentment inside her is capable of doing anything to make a change in her life. Maybe even killing off her—'

'Gosh, what a lovely outfit,' exclaimed Margaret rather loudly in regard to nothing. The words stopped Violet mid-flow. This was just as Margaret intended, which became clear when the group turned to see who Margaret was aiming her words at. Belinda Flatt was approaching the group, the look on her face more than a fraction or two away from friendly.

Violet mouthed 'thank you, dear' at Margaret when she realised the reason for her rather loud interjection. Samuel hurriedly jammed his phone into his jacket pocket.

Belinda smoothed her hands down the creases of her dark suit and attempted a smile. 'Oh, thank you, d'you think so? I wasn't sure what to wear. It's designer.'

'Well, it's lovely, dear,' said Margaret, sparking a murmur of rather overexaggerated agreement from the entire group, including a bemused Samuel who didn't know his Primark from his Prada.

'I thought I had better come and say hello properly, seeing as you and I will be sharing a lot of time together, it seems.' Belinda was targeting her comment at Sheena. She sounded far from thrilled with the idea. 'Mind if I sit down?'

Jimmy shifted his seat so that Belinda could

manoeuvre herself into the group. He held out his hand as he did so. 'Hi, I'm Jimmy, from the farm, this is Margaret Millsop. That's Sergeant Pollett, who is Sheena's dad. I believe you know Violet, of course.'

Belinda ignored his words and merely sat down. She crossed her legs, immediately drawing attention to the price tag on her shoe again. No one said a word. They were pricey. Sheena couldn't help but think that she could purchase half of her own wardrobe with that kind of money. The rather pleasing thought occurred to her that now she actually could. Mind you, she guessed she would still love a bargain whether it was House of Fraser or House of Versace.

'So, you and my son Sage are going to own this place. First off, I want to know what you're going to do with it?' Belinda's words were blunt.

Sheena was quick to respond. 'I have no idea. This is probably more of a shock to me than it is you.'

Belinda scoffed. 'I doubt that. It's quite a shock to the system when your dead father tells you that the cleaner gets the house you grew up in in his will.'

Albeit a little taken aback, Sheena could understand the tinges of resentment in Belinda's words. 'I will be sticking to your dad's wishes, though. This place is the very heartbeat of Rooney-at-Burrow. Nothing should change that. I was extremely fond of Sir Buster.'

Samuel put his arm around his daughter and gave Sheena a comforting and proud hug.

'I'm sure you were,' said Belinda. 'Very fond. Fond enough to manage to get him to give you this place. Are you sure you were just the cleaner? Or were there other duties you had to perform for him to earn your pay?'

Sheena's mouth fell open and a series of tuts and gasps Mexican-waved around the group.

Samuel removed his arm from around her and pointed his finger directly in Belinda's face. 'Now, hang on a minute, what are you suggesting? My daughter is not that kind of girl.'

'Well, she's the kind of girl that managed to get a seventy-year-old man to change his will at the last moment. Are you sure she didn't write those threatening notes herself and then feed my father with words of how horrible Alexi and I are to make us lose what is rightfully ours? It's easy to warp a man's mind when you look like that.' She waggled her fingers in Sheena's direction.

'Now, look here...' Samuel stood up to show his protectiveness. 'I am not having anyone talk to my daughter like that.'

'It's okay, Dad.' Sheena interrupted her father by standing up and placing herself directly in front of Belinda Flatt. 'I can handle this.'

Samuel fell silent, as were Violet, Margaret and Jimmy, all wholly enthralled, if also concerned and somewhat appalled at the accusations being thrown.

'Okay, first off, Belinda, I'm sorry about your dad. I really am. Because Sir Buster was a brilliant man, and I will miss him enormously. So... I'm going to put your rude, ridiculous accusations down to the fact that your brain isn't exactly working clearly after what has been a really surprising day for us all. And I hope that when you wake up tomorrow and it's a new day, you'll realise just how nasty and idiotic your suggestions are. And maybe you'll apologise. I'm not going to get embroiled in your family affairs. What's gone on before and any issues that have arisen between you and your dad and your brother are not my business. And my friendship with your dad is none of yours. As for this place. I intend to do my best to make sure that Sir Buster's last wishes are always granted and anyone who tries to make me do otherwise will be in no doubt about how I feel. I look forward to meeting Sage, I really do. Let's hope the bitterness and foul-mouthed rants that seem to have afflicted both you and your brother have skipped a generation. In the meantime, if you have any more advice you'd like to pass onto me, then I suggest you do it through Mr Cushing over there. Now, if you don't mind, my friends and I were having a decent conversation. So would you kindly leave us alone?'

Jimmy wanted to applaud as Sheena sat back down but halted himself from doing so. Violet and Margaret, both rather thrilled by Sheena's gall too, merely gazed into their laps awkwardly. Samuel puffed out his chest with paternal pride and held Sheena's hand tight once she was seated.

Belinda's face was stony and pinched in its appearance. A tremble of fury threatened from her bottom lip. She stood up without saying a word and smoothed down the creases of her suit again.

'I'm sure Sage will have exactly the same impression of you as I do. He's a good judge of character. You're the stranger in our family home.'

'Hardly a stranger. I've spent more time here than you have over the last few years. I'd never even seen you before this week.'

'I hope you're happy with what you've done,' stated Belinda, before turning to walk away.

'And I hope you've kept the receipt for those shoes because they're not worth the price you paid,' said Sheena cuttingly, pointing to the tag on Belinda's shoes. 'You should try to get your money back. You may need it.'

Belinda looked down, saw the tag, huffed and strutted off towards the study door.

Sheena could feel her face flushing. 'Well, that was unexpected.'

This time, Jimmy did applaud. 'OMG, you were fabulous. I wish I'd recorded it as Bailey would've loved that.'

Samuel asked his daughter, 'Are you okay?'

'Totally. I've dealt with enough jealous girlfriends and school bullies to cope with women like her before. If she wants to start a fight, then bring it on.'

'Well, I thought you were marvellous, dear Sheena,' said Margaret. 'Just the right side of feisty with a little dash of soap opera catfight thrown in.'

'As did I,' agreed Violet. 'But if you will excuse me, I need to go and chat to the enemy a little more.'

'What about?' enquired Sheena.

'Just about something Sir Buster said on his video. Now, if you'll all excuse me.'

Violet stood and rushed off after Belinda. She reached her just as she had exited the study. Not an easy feat given the speed of Belinda's furious strut. She was resting her hand on a table with her leg angled upwards, yanking frantically at the tag on her shoe.

Violet turned on the charm. 'Well, I thought they're a rather lovely pair of shoes. Mind you, I could buy a lot of wool for my shop at that price.'

Belinda finally detached the tag and chucked it onto

the table. 'You pay for quality, what can I say.'

'Would you care for a walk? It seems like you could do with a little time to destress. I need to flex my aging bones regularly if you'd care to join me. I was thinking of walking down to St Charlotte's and back if you fancy. Perhaps it will take your mind off today.'

Belinda let the idea run lazily around her brain. She sighed and then agreed. 'Why the hell not.'

The two women were just walking out onto the gravel when they spied WPC Horton walking towards them. She smiled and waved on seeing Violet.

'What does she want?' huffed Belinda.

Unable to answer, Violet ignored the question. But she was keen to find out.

'Hello, Paula, how are you? I assume you're here officially given the fact you're in your uniform.'

'I am, and it's you I need to speak to.' She pointed at Belinda.

Belinda huffed again. 'As long as it's to tell me who this man is that is supposed to have killed my father. God, could this day actually get any more draining?'

Chapter 49

It was clear to WPC Horton that Belinda was not in the best of moods to undergo a grilling from her. The deep frowns of annoyance slashed across her face emphasised that. It was also a fact that Violet was more than aware of, so in the interest of Paula pertaining the information she required and Violet being able to earwig every detail, she suggested that the three of them retreat to the calm of the veranda on the side of Burrow Hall overlooking the lawns.

Within a few moments, the three women were sitting at a small round table, the heat of the sun kissing their skin with a warm and welcoming glow.

'Is Sergeant Pollett still inside?' asked Paula to Violet as they took their seats. She was eager to conduct the interview on her own. To showcase her own skill.

'He's with Sheena. It's been quite a morning, dear,' replied Violet. 'But let's discuss the affair in hand, shall we?'

Sheena was not exactly part of Belinda's friendship circle right now and Violet was keen to steer the conversation away from what had materialised at the will reading. Sadly, the damage was already done.

'Yes, he's looking after the new owner of Burrow Hall?' There was malice glued to every one of Belinda's words.

'Sorry? You mean that...' Paula started her sentence but left it dangling, not really knowing what the jumbled thoughts in her mind were doing.

'Yes. I do. Sheena is the new owner of Burrow Hall. Well, fifty-one per cent of it anyway. It seems that being a cleaner here, if that's all she was, pays dividends.'

A dumbstruck Paula said nothing.

Violet did, aiming her words at Belinda. 'Now, now, dear, I can guarantee that Sheena is a good girl. There's no way she would be involved with...' It was now Violet's turn to leave a sentence dangling.

She turned to Paula and surreptitiously tried to shush

her from making any further comment. Luckily, the police officer took the hint.

'I'm afraid I can't give you any information about the man who has apparently confessed to killing your father as I'm not directly working on that part of the case, but I do need to talk to you about something else.'

'Well, it had better be quick because I have a funeral to arrange for the man who has just left me out of his will. The man who has pretty much accused me or my stupid brother of sending him threatening notes to want to finish him off. Plus, I'm not overly thrilled to think that someone may have actually killed my father. So forgive me if I'm not really in the mood to talk.' Belinda's voice cracked slightly. Was her hard exterior cracking somewhat?

Paula pressed on. 'I need to ask you about the gun that Sir Buster kept in his shed on the allotment.'

'Oh, that damned thing. It shouldn't even be here any longer after all of the damage and heartache it's caused. Why he insisted on keeping it, I will never know.'

'Is it the gun involved with your mother's unfortunate accident, dear?' asked Violet.

'Yes, it was.' Belinda's face softened, just for an instant, at the mention of her mother. A momentary tenderness breaking through. It vanished as rapidly as it came. 'It was the gun that killed her.'

Not shocked by this revelation, Paula was keen to crack on. 'I've been doing some fingerprint tests on the wellington boots and the gun from the shed and we've had the results through.'

'What did you find on the boots, Paula?' asked Violet, eager to hear the outcome.

'Just Sir Buster's on the boots, unfortunately.' As ever, Paula wasn't totally sure why she was telling Violet, but she was unable to stop herself.

'And the gun?' asked Violet, enjoying the facts on offer.

Paula directed her answer at Belinda, keen to revert the conversation back to her original line of questioning. 'The prints we found on the gun belonged to Sir Buster, Herbert the butler and yourself, Belinda. What do you have to say about that?'

Belinda seemed non-plussed. 'That they're mine. I

handled the gun the other day. I went to look around the estate the first day I was back. I went down by the lake to see where father died. Or was killed… I wandered down to the church and then I meandered off to father's allotment too. I went into the shed, saw the gun and picked it up, bringing it back to the house. I asked Herbert to get rid of it for me. I don't want it here. It's the gun that shot my mother. Why would I want to see that?'

'So, Herbert handled it too?' asked Paula.

'He did. But he refused to get rid of it. He said he would as soon as he felt he could. Apparently, it's too raw for him to throw anything away that reminds him of my father right now. I suppose I can understand that. He has worked for him for his entire life. Mind you, he's been well paid for it now, hasn't he? He bagged the vintage car and more money than me in the will. The butler? I ask you. What a joke. Are you sure he didn't kill Daddy off? I'm not sure I trust anyone anymore.'

Paula could see that she obviously had a lot of catching up to do on what had happened at the will reading. She'd have to go into the house and find out everything as soon as she had finished grilling Belinda. But it certainly sounded like it had not gone to plan. Well, not Belinda's plan anyway.

'So, he returned it to the shed?' Paula resumed her line of questioning.

'I guess he must have done.'

'When you were in the shed, did you not think it a trifle odd that there were wellington boots in there that had marrow squashed all over them?'

'I saw the gun and nothing else. There could have been a baby dinosaur in there and I wouldn't have noticed. My attention was on the weapon that killed my mother. I get quite red misty when I think about that day or anything to do with it. It's the very reason I don't come back here really. Too many bad memories.'

Violet was keen to chase up on something that Sir Buster had mentioned in his video. 'Belinda, why do you blame your father for your mother's death? Why do you feel such anger towards him? It's not like he shot her, is it? Sir Buster loved Fiona. It had been such a lovely day.'

'It shouldn't have happened. I remember it like it was

yesterday. It all happened out here, you know.' She motioned out across the lawns. A blending of sadness and reflection coated itself across Belinda's as she recalled the day ten years ago…

* * *

Belinda Flatt was talking into the microphone on the purpose-built stage she was standing upon on the lush green lawns of Burrow Hall. Alongside her stood her husband, Rupert, who some of the crowd gathered seemed very excited to see – such was the drawer of someone who's been on the telly – and her son, Sage. Neither of them really wanted to be there. Rupert had returned at his wife's insistence, just for the day, from a village-building exercise he had been working on in some remote area of Africa. But Rupert Flatt was one of Belinda's main attractions for the day and if people were willing to pay good money for a photo and an autograph with the famous telly conservationist, then Belinda was not taking no for an answer. Sage would have rather been inside trying to collect a million coins and saving a princess on his Super

Mario game. What ten-year-old wouldn't? But Mother was again insistent that he show willing and family togetherness when she delivered her speech to the crowd assembled.

'And, in conclusion, I would like to thank each and every one of you for coming to our Earth Day celebration. All of the money raised from today will be going towards charities and schemes that demonstrate support for environmental protection. I would like to thank my parents for allowing us to literally erect a fairground on their lawns and I would like to encourage everyone to please buy as many raffle tickets as possible for all of the wonderful prizes on offer, which include...' Belinda unfolded a sheet of paper in her hands so that she could read what she needed to remember. 'Er... a free slap-up meal, including drinks, at The Six Pennies pub, a patchwork quilt made from materials donated from the ladies at Brewer's Loop, a skydive experience courtesy of the owner of Coates Farm and also a signed helmet and T-shirt that my husband wore on his most recent adventure in Africa. He is also posing for photos and signing autographs for a small charitable donation. Plus, Mrs Turner has made a huge batch of her famous plum flapjacks that she is selling for £2 a piece, so please dig deep, everyone. Now, please go and enjoy yourselves and celebrate Earth Day.'

Belinda applauded the crowd and switched off the microphone. She was pleased with how the day was going. It had been her idea to hold an Earth Day celebration at Burrow Hall. It was free to hire after all. And seeing as not all of the attractions on show had donated their services for free, she needed to try to cut as many corners as possible in the name of both the charity and her own family bank balance. But people seemed to be having fun and enjoying the attractions – a helter-skelter was alive with joyous whoops as children looped down its slide. A coconut shy and test your strength seemed equally busy, with the sounds of ball-on-coconut and mallet-on-button and subsequent ting from the bell filling the air. The hook-a-duck and duck shooting galleries were also particularly busy. Although Belinda was wondering if the day would pass without some sarcastic clever clogs mentioning the fact that perhaps an attraction where shooting ducks, albeit bright yellow mechanical ones, was particularly befitting for such a green eco-friendly cause. But people were spending their money and that was all that mattered.

'Can I go back inside now and play my game?' asked Sage. His tone was nasal and whiny.

'Why don't you go and play on the helter-skelter? There's lots of children over there. Go and have some fun,' said Belinda. 'It's a beautiful day.' It was, indeed, the sun even hotter than Belinda could have wished for, given that it was April.

'I don't want to. I did it earlier. It's boring.' It was true, he had, about half a dozen times, but when a girl roughly his own age, one that Sage found incredibly pretty, had offered him some candyfloss and smiled, he had blushed bright red and run a mile. Sage now merely wanted to play his computer game and not talk to girls. Even if they were prettier than the princess that Mario was trying to rescue.

'Let the boy do what he likes,' said Rupert. 'How much longer is this going on for?' He sounded equally whiny.

Belinda checked her watch. 'Another hour. So, I suggest you get back to your stall and let some more of these villagers have their photo taken with their favourite TV conservationist. And do try to smile. And can you make sure you're ready to draw the raffle at five o'clock. Although quite why someone would want to win your sweaty old T-shirt is beyond me. I've had enough of them in the laundry basket over the years to cover these lawns twice over.'

Belinda watched as both her husband and her son disappeared out of sight. She reprimanded herself for letting her smile slip. She had needed to emboss it across her face all day. She forced it to return as she looked out at the crowds mingling happily in between the attractions. This was not her kind of event. It reflected well on her that she had organised it and that was what counted, but deep down mixing with the locals was not really her bag. They just all seemed a little provincial these days.

She waved at the two ladies who owned the wool shop. They seemed to be loving the day. And then there was the woman who made the patchwork quilt. Margaret, was it?

She had been banging on all day about how much she had enjoyed making it and that she hoped it would raise a lot of money. She'd met her husband too. Belinda was sure that he was flirting with her and found him a tad smarmy. He reminded her of her own brother. Who, not surprisingly, had not turned up today. This was to be expected. As Belinda had not invited him. He had made it clear a long time ago that green issues were not his thing. The only green he cared about was the green of dollar bills, or whatever currency he was currently dealing with. Belinda may have always tried to be green, but yet somehow her brother always made her see red, so she was grateful he wasn't here to spoil the day.

She spied her mother and father at the shooting gallery. Sir Buster had the pistol in his hands and was merrily firing as many pellets as he could at the mechanical ducks. As another fell to his shooting skill, he cried out, 'That got the feathered bugger, he's quacked his last' at the top of his voice. Belinda's mother laughed joyously.

Belinda cringed. Yes, the shooting gallery was definitely a brutal and violent idea that she hadn't thought through.

She checked her watch and smiled again. Less than an hour. She could do this. She'd been planning it for weeks. It was nearly over. Then when it was done and dusted, she could get away somewhere nice and sunny. Where she could be pampered. And alone. Gosh, that would be wonderful.

Sir Buster shouted across at his daughter, 'Belinda, get over here and watch your mother trying to shoot these ducks. She's bloody terrible. She couldn't shoot a pig in a passage!'

It was about two hours later that Belinda sat down on the veranda of Burrow Hall with her mother and looked out over the now empty fairground attractions. She was glad it was over, but they had raised a good amount of cash for Earth Day, plus she was pleased that she had made the effort. Although she wasn't certain she would attempt another one for the longest time.

'Your tea, madame,' said Herbert as he placed a tray on the table containing a pot of tea and two bone-china cups.

'Thank you, Herbert,' said Fiona Burniston. Just

turned sixty, she had her shiny grey locks tied in a tight bun at the back of her head. She radiated class and elegance. She sat upright, her posture perfect, as she poured the tea. Fiona was a lady, in every sense of the word. 'Well, you must be thrilled about the amount of money you've raised,' remarked Fiona to her daughter, before nearly jumping out of her seat as the sound of a gunshot cracked across the air. The stream of tea she was pouring escaped from the cup it was flowing into and began to fill the saucer. 'Oh, for heaven's sake, look what your father had made me go and do.' She shouted across at her husband: 'You've made me spill the tea, Buster.' Despite the spillage, there was no displeasure in her voice.

'Sorry!' called Sir Buster from across the lawns where he had set up a row of tin cans on an old table. 'Just having a practice. Your turn next Fi-Fi.' It was his affectionate name for his wife.

'What is he doing?' asked Belinda.

'He's appalled that I'm such a lousy shot apparently. Reckons that any lady living in a big house like this should be able to shoot a gun. Apparently, I let too many mechanical ducks live to quack another day.'

Belinda smiled. 'He enjoyed himself today, didn't he?'

'Oh, you know your father, always the life and soul of any event.' Her words were wrapped with warmth.

Belinda contemplated her mother's words. Actually, she didn't particularly know him that well. She had always been a mummy's girl really. Her dad always someone she felt a little disconnected from. It had been her mother that had been there for the hugs and bedtime stories. Maybe other daughters felt the same about their dads. She didn't really know. He just seemed to be much more into the more machismo side of life. Maybe there was a stronger bond between him and her brother, though she wasn't close enough to her brother either to know.

Fiona must have read her daughter's thoughts. 'Have you spoken to your brother recently? The pair of you are pretty useless at coming to visit, but at least you stay in touch on the phone with me all the time. I can't remember the last time Alexi actually phoned me up. Your dad speaks to him now and again, but it's normally when Alexi needs something. Or we receive a begging letter. He's been quiet on that front for a while, though.' Ever maternal, Fiona's words were peppered with worry.

'No, I've not spoken to him for quite some time. He's still sponging then. Where is he living now?'

'Back here, I think, in this country. He was away in the Caribbean, but I'm sure your father said that he was back. I've no idea what he's doing, though. I never really have. Your brother has always been an enigma to me. Well, since about the age of thirteen he has anyway.'

'Gunshot coming!' shouted Sir Buster again before another explosive crack filed the grounds. A tin can zinged off the table and landed with a soft thud on the floor. A jubilant whoop followed from Sir Buster.

'At least he warned us this time,' smirked Belinda, before her expression turned darker. 'No, Alexi was all vague the last time I spoke to him about his whereabouts. I'm not sure I really care. It would be nice if he wanted to see his nephew once in a while, though.'

'Where is my favourite grandson, Sage?' enquired Fiona. 'Probably my only one unless you're thinking of having another or Alexi decides to settle down with somebody. I don't think he has. He doesn't seem the settling type in any area of life.'

Belinda couldn't help but immediately think that no woman in her right mind would want to settle down with Alexi. 'Sage has gone back to London with Rupert. Did he not come and say goodbye to you? I told him to. Rupert had to get back home because of some campaign he's working on and Sage said he was bored, so he's gone too. Plus, he doesn't get to spend that much time with his dad on his own these days. And, no, we're not contemplating any others. I think one is enough when you're on your own most of the time.' Belinda had to admit that she missed her precious me-time as it was having one child, so another was not an overly appealing thought.

'It's nice that Rupert's away doing worthy things,' said Fiona.

'I just wish he could see my worth when I'm at home bringing up Sage and literally running rings around myself trying to do everything. Mind you, Sage will be off to boarding school soon. Maybe then I can get a moment's peace.'

Fiona looked at her caringly. 'Has the romance disappeared from the marriage then? I thought you too didn't seem particularly lovey-dovey today. You have to work at a marriage, Belinda. And appreciate each other. Your father and I laugh and joke with each other each and every day and we always treat each other with respect and dignity. It's the secret to success.'

'It's hard to find something funny when your husband is a dozen time zones away or fifteen feet underground or underwater or up a tree in some country you've never even heard of,' Belinda moaned.

'Another shot then it's over to you, Fi-Fi,' boomed Sir Buster, again followed by an ear-splitting bang as a third shot slashed the evening air.

But Fiona was focused on her daughter. 'Well, you used to be inseparable.'

'I didn't use to have to worry about school runs and trying to get someone to football practice on a Saturday morning and do the weekly shop, did I?'

'Keep it fun, dear, always remember why you fell in love. And always be grateful of the time you have together.

And appreciate each other.'

Sir Buster came bounding up to the table. 'Right then, Fi-Fi, I think it's time you learnt how to shoot in a straight line. Can you believe your mother is such a dreadful shot, Belinda? Hardly hit one bloody duck today. I bet you know one end of a gun from the other, not like your mother. I'm sure you and that husband of yours have had to shoot wild animals away from your tent in some of those remote places you've been to.'

Actually, Belinda hadn't. She was as clueless about a weapon as her mother. And glad of it.

Sir Buster bent down to kiss his wife on the cheek. 'I'll be right back. Just got to answer a small call of nature and then it's you and me, kiddo.'

'Okey-dokey. Let's do this, shall we?' said Fiona. She winked at her daughter as she spoke.

Sir Buster ran off to do whatever he needed to do. Fiona and Belinda stood up out of their seats and walked across to where the table was set up on the lawn. A trio of cans still stood on the table like a little metallic firing line. But Belinda was less interested in the cans and more in the conversation she'd been having with her mother.

'How do you make sure that you stay in love with someone?' asked Belinda.

Fiona answered her daughter. 'Darling, there is no rule book to make sure that you stay in love with someone, you just have to know that you are in love. You can never force the issue. You just wholeheartedly love that person, faults and all, because you heart says it's impossible to do otherwise. You father drives me insane sometimes, but I always love him. I can't help that.' Fiona looked down at the gun that was lying on the lawn. 'Now, what on earth am I supposed to do with that?'

She bent down to pick up the gun.

Belinda would never know exactly what happened next even if she relived it in her mind for a thousand years.

Her mother had picked up the gun, turned it in her hands and fiddled with something. The gun had sounded. The only noise that followed was not that of a tin can zinging off into the distance, it was that of Fiona Burniston falling to the floor and her daughter's subsequent screams.

Belinda was still screaming when Sir Buster came running back out of Burrow Hall having heard the sound of the gun…

'You must know that it was an accident,' said Violet. She reached into her pocket for a tissue. She could see that tears were teetering, ready to fall from Belinda's eyes now that she had finished telling the tale of her mother's premature death.

'That's just it,' said Belinda, talking the tissue from Violet's hand and dabbing her eyes. 'I know it was an accident. I know that my father said that he had flicked the safety catch to on. But it went off. Maybe my mother flicked it off. Maybe she didn't. But my father shouldn't have left that gun on the ground loaded. He shouldn't have left it for my mother to pick up. He shouldn't have disappeared, leaving me and Mum there with the gun. He shouldn't have been so bloody stupid and careless. That was his fault. And I know I should love him despite his faults, but I can't. Every time I look at him, I see my mother falling to the floor and I see her dead body lying there. I hate him for it. And that's something I can't help.'

Belinda stood up and pushed herself away from the table she was sharing with Violet and WPC Horton. The chair she had been sitting on fell to the floor with a clatter.

'Excuse me please,' she uttered between sobs before running off and out of sight around the corner of Burrow Hall.

Violet and Paula stared across the table at each other.

'She is one tormented woman,' remarked Violet.

'I should say. Imagine seeing your own mother drop down dead in front of you. That's enough to scar you for life. I get hysterical when Mr Bublé sicks up a massive furball,' offered Paula.

'She's scarred indeed,' replied Violet. 'Scarred enough to threaten her own father?'

'She could be.'

'She could even be scarred enough to kill him,' suggested Violet, raising her eyebrows in contemplation.

'It's all becoming quite a mess, isn't it? Blackmail and threatening notes,' pondered Paula.

'It is, dear, it is. Put it this way. If this entire messy situation was a ball of wool in my shop, then I wouldn't use it to make a jumper quite yet as there are way too many loose ends that would need some serious unravelling. Sir Buster's heart, the squashed marrows, those threatening notes, siblings who obviously dislike each other and the convenience of a suicide note blaming it on a scoundrel like Jeremiah Halliwell. There's too many things pinging around my mind right now that are making me think that we are nowhere near unravelling the entire murky truth about poor Sir Buster.'

Chapter 50

The back room at Brewer's Loop was a hive of activity as the clock on the wall ticked to 6 p.m. Jimmy, Pearl, Margaret and Violet sat around the table, glasses of rhubarb gin in their hands, discussing the events of the day.

Sheena and Samuel were stood by the doorway, deep in conversation about her inheritance of Burrow Hall, a fact that had still not fully sunken in and would no doubt take a mammoth amount of time to do so. Both were drinking tea.

Paula Horton, herself with a much-needed glass of sloe gin in her hands too – well, she wasn't on shift anymore – was browsing the shelves of crafty delights in the back room. Was that a sheet of pussycat pictures she saw? It was. She picked up the packet. One of the ginger cats looked identical to Mr Bublé. She read the top of the sheet. Feline toppers, it said. She had no idea what toppers were, but she liked the ginger cat so she would ask Violet if she could have a sheet. She stared across at Violet, who was mid-flow telling the others what Belinda Flatt had said about her mother's death. Maybe she'd ask another time.

Paula looked at some of the other things on the shelves. Bottles, tubs, tins and brushes. She read their names, again oblivious to what they were. Glossy accents. Gesso. Finger wax. Glitter wands. It really was another world. A rather colourful, somewhat enticing other world. Maybe one day she'd give it a go. Maybe knitting. That seemed fun. Lots of people did it. She could knit Mr Bublé a winter jacket. Not that she thought he'd actually wear it for one second. He could be quite the cantankerous puss when he wanted.

She wandered over to where Sergeant Pollett and Sheena were talking. Just as she approached, her boss's phone rang. He pulled it from his pocket and looked at the screen. He held his hand in the air, drawing the attention of those in the room. All conversation ceased.

'It's the Sergeant from Darrochdean. This should be about what she's found at Jeremiah Halliwell's caravan.' The room remained hushed.

Everyone watched on in silence as Sergeant Pollett answered the phone. He didn't say much other than the odd 'ahem', 'I'll let you know' and 'okay' throughout the phone call. All of them were on the edge of their seats by the time Samuel hung up.

Violet burst forth as soon as he finished the call. 'What did they find?'

'Well, there was a newspaper spread out all over the bed in his caravan,' started Samuel.

'With letters cut out,' shrieked Pearl. 'So it was him. Heavens above.'

'Pearl Wheeler, will you let the man finish?' said Jimmy, fully aware that Pearl had interrupted the police officer in mid flow.

Samuel raised his eyebrows and nodded in agreement with Jimmy. He then continued.

'They couldn't find any letters cut out from the newspaper and even though there were some magazines in the caravan – some of quite a distasteful nature, apparently – none had been cut into.'

'Distasteful?' questioned Pearl again.

'Porn. Now shush,' whispered Jimmy.

Samuel continued yet again. 'What was unusual, though, was that the newspaper on the bed did have a large scribbled ring that had been drawn in pen around one of the headlines. It was the story about Sir Buster's death.'

'Well, that is very interesting. So we now know that Jeremiah Halliwell was definitely interested in Sir Buster's death. But for what reason exactly?' mused Violet.

'Maybe he was blackmailing him. You found a blackmail note near Jeremiah's body, didn't you?' asked Sheena.

'If he was, it wasn't with that particular note, because Sir Buster was long gone by then,' replied Samuel.

'But it's a possibility that he may be a seasoned blackmailer,' offered Margaret.

'What else did they find?' asked Violet. 'Was the newspaper story the only connection to Sir Buster?'

'No, Aunty Vi, it wasn't. They also looked inside his freezer and found something—'

'Not a body?' shrieked Pearl again, unable to stop herself.

Samuel eyeballed Pearl, giving her his fiercest 'do not interrupt me again' glare.

'Yes, they did, they found six, Pearl...' He left a moment's silence before continuing, allowing the intended shock factor to coat the room. He smiled momentarily at the look of horror on Pearl's face. 'Six massive trout. No doubt poached from Sir Buster's private lake. Sir Buster hardly let anyone use his lake, so I'm very sure that a lowlife like Jeremiah Halliwell hadn't been invited there'

'Very interesting indeed,' cooed Violet. 'And what about the blackmail note. Do we know whether Jeremiah actually wrote that? Did they find a sample of his handwriting?'

'They did. Sergeant Sheridan said they found a shopping list. She wanted to know why I requested to see it. I said I'd let her know, but she is going to send a photo of the list through to me. To see if the handwriting matches the note.'

'Seeing as you're sharing all of this with us, Samuel, will you be showing us the blackmail note?' probed Violet.

'I don't see why not. I hate to admit it, but you lot make quite good sleuths, don't you?' He smiled and walked to the table, placed his hand into one of his inner jacket pockets and pulled out the clear bag with the note he had found while searching the woodland with WPC Horton. He placed it on the table for all to see.

Just as all of Team C.R.A.B. stared down at the blackmail note with intrigue, Samuel's mobile phone beeped, signalling the arrival of a message. It was the photo of the shopping list found at Jeremiah's caravan. He opened the picture and smiled. He placed his phone down on the table alongside the note. The handwriting on both the blackmail note and the shopping list was identical, proving to them that Jeremiah Halliwell had indeed written the note.

'Well, this is all starting to piece together, isn't it?"

acknowledged Violet.

'Is it?' asked Jimmy.

'Yes, indeed. A freezer full of trout which undoubtedly came from Sir Buster's lake and the fact that we now know that Jeremiah did write that note proves that he was blackmailing someone to the tune of £50,000. Probably the someone that he was looking for in Rooney-at-Burrow when you and I saw him, Paula. Which means that someone else was definitely involved. And it was probably that person who stuck the confession to Jeremiah's dead body to try to frame him for Sir Buster's death.'

'So it definitely wasn't a heart attack then?' asked Margaret.

'It looked like one. Dr Roberts thought it was. But why would someone want somebody else to cough up £50,000 to cover up a death caused by a heart attack?' asked Violet.

'If in fact it wasn't?' answered Samuel, not totally sure of where Violet was going with her theory.

Violet carried on. 'I think that Jeremiah Halliwell was at the lake the morning of Sir Buster's death and saw something that he was then trying to blackmail somebody about. But £50,00 does not signify an unfortunate event like a heart attack, it signifies something much more sinister... A murder. But we need to work out how this murder looked just like an elderly gentleman's heart giving in.'

'And of course we need to try to work out who was being blackmailed,' stated Margaret.

'Well, I think we can safely guess that it was somebody who more than likely wrote all four of the threatening notes to Sir Buster and definitely thought that life would be easier and more beneficial without poor Sir Buster around,' pondered Violet.

'And who would probably be certain of gaining a lot from Sir Buster's will?' suggested Sheena, horribly aware that she had gained the most and hoping that eyes wouldn't fall on her. She shuffled a little awkwardly, rocking on her feet.

'Exactly, and I can think of two people who fit that description right away,' said Violet. She spotted the worry on Sheena's face and added, 'Dear girl, you are most certainly not one of them.'

Chapter 51

'So, it's been pretty eventful as you can imagine, Betsy. Not quite the day we expected, mind you, but certainly a lot of surprises.'

Betsy, who was sitting in the passenger seat of her car, with Rod at the wheel, was stunned by Violet's summary of the day's events in Rooney-at-Burrow and the subsequent findings of the search at Jeremiah Halliwell's caravan.

'So, let me get this right. It appears Sir Buster was in fact murdered. Top two suspects are his son Alexi, who is broke and wanted to demolish Burrow Hall and turn the land into a housing complex or a new town, or whatever those places are called. The other is his daughter Belinda, who has held a grudge against Sir Buster since the day her mother died and can't help but blame him for her death. And there's now four cut-out-letter-notes, including one which was attached to a dead man found hanging from a tree who has confessed to the killing that he seemingly didn't actually do. But he was trying to extort cash out of whoever did. Oh, and Sheena, my granddaughter, has been left Burrow Hall in the will?'

'Fifty-one per cent of it, yes.' Violet, again FaceTiming from her bed, nibbled on a malted milk as she spoke. She always found there was something macabrely satisfying about nibbling into where the cow's head began on the biscuit's design. 'Belinda's boy, Sage, was left the other forty-nine per cent. That is great news for the village. Could you imagine all of that being demolished?'

Betsy didn't answer. She was too busy contemplating the fact that her granddaughter was now the main owner of Burrow Hall. She was also smarting over Belinda accusing Sheena of sleeping with Sir Buster, which led to her next charge.

'My money is on Belinda being the killer. I'll demolish her myself if I get my hands on her. Accusing our Sheena of all sorts. What a piece of work. I bet Samuel went wild, didn't he. He's not phoned me yet, you know. If it wasn't for you, Vi, then I'd still be very much in the dark about the entire sordid affair.'

'Samuel leapt to her aid, but, to be fair, Sheena was more than proficient at looking after herself. She certainly put Belinda in her place. Sheena has a tongue as sharp as a darning needle when required, it would seem.'

'She obviously gets that from her granny,' laughed Rod from his position in the driving seat. 'This one's got sass by the yard full when she needs it. But you know that, Violet.'

'You cheeky devil. You just keep your eyes on the road,' observed Betsy.

'Where are you two off to this morning anyway?' asked Violet.

'Rod's taking me to the set of *Cheese Wire*. We'll be at the studio in two minutes. We left early from Willow's Spit. Rod's recording a few scenes today and he asked if I'd like to come along. It was that or start on a new embroidery for Rod's mother. She loved the one I did of Sydney Harbour Bridge for her, so I was going to start another, but that can wait. It's not every day you get to go to a horror film set,' Betsy enthused.

'Indeed,' said Violet, hoping that the new embroidery was not of a wombat like the one that she was doing for Betsy. She decided she would attempt a little more of the creature before turning in for good for the night. She needed to visit the tranquillity of her craft bubble after a day like today.

Rod spoke. 'Yes, my character – you remember, retired cop Peter Beacham – well, the scenes today are in hospital after the *Cheese Wire* killer poisons him with some kind of rotten cheese and then tries to take his head off with the cheese wire while he's feeling crook in his hospital bed. It's one of the most dramatic scenes in the entire movie. He doesn't kill me, of course, I survive. The producers are thinking that this could be a franchise. How cool would that be. So I'll be back for a second one. And it would open me up to so many new parts, I'm sure.'

'Yes, you said it might,' said Violet, continuing to nibble as Rod enthused.

'Then I've got another scene where I'm visiting the

kitchen of one of his victims. There's blood all over the room as the killer has attacked the victim with a set of bread knives and it's a complete disaster zone, but I've got to look for clues. Which I find, naturally, being a totally brilliant sleuth.'

'It sounds like you've got the perfect day planned,' mocked Violet. 'We've got the memorial night at The Six Pennies tomorrow. Sheena's singing, of course. It'll be interesting to see what happens now that doubtless word will have got round about her and Burrow Hall. I imagine everyone will be incredibly pleased. I'm sure there will be a few tears tomorrow night about Sir Buster, though.'

Violet watched as her sister and Rod pulled the car to a stop and disembarked from the vehicle as Betsy spoke. They had obviously reached their destination. 'And a few sherries too, no doubt, Violet Brewer,' laughed her sister. 'Just make sure you can remember every word of what's said, especially if Alexi and Belinda turn up. Do you think they still will?'

Violet wasn't sure. 'Well, now that Alexi knows what he's getting in the will, or not getting more to the point, he may not want to stay. Pearl and Jimmy said that he was ready to quit the village after the reading, and that was before Pearl told him he has to stump up £100,000 to pay off somebody he owes money to. And the last we saw of Belinda was her running off in tears from me and Paula Horton after saying that she hates her father. Whether they turn up tomorrow night or not to honour their dad's life remains to be seen – your guess is as good as mine.'

'I shall expect a FaceTime straight afterwards, if you're still able to make any sense,' giggled Betsy before flipping the camera on her phone. 'Oh, look, Vi, we're at the studios, how exciting. That's make-up over there apparently, and that's the canteen area and this is the studio door.' Violet could hear that Betsy was merely repeating what Rod was saying to her out of shot. To Violet, it looked like some drab service station, but she kept her thoughts schtum. 'We'll take you to Rod's dressing room via the set. Did I tell you that this might be a franchise if it takes off? Isn't this just thrilling?'

Violet would have more excited about doing the wordsearch in her crafting magazine but again bit her tongue. This was her sister's moment, but Violet couldn't stop her own braining whirring into action about how many kitchen gadgets there were available to a killer. She had to admit she'd had her own near misses with a paring knife in the past.

Betsy and Rod entered into the building. It was dark until one of them switched the lights on.

'It looks like we're the first on set. I guess we are a little early. The crew are probably all still in the canteen having breakfast,' declared Rod. 'D'you wanna see the kitchen set, Violet?' He took the phone from his wife.

Violet knew that it was merely a rhetorical question. Her only choice was yes, but she didn't get a chance to answer anyway.

'Right then, Betsy, don't touch anything as continuity will have my head on a stick. This is where I have to look for clues later. There will be a body lying on the floor down here. The actor's probably having breakfast too right now. But, apart from him and me, the scene is set.'

Violet could feel her stomach turn a little as Rod passed the phone over the kitchen counter. It was splattered with blood.

Rod was keen to share details. 'The blood isn't real by the way. It's made from something like corn syrup and food colouring.'

'Oh, I see.' It was all Violet could say as she took in what she saw on the screen. A wooden rolling pin, a box of cling film, a set of knives, a bread bin, a roll of foil, a kettle, a pestle and mortar. All of them splattered with pretend blood.

Betsy grabbed the phone again. 'Oh, my word, Vi, isn't it just fascinating. It's incredible to see behind the scenes, isn't it?'

'Fascinating is one word for it, Betsy. I am sure there are others.'

'Do you want to see Rod's dressing room now, too? He's got a minibar and one of those showbiz mirrors with light bulbs around it.'

For a moment, Violet was silent. She was thinking. A series of thoughts ricocheted through her head. Something had triggered her grey cells into action.

'Violet? It has light bulbs...'

Violet snapped back into the present moment. 'Oh, I'm sorry, dear, I was getting sleepy. It's been a long day. Can we look at Rod's dressing room another time? I'm sure there will be lots of chances, especially if *Cheese Wire* is set to be a franchise, eh? I think I need to get my beauty sleep.'

A little crestfallen but totally understanding, Betsy and Rod bid Violet goodnight and clicked off the screen.

Violet wasn't at all sleepy, in fact her brain was more animated and buzzing than it had been all day. And that was saying something considering the events up at the Hall.

Violet tried to get some clarity on the thoughts frothing in her brain. She needed to concentrate. A little piece of quality embroidery time would allow that.

She reached into the bedside table drawer and pulled out her wombat work in progress. Violet was embroidering solidly for the next two hours. By the time she settled down to sleep, the wombat was more or less complete and Violet's brain was more or less in some semblance of order.

Chapter 52

Margaret Millsop loved The Six Pennies pub. She always had. The village pub was the very life force of any small community. But even though it had been years since her husband had decided to run off with former Six Pennies barmaid Cheryl, there was still a tiny little piece of Margaret's heart that automatically flared up with recollective anger every time she stepped through the doors of her local inn.

But thankfully the distressing memory never lasted. It disappeared as rapidly as it came. And today was no exception, it had vanished by the time Margaret had pushed the front door of the pub open and wandered to the bar.

It was still before opening time, but she had guessed

the door would be open as no doubt Steph and Phill would be in full swing preparing for that night's memorial for Sir Buster. Margaret, always keen to be at the epicentre of any organising, had decided to pop by to offer her services.

A glum-looking Steph was behind the bar. In between drying another batch of freshly washed glasses, she was attempting to swat away a rather well-built bluebottle that seemed to be encircling her head with its maddening buzz.

'A squirt of fly killer will sort that pesky thing out,' offered Margaret. 'Where do you keep it?'

Steph looked up at Margaret. Her eyes were red and puffy. If Margaret was to hazard a guess, she would have said that Steph had been crying.

'Oh, morning, Margaret. It'll fly off eventually. Although it doesn't seem to want to leave me alone.' Her voice was as gloomy as her face.

'Maybe it's attracted to your perfume,' remarked Margaret. 'Or perhaps your misery. Are you okay? No offence, but you look dreadful. I've come over to offer some help with preparations for tonight.'

'Thanks, another pair of hands is always welcome. I'm

on my own right now as Phill's at Dr Roberts' surgery. His shoulder is playing up again. It has been for weeks. And then he's off to the wholesalers to pick things up for Sir Buster's tonight.' She sighed before adding, 'And is it really that obvious that I'm not feeling too good?'

'Stephanie Brooks, I may not have Dr Roberts' medical qualifications, but even I can spot a solemn dose of misery when I see one. Especially given your eyes are as red as a couple of tomatoes.'

Unable to stop herself, Steph's bottom lip began to tremble and tears started to cascade from her eyes. The bluebottle targeted her face again and she tried to bat it away between her sobs.

'Right then,' said Margaret. You take a seat and I'll put the kettle on. I think somebody needs a listening ear and a shoulder to cry on.'

Without waiting for a reply, Margaret headed through to the pub's kitchen and stuck the kettle on.

When she returned with two steaming mugs of freshly brewed tea and a plate of biscuits, Steph was perched on a high stool at the bar. Her eyes were still red, and the bluebottle still orbited.

'I know they're not my kitchen cupboards, but I always think there's room for an emergency sugar rush when misery hits, don't you? Nothing can banish a grim moment like a plate of bourbons. I hope you don't mind.'

'Of course not, thank you.'

Margaret pulled up a stool alongside the landlady and for a moment both of them sipped at their tea and nibbled at the biscuits. The bluebottle landed on the plate of biscuits, momentarily quiet as it contemplated a mid-morning snack.

'So, what's the matter, Steph?'

Steph paused for a second or two and then sighed. 'I just feel suffocated by everything. Have you ever been in a position where nothing seems to make you happy anymore? Because that's how I feel, Margaret.' The tears continued to roll down her cheeks to prove her point. 'I just don't feel good about myself. Like I don't count. That nothing I do really matters. It's like I'm just acting out a part in my life, but it's not really my life. Well, not the one I want, anyway. I feel like this is all supposed to be for somebody else and not me, because none of it makes me happy anymore. And I hate myself for being so miserable.'

Margaret could almost feel the misery in Steph's every word. It was that tangible. Her words immediately took her back to the horrid business with Cheryl.

'Steph, you and I have known each other a long time. You know how low I was when that scumbag ex-husband of mine ran off with Cheryl, your barmaid. I felt like such a failure. Why was he wanting to go off with somebody else? What was I lacking in to make him look elsewhere? I felt wretched. So, I understand suffering, believe you me.'

'That was such a horrible time. I wish we'd never employed her,' said Steph, flicking at the now in-flight bluebottle again.

'Poppycock. How were you to know that my husband was going to be a total pushover for a push-up bra and a loose set of family values. I don't blame her at all. She knew no better. I didn't even blame him at first. I immediately blamed myself and thought that I had done something wrong to force him into the arms of another. I thought that I had caused my own misery. So, I fully understand you beating yourself up. It's a natural thing to do, if misdirected. But why are you feeling like this in the first place?'

Steph picked up a serviette from the bar and dabbed at her eyes with it. She sniffed loudly and began.

'I've been dissatisfied for years. Every person in this village is lovely and I have had some truly fabulous times here, but I want more than this.' Steph waved her hand in the air attempting to hit the bluebottle. The action appeared more angry. 'No offence to anyone, but I'm bored. So terribly, mind-numbingly bored. I always thought this would be a stepping stone not a final destination. I feel like there's nothing to look forward to anymore. I want excitement and something different.'

Margaret was a villager through and through and couldn't really understand why anyone would be dissatisfied with life at Rooney-at-Burrow, but she could see from Steph's expression that she meant every word. Margaret may not have been able to comprehend it, but she knew she had to respect it.

Steph continued, 'When Phill and I fell in love, we

had such big ambitions. We were going to be running the best bars, the swankiest clubs, the places that all of the famous people wanted to go to. When we had our first pub, even though it was a local run-of-the-mill boozer, we had dreams of what the future held, of where our careers could take us. We aspired for so much. But it never happened,' she sighed. 'One pub rolled into another and then another and then we came here. I always believed that one day we would find ourselves in London or in one of the big cities running the go-to bar. I wanted celebrities lining up outside and VIP areas. I wanted us to be something. To be that *it* couple.'

'Oh, you sound just like Sheena, she loves all that celebrity stuff, doesn't she? Mind you, now she's going to be in charge of Burrow Hall, maybe she can hang out with a few of the rich and famous, we'll have to see. I suppose you have heard about yesterday's will reading, haven't you?' Margaret's words were an attempt to distract Steph away from her melancholy.

'Yeah, I heard. I bumped into WPC Horton in the village square last night. She told me all about it. Sheena's a lucky girl. She has her entire life ahead of her. What an opportunity for someone of her age to have so much pushed upon her. I wish I was in my twenties still. I feel so washed up these days. I'm in my forties and life just seems to have slipped by. What is there to look forward to?' The melancholy was evidently going nowhere.

'You and Phill are such a great couple though, and forty-something is not past it, believe you me. Why don't you look to move on if you're so dissatisfied here? Try to find something… swanky, as you call it.'

'Phill's lovely.' The way Steph said it made it sound as if she wasn't being fully complimentary. 'But that's just it. He is lovely. In the same way that the ducks in the village pond are lovely, and the cakes from Burrow Bites are lovely, and the crowning of the Ravishing Rooney Queen is lovely. It's charming and it's cosy and it's utterly delightful and *lovely*. But it's not exciting anymore. I'm so sorry if I'm sounding harsh and I truly dislike myself for saying these things about the village you love. That *I* love. But I just don't love it enough to want to stay here. And Phill does. He's lost his edge, his drive, his aspiration and his ambition. He's happy to settle here for good. And I just feel that that would be settling for second best. I want more.'

'Have you tried speaking to Phill?' asked Margaret, a little peeved that Steph was putting life in the village under a rather dreary microscope lens. But Margaret had always been a listener, even if she didn't always agree with the words she was hearing.

'On countless occasions. I think he knows how unhappy I am, but he doesn't seem to consider the fact that I need to find something else to make me happy again. Maybe someone else. He doesn't see that he is part of the problem. He's lost his drive and that was so much of his appeal to me. Does that make me a horrid person?' Steph tutted as she tied to swat the bluebottle again, its buzz still irritatingly incessant.

'It makes you an honest person. That's one better than my lousy ex was. At least you're not cheating on Phill.'

Steph remained silent, for a little too long, prompting Margaret to ask. 'Are you?'

'Well, no, not cheating exactly, but I think he knows

that I've fallen out of love. I don't find him exciting anymore.' There was genuine remorse in her voice. It was a situation that she couldn't help.

'And you find somebody else exciting instead, is that it?' Margaret could feel that perhaps she was on the edge of a confession.

'I find anyone exciting that talks about celebrities and life beyond the village. I love it when I chat to Jimmy's boyfriend, Bailey, about his clients. I loved it when Alexi came here to the pub and talked about making deals and hanging out in celeb-filled bars in London. He knows people that I read about in the magazines and online. He was sat in the beer garden smoking his funny cigarettes and I found it exciting.' Steph shook her head. 'That's so wrong of me. I just wanted to be part of his world. Because it's one beyond the walls of all this. It's beyond village life.'

'But it's not too late for you and Phill. Surely, if you really told him how you felt, then he could find a way for you two to be happy. It seems such a shame to just give up so easily.' Again, Margaret was reminded of how easily her own husband had given up on their own many years of marriage. He hadn't even tried to explain his actions and beg forgiveness from his wife. He had just run off into the distance with Cheryl. Margaret sometimes wondered if they were still together. But not enough to care.

'I think it is. Either I just stay and remain miserable and resent him. That would hurt him because he knows he's the root of the cause of my misery. Or I leave him and break his loving heart. I was going to do that, you know. I was ready to break it. So, it is too late. I've gone past that stage.'

Steph watched as the bluebottle landed on the bar again and walked its way across to where a few crumbs of bourbon biscuits scattered the surface. It stopped in position to contemplate its next move.

Steph lifted up a glass from the bar, upturned it in her hand and began to talk. As she did so, she moved the glass to hover over the unsuspecting fly.

'I was ready to go. Sir Buster was about to make that happen for me. Sweet man.'

'You were having an affair with Sir Buster,' spluttered Margaret, nearly spilling her tea.

Steph never moved, her actions slight and calculated, despite the accusation. 'Not really an affair. There was nothing physical, but he made me feel special, made me think that I could do anything in life and that I should follow my dream. I told him everything about my hopes and aspirations and how I longed for a more glamourous life. It's silly, isn't it? If I said that to anyone else, I felt as if they were pitying me and just thinking I was being daft and middle-aged, but with Sir Buster it was different. He was in his early seventies, yet he was still so full of life, so full of energy. No was never an option to him. I loved the fact that he was interested in me and my dreams. I loved the fact he showed me care. Flirted with me, even. It made me feel worthwhile. Relevant.'

'But, Steph, Sir Buster flirted with everyone. That was just how he was.'

Without saying a word, Steph lowered the glass in her hand over the fly and the crumbs. Aware that he was suddenly imprisoned, the fly seemed to buzz into action and flew frenziedly around its glass cage. Steph smiled as she watched it for a second and then returned her attention to Margaret.

'But he didn't offer to help everyone, did he? He said he'd help me with a bar, set me up in London. He said that if he was twenty years younger he'd whisk me away and look after me and give me everything I needed to make me happy. He said it in front of Phill many times. We laughed about it. He even said he'd leave me some money in his will to make sure I was all right. We laughed but I know that he meant it.'

A crease of concern engraved itself across Margaret's forehead. She could see that Steph was being serious. She was sure that Steph's own misery had muddied her clarity when it came to Sir Buster.

'Steph, dear, surely you know that Sir Buster was joking. He was like that with a lot of people. He was very fond of you, there's no doubt about that. But I don't ever think he would have left you anything in his will or wanted to devote his cash to building a new life for you. He offered to marry me after my louse of a husband ran off with Cheryl, but he was joking. You did know that, right? You didn't really think he would leave something to you in his will, did you? To help you...' She searched for the apt word. 'Escape.'

Steph blotted the serviette against her eyes again as the tears returned with more force. 'No, no, of course not.' Her words sounded hollow and unbelieving. 'And he didn't, did he. WPC Horton told me exactly who got what. There was nothing for me. Why would there be, eh? He was just messing around. He didn't care about me being...' Now Steph searched around for the right word. She chose 'trapped'. Steph placed her hand back on top of the glass where the bluebottle was still circling crazily. 'No one deserves to be trapped, do they? No one.' She lifted the glass and let the bluebottle fly free. 'It's just nice when somebody who cares for you actually comes along and is able to really let you fly free. Except that doesn't always happen, does it.'

As the bluebottle wisely disappeared from sight, the two women sat in silence for a few seconds. Margaret reached out and tenderly touched Steph on the leg. It was clear to see that she was a woman on the edge. Margaret couldn't help but wonder just how much a plainly disturbed Steph was capable of doing to rush her escape along. Sir Buster could have lived for years before Steph found out whether he was being true to his word. Would she have tried to hurry things up? For the moment, Margaret tried to sideline the idea from her thoughts.

It was Steph who broke the silence. 'Well, that was unexpected. I suppose it's good to talk. I do feel much better for having done so.' Her words sounded like she was trying to convince herself. 'Now, shall we crack on? Are my eyes still as red as tomatoes?'

They were visibly bloodshot. 'They are. Talking of all things vegetable,' said Margaret, keen to change the subject. 'How are your marrows coming along? I know everything is supposed to be swathed in secrecy until next week, but nothing is normal right now, is it? Mine are doing fantastically well, but I'm not sure they're winners. We'll see next Saturday.

'Come and see if you like. I know Phill would kill me for showing them to you, but I think we may have a couple of winners this year.' Steph smiled for the first time that morning. 'Just don't tell him I let you. Like you say,

555

nothing is normal right now. It was dreadful to hear someone squashed Sir Buster's. Do you think the man who confessed to killing him did it? I can't get my head around that at all.'

Margaret chose not to comment, especially after the revelations of what she and Team C.R.A.B. had learnt from Sergeant Pollett the night before about the findings in Jeremiah Halliwell's caravan.

The two women walked through the back of the bar and out through the beer garden to the small allotment area hidden away at the back. The vegetable patch was looking leafy and green and sitting in pride of place in the centre were two rather splendid marrows.

'Oh, they are magnificent,' cooed Margaret, trying to calculate in her mind whether hers were indeed bigger or not. 'Mind you, the soil looks a bit dry, dear. Parched, in fact. You should get a watering can on that straight away.'

'There's one in the shed. You get it and I'll uncover the bench for Sir Buster. You've not seen it, have you? It looks fantastic. We've been hiding it behind the shed. Phill's keeping it a secret until tonight, but we'll have to move it onto the stage before the memorial event starts and then cover it up, so if you're helping today, you're bound to see it anyway.'

'Oh lovely. Yes, I'll get the watering can and you uncover the bench,' said Margaret, heading into the shed.

Margaret came out a minute or so later with a watering can. She looked a little flushed.

'Oh, that took some finding. Now where's the tap?'

It was alongside the shed, near the brightly coloured bench. Margaret had to admit it looked superb.

She filled the can and then watered the marrows. Her actions were a little rushed. Her words were hurried. 'Look at me, helping out the competition. If you beat me next week, I will be turning the air blue. But I guess that's what's neighbours are for deep down. Helping each other. Talking of which, if we're going to move benches and things like that, you'll need more help than just me. I think I'll go and fetch Violet. She's always good with a bit of grafting. See you in a minute, dear. It's a lovely bench and well done on the marrows. Simply marvellous.'

Margaret placed the can on the floor and hurried off

back through the beer garden and the pub, leaving a bemused Steph wondering why Margaret was acting so strangely. But maybe it proved yet again that indeed nothing was normal right now.

Five minutes later, Margaret was knocking rather forcefully on Violet's front door.

She barely waited for Violet to open the door fully before bolting her way inside.

'Oh, my word, have I got some things to tell you,' said Margaret.

'As have I, Margaret, as have I. Why don't you come on in? Oh, I see you already are.'

Violet shut the door behind her.

Chapter 53

'You're lucky you've caught me in, Margaret. I'm just this minute back from the post office. I was sending a parcel over to Betsy and Rod. Now, what on earth is causing you such a panic?' asked Violet, as she sat down on the armchair in her front room. 'And do park yourself down, you're like a coiled spring, fidgeting around making me all nervous. Have you got ants in your pants? Or have the findings of last night maybe unsettled you a little too much?'

'No,' countered Margaret, her face still flushed with colour as it had been ever since she'd rushed into her best friend's flat a few minutes earlier. 'Not ants, but I have got this.' Margaret lifted up the hem of the T-shirt she was wearing and pulled out a rolled-up magazine that she was hiding, jammed into the waistband of her trousers. She passed it to Violet and then sat herself down. 'Can you believe that?' she asked.

Violet's face folded into perplexity. She unrolled the magazine. *Create and Craft Monthly.* 'Believe what? That it's Saturday morning and you've got a crafting magazine tucked into your knickers. Given that you adore quilting and are two balls of yarn short of a knitting basket half the time, then, yes, I can believe it. Why is that such an odd thing? Although the reason you have it down your trousers is confounding me, I must say.'

'I was hiding it. I couldn't let anyone see it until I gave it to you.' Margaret looked at her eagerly.

Violet, more than perplexed, found herself wondering if her friend had been on the sherry last night.

'Why? I've read this one a few times cover to cover in the shop. I think I know every sewing pattern or card making idea in there off by heart already.'

'Turn to the competition page.' Margaret's face was now ashen.

'Oh, this is the magazine with the competition to win

the…' Violet's words faded away to nothing as she suddenly considered what Margaret could be suggesting. She hurriedly flicked to the page. There was the headline 'WIN A LIMITED-EDITION DIE-CUTTING MACHINE' in the bright yellow letters on a purple background. 'Oh, my word, well, will you look at that.' Violet felt her mouth fall open. The W in the word WIN and the M in the word MACHINE were missing, having been cut out with a pair of scissors. It was obviously the magazine that had been used to help compose the third threatening note to Sir Buster and the one found on Jeremiah Halliwell. 'Where did you find this?' asked Violet, her mind kicking into fifth gear with the thought that perhaps she and Margaret were another step closer to solving the mystery of the notes, the blackmail and Sir Buster's death.

'Well, I've spent the morning in The Six Pennies…' Margaret explained to Violet about her revealing conversation with Steph and her invitation to see her and Phill's marrows and the commemorative bench for that night's memorial event. She unfurled the story to explain how she had ended up alone in Phill and Steph's shed.

'And you found this in their shed?' stated Violet, gripped by Margaret's every syllable.

'Well, I only went in there to fetch the watering can and when I went inside, I just found myself having a little look around. Normal kind of garden paraphernalia in there, a few tools, tins of paint, loads of paint thinner, actually rows of it, and then I saw a pile of magazines in the corner. Mainly garden ones and brewery ones. *Brewers Journal*, that kind of thing. I started to flick through the pile and then I saw the crafting magazine. Well, that's like a moth to the flame for me as you know, so I had to have a look inside. When it fell open at that page and I saw the letters missing, I panicked and shoved it down my trousers and ran off. Steph must think I'm an absolute fruit loop.'

'Did you look through the other magazines at all? They may have been used to cut out the other letters,' suggested Violet.

'No, I just made my excuses and fled. I'm such an idiot, I should have thought and grabbed a couple more. I was so worried about getting caught snooping. So do we think Steph wrote the notes. That she's the killer? She sounds like she was besotted with Sir Buster. She genuinely thought she would be left some money by the sound of things. I have a suspicion that Steph is a little more unhinged than maybe we realised. Actually, make that a lot.'

'It sounds like she is,' echoed Violet. 'But I don't think she is behind the notes. I think it could be Phill. We just need to try to find out if the other magazines have been used for those notes. It's odd that he has a crafting magazine. Neither he nor Steph come into Brewer's Loop, so it's unlikely that they bought one there and the only other place that has them around here is Dr Roberts' surgery as I give him some for the wating room. I always have done.'

Margaret clapped her palms together and placed her hands to her lips. Her eyes opened wide as a thought struck her. 'Phill is at the doctor's this morning. He has a bad shoulder. Apparently, he has done for weeks. Steph said this morning. Perhaps he picked up the magazine from the surgery.'

'Well, seeing as he's never taken any interest in die-cutting and embossing machines, I'm thinking you may have hit the nail on the head, Margaret. It looks like Phill Brooks has just become prime suspect in the mysterious case of the threatening notes and the murder of Sir Buster.' Violet was loving playing detective. Even if the local landlord hadn't initially been high up her list of suspects, or indeed even on her list, but the magazine changed all that.

'But why would he want to kill poor Sir Buster. I thought the two of them were friends. They loved a lock-in together, didn't they, on their poker nights. Quite the drunken duo on occasion, if rumours are to be believed. And I find it hard to believe that affable Phill could be behind two killings in as many weeks. I'm not sure he's capable,' Margaret remarked. 'It is always the nice, quiet ones, isn't it.'

'I think one of us needs to find our way back into that shed without anyone noticing to riffle through those other magazines,' suggested Violet. 'If they have letters missing too, then we know that Phill is our man.'

'Well, that's easy enough. I've volunteered your services to help with arrangements for the memorial tonight. You and I can spend the afternoon at The Six Pennies and hopefully one of us can sneak into the shed when Phill and Steph are busy.'

'Perfect,' said Violet. 'I'll grab my coat and bag and we'll get back over there.'

'You won't need a coat; the sun is blistering the paintwork out there. It's glorious Summer weather,' observed Margaret, a little perturbed by Violet's choice of daywear.

'Oh Margaret, if I'm to sneak a pile of magazines out of somebody's shed without them noticing, then I think an overcoat to hide them under and a big bag to shove them in may be a wise move, don't you?'

'Oh, aren't you clever, Violet Brewer?' cooed Margaret. 'But do we really think that good old Phill Brooks, who wouldn't say boo to a goose, could be the horrible person behind all of this?'

Violet's features rolled in contemplation. 'Margaret, if we take into consideration the clues and look at Sir

Buster's appetite, the drunken lock-ins, my brother-in-law's horror film, Mrs Turner's dislike of cling film and what seems like a rather unnecessary amount of paint thinner, then I think he might be the person who killed Sir Buster. And indeed then killed Jeremiah Halliwell. We just need to uncover some kind of proof.'

A thrilled Margaret, none the wiser but now fizzing with twice the excitement at Violet's list of clues, looked on animatedly as her friend grabbed her seasonally unnecessary overcoat and her bag.

'Right, back to the pub we go, Margaret,' said Violet as the two women headed to the front door. 'But you must keep a poker face and act normal all afternoon. We mustn't let Steph, and more importantly Phill, know that we suspect anything.'

'I will be the dictionary definition of stoic,' smiled Margaret. 'Are you going to tell Samuel and Paula or any of Team C.R.A.B. about your suspicions? Jimmy, Pearl and Sheena will be stunned.'

'Let's try to compile some solid evidence and then maybe when everybody is at the pub tonight, we can reveal all. But not until the time is right. I don't want to spoil the evening before it's even begun. I know that Sheena has been working so hard on her set list for Sir Buster for tonight, it would be such a pity to spoil all of that. She's working on it today. I've shut up the shop as a mark of respect. Let's see what we uncover this afternoon and then maybe we can shine some more light on things tonight. But you're right, Team C.R.A.B. will be gobsmacked if it is Phill. But maybe we shouldn't discount a delusional Steph either. Let's see what the day brings.'

Violet shut the door behind her as the two friends stepped out into the warmth of the high street.

'Gosh, I feel like Cagney and Lacey,' beamed Margaret as they walked towards the pub. 'What a buzz.'

'Oh, these are hardly the crime-filled streets of New York, dear, but foul play can happen in even the sleepiest of places, it would seem,' smiled Violet.

Chapter 54

'Remember me when you drink the wine, remember me as a good thing…'

The exquisite last note of the Diana Ross classic 'Remember Me' cut a beautiful stripe of love, respect and admiration through The Six Pennies as Sheena faultlessly brought her final song of the evening to a close. Love, respect and admiration for her own vocals and the beautiful set of songs she had just performed and for the man they were all dedicated to, the late Sir Buster Burniston.

Sheena had chosen the final song especially as the lyrics seemed to strike the right note about how she thought Sir Buster would like to be remembered. Plus, he had told her during one of their chats at Burrow Hall that he had always fancied Diana Ross, especially when she 'had that cute little haircut as a Supreme'.

Every person in the pub stood on their feet and applauded as Sheena took a bow. She turned around to the large photo of a beaming Sir Buster that had been framed and placed on an easel behind her on the pub stage and smiled. She would miss him so much. And she would do him proud in her new role as the majority owner of Burrow Hall. Even though she still hadn't really been able to get her head around exactly what the role would entail, she knew that she would never go against the wishes of what he had so clearly stated in his last will and testament.

A lot had changed since the last time Sheena had sung at The Six Pennies. In fact, it seemed everything had, even though it was barely a week ago. Life would never be the same again. There were responsibilities placed upon her that she had never possibly considered. The thought both thrilled her and terrified her in equal measure. Only time would tell how things would work out, but she knew that it would always be for the good of the village.

Sheena turned her attention back to the crowd

gathered in front of her. Some things never changed and that was something that Sheena was feeling incredibly thankful for.

'Let's raise a glass to the much-loved Sir Buster Burniston. He will be deeply missed. May he rest in peace.' Sheena grabbed her glass of wine from alongside the bench that also sat on the stage with her. It was still covered with a large sheet of cloth ready for its grand unveiling at the end of the evening. She raised her glass towards the crowd. 'To Sir Buster.'

Her friends, Team C.R.A.B., beamed back at her. Jimmy, who was sharing a table with Bailey, Hannah and Oscar, was in floods of tears. He had been ever since Sheena's opening Streisand number. She'd chosen 'Memory'. It was a song that always made Jimmy cry. A huge amount. Bailey too appeared to be crying, mopping his tears carefully with a silk handkerchief. As he dabbed at his face with one hand, he used the other to air-click his applause. Hannah and Oscar, both looking catwalk-ready in head-to-toe black, held their champagne flutes aloft. The entire table had been on the fizz all night, even though complimentary wine had been provided by Steph and Phill. Bailey had ordered the best bottles of quality champers that the pub sold in honour of Sir Buster.

Pearl and Noah were sharing their table with Violet and Margaret. They all seemed rather red of eye and a little teary too. Although for once it did seem that Violet had not been hitting the sherry to excess as she didn't seem to be her normal overemotional, wobbly-on-her-feet teary self. They were genuine tears of sadness that gilded her cheeks. She had recorded a lot of Sheena's performance on her phone, doubtless to play back to Grandma Betsy on their next FaceTime conversation. Meanwhile, Margaret seemed a little occupied to Sheena. She had been all night, as if something was playing on her mind. As ever, though, the beauty of Sheena's voice and the added sombre nature of the occasion had reduced her to total tears.

Sheena's dad and mum, Samuel and Rita, were sharing a table with Paula Horton. All three of them were also in tears. Samuel and Rita had never been prouder of their daughter than over the last few days. Their little girl had certainly had to prove herself as a fully grown, mature woman. She had dealt with the death of Sir Buster, a man that she loved and admired, the will reading and the accusations and the responsibility of preparing her set and entertaining the memorial crowd in her stride.

Sheena had noted that neither her father nor Paula Horton had been drinking alcohol throughout the evening. Neither of them was on duty, but yet they had abstained from the free bottles of wine that dotted every table. Odd. Rita hadn't and looked decidedly unsteady on her feet as she applauded. Hardly surprising seeing as she'd had all the wine to herself. Sheena wasn't sure why neither her dad nor Paula weren't drinking, but she had noticed that they had both spent a lot of time in deep conversation with Great-aunty Violet.

Mrs Turner and Herbert were seated at a table together and both appeared to be having a joyful time reminiscing about their old boss. Mrs Turner had spent a lot of the night appreciating the free wine and mingling among all and sundry, telling them how it had been the biggest honour and privilege to work for the Burniston family and fending off anyone who tried to wheedle her top-secret recipe for plum flapjacks out of her when her cheeks started to redden with the effects of alcohol. She may have been giddy and tipsy, but some things she would take to her grave.

Herbert was revelling in the chance to loosen up his usually starched collars for once and had been up and dancing to Sheena's rendition of 'Yes Sir, I Can Boogie', another of Sir Buster's retro favourites.

The major surprise of the evening, as far as attendance was concerned, had been the arrival of both Alexi Burniston and Belinda Flatt. And if their attendance had sent a massive wave of surprise throughout The Six Pennies, then the fact that the siblings had actually arrived together and were sharing a table caused a tsunami. In fact, it seemed like the last twenty-four hours had given both of Sir Buster's offspring a chance to realise their own faults.

On arrival at the pub, Belinda had marched straight up to Sheena with a young man by her side and immediately apologised for her behaviour towards her the day before at the will reading. She put it down to shock mixed with abject grief. There was no mention of the rage she had showed towards Sheena, but the new majority owner of Burrow Hall was not going to hold that against her. It couldn't have been easy to have your own father practically cut you out of his will in front of a room of virtual strangers.

Once she had finished apologising, Belinda had pushed the young man with her towards Sheena. His cheeks had immediately turned double the colour of a tiddly Mrs Turner's. Belinda introduced him as Sage, her son, who had decided that flying home for the funeral next week from the other side of the world was a good idea after all and had phoned his mother from the airport when he had landed the night before. It was then that he had found out that he was now the part owner of Burrow Hall with Sheena. According to Belinda it was best that her son and Sheena became friends as that would be best all round for both the past and the future of Burrow Hall. Sheena agreed, although she found it hard to imagine how the bumbling, scarlet-faced boy in front of her would deal with lavish affairs at a manor house when he could barely say hello to her.

When Sage had sat down at the table with his mum to watch Sheena perform, he couldn't help but feel that he had met the beautiful apparition in front of him before. After two glasses of wine, it suddenly twigged that a ten-year-old Sheena had been the pretty girl who had intimidated him with her offer of candyfloss at the helter-skelter a decade ago. Another glass later and he was wolf-whistling at her on stage, all coyness suddenly vanished into thin air, shouting out that she was the most beautiful woman he had ever seen.

Alexi had made his first port of call on arrival at The Six Pennies the table where Pearl was sitting. Her conversation with him the day before about his former life in Barbados had stuck in his brain and after a night of virtually no sleep, tossing and turning in bed, he had made the decision that he would pay Vin Sutton the cash he requested as soon as the will money landed with him. Pearl had told him that she would inform her Uncle Josh that man mountain Vin would not need to fly to the UK.

Alexi had spent the rest of the evening drinking the

free wine on his table and managing to swerve putting his hand in his own pocket and going to the bar. For a few hours, he and Belinda had put their dislike of each other to one side, aware that the night was about their father's much-adored existence when he was living and not about the almighty mess he had decided, in their eyes unnecessarily, to leave them both in after his demise.

Sheena looked across at Steph, who was stood behind the bar, nibbling at the bowl of Bombay mix on the counter. Sheena wasn't sure she was enjoying it judging by the look on her face. It was devoid of any kind of emotion. She was the only one in the bar not clapping. Oh well, each to their own, mused Sheena.

She knew what she had to do next. Having finished her set, the end of the evening was to culminate in the unveiling of Sir Buster's commemorative bench. Sheena had been given her orders that she was to invite Phill Brooks up on stage to make a speech about Sir Buster's popularity in the village and then he would invite someone, probably Belinda or Alexi now they were here, up to unveil the bench.

Sheena scanned the pub to locate Phill. She couldn't.

Undeterred, she continued with the events. 'Thank you, everybody, it's been such an amazing evening and there's only one thing left to do and that's unveil a special something that has been created in Sir Buster's honour. I'd like to invite to the stage the man who created it. Our pub landlord, Phill Brooks.'

A round of applause sounded again. But still no sign of Phill.

At their table, Violet and Margaret looked at each other, trepidation emanating from their features. Neither of them had seen Phill for about half an hour. And Violet knew that she, nephew Samuel and Paula Horton needed to talk to him once the evening was done. They were the only people she and Margaret had shared their disturbing news with so far. A sneaky trip into Phill's shed that afternoon and a bag full of magazines that now sat in a bag at Violet's feet under the pub table had fortified that necessity.

'Er, Steph, where's Phill?' asked Sheena as the landlord still failed to show.

The applause subsided to nothing.

Steph looked blankly at her. 'He's gone.' There was still no discernible emotion on her face.

'Gone where? He's due to present the…' She pointed at the covered bench on stage behind her, keen not to give away the surprise.

'He's gone,' said Steph again, her voice still monotone.

Hush reigned across the pub. Samuel stood to his feet, as did Paula and the two of them approached Sheena behind the bar.

'What do you mean Phill's gone, Steph? Gone where?' asked Samuel.

'He's gone. He's not here. He's downstairs.'

'Downstairs?' queried Samuel.

Steph stared directly at Samuel. Her eyes were cold and glassy. 'He's in the cellar.'

'WPC Horton, you stay with Steph. I'm going down to find Phill.' Samuel's words, chest puffed again, were suddenly delivered with an air of authority and professionalism.

'Will do, Sarge…' Paula stood by Steph, who merely

smiled politely at her.

The silence in the air rested there drum-tight across The Six Pennies until Sergeant Samuel Pollett came back upstairs from his visit to the bar's cellar. It was there that he found the body of Phill Brooks lying on the floor, blood pooling from his head. Samuel had checked his pulse. He was dead. An unopened bottle of champagne lay by his side. It too was stained with blood.

Samuel announced to the pub, 'Can everyone stay seated and not leave the bar please. I'm afraid we appear to have a murder on our hands.'

A collective gasp ricocheted throughout the crowd.

Despite her nephew's request, Violet Brewer was on her feet and walking towards the bar, bag in hand, almost before he had finished the sentence.

Chapter 55

Violet placed the bag down on the bar. It made quite a considerable thump as it landed on the surface. She immediately marched over towards Samuel, who didn't seem particularly thrilled by her disobedience of his orders.

He leant forward and whispered into her ear through gritted teeth, 'Aunty Violet, could you sit down with everyone else please, this is police business and I need to show some kind of control here. Phill Brooks has had his head smashed in with a champagne bottle down in the cellar and somebody in here is more than likely the one who whacked him over the head. I need to start asking some serious questions.'

Violet was a cocktail of firm, dismissive and slightly sympathetic in her reply. 'Oh gosh, with a champagne bottle. Poor man. How ironic after he'd given his life to the brewery business. How truly awful and what a sad way to go. And yes, dear, of course, I know it's serious police business.'

She turned to the crowd of people gathered, a sea of bewildered expressions, and began to speak, choosing to ignore her nephew's plea for her to be seated.

'I'm sure we've all read the story, have we not, in the papers. The one about the discovery of a body in the woodland not far from here. A body as yet unnamed to most, but apparently the man had left a suicide note confessing to the death of Sir Buster. I always knew myself there was more to Sir Buster's death than just a heart attack. I just felt it in my very soul. Some called it a silly woman's intuition, but I just knew it.' Violet was tempted to look in Samuel's direction but chose to ignore the temptation. 'I think I can tell you exactly what has happened. I should have done it earlier maybe, as it's too late for our landlord Phill now. But he really did bring this situation on himself, I guess. He's been the master of his own tragic destiny. And caused that of others along the way.'

Despite his annoyance at his aunt, Samuel was more than intrigued by what she was saying.

'What do you mean? What has the landlord of this place got to do with my father's death?' shouted Alexi. 'We've all read that some man has confessed to it. Not that anyone has actually confirmed who he actually was yet.'

'That man in the papers who apparently confessed to Sir Buster's death is con artist Jeremiah Halliwell. He lived about fifteen or so miles away from here in a caravan. But I'll come back to him and explain what has happened. But he is no more the killer of Sir Buster than I am,' answered Violet.

'Then who is?' shouted Belinda, joining her brother in his questioning.

Violet remained calm in her reply. 'I think I can give you all of the answers you need, including who killed Sir Buster, Jeremiah Halliwell and now Phill Brooks,' said Violet, curling her lips.

'Really?' said Samuel. 'You know exactly what happened?'

'I think I know what has occurred,' replied Violet. 'It's a very tragic tale. One that simply got out of hand. That snowballed into death and disaster. So why don't you pour Steph here a stiff whisky for her nerves and I'll tell you everything.'

Samuel knew he had no chance. His aunty was not taking no for an answer. She never did. He grabbed a glass and began to pour.

Violet moved back to the bar, where Steph was standing with Paula. The landlady's face was just as glassy and empty of emotion as it had been before the news of Phill's death had broken. Her body was present, yet somehow her feelings and emotions were missing in action. Paula smiled at Violet, a cloud of confusion hanging over the gesture.

Violet touched Steph on the arm caringly and then turned to those gathered. She knew exactly what she needed to do. She coughed to clear her throat and then began to speak.

'What horrid news. It appears that our landlord has poured his last pint. Such a shame, especially as we were here tonight to celebrate the life of another recent loss to the village, Sir Buster. But I have thought for a while that there was more to Sir Buster's death than just a heart attack. And it turns out that I was right.'

All eyes in the pub focused on Violet, silence pocketing the air, knowing that revelations were to follow.

'But I'll come to Sir Buster in a moment. First off, we need to talk about who killed Phill Brooks. Hit over the head with a bottle of champagne.'

Murmurs of disbelief sounded across the room. At Jimmy's table, Bailey let out a tut, a little disgusted by such a lavish beverage being using for something so squalid.

'I think I'm right in saying that I know exactly who killed Phill.' Violet turned to face the two women beside her. 'It was you, Steph, wasn't it? You killed him.'

Samuel, who had been in the process of handing Steph a whisky, nearly dropped the drink at Violet's accusation. A few drops splashed to the floor as he regained his composure. Paula's mouth fell open in surprise too. As did pretty much every mouth in the pub. Except Steph's.

Steph took the drink, sipped a little of the whisky and

then merely nodded. Despite her confession, it was a thread of sympathy and not abhorrence that stitched its way around the pub. Everyone could see that she was a woman broken.

Steph placed the drink on the surface of the bar and spoke. Her voice was clear, yet a dryness coated it. 'I didn't mean to. I just snapped. He was talking and talking, telling me what was good for me, that I should be so grateful for what I have and then I saw the bottle and the next thing I know Phill was laying there on the cellar floor.'

'Did he tell you about Sir Buster and Jeremiah Halliwell?' asked Violet.

'He told me everything. Just now, downstairs in the cellar. We were sniping at each other, I was telling him I was unhappy and he just snapped and confessed. He told me that he was the one responsible for Sir Buster's death and that he killed this other man and tried to frame him.'

Another gasp, this time a much louder one than previous efforts, sounded across the pub. Both Belinda Flatt and Alexi Burniston leapt to their feet, ready to step forward and confront the landlady. A cacophony of reactions burst from every table.

Steph was oblivious to them all and began to repeat what Phill had said to her. As she did so, all details of her surroundings smudged into nothingness as her mind wound itself back to her husband's revelations in the cellar earlier that evening...

Even though Steph had lived in The Six Pennies for the longest time, the air in the pub cellar never failed to chill her skin slightly as she descended the bar stairs and entered into the cellar. Even in the height of summer, as they were now, the air was always a little cool against her flesh.

But Steph knew it wasn't just the chill of the cellar air causing a frisson of frostiness in her veins tonight. She should be enjoying the evening. Sheena was on stage singing one of her favourite songs, 'Kids In America', the pub was full of life and the memorial to Sir Buster seemed to be passing off just as planned. And Sir Buster deserved a fitting send-off. He was a good man deep down, even if he didn't keep his promises. The bitterness and disappointment from the previous day's will reading was still inking her every thought. But that wasn't purely what was washing over her now.

No, her chill was heightened tonight, as it had been all day, ever since the visit she had made to her husband's shed after Margaret Millsop had run from there ever so weirdly earlier that day. Something had spooked her. Steph had entered the shed and found the pile of magazines spilled onto the floor. Maybe Margaret had knocked them over. It was when Steph picked them up that loose pages fell out, sheets cut into with a pair of scissors. Steph knew instantly what they had been used for. Word had woven its way across the village about the hostile notes and the cut-out letters spelling out threats. She had known immediately that Phill had sent them to Sir Buster. Then she had been speaking to Sheena when she had been doing a soundcheck and had casually mentioned the notes. Sheena hadn't meant to but had let slip that the confession note on the body that had been found was also written in cut-out letters. Steph immediately knew that Phill had done that too. That he had killed someone else. She couldn't think of any alternative.

She hadn't planned on confronting Phill that evening at first. She was going to let the memorial pass and then ask him, but there was something about the way he turned and smiled at her as she descended into the cellar. Something smug appeared to stain his features. Something arrogantly happy that the evening was going well. Ecstatic that Sir Buster wasn't around anymore, joyful that his wife's chance of freedom away from the groundhog monotony of life as his wife in the local village boozer had been erased. At least that was how Steph was seeing his expression. That seemed to be all she could see. It had been ever since her tell-tale visit to the shed and her subsequent conversation with Sheena.

She pressed play on her feelings, the words spoken before she could stem their flow. 'Why did you send those notes to Sir Buster?' she asked. 'I found your stash of magazines in the shed.'

His smile vanished, but, to Steph, his smugness

remained.

He didn't even attempt to deny his actions. He could see that it was pointless and a part of him was glad that he could finally share the news with someone else. 'Because he made me feel useless and I wanted him to leave you alone. He could never love you like I do.' He let the words settle for a moment before continuing. 'I knew you two were having an affair. How do you expect that to make me feel? He was over seventy and yet managed to make my wife smile more than I've done in years. That's not an easy thing to deal with, Steph. Not for any man. It's a real ego-crusher.'

Steph looked at her husband. She knew that this moment would come. The moment when he rightly admitted that he couldn't make her happy anymore. Steph had felt so guilty about it for so long. She was bored of life with Phill. The pub, the lack of excitement, the anticipation of what the future would bring. He couldn't please her anymore. Whereas she knew exactly what the future held with Phill, she could only imagine a future with others. And sometimes her imagination would get a little crazy and out of hand. But life with Phill was not an option anymore. As she heard him say that her actions had crushed him and spurred him into spite, she didn't feel pity for him. She couldn't. She had tried to explain how she felt, but he would never understand. He couldn't. They were a recipe that just didn't work anymore. The love was gone. The sell-by date had passed.

Upstairs, she could hear Sheena now singing the opening lines of her next song. It was Ella Fitzgerald's 'Summertime'. For a moment, she listened to the words, Sheena's vocals as crystal clear as ever. 'Summertime and the living is easy...' Oh the irony of it. Living didn't seem easy in the slightest recently. Not to any degree of happiness anyway. Not for Steph. Things had to change, starting with Phill.

She was keen to correct him. 'There was no affair. Sir Buster made me smile because he cared for me, cared what I wanted, cared about my future. Cared about my life beyond the end of the village high street. He wasn't my lover. He was my excitement. My hope.'

'I know, I heard him, rubbing my nose in it about how

unhappy you are.' It was the first hint of real venom in Phill's voice.

Steph knew now that Sir Buster had been joking, flirting, as he did with everyone. He never intended to be her heroic knight in gleaming armour. He didn't want to be. That was a fairy tale that Steph had created her own imaginary romantic happy ending for. In retrospect, it now seemed so clear. But Phill had obviously felt the same and Sir Buster was a threat to everything he had built with Steph. The dragon who needed slaying.

An angry thought flashed into her mind. It had been doing so all day. No matter how many times she had tried to push it away, it kept springing back like an evil jack-in-the-box. Now it bounced back for good. 'Why did you kill him? You're not a killer.' The question was simple.

The reply wasn't as straightforward.

'I didn't mean for it to happen; I just wanted to scare him and make him suffer.' There was a vulnerability and a frailty in his voice that had been previously missing. But it wasn't enough to evoke compassion from his wife.

Steph listened as Phill gave her a detailed blow-by-blow account of his role in the demise of Sir Buster. As she let his maze of words settle dangerously onto her thoughts like angry embers, she could hear Sheena's sumptuous vocals matting and layering on top of them in her head as she reached the rousing last moments of her song. 'Oh don't you cry. Don't you cry.' The vocals and her husband's confession blurred into a knotted ball of confusion as the two entities criss-crossed inside her brain. The beauty of the song at odds with the horror of his words and the results of his actions.

Phill finished his confession. 'So, I left Sir Buster there, dead. And there was a part of me that wasn't sorry. I knew we were free of him, his meddling and bragging, and you and I could concentrate on life together. Just you and me. How it should be. Forever.'

His final words synchronised with the end of Sheena's song. As the applause sounded from above, Steph contemplated a forever with Phill. She couldn't. Not now. Not after what he had just told her. The thought petrified her. A red mist descended across her brain and before she had a chance to block it, or indeed to question him further, the champagne bottle was in her hand and she had smacked it as hard as she could across his head. He fell. Steph let the bottle fall too. Remarkably it didn't smash on the stone floor.

Steph returned upstairs to hear the opening bars of Sheena's next song. Ironically Gloria Gaynor's 'Never Can Say Goodbye'.

Chapter 56

Stephanie Brooks had been unnervingly calm as she retold the story of what had happened in the cellar of The Six Pennies. As if detached from her own actions. There was no regret in her voice as she spoke, but there did seem to be a genuine sadness that things had crumbled in her life as they had.

But her confession was still missing some vital information. Her words to the gathered jury in the pub had not explained fully how Phill had managed to leave 'Sir Buster there dead' or indeed how he had come to kill Jeremiah Halliwell and why. In the same way that Steph's brain had blurred during Phill's confession, her retelling of the events had blurred when it came to Phill's explanation. Which spiked fury from some gathered.

It was Belinda who shouted, her words ripe with anger, 'How did he kill our father? I think you owe us a full explanation, seeing as the murderer himself can't.'

When Steph failed to reply, her stare glazed once more, Violet took her chance. 'It appears that the combination of a bored and despondent landlady, frantic for a little excitement in her humdrum everyday existence and a deeply devoted yet stupidly misguided husband putting two and two together and making way more than five has now ended up with three dead bodies, two of them here in our very own village.'

Violet turned to look at Steph, who had silent tears running down her face. Maybe finally her emotions were coming to the surface.

'I think we have all had conversations with Steph where she has admitted that she gets a little bored with life here in Rooney-at-Burrow. Personally, I couldn't imagine life anywhere else, but obviously some do. Each to their own. But it appears that Sir Buster, in his idle flirtations with Steph, as he indeed flirted with everybody, allowed poor Steph here to believe that he was going to leave her something in his will.'

'Why not? He left something to most other people instead of his family.' The outburst came from Alexi, his words both bitter and throwaway, his uncharacteristic pleasant air from earlier in the evening now definitely extinguished.

Violet was quick to shut his heckle down. 'I don't think this is the time for that, do you?' She returned to her ponderings. 'Steph misread Sir Buster's flirting and maybe even Sir Buster played on it a bit too, giving it the big man talk in front of Phill. Making Phill feel small. Not intentionally, but Sir Buster was a highly indomitable force, and if you're feeling somewhat weak anyway, it would be very easy to see Sir Buster as intimidating. Phill was convinced his wife was having an affair. So that's why he created the threatening notes. He wanted Sir Buster to feel intimidated too and perhaps a little scared. Almost to make him go through what Phill himself was feeling.'

Violet emptied the magazines from the bag onto the bar.

'I took these from Phill's shed this afternoon. Margaret

found one there earlier when she was watering Phill's marrows. It was a craft one so completely out of place as neither Phill nor Steph have ever shown the slightest interest in anything at Brewer's Loop. One of the pages had been cut into to use letters for the notes. Most of the magazines have been butchered for the same use. I suspect Phill picked up the magazine from Dr Roberts' surgery as I always lend some for the waiting room. He's had a bad shoulder recently, I believe, and made a few visits.'

'I was so shocked to find it there,' said Margaret, unable to resist an interjection. 'I had to rush right round to Violet's straight away with it.'

Samuel, who was now standing over Steph, protectively flanking her on the other side of WPC Horton, tutted loudly. He'd been saying to both Margaret and Violet all night that maybe they should have brought the evidence to him first. As ever, they had disagreed. The two women had filled in both him and WPC Horton on their suspicions of Phill Brooks and they were going to all approach the landlord after the memorial evening ended. Hence why they hadn't touched a drop of fizz all night. Naturally, they hadn't planned on Steph killing her husband before the night concluded.

'But the notes don't explain why Sir Buster is dead,' cried Jimmy.

'No, they don't,' replied Violet. 'Because Sir Buster would never give in to threats, would he? It's not in his nature. But I think that not even a man like Sir Buster could avoid succumbing to a bit of poisoning.'

Another horrified communal gasp swept the bar at the sharp turn of events.

'Poisoning? You think Sir Buster was poisoned?' cried Mrs Turner, a little indignantly. 'Not by my food, he wasn't. He was always so particular about what he ate. I always made the healthiest of things.'

'Well, no, quite, Mrs Turner, we all know that Sir Buster had a rather wonderful appetite, but he did watch what he ate, didn't he? He'd never eat anything fatty, or highly calorific. Heaven knows I tried to tempt him with many a Jammie Dodger over elevenses. But you, Mrs Turner, have been very helpful in my deductions on what caused Sir Buster to die, but I'll come on to that.'

Mrs Turner's expression moved from indignance to intrigue and she remained silent.

'So, first off, I need to have it confirmed from you.' Violet turned to Steph. 'Did Phill try to poison Sir Buster with paint thinner? There's an extraordinary amount of it in Phill's shed, more than one man would ever need. Margaret mentioned it today and when I went in there this afternoon there are so many tins of it. So, I'm guessing it wasn't just being used for thinning paint. Plus, it would be very easy to administer without anyone really knowing. A few drops in his beer every time he came in here. That kind of thing. You mentioned, Steph, that Phill said he didn't mean to kill Sir Buster and that he just wanted to scare him and make him suffer. Well, a little poisoning would certainly do that.'

Steph sniffed and moved her hand to her face to dry her tears. She nodded. 'Yes, stupid Phill said he tried to poison him. You're right, he used the paint thinner. He told me that he kept a glass of it under the bar and would add it to whatever drink Sir Buster ordered. Just to make himself feel a little better. A little more in control. How pathetic. He didn't mean to kill him. It was just spite. Stupid idiotic spite.'

'It's as I thought,' said Violet. 'Didn't Sir Buster say on his will reading video that he had been suffering stomach upsets recently. Strange for such a healthy man who watches what he eats. Well, that could be from a little too much paint thinner in his system. The idea came to me when I was speaking to my sister, Betsy, in Australia. She sends her love by the way. Her husband, Rod, is in some creepy horror film about a man who kills with a piece of cheese wire or something. Anyway, that's by the by. But in the film my brother-in-law's character gets poisoned and that reminded me of that story that Paula told me about the duck on the village square who was killed mistakenly by being fed avocado by Phill and Sir Buster after one of their drunken lock-ins. The duck had some kind of fatal reaction from the avocado. Apparently, it's highly toxic to ducks.'

'That was supposed to be confidential, Violet,' said Paula, her cheeks reddening.

'Yes, it was,' agreed Samuel, aiming his glare at his

WPC.

'That hardly matters now. In this case, loose lips give tips. I got to thinking,' continued Violet, 'that perhaps if a duck can have a fatal reaction to something toxic, then a human can too. I think Phill thought the same. I suspect the episode with the poor duck may have been in Phill's mind when he hatched the plot. So, I went on the shop computer this afternoon after finding the paint thinner to see if it can cause a heart attack. Apparently, it's highly unlikely unless drunk neat by the glassful, so I was trying to work out what might have occurred.'

'Bloody hell, she's good...' said Bailey, swigging back more fizz. This was turning out to be one of the most eventful evenings out he'd experienced in ages. Jimmy shushed him so he didn't miss a word from Violet.

'Which brings me to the morning of Sir Buster's death. At the lake. Poor Noah found him face down floating in the water. It must have been awful for him.'

Violet pointed to Noah, sitting alongside Pearl, who squeezed his leg under the table appreciatively. He flinched slightly, her grip a little tighter and with more added pinch than planned.

'It seemed odd to me than Sir Buster's heart should give out whilst he was doing something as tranquil and peaceful as fishing. Also, it seemed peculiar that his cool box should still be so full of food. Paula, you mentioned to me that you thought there had been two lots of sandwiches in his cool box. One in foil and one wrapped in cling film. That's odd in itself. Who wraps two lots of the same kind of food in two different materials? Unless you run out of one or the other mid-preparation. Which is why I was keen to talk to Mrs Turner as she would have prepared all of the food for Sir Buster's fishing trip. She told me that she doesn't use cling film as it gets the food *too sweaty* and is *horrid stuff.* So how can it be that WPC Horton here told me that she had seen a screwed up ball of cling film inside the cool box that had breadcrumbs inside it? It didn't make sense. Unless somebody else gave him the sandwiches.' Violet turned to Steph again. 'Is that what happened, Steph? Did Phill go to the lake with Sir Buster?'

Steph could feel herself tearing up again. 'I didn't

know he had. He told me he was at the wholesalers like he is every Saturday morning. But he admitted to me down in the cellar that he had gone to see Sir Buster at the lake the morning of his death. Sir Buster had told Phill that he was going fishing when he was in here one night and Phill thought it would be another opportunity to make him suffer at his expense. He took some sandwiches and a flask with pure paint thinner in it. He lied and told Sir Buster that the sandwiches were some kind of superfood, and he should try them. He even told him that I'd made them. He added some superhot chilli or something to one of the sandwiches. Phill ate his half of the sandwich and offered the other half with the chillies to Sir Buster. He bit into it and it was way too hot, so he needed a drink. Phill passed him the flask of pure paint thinner, and he took a massive swig. Phill told me that it was supposed to end there. That he'd say he must have picked the wrong flask up as he was using one in his shed to keep paint thinner in. That it was just a silly little mix-up. He really didn't mean to kill him. He just wanted to cause him pain.'

Steph plunged into silence again. It clung to the air in

the pub like smog. Everyone waited for more information.

'So, what happened? Did Sir Buster become dizzy and fall into the water?' enquired Violet. She had read online that it could happen if paint thinner was consumed. Dizzy and delirious and as if you were drunk, it had said.

Steph nodded, Violet's questioning causing her mind to jolt back into action. 'Yes, he did. Phill said that Sir Buster started stumbling around and fell into the lake. He must have passed out and drowned.' Steph burst into tears again at the thought. 'I know Phill didn't mean for Sir Buster to die. He was only trying to poison him because he read this bizarre story online about some man who had done a similar thing to his wife to try to get an insurance policy to pay out. He was just stupid and spiteful. But he panicked and left kind Sir Buster there to die. But he could have stopped it. He could have pulled him from the lake and saved him. But he didn't. His decision was to let poor Sir Buster die. When I saw red downstairs and killed Phill, I couldn't stop myself. But Phill could have stopped and saved Sir Buster, but he chose not to.'

'What do you mean?' asked Violet.

'He must have been so calculating in his actions. He threw away the half-eaten sandwich, he must have thrown the rolled-up cling film into the cool box, grabbed his flask and then he ran. He left Sir Buster in the water to drown, not able to save himself. And Sir Buster's last thoughts might have been that I made that actual sandwich. Someone who cared for him had chosen to make him a sandwich that ultimately caused his death. That makes me sick to the core. Phill panicked and ran. He says he didn't know he was going to die and that he didn't mean to kill him, but he condemned Sir Buster to a watery grave by running off and leaving him face down in the lake. How could I ever choose to spend the rest of my life with a man who made choices like that? And then, of course, things took an even darker turn…'

'You mean the business with Jeremiah Halliwell?' coaxed Violet.

Steph nodded again. 'Yes. He was at the lake that morning too. I don't know why, but he saw what happened with Phill and Sir Buster and he tried to blackmail him. He wanted £50,000 for his silence. He said that he would tell the world about Phill being there and leaving Sir Buster to die. Phill knew if that got out, then he'd be ruined. That would be his nice guy image obliterated for good. This Jeremiah told Phill to meet him and hand over the cash. But Phill panicked again. We haven't got that kind of money. So he took the matter into his own hands. Literally. He met Jeremiah and strangled him with some rope from the shed. And then he hung him to a tree to make it look like suicide.'

The thought of her husband's callous actions caused Steph to break down and she began to sob. Paula steadied her as Steph started to wobble on her own feet.

'And he even created another note from cut-out letters to frame the dead man for Sir Buster's death. Which was a silly mistake,' said Violet. 'Nobody would have connected the deaths had he not done that. And the fact that he must have dropped the handwritten note that Jeremiah Halliwell gave to him. Luckily, Samuel found that. Silly mistakes all the way through this sorry tale that cost Phill so much. Phill Brooks was not made to be a criminal, was he?'

Steph spoke through her sobs. 'He wasn't. He was a good man at heart. I know he was. But killing a man with his bare hands. Who can justify that? Sir Buster's death wasn't supposed to happen but the second one was pre-planned. It was that thought that made me reach for the champagne bottle downstairs. The fact that it was so cold-blooded. I knew that Phill had gone too far. He couldn't be allowed to do it again. I saw red. A deep horrible red. And I hit him with the bottle.'

'You killed him, just as he had killed Jeremiah Halliwell. In cold blood,' summed up Violet. There was a modicum of sympathy in her words.

'Yes, I did, didn't I?' Steph let out a nervous, slightly maniacal giggle. 'I did exactly what he did. Maybe Phill and I were a perfect match after all. Maybe we were supposed to be together for a lifetime.' She started to laugh, but it swiftly turned to tears. Her sobs were the only noise filling The Six Pennies as those gathered attempted to take in everything they'd heard.

It was Samuel who spoke next, now that the moment finally felt right. 'Stephanie Brooks, I am arresting you for the murder of your husband Phill Brooks.'

She didn't put up a fight. In fact, she went willingly. She had murdered Phill. And he had murdered Jeremiah Halliwell and Sir Buster. One by choice. One by accident. After everything, it appeared that she and Phill were indeed cut from the same cloth.

Steph looked at the sea of faces staring at her as Sergeant Pollett and WPC Horton ushered her from The Six Pennies. Most with shock, a few with anger, a few with peppered sympathy. A half-hearted smile found its way across her face as she left The Six Pennies for the last time. She knew she would never return. She had no wish to. She would be glad to see the back of it. In a remote corner of her mind, a bizarre sense of satisfaction came over her. At least she had managed to bring some excitement and thrills to the sleepy village of Rooney-at-Burrow on her last night there.

Chapter 57

Team C.R.A.B. were sitting in the back room of Brewer's Loop the morning after the revelations in The Six Pennies. Five steaming mugs of tea and a tray of HobNobs sat on the table. It was only Margaret who was diving into the HobNobs, spreading them, much to everyone else's eternal disgust, with marrow chutney, supplied once again by Jimmy. The others around the table were all enjoying a plate of coconut bread, freshly baked by Pearl. Well, fresh in the fact that she had made it at 3 a.m. that morning, powerless to sleep after the revelations about Steph, Jeremiah Halliwell and the murder of Phill at the pub.

'This really is rather delicious, Pearl,' said Violet. 'It's from your homeland, I'm guessing. You must give me the recipe as I will have to share it with Betsy.' She placed her finger over a final crumb on her plate and squashed it onto her skin before placing it into her mouth. 'It's devilishly moreish.'

'It's Bajan, yes. I used to cook it all the time back home. The cottage smells completely of coconut now. I'm glad you all like it.'

A murmur of approval circulated around the table, even from Margaret, who, as yet, hadn't tried a slice.

'I couldn't catch a wink of sleep last night. My mind was buzzing after all of the goings-on. I must say, Violet, you really were incredible to work all of that out,' remarked Pearl. 'Quite the sleuth. I can see where Samuel gets it from.'

'I think we all did our bit in piecing the story together, so I am marking it up as very much a team effort. It's so very sad, though. Poor Phill really didn't realise what he was getting himself into, did he. Oh, the insecurity of man. One minute he's panicking about his marriage and the next he's actually strangling somebody and tying them to a tree. It's all incredibly tragic. If only he and Steph had talked a bit more about how they really felt, then maybe none of this would have happened,' lamented Violet.

'I still can't believe that Phill tried to poison Sir Buster in the first place,' said Sheena. 'He always seemed like such a sweet and placid man. And he was the one who restored and painted the memorial bench for Sir Buster. Why would you do that for someone you dislike so much?'

'Phill didn't dislike Sir Buster deep down, he just disliked how Sir Buster made him feel about his marriage and the fact that Phill felt he couldn't make his own wife happy. Phill had spent a lifetime making people happy in his pubs, so the fact his marriage was failing and that he couldn't make Steph happy must have really cut at him,' said Margaret. 'It's what caused his entire catastrophic downfall.'

'When he had killed Sir Buster by mistake, I suspect he thought making the bench might help to ease a guilty conscience,' offered Jimmy. 'But still, Phill is the last person in the village you would expect to do something like this. I still can't get my head around the fact that he felt he had to kill Jeremiah Halliwell when he tried to blackmail him. That's hardcore stuff.'

Violet replied, 'I suspect by that point he was such a lost man, caught up in the almighty whirlwind of everything that had happened, that he was unable to see right from wrong. The line between them had very much blended together. Causing one death, accidental or not, can very easily lead onto causing another. Everyone has their good and bad sides, Jimmy. Those hidden inner demons. Just like Dr. Jekyll and Mr. Hyde. Sir Buster was spot on picking that as his favourite book given what we know now.'

'There is one thing puzzling me though,' said Pearl, her voice questioning. 'Who stamped all over Sir Buster's marrows? That just seems so mindless and vindictive. It was the one thing that wasn't revealed last night.'

'Oh, I forgot to say,' said Violet. 'I spoke to WPC Horton this morning. She and Samuel are going to be very busy today sorting out what happens next to poor Steph. They asked her about the marrows, and she said that Phill had confessed to her that he had done it. Apparently, he did it that Saturday morning before joining Sir Buster at the lake. Sir Buster had been bragging about the size of them in The Six Pennies and Phill must have felt small and insecure again and thought that he would sabotage the competition. He knew thar Sir Buster would be at the lake, so he went to the allotment first thing and trampled all over them using Sir Buster's wellingtons. It was a risky thing to do, but I guess he couldn't stop himself. I think his mind was awash with anger and confusion and ultimately rage and desperation.'

'Pulverising those marrows was the biggest crime of all, if you ask me,' said Margaret, not really meaning it. She was fully aware that vegetable destruction didn't really rank alongside trying to poison someone and death by strangulation when it came to penal sentences. 'Squashing another man's prize marrows. Scandalous. Ironic too given that I suspect that Phill's specimens might have won at the fayre next week, having seen them with my own eyes.' She shook her head. 'I would have never thought that Phill Brooks would be capable of being such a dreadfully bad penny.'

'A bad penny at The Six Pennies,' said Jimmy, amusing himself. 'Actually, two bad pennies, now we know about Steph as well.'

'Let's just say that they weren't so much two bad pennies, just one good one who let his insecurities turn him horribly bad and one who was definitely a little tarnished by her dislike of her own life,' said Violet.

A contemplative hush enveloped the group as they considered Violet's verdict. Margaret reached for another HobNob as Jimmy eyed the final slice of coconut bread.

'I have a question too.' It was Sheena who spoke. 'So, when we realised that one of the threatening notes had used a letter from a crafting magazine, did any of us really think that one of us could have been behind it?' Sheena was smiling, the action minxy, as she asked. She was certain that they had all experienced a momentary flash of 'what if?' when they had discovered where the tell-tale W on the third note had come from.

A general echo of 'no, no, not at all' erupted around the table. Sheena grinned. She was sure that every one of them had given in to a nanosecond of suspicion. But looking at her crafting friends around the table she knew that the suspicious niggle had rightly disappeared in a heartbeat.

It was Violet who summed up everyone's thoughts perfectly. 'Dear Sheena. Crafters are people who would never swap découpage and quilling for deception and killing. It's just not in our nature. Now, who's for another brew?'

All of Team C.R.A.B. raised their hands.

Epilogue

One week later…

'And the prize for best marrow in show at this year's Rooney-at-Burrow village fayre goes to…'

It was Sage who had spoken. But it was Sheena who wavered a second before giving the result. As the new joint owners of Burrow Hall, they had been picked by the fayre organisers, namely Margaret, to be the ones who would deliver the good news about the winners of this year's veggie top spot.

Normally, Margaret would do it herself, but this year she had good reason to ask someone else to provide the result.

'Congratulations to Margaret Millsop,' smiled Sheena, beginning to applaud as she invited Margaret to the microphone set up in front of St Charlotte's, the site of the annual fayre.

Margaret was fully aware that she had won. It wasn't hard to guess when only two sets of marrows had been entered. Hers and Jimmy's, and it was plain for all gathered to see that Margaret's were at least two inches thicker in circumference.

Margaret was beaming as she settled herself in front of the microphone. Sage handed her a small silver metal trophy, about four inches in height. It was the same prize every year. She held it aloft and squinted a little as she looked out, the intensity of the summer sun in the sky above hitting her eyes.

'Well, thank you, everybody. I must say I am rather chuffed to have won, even though I am fully aware that I wouldn't have done so if we weren't so marrow light. I know for a fact that the marrows from the pub might have pipped me.' Margaret refrained from mentioning either Phill or Steph given the rawness that still hung over the village following the proceedings of the week before. She felt it best not to toss murderers into the mix on such a wonderful afternoon. 'As would have, I suspect, the marrows from dear Sir Buster.'

A nod of acknowledgement swirled with sympathy flowed from the crowd. Many of them had attended Sir Buster's funeral earlier that week. It had been a somewhat jolly affair considering everything that had gone before. It had been another of the instructions that the late Sir Buster had insisted upon to Jonas Cushing. The funeral was to be a celebration of life, not a commiseration of Sir Buster's death. No black was to be worn, which had pleased Violet hugely as she had recently bought a very smart baby pink blouse from Marks and Spencer's that she'd been desperate to find the right occasion for. It hit the perfect note for the ceremony. Sir Buster's directive, however, hadn't pleased his daughter Belinda Flatt, who had already purchased a power-dressed black trouser suit to wear. She was forced to ditch it in exchange for a flowery summer blouse that she seemed most ill at ease in throughout the entire funeral. Margaret suspected that if Sage hadn't been there keeping his mum in tow, things could have turned out differently, and though quiet and unassuming, Sage was proving to be a calming influence at Burrow Hall.

Margaret continued with her speech. 'On the subject of Sir Buster, I would just like to say that today's fayre, and indeed every Rooney-at-Burrow village fayre from now on, will be in honour of the great man.'

She turned her gaze onto both Sheena and Sage to let them know that this was more of an order than a request. They both nodded in unison. The two of them actually been getting on very well over the week. Sheena would have had to have been both blind and deaf not to have realised that Sage obviously found her highly attractive, given his appreciative heckles during her performance at the pub the week before. And she had to admit that there was definitely something deeply handsome about Sir Buster's grandchild. Not that she had told him as yet, but she definitely enjoyed his company, which was more than handy given the situation Sir Buster's will had thrown them in together.

'Sir Buster was this village's very heartbeat and I'm sure that if he had been here now, he would have been filling the air with the sound of his laughter and doubtless looking forward to judging the Ravishing Rooney Queen pageant as ever.' This year's pageant had been cancelled due to a lack of entries, but Margaret had chosen to spin it that it had been postponed until next year as a mark of respect. 'I'd like to thank his daughter, Belinda, and his grandson, Sage, for being here with us today. It genuinely means a lot. To have a Burniston family presence at the village fayre has been a tradition unbroken for as many years as I care to remember, so it's fabulous to see that the family are still here with us today. Well, some are at least...'

Belinda smiled a tad awkwardly, both at Margaret's comment and also at the ripple of applause that sounded from the village fayre crowd. Belinda was pleased to have stayed for the fayre, but she was doing it for Sage and not for any reason of tradition of harmony with the villagers. In fact, she had a flight booked back to Dubai in a few days' time. A little retail and relaxation therapy in the Arabian sunshine was just what was needed. On the joint account card. She needed to have a conversation with her husband Rupert at some stage soon about their marriage and the card would doubtless be an early casualty, but for now, the card was still at her disposal.

Margaret's comment had obviously been aimed at the absent Alexi, who had taken off from the village in a cloud of funny-smelling smoke literally the moment the last word of the funeral service had been uttered. Rumour had it – the source being Bailey's reality TV friend Tanya – that Alexi had flown to Germany to manage a failed glamour girl pal of hers who had been promised a career revival as a techno singer in Germany's rave clubland. Bailey had taken great delight in telling Jimmy, who then took great delight in telling all he could, that Tanya had already warned her friend against Alexi's bad management skills and she would doubtless be dumping him before you could say glow stick.

Margaret carried on, 'I'd just like to say as well, if I may, a massive thank you to everyone who has helped make today a success, especially my best friend, Violet, who has proved herself invaluable as ever. And a rather nifty detective too, it would seem. It looks like you've got some competition there, Samuel and Paula,' laughed Margaret.

She stared across at the grouping of Samuel Pollett, Paula Horton and Violet, who were all stood together. Violet was fanning herself with an electric fan in an attempt to try to keep cool. The three of them smiled, although Samuel couldn't help but inwardly wonder if people really did think that Violet was better at crime solving than he was. He'd be fooling himself if he didn't admit that the past week's activities after the arrest of Steph Brooks had definitely made him feel like he was playing with the big boys. He hoped that others thought the same of him, even though it was thanks to his aunty that he'd got the leg-up.

Margaret concluded. 'So, enjoy the rest of the fayre and I shall let you know what I do with the marrows. I am hoping I can tempt Pearl and Noah into inviting me around for a delicious Bajan marrow sensation at some point soon. And thank you.' Margaret held the small trophy aloft again.

Pearl knew that she would be given the task of creating

something wonderful with Margaret's marrows. It was the same every year. She'd already planned a meal in her head and had extended an invitation to Team C.R.A.B. to come around for dinner at the cottage the next evening. They could do with a good celebration after all. And maybe they could open the Mount Gay 1703 Master Select rum that a grateful Vin Sutton had shipped over.

It was a few hours later that Violet found herself staring at the duck pond in the village square. She had gone there to see Sir Buster's bench which had been placed there, replacing the old one, after his funeral. Even though it had been made by Phill Brooks, it still seemed a fitting tribute to have the bench displayed in the very centre of the village and not in The Six Pennies beer garden, as originally planned. That way, it could be used and seen by everybody on a day-to-day basis and not just when someone wanted to go for a sly pint. Also, it was unclear what would be happening to the pub now that the Brooks were no longer the landlords. She just hoped that whoever took over would keep the local spirit and not turn it into one of those ghastly chains or even one of those gastropubs, or whatever they were called.

Violet had to admit that the bench looked lovely. It gave the viewpoint a new lease of life. As the evening light started to fade a little, she sat herself down on the bench. It felt good to sit and relax, the fayre was always fun but quite exhausting.

A miaow sounded from beneath the bench and Mr Bublé, WPC Horton's cat, appeared from under the wooden beams before jumping up onto the bench, circling slightly and then settling down into a crescent of comfort and content against her. It was a strange thing for him to do as normally Mr Bublé hardly ever ventured from the familiar surroundings of Paula's front garden. But Mr Bublé had immediately made it his home. Some feline mark of respect for dear Sir Buster? Or just a ginger tom being an odd little puss? Paula wasn't sure, but she had informed Violet at the fayre earlier on that he had been doing it ever since the bench had been moved into its new position. The act seemed both cosily charming and magically mysterious.

Violet could hear Mr Bublé's purring increase in volume as he dozed alongside her. She slipped her phone from her pocket and looked at the time. She did a quick calculation in her head and worked out that it would be the early hours of Sunday morning in Willow's Spit, Australia. She knew that Rod would more than likely be up for his early-morning swim, and that Betsy would doubtless be up too.

Violet chanced her luck and FaceTimed. Her hunch paid off as Betsy answered within a couple of rings. She was already busy beavering in her kitchen stirring vigorously at a large bowl. She greeted Violet with a cheery 'Hey, sis.'

'Hello there, Betsy, oh I am glad I've not got you out of bed. I guessed Rod might be up for his swim. I thought I'd phone and show you Sir Buster's bench. It's the one that was supposed to be uncovered when we discovered Phill Brooks' body last week. They've moved it here to the village square. The bench, not the body, I mean...'

'I guessed that, Violet. The body would not be looking too good by now, would it? It'd be like something from

Rod's horror film. And yes, he's out the back swimming before heading to the studio. I thought I'd crack on with a cake. Did I mention that the movie is hopefully going to be a franchise, by the way? I'm so proud of him.'

'You may have mentioned it,' deadpanned Violet. She moved the phone across the bench so that as much of it as possible appeared on the screen for Betsy to see. Mr Bublé was still curled up asleep, blissfully unaware that his image was being seen thousands of miles away. 'Here's the bench. Oh, and this is Paula Horton's cat, Mr Bublé, by the way. You may remember him. Apparently, he's taken to sleeping on Sir Buster's bench. It really is rather poetic.'

Betsy stopped the spirited stirring she was doing and stared at Mr Bublé. 'Oh yes, he's as adorable as ever, I see. And the bench looks lovely too. Such a good spot by the pond. Shame it was made by a murderer, but I suppose with time most people will forget that. Now, talking of animals, I must thank you, Violet.'

Betsy put down the spoon, grabbed the phone and moved to the back door. Hanging above it, already framed, was the wombat embroidery that Violet had completed for her sister and her husband.

Betsy moved the phone in to focus on the embroidery. 'Oh Violet, we love it. Thank you so much. It's perfect. And we've had it framed above the back door as that way Rod can remind himself to keep that fence in order from future wombat invasions every time he nips out for his daily swim.'

Violet couldn't help but let a smile as large as the Great Barrier Reef spread itself across her face. Her handiwork looked lovely and was indeed perfectly placed. 'Oh, that does look wonderful. And it arrived quickly. I only sent it last week.'

'Well, I think we all know wombats can be pretty speedy when they want to,' chuckled Betsy. 'Just ask Rod. Would you like to say hello?' Betsy threw open the back door and held the phone up so that Violet could see Rod front-crawling the length of the backyard swimming pool. She called out to him, 'Rod, say thank you to Violet for the wombat!'

He stopped swimming for a second, raised his arm at the phone, shouted 'Cheers, Vi!' and then continued to swim.

Betsy's face filled the screen again. 'So how is life in Rooney-at-Burrow? How was the fayre?'

'Well, first off, Margaret won the trophy for the marrow competition. She was ever so thrilled, even if there was hardly any competition. We're all going to Pearl's tomorrow night to have dinner made from them. All of Team C.R.A.B. will be there. It should be lovely.' Violet went on to give Betsy the ins and outs on the day.

Nearly an hour later, Violet clicked off the conversation with her sister, having filled her in on all of the latest village news. Virtually all remnants of daylight had disappeared. It was time to go home to bed. Violet was planning a little bit of knitting before settling down for the night. She'd had delivery of some lovely balls of bright pink yarn in Brewer's Loop and she was determined to put them to her own good use. She was thinking about a lovely cardigan to co-ordinate with the blouse she'd worn for Sir Buster's funeral. Well, she would need it when the weather turned.

She stood up, doing her best not to disturb Mr Bublé. She kissed two of her fingers and placed them on the bench. 'Goodnight, Sir Buster. Sleep tight.' She would miss the old boy.

As she walked back home Mr Bublé purred blissfully on in the warm night air.

THE END

If you'd like to keep up to date with my latest releases, just sign up at the link below. I'll never share your email address and you can unsubscribe at any time.

Sign up here!

www.nigelmay.net

Also by Nigel May

TRINITY

https://mybook.to/trinity-nigelmay

ADDICTED

https://mybook.to/addicted

SCANDALOUS LIES

https://mybook.to/scandalouslies

DEADLY OBSESSION

https://mybook.to/deadlyobsession

LOVERS AND LIARS

https://mybook.to/loversandliars

REVENGE

https://mybook.to/revenge-nigelmay

THE GIRL UNKNOWN

https://mybook.to/thegirlunknown

Letter From the Author

Thank you so much for choosing to read Quilling Me Softly.

I've been involved in the world of craft for many, many years and if somebody had said to me way back when that I would get excited about the thought of glue, glitter and cardstock then I would have laughed myself silly. But I can honestly say that the crafting world has always been such an amazing place and that it made sense that I would eventually write a book with its roots in the many fabulous decoupaged layers of crafting. I hope you enjoyed meeting the characters as much as I enjoyed creating them. Who knows what adventures may be yet to come for them all. Watch this space.

I always love to hear from my readers, so do please get in touch and let me k now what you thought about the book and please leave reviews too – I adore to read them. You can get in touch with me on my **Facebook page**, through **Twitter**, **Instagram** or my website.

If you did enjoy the book, and would like to keep up to date with my latest releases, you can sign up at the following link. Your email address will never be shared and you can unsubscribe at any time.

Sign up here!

www.nigelmay.net

Thank you to all of you for joining me in Rooney-at-Burrow… until next time. Happy crafting!

Nigel

X

Acknowledgements

Crafting this book has been a total joy and there are many people I would like to thank for guidance and support along the way.

First off, to every crafter I have ever had the joy of sharing time with. The warmth and happiness the world of crafting has given me has always meant such a lot and I thank you all from the bottom of my heart. I never dreamt there was so much magic to be had in a world of glue and glitter. Embossed love to all those I have worked with along the way. Some of you may recognise names featured in this novel. The inclusion of the names was intentional but that is where any similarity ends.

On a publishing front I want to say a massive thanks to Team Quill who helped push and shape this book to where it is now: the outstanding Kim, Jade, Lisa and Rachel. Die-cut hearts and flowers to you all.

Ulti-Mate love to Lisa Horton for total support. And to the craftily gorgeous Debby Robinson who was one of the first to read this novel and made me fizz with glee at her reaction - I'd like to say I love you.

To my friends, my family, my second A-May-Zing family and my rock Al – you are every page of the scrapbook of my life and you make my world shinier than a tote bag full of sequins. Loving you all.

I hope you enjoy Quilling Me Softly and its characters as much as I do. Please leave a review if you like and here's to potentially another crafty adventure in the future. You never know. Oh and tell your friends. Share the love, share the drama, share the craft.

Printed in Great Britain
by Amazon

19524401R00366